DARK MOON RISING

Saga of Storm - Bk 1

- PART ONE -

ANTHONY LARIVA

Editing by The Pro Book Editor
Interior Design by IAPS.rocks
Cover Design by Brad Fraunfelter

eBook ISBN: 978-1-957838-01-4
paperback ISBN: 978-1-957838-00-7

      1. Main category—Fiction
      2. Other category—Epic Fantasy

First Edition

This novel is dedicated to my confidante Jack, with whose enduring encouragement and honest advice I was able to transform a simple manuscript into an epic novel…

And also to my good cat Django, whose indifference toward all the passages I read to him over the years led to the many rewrites and self-edits this story needed.

TABLE OF CONTENTS

Preface

The Stormlands

WHEN TORLV'S THUNDER SHAKES ELDARIA as though Valkyrie have descended from the Halls of Halvalkyra, the faint cower in fear. Yet, for those born by the timeless siege of storm, nothing is sweeter than the sight of white lightning igniting the kindling of fear. Stormborne do not waste what Torlv relents, for the Stormlands are forever brimming with his tinder and wrath.

Nestled like the Breidjal eagle's perch in the north lies this antediluvian land. The Range of Tjorden lies to its west, encumbering sky's remorseless wrath. Sprawled across its heart, the Range of Valdhaz endures the far north where rules Jüte, the runic god of frost. In the most difficult times, its beauty is shrouded beneath the bower of frozen pine, yet rain from winters ever receding renew the Stormlands time and again.

The Wrathgorne Wilderland coats its breadth like dust coats a hunter's refuge, forever awaiting its primordial owner's return. Forests of pine swathe fjord cliffs. They overlook the three seas that carve out the shape of Hælla Dwolv, runic god of the earth. At the impregnable temple of the runic god of war, Helti, sealed behind the Great Gates of Tjorden, endures the Stormborne, a runefolk` molded by the same moon-lit dust as the savage land which birthed them.

The Stormborne are a militant people who know war's many faces, the faces of Helti, the runic god of war. Patience and wrath are a berserker's only armor besides his furs. Treachery and trust, the jarl's chief tomes. Siege and onslaught, the thatching on which the Stormborne slumber until peace trounces them both. Shining valor is the crown that rules above them all. Their iron grit leaves no room for the dread of Drur's Abyss. In pursuit of glory, the Valkyrie claim all.

Where the Stormborne march, the ground is soon to be soaked in blood. Wise men are familiar with the abominable sting of runeforged steel that has been blessed by Helti's seers. It is like a score that ices the veins the precise moment it splits flesh. Lesser men cringe at the mere thought of fighting Stormborne beneath the endless clash of Torlv's resilient thunder and Jüte's bitter chill. Eldrahg the Draconic Father drew forth a hardened folk, men who broke lesser men who could not withstand the wanderer's stunning roar into subservient thralls.

Stout villages dust the fjords and the edges of the Wrathgorne Wilderland where most of the Stormborne dwell. Their domiciles are built with crested roofs that look to stab the sky in defiance while some shield themselves with sward. Firmly entrenched against the fjords, there is little which can break their steadfast hold over Hælla Dwolv.

Their mountain holds and fjord fortresses delve into the depths of Eldaria. They are all rooted like the pine, birch, and ash forests that envelop them. Stormborne fortresses exhibit the spirit of those who call them home, hard like the uncultivated monsters roaming the lands of Dwevland and the Broken Fjords, voracious like the Great Etin Kazbel himself, and as indomitable as Frosthammer dwarves.

Spread throughout these frost-stricken and storm sieged slopes lie groves untouched by the lands own scorn known as the Vales of the Eversong. They are timeless enclaves encroached upon by Frosthammer dwarves, mindless mountain trolls, and the ældrik of the Broken Fjords. They exhibit their brilliance like the runic goddess Freyja as she stands beside the passage of her Draconic Father's hand. They are also the most perilous spread of land, for within the Vales of the Eversong dwell mischievous fae. Fae folk sleep peacefully to the envy of those who dwell in neighboring lands, so long as those peoples don't disturb their domains. Yet, the fae are devious like Eldrahg's second son who wears all names except for the name of Lok, the trickster god, blood brother to Eldrahg, and most beloved brother of Torlv.

The Vales of the Eversong lie scattered across the high country—extensive stretches of sub-alpine forests, montane glades, and Highland plains. The Nordland high country overlooks the Jüteheln, an arctic sea ever forbidding the advance of the runic god of frost's icy fangs. The Soudland high country extends above the Thunder Falls—a series of massive waterfalls that spill over tall basalt cliffsides, split the Wrathgorne, and carve the realm's greatest of fjords.

The Thunder Falls divide the high country from the Wrathgorne Wilderland. Stormborne claim the falls are like threads of leather that bind the Stormlands together, threads binding the true realms of men to those untamed portions of the world men could only dream to conquer. The falls feed massive rivers that weave through the land like snakes caressing the ground, and the land endures their percolating scorn. The rivers eventually widen to form sun-scorned firths and breathtaking coastal fjords from where the Stormborne row out to plunder the world.

In the southeastern Stormlands lies the aerie peak of Valheim, from which the Range of Valdhaz springs across the land. At the mountain's peak high above the clouds there lies a portal to the Halls of Halvalkyra. Laid against Eilíft Vatn—the Eternal Falls—the Halls of Halvalkyra house the valorous dead in eternity beside Valvítr, her Valkyrie, and most of the runic gods. It is a city of ore-pine posts, wattle-walls, towering holds of timber, luminescent moonstone, granite pillars, gneiss foundations, sward-roofs, and longhouses both striking and eternal. It is a bastion ruled by the Draconic Father Eldrahg and a sprawling afterlife pulsing with valor at its heart.

The Stormborne, a people ever deserving of Halvalkyra, revere the audacious lord who first opened to them its doors. Erun Runeheim, whose line forever rules as the Storm King after he won the Stormborne's eternal obedience and trust. His was the line that fought for the right to rule the most resilient folk. His fortress of Stormguarde was crafted in an age of antiquity by Dwarf Lord Harnik of the Frosthammer clan and the line of Folkenarr, who ruled Dwevland between the Nordland and the Broken Fjords, who became runic god of the forge.

Since Erun Runeheim abandoned blighted Stormurgall to claim his seat in Stormguarde, his line has ruled from the Tempest Throne. The throne is inscribed with rarefied runes in some ancient Frostheim Dwarvish tongue. A vestige to the grace of Monomua the Crescent Lady, the might of Eldrahg the Draconic Father, and the strength of his pantheon of lesser runic gods, the Tempest Throne sanctions the Storm King's solidarity in rule. Every Storm King to find strength in war has reigned from its mantle true. The throne's power is bound for all the world to rue, for a saga sings that within the Tempest Throne dwells Torlv, runic god of storm, who imparts the valor with which the progenies of Erun Runeheim rightfully rule.

Within these realms where tempests writhe
Lay a kingdom sieged by storm,
In which the blizzard's frigid scythe
Leaves spring in darkened forlorn.

On bliss's threshold where shadows lie
The mighty Stormborne make their home,
In one true service to their Storm King,
Upon his ageless Tempest Throne.

A fjords' secrets, a seer doth unearth
Where thy mighty bastion Stormguarde stood.
The solemn crest of a king's lost mirth
Which no Jarl, karlar, nor thrall withstood.

Darkness falls athwart those realms untold
As shadows claim enfeebled minds
Due forth into wars to still unfold
With the Dark Moon mourned and maligned.

Withdrawn the wolf to answer love's call.
Unseemly the thrall to rise above the gall.

Honorable the heiress, her dominions since shattered.
Valorous the heir, his dominions to be battered.

In the heart of sundry kingdom, three chosen make yield,
But by hands of blaze and shadow, one chosen thus wields.

MAP - ERUNHEIM & AIDELGARD

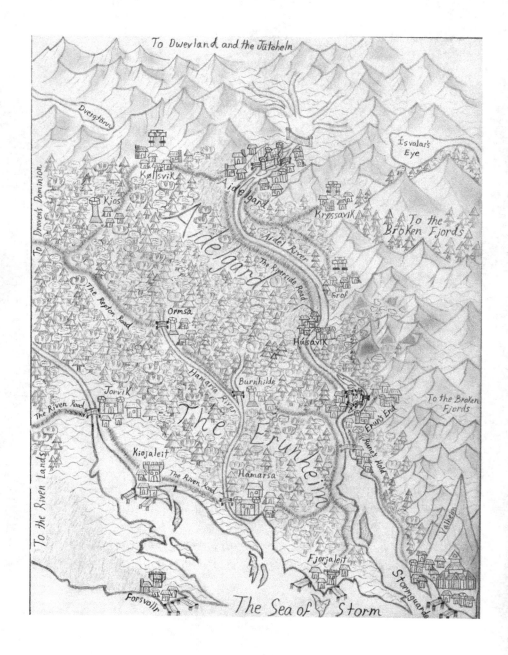

MAP - NORDLAND & SOUDLAND

PROLOGUE

FALLING SKY

"WAKE UP. DARIUS, WAKE UP. Andurial damn you, brother. Wake up!"

Darius split the crust of dried blood from his tired eyes. His body felt heavy and the air abnormally warm. A red-orange blur raged around him. Like an ocher brush over an oil canvas, it guttered behind the figures kneeling by his side. He blinked in rapid succession to restore his vision. Gold strands enfolding a sharp but pale visage manifested within the haze and behind it shimmered a divine almost as familiar as his sister Thyra's face.

"Thank the God of the Skies you're alive. Now we need to get out of here."

Darius blinked again as Thyra heaved him to his feet. His balance was severely lacking, so he forced his legs to lock while he steadied himself against her armored shoulders. Mother's quarters were aflame. Her life's every possession rapidly burned away. He saw no one but Thyra amongst the sweltering carnage, only her and her personal core of grizzled warriors from the Imperial Lysian Guard.

Darius extended a hand toward the mightiest of the fires devouring Mother's shrouded bedstead, inhaled the flames with solar sorcery, then swiftly decimated their spread. Thinking it appropriate to transition to the next, he swiveled right. A large portion of the ceiling collapsed above Mother's bed. Flaming logs and melting stones plummeted, revitalizing the fire he'd only just extinguished. Cursing the avaricious bastard who wrought this destruction, he lifted an arm to extinguish the flames again.

"Look at me!" Thyra shouted, pulling him in until their noses nearly bumped. "Thalynn's dead. We killed him scarcely minutes ago, but the Archdemon interred inside him escaped. It has already begun opening portals to its nether hell. We need to evacuate Ellynon now."

For the first time since before his descent into insentience, he stole the time to recollect all that had happened prior. Thalynn was dead. The Voevoda Princip still leaked defiled blood upon the floor twenty paces away. But where was their mother? Thyra had received his Golden Legions at the southern gates of Ellynon upon their triumphant return from Carradinia and the Moorelands specifically to return him to her. That was why he, Viktor, and their most trusted golden knights had followed her here. And where were Viktor, Idrik, and Valil? They three comprised the vanguard that confronted the Voevoda Princip Thalynn beside him. Thalynn was dead, his mother was missing, and among all of Thyra's subordinates, none of Darius's golden knights remained.

"What happened to Mother? Where are Viktor and the— Aahh!" Blood spilled from a wound along his left oblique that his wrenching voice reopened.

Thyra gripped his side with a flaming hand, cauterizing the wound before he could think to scream. "Viktor went ahead with my second, Grigory, to find Tanya and Ryurik. Valil's taking Idrik to the infirmary, but, God of the Skies, I doubt either of them will live."

A spear of shadow driven through the heart and a myriad of lacerations did tend to kill a man, but both Idrik and Valil had understood the consequences of following him into any engagement. His Golden Legions had become criminals the moment they'd followed him from Ellynon to the Rivermark. Although they fought for the emperor, Edvuard was not a forgiving man. Neither were the high lords in open rebellion or the demonic filth long operating in the shadows through Thalynn. Only by the grace of Andurial would they live, but a million people lived in Ellynon who could still be saved…as did his family.

After beginning the operose task of fleeing his mother's burning quarters, Darius grunted, "Andurial save them, but I can still fight."

Thyra's hand came to clasp his own, pulling him along faster while his body wailed to be left alone. "I'll need you to if we are going to make it out of this alive."

Darius nodded as he forced himself to maintain her pace. "I am sorry

I ever doubted your heart. War may have devastated my judgment, but I should have known your benediction would never buckle like I thought it had."

Thyra forced him and her entire contingent to a standstill in their mother's antechamber when her fury overtook her. "I know," she growled. "Half of the empire might think you started this war, but I know you have only ever done what you can to bring it to an end, though your lack of faith in me and your family is exactly what wrought this sky-damned predicament!"

"I know..." he murmured.

"Then how could you ever believe I was working against you?!"

"Commander." An officer of Thyra's stumbled in to cry out, "Ellynon is being overrun. We must leave now!"

Thyra tersely nodded before returning her fiery focus to him. "You must trust me this time. No more sprinting off to fight fate by ourselves. I cannot do this without you, and I won't lose you again." The fear behind his sister's stalwart façade of resolve flickered as brightly as the slight quiver in her amber, star-like eyes.

Their situation was growing increasingly dire, but he could not fault her for succumbing to her heart's distress. Hundreds of thousands of Lysians were dead because of his mistakes. It had been those same mistakes that led him to march the Golden Legions to the Rivermark three years ago, leaving her behind to address the political fallout and their father's wrath by herself. The first promise he'd ever made was to stand beside her always. He had failed that promise the same as he had failed Lida Baelviche when he failed to save her from the executioner's blade. He clutched the phoenix necklace Lida had given him as a gift the night they'd first made love to remind himself of her undeserved fate and of everything that decision to love her had caused.

"Together," he whispered through sharp pain.

"Together," Thyra reaffirmed, softening as they recommenced their escape.

They sprinted down the long antechamber where Sorcerer Selvik Drazhan's and the servant girl Tolina's bodies grew cold. Broken columns of marble passed them by as Darius entered the central courtyard of their mother's palace ward. Several imperial guardsmen splintered off to collect the frightened servants scattered across the gardens. Darius, Thyra, and

Ser Grigory—the tall, stocky brute his sister called her second—continued on. They dashed through a large, foyer and descended a spiraling staircase that connected to a long balcony overlooking the ocean from high above. Fires raged just beyond the docks in the merchant's district of Ellynon, and plumes the likes of volcanic ash rose along Bael Street south of that. They descended a second spiraling staircase to move from one bastion to the next. Soon after, they broke free of their mother's ward to the welcome of more of Thyra's men.

"Commander Thyra, Fourth Prince Ryurik, Second Princess Tanya, and their retainers are being escorted through the seaside markets to the harbor docks as we speak."

"What of my mother?" Thyra asked.

"She is with the Black Prince's knight in route to the harbor as well," conveyed the same burly imperial guardsman.

"And the emperor?" Darius interjected, fiercely perturbed that nobody had yet addressed the whereabouts of their father.

"Emperor Edvuard is…" another imperial guardsman said before losing her voice in some unspoken, dread thought.

"He is where?!" Darius demanded. "Where is my father?"

"In the throne room. He refused to leave," the woman nervously sputtered.

"Lysian will endure. Long live the emperor. Long live Edvuard. He repeated those words and nothing more," another guardsman informed.

Darius's gut coiled until he almost expelled the venom roiling within him. "Those were the last words the Archdemon possessing Thalynn said before it fled." He twisted to face Thyra. "That shadow fiend has gone after our father!"

"Darius…" Thyra briskly stepped in. "Listen to them! He has already been possessed."

"Then we will rip its vile soul from his body like we did with Thalynn!"

"It will kill him!" she shouted.

Darius gripped her shoulders amid a burning furor sprawling leagues below. "It won't, not if we work together from the start. Not if we remind him who he was. He loves you, Thyra! Our father loves you more than anything else in this world, even if you weren't born his son."

"You've always hated him, and he has always despised you. Why strive to save him now, after everything you have done to spite him before?"

She tried to pull away, but he held her firm. "Because he's our father first and Emperor Edvuard Ehlrich of the Lysian Empire second. We cannot leave him to wither and die when there is still a chance we can save him and our line."

"He won't thank you for it. He'll be the same man who compels Durel toward cruelty, Ellyan toward violence, beats and berates Mother, and searches for any opportunity to disown you, even if we somehow succeed."

Darius swallowed the horrid truth of those words. "I don't do it for myself. I don't do it for our mother. I never have, even though I have always wanted to. I do it for Lysian, for Tanya and Ryurik's futures, and I do it for you."

Poignant understanding glazed his sister's stare until a tear leaked down her pale, beaten cheeks. Before Lida Baelviche, only she had known him for what he was and everything he aspired to be. In equal fashion, only he knew her in the same. He'd learned how to wield the sword while she'd learned how to wield Heaven's Halberd beside him. God of the Skies, they'd learned the record of the world before traveling half of it together also. They'd faced the world side by side for all of their lives before the Lysian War of Ire consumed him for three years, whereupon he left her for his own ambitions without so much as a goodbye, only to return to this obliteration of their lives.

"We go together, just you and I," stated Thyra firmly.

"Together, and then on to save Ellynon," Darius agreed in full.

⊰⊷⧫⊶⊱

Darius and Thyra rushed through the lofty, Pentland red-cedar doors reinforced with iron, rimmed in white diamond, and left open to the throne. Twisted pillars of white, ascendant marble upheld the room's cathedral like ceiling, dwarfing brother and sister both as they walked down the darkened hall. Light disappeared against the crimson buttresses reinforcing the ceiling above. Stained glass forgotten of all its golden glory dwindled amid the sprawling shadow. The crimson strokes of Lysian's heritage bled down the silvers, whites, and golds, and even the crimson stone intertwined with white, ascendant marble bled an unnatural, nether-like hue.

Darius stepped onto the tail of the imperial phoenix whose wings spread to the steps of the throne. He paused when the air turned musky, and he inhaled his final clean breath. The bloody history of Lysian's conquests echoed sharply with their every step atop the elegantly painted stones. The line of Ehlrich had known nothing but violence in the pursuit of Lysian's throne. He wondered in the millennium that followed First Empress Aernika's rule, how many times had another unfamiliar with the privilege of being first born walked these halls to violently succeed Eldaria's most powerful throne.

Darius was unlike his ancestors in more than just the color of his eyes and hair alone. He did not come to conquer. He did not come to usurp the throne. He did not want it nor had he ever before. There was only one among the six children of Edvuard Ehlrich and Valyria Runeheim fit to rule. She alone bore the adulation of their father's approval and love. Only she should succeed the emperor now glaring down at them dubiously yet apathetically from atop his diamond-encrusted, gilded, marble throne. Still, only together could they drag Father's mind back from the nether hell the shadow fiend had drawn it into. Only together…or not at all.

Fear was a stench Darius knew well. Men sweated it profusely in the face of uncertainty. Women wilted phantom tears when facing their fears. Behind the strength they wore so well, a keen eye could see it still. Children's faces soured like milk when fear overtook their innocence. It was wretched to watch a young girl's eyes close when fear was the last thing she ever saw. When a young man's courage crumbled against the fear of death and what lay beyond, it spread like a contagion unshackled by any moral code.

Contrary to what Darius anticipated, their father did not wear fear at all. It was as if he shed it completely the moment they entered the throne room. Apathy was equally inapt. Behind the stale glare he exhausted for them both was a malice pure and strong. Suspicion and distrust alone weighted the emperor's countenance. It gave him a grievous look. Fear knew not the fiend hiding inside their father's soul. It descended upon Darius, however. When he glanced to Thyra, he saw it was descending upon her also.

Edvuard Ehlrich was, perhaps, the most feared and dangerous man presently alive in all of Eldaria. He was not righteous in his convictions like Paladin Supreme Urien Aylard. He did not command holy benediction like Pharophah'll Prudente. The Old Alderian Empire existed for centuries before Lysian, and its predecessors millennium before that. The elves in all of their grandeur boasted martial strength and magical prowess superior to all of Lysian's. Trolls boasted numbers more vast than the grains of sand on a beach. Dwarves boasted tougher skin, jütengolk larger stature, centauri hardier bodies, gnomel superior technology, and fae craftier magics. Less Divines were held within Lysian than without, although few were as powerful as the ones within.

Edvuard simply possessed something the whole of the rest of Eldaria did not. He ruled the disparate spread of men who comprised an empire in the most vicious corner of the world. Their lands were more vast, consisting of a coalition of territories, principalities, and kingdoms either conquered or annexed. The realms were richer in resources like timber, oil, cattle, and ore. Portions were fertile enough to serve as breadbaskets for the whole of Lysian. Their people were more intellectually and ethnically diverse, and although it was nigh forgotten, it was the strength in unity amongst peoples of infinite strengths which made them stronger than the rest. None of the other races ruled over Eldaria's most potent empire nor fathered three princes, each feared in a different light.

Notions of superiority was Lysian's strength, and it was also their father's weakness. Edvuard Ehlrich had engrained it into his sons and daughters so severely that their own twisted notions of superiority tore the empire's unity apart. From the Pentland coast to the Moorelands and the Eastern Plains the empire was at war with itself, and all the emperor apparently cared to do was smile while a more insidious entity assailed Ellynon through him. Father was gone. Their only chance to save him now was to sever an Archdemon and his soul when it genuinely seemed to belong there.

"Three years has it been? You left us an insolent prince intent on destroying the Ehlrich name. You've returned to me a black one who some now fear more than your brother Durel," Edvuard said.

"I would not have been considered an effective adversary if I were not feared. That was all you ever desired from Durel. I expected it would have been enough for me," Darius replied.

Edvuard's slightly bulbous nose shifted a long shadow when he cranked his head to scoff. "You are not Durel. He is my first born, inheritor of Lysian when I die to someone more inspired and ferocious than you."

"I've never sought your throne."

"Is that so?" Edvuard crooned. "So that was not why you stole the Golden Legions to march against High Lord Carradinne at the Rivermark?"

"I marched them to prevent Carradinne's convergence with High Lord Ulmoroch at Attal. I didn't want to see Ellyan fall while winning Durel's senseless war."

"What would an insolent teenage boy understand of winning a war?" Edvuard rumbled at precisely the same moment as when something massive toppled in Ellynon far below.

"I reconquered the southern principalities through the Rivermark, into the Moorelands, to the port city of Moore, and the seat of Carradinia itself. I did it to preserve your throne!"

"And this made you think you are fit to rule?"

"No better than the others in this room."

"Your victories against beaten dogs do not impress me and neither did the lust and envy that began my empire's downfall."

"No. You're too sharp to believe Durel's lies, even now, even after acknowledging what you have become," Thyra interjected sternly, having finally found her voice.

"So, the only woman I have ever favored decides to speak at last, seeking to transform me through the love I reserve for her and her alone."

"She has. I am your daughter, your first daughter, and Darius your third son. You cannot cast him aside like an abandoned ship upon the empty shore that is your heart, no matter what now rots the core."

"No!" Edvuard thundered. "Not here. Not now. You will not name him my son after what he has forced upon us."

"This is not his doing, nor is it yours. There's still time to save Ellynon. There's still time to turn the tides of the battle raging below."

"And why would I do that?"

"To save your empire! To save your people!" Thyra shouted in verve.

Edvuard twisted his broad shoulders until his back nearly cracked in half, then he lifted a stout, grizzled chin until his neck nearly cracked as well. "To protect this ingrateful swine who stands against me. A phoenix does not concern itself with the squawks of lesser fowl that burn when it spreads its wings above them."

Darius lurched forward until his father's eyes descended upon him. "We only stand above them because they choose to submit to our rule. Once they learn what you have allowed Thalynn to bring unto the foot of Andurial's home, they'll all begin to rebel against your reign, plunder Baelric's legacy, and tear down Aernika's throne."

Edvuard stood, the shadows began to crawl, and a blaze sprawled underneath their folds. "You speak of Baelric as if you were his falsely augured son? Leave, you faithless, treasonous cur! I will not tolerate your insults! I will not tolerate your blood in my home!"

Darius laid his fingers over the hilt of his sword when, by his sister's hand, the Heaven's Halberd was drawn. "I will not tolerate you tainting my father's soul any longer, and I will sever you from his body like I did with Thalynn before she butcher's your soul, shadow fiend."

The shadows thickened around the edges of Father's throne until the diamonds reflected light no longer, the gilding turned sallow, and the white, ascendant marble descended into dusk. "This soul was tainted long before I ever set foot upon Eldaria, and it will continue to rot long after I'm gone. So long as I live, Edvuard will rule."

Exhausted of the lies the Archdemon spewed, Darius strode within the shadow's crawl until Thyra blocked his path with the Heaven's Halberd. Bewildered beyond words, he paused. Fear no longer stained his elder sister's countenance. The yearn for vindication glazed her soul. It was fair for him to have forgotten this was not his fight alone, as it was fair for her to remind him he was not the only sibling of six their father had repeatedly wronged. His peace with this uncertain future was set in stone, but he withdrew a half step to offer his sister her own.

"Do you remember when I was little girl? You summoned me to your chambers the night you returned from the last war with the Asmoduil you personally commanded. Two legions, ten thousand Lysians, died to secure the long stretch of marshes between the Moorelands and Delrim Bashat. You did not think to summon Durel to teach him what it meant to rule— Ellyan or Darius either. You sought me alone, to share in your mind what it meant to rule the greatest empire this world has ever known. Do you remember what you told me, Father?" Thyra queried in a voice as smooth as the edge of a jittering stall.

The shadows receded ever slightly upon a breath unheard, and Father's face became clear within their folds. He wore the tight eastern side shave of the Pentland coast, the bushy top of the Rivermark, and the dense, short but evenly trimmed beard popularized by his great-grandfather. Deep furrows traversed his stern forehead, and his flat cheeks were sunken with the weight of his sundered soul. A wide bridge, bulbous nose, and harsh amber eyes scowled with dispirited furor. Behind those blazing eyes of the shadow fiend, Father gazed out of his own twisted accord.

"When my sons inevitably fail to prove themselves worthy of Lysian's throne, it will fall to you to rule." Father licked his lips as though they were candied pecans. "Then have you come to succeed me, Daughter? Do you think I've failed in preserving Baelric's legacy and Aernika's charge?"

"Yes, but that does not mean you cannot free yourself of this infection, save Ellynon, and restore the empire as a whole. Fight it! Fight it like you have fought every other rival before and show me the legacy I'm meant to succeed when you fall to someone more inspired and ferocious than the Archdemon that has burrowed into your soul."

Father's glower churned until a punitive grin was formed. "You have always possessed an ornate charm, one which belies the ambitions that fuel the fires of your own heart. I know no rivals here but the black-haired saboteur you call brother and a daughter who would choose to stand beside him instead of me." Edvuard began descending the steps before his throne like an oarsman from the deck of a ship lost to the Sea of Storm for centuries. "Our war was lost the first moment I entrusted it to sons who held less merit than you—a child of the lesser sex who could still slaughter them each, should you choose. I will not be the Ehlrich who reigns over the age of Lysian's fall, so Thalynn found me the allies I needed to win this war."

A tear struck his sister's cheek, trickling into the creases of youth long tested by all those she held dear. "No…" she muttered with a spirit dashed and a hope for rectitude sundered in full.

Father smiled, and Darius stared into the horror which was his dusky maw. "Look to your mother's filthy blood. Hers is the only infection I have ever regretted bringing into my home."

"You deserve him, this demon you've chosen to befriend and allow into your soul. I can barely distinguish where its malice ends and yours begins, but I can see yours still." Darius lifted and ignited his sword. It felt heavier than the hatred and mistrust Father had always allotted him. "I see enough of you to know how to carve out the rest, so face me fiend and let time determine which of us should truly be feared."

Unwise as it was to divert his attention away from the enemy within their father, Darius turned toward his sister to return her to the fight he knew he could never win alone. Columns twice the size of mammoth pines cast their own shadows over the dejection hemorrhaging from her heart. Father began to laugh in a barbaric tone, and the shadow magic of his parasite lurked forward until it blotted out the whole of Lysian's throne. The torchlight around the column's and along the outer walls dimmed until Thyra's face grew dark also. Within that swollen darkness, his sister recovered her courage. She shook herself of helplessness with Father's betrayal to light the Heaven's Halberd and drive back the mounting shadows. Edvuard's laugh deepened until he inexplicably paused, Thyra withdrew the pure light emanating from her divine halberd, and Darius rekindled the flames along his blade that the darkness from the demon's hands deigned to smother whole.

"Do you hear that? A retribution greater than yours has decided to make itself known," Edvuard crowed behind a subtle smirk.

Darius turned his ear toward a distant whirr as light began to bleed through the stained glass arranged in the walls high above them. The sky began to shudder before it trembled in full. Glass shattered against the cascading boom. A flaming meteor crashed through the ceiling and the upper buttresses, laying a trail of broken marble and red stone across the floor between them and their father. Another dozen whirrs reached his ear, and Darius gawked through the blinding light plummeting from Sky's Throne as the sky itself began to crack and fall.

"You bastard! What have you done?!" Thyra screamed after rising from where she rolled to avoid being crushed by celestial rock.

Edvuard recommenced his barbarous laugh.

Darius crawled across the floor to seize his sister's trembling hand. "We cannot fight him here. We must flee at once."

"If we do not separate them and kill the demon here, Andurial will destroy all of Ellynon in his attempt to kill them himself."

Another meteor crashed through the ceiling, obliterating the nearest column holding it up. "Thyra." He cupped her cheek in his hand. "He is lost. We must save our people now."

A clammy chill overtook her face, and she slid a revitalized hand into his when he helped her to stand. "The exodus was already underway before you and your legions returned," she said.

"Then we go to the docks to see that Mother, Ryurik, and Tanya are made safe."

Taking the lead like his heart told him he should, Darius sprinted from the Gilded Citadel toward Bael Street where all havoc was breaking lose. A meteor hurtled through the peak of an orangish-yellow dome older than Carradinia. A spray of stone splashed the city, crushing the citizens frantically scattering below. Darius and Thyra scarcely beat the tower's fall. Brick and stone crushed the lines of his golden legionnaires and Thyra's imperial guardsmen who fought against the immeasurable tides of demons rushing up Bael's street and crossing Ellynon from east to west. Their screams of agony pierced the soul, but Darius refused to let Thyra swivel to their aid and continued leading them forward.

All of eastern Ellynon was lost. If not by the demonic abominations ravaging the capital and its people alike, then by the chaos meteors plunging down from above. Thousands of years of sky-sworn magnificence smoldered beneath the repeated strikes of the God of the Skies. Above the capital from where they descended, the Gilded Citadel stood as a testament to the fiery brutality strewn across the surface of the sun.

Darius did his utmost to direct the defenders along the way where he could. Both he and the soldiers he left behind understood their responsibility was to stand until the last man or until cataclysm consumed them all. Light steel sabatons strapped with twinned golden phoenix wings slid atop the ground. They did not buckle as their wearers slashed the demons down.

Blistering shoulderguards affixed with twinned, golden, phoenix epaulets withstood the relentless onslaught. One quietly cried toward the conquered sun and her sister moon while the other silently shrieked at the rivers of blood pooling ahead of their lines. God of the Skies, forgive them for these fiends they allowed to cross into Ellynon—monument to his greatness within this mortal realm. The valiant Lysians who held the line deserved better than a death spent defending against the mistakes wrought by men worse than them.

Darius continued on, and the crowds of refugees swelled with every street they crossed. The seaside markets were congested with numbers far beyond what they could sustain. He soon realized there were not enough ships in harbor to ferry them all. Too much of the imperial navy was with Durel along the Pentland coasts.

He thought to begin redirecting the masses toward the southern gates of Ellynon until a blazing meteor collided with that polished iron. Through the blazing wreckage another horde of demons surged forth. They slashed down the unarmed civilians like a scythe through wheat dryer than a desert's cloak. A panic unlike any which came before it spread through those desperately vying to escape. Caught between the blistering demons and thousands of other Lysians, hundreds died to the malformed, sharply pronged, grotesquely bespectacled fiends.

"Clear the way!" shouted Ser Viktor, his toughest, most valuable and ferocious friend.

Darius shoved his way through the sheer panic. They were verging upon the edge of the seaside markets where Ser Viktor was supposed to have escorted the rest of their family. He ran through the shadow of the Lighthouse of Ellynon, an ancient structure predating the formation of the Lysian Empire. Just beyond the most striking ridgeline of the Ushbah, against which Ellynon sprawled, their father's personal docks extended into the Sea of Storm.

A ten-man contingent of his golden knights stood guard around Mother, Ryurik, Tanya, and a scarred assortment of nobles who'd escaped the slaughter mounting within Ellynon. Viktor, in all his bravery, led the remaining knights alongside two cohorts from one of Darius's five Golden Legions against the demonic rout surging in from the south. Their foray struck fast and hard, but the numbers they faced were overwhelming and they'd only just returned this same night from a two-day march.

"Viktor!" Darius shouted.

Amid the chaos of battle, Ser Viktor turned to offer him an extremely soured variant of his typical, convivial smirk. His long face was drenched in blood where some ossified talon had sliced through his forehead and under a jawline sharper than the tail of a shooting star. His pale blond beard dripped crimson gore. Hooded brows overhung close-knit, shallow gray eyes that understood the futility of the fight they oversaw. Viktor intimidated most men, but to intimidate fiends born in a shadowy or blazing abyss was something even his best knight could not achieve.

Ser Viktor withdrew, though not enough that he couldn't return to the action if his heart demanded he should. "Darius, I would thank the God of the Skies for keeping you alive if only he weren't slaughtering us quicker than these demonic spawn."

"We failed him in some indecipherable regard. This must be how he thinks he can purge Ellynon of both these demonic armies and his traitorous Lysian sons."

"He can slaughter them all, for all I care, but I wish he would have given us the chance to abscond before he did. Where are the Sorcerers Selvik? We will never hold back these wretched fiends long enough for the conquered sun to rise without their aid."

"My imperial guardsmen escorted as many down from the Gilded Citadel as they could while we went to recover my father. The rest are either dead or have fled of their own accords," Thyra informed.

"How many?" asked Viktor.

"No more than twenty, and less than a quarter of those have heat and light reserves..." said Thyra.

Viktor's face sunk until it morphed into that of a creature more ruthless than those which roamed the swamps around Delrim Bashat. "You must leave. The rest of us will hold against the demons until our armor is rent and our gold glints no more."

Darius declared, "Leave the captains to command the rearguard themselves. I'll need you by my side after we sail north and land to join with Ellyan or Durel to fight back on better ground."

"I won't leave the men."

"Then you will die without cause or reason!"

"Have more faith in me than that." Viktor gripped the back of his head. "I followed you from Ellynon to the Rivermark at the beginning of this war. Get your family on a boat and make your way ahead. I'll see that we and the rest of Ellynon follow when we can."

In a matter of seconds, Darius was forced to choose between his loyalty to his family and his loyalty to his soldiers and best friend. Andurial, who was ruthlessly bombarding all of Ellynon with meteors and sky fire from above. Darius hoped he was making the right choice. He pushed into a brusque embrace with his most loyal of friends.

A barrage of molten, celestial rocks peppered the remaining lines of his golden knights, legionnaires, and the malformed, chitinous demons they fought. He swiftly withdrew to broach his goodbye without a word. He joined Thyra, and together they pressed through the shifting crowds to reach their mother, brother, and sister at the port side of a large, ocean-faring vessel. His family's escort of golden knights and imperial guardsmen split ranks, recognizing both his and Thyra's battered faces.

"You're alive. Thank the runic gods you're both still alive!" their mother Valyria sniveled and sobbed.

Ever the vigilant hawk, Thyra moved in to inspect Mother's injuries first. "Are you hurt?"

"No, Thyra. None of us are," Valyria responded.

"Find your courage, Mother. This fight is far from over. Ryurik and Tanya need to see you strong." Thyra then strode directly toward their little sister whom she adored the most of all.

Darius stepped into his mother's rushed, constricting hug. "We couldn't save Father. Not because we wanted to leave him behind. That…shadow fiend, which consumed Thalynn's mind and soul, has infested Father's also. Thalynn was never operating on his own. They were working together from the start," Darius spurted in a terse mumble.

"This is my fault. I brought the very thing to Ellynon that he believed he could use to win his civil war."

Darius furiously retorted, "This is not your fault! He was a wicked bastard long before he overplayed his hand by making allies out of Archdemons of blaze and shadow."

"He only knew how to speak with an Archdemon of shadow because of what I told him. Of all the mistakes in his life he might have made, this is not one of his."

"What…what do you mean?"

"I am taking Ryurik and Tanya to the Stormlands. This city is lost. All of the High East will soon be lost as well."

"You cannot lose hope. Durel still commands half of the loyal legions, and we can still win if Ellyan assumes absolute control."

Mother shook her head while her eyes trickled with waning hope, and she disregarded his plea without betraying a single pretense that she might be wrong. "I won't ask you to come with us. I won't ask Thyra to either. I know you both love this country too much." Valyria shakily withdrew a small iron coffer from a sack hanging from her right hip. "If you choose to stay, take this. I will not bring it back to the Stormlands. I cannot destroy my home like I have destroyed yours." Valyria openly sobbed and tears streamed down her cheeks as the strength his sister had just demanded evaporated into dimly lit air.

Unsteady hands came to clutch the clandestine source of all his mother's suffering. She did not initially let go. Deep blue eyes streaked with wisps of verdant green latched onto his like heat to the coals of a dwarven foundry. Darius steadfastly reassured her it was an obligation he was willing to undertake, though behind the lie, he was disconcerted and nervous without repent. She released her talon-like grip, and he slipped the inscrutable iron coffer and its faint, indiscernible whispers into a tight pocket upon his leather tunic.

"Darius…I'm scared. I don't want to leave without you," Tanya cried out from where she trembled beside her older sister's legs.

Bright amber eyes so ill-equipped to handle the death and destruction raining down around them commanded his gaze. He came to crouch beside her, the spitting image of their older sister when Thyra was also ten years of age. Tanya grabbed his hands with an iron grip, and he felt the tremble in her youthful heartbeat. God of the Skies, at times he felt like a child just like her, but the Lysian War of Ire had stripped most if not all of that innocence away. He knew he needed to leave, but he would do so with an assurance that Tanya would never forsake her inner strength.

Darius lifted the golden phoenix heirloom hanging above his chest. "Do you remember the night which marked the ball of Durel's engagement? You stole my second dance after I stole Lida Baelviche's first. She gifted me this necklace not long after, alongside the promise it would remind me of us wherever I went." He unclasped the necklace to lay it around Tanya's neck. "I want you to have it. Know that for as long as you wear this, it will keep you safe, and after I've done what I must here, I'll return to you and life will return to what it was like before this."

Tanya wavered amid the enormity of the promise he placed upon what was once a high lord's most prized family relic and now his little sister's necklace. "You cannot come with us?"

Darius kissed her forehead, then he kissed her cheek. "Not yet, but I swear by Andurial and the Goddesses Seven I will return to you after I have saved our homeland."

Tanya gulped down fear and nodded until her eyes grew wide with mystified horror.

Startled, Darius swiveled into the breadth of an aquatic monstrosity of torrential shadows rising from the ocean's floor. With what scarce solar energy was still stored within his core, he began forming a sphere of solar sorcery to hurl against the beast. The shadowy demon released a colossal screech, and the whiplash from the shockwave distorted his sorcery before it could form. He collected the remnants into his palms to restrike the spark when an untainted light lanced through the demon's heart. It screeched again, only in agonizing pain rather than to spread fear and dread like before.

Standing breathless and devastatingly exquisite, Thyra glanced to him until her eyes shot wide and scaled the sky behind him. "Darius, look out!" she shouted.

His ear began to twitch against the all too familiar whirr of a meteor plummeting directly toward them. A haze of blinding light tailed the blazing rock, which his eyes struggled to ignore. Tanya screamed, and legionnaires who had survived three years of war began shouting and panicking like little boys. A lance of light whipped from the Heaven's Halberd soared against the meteor, slicing away a minuscule chunk off the meteor but otherwise leaving its path totally undiverted.

Solar sorcery was useless to him now, but the conquered sun was not the sole source of heavenly power his hands could command. For millennium, the Goddess of the Sun was seen as supreme until a vengeful sky subdued Eshkalah and made her his second queen.

Darius inhaled the full breadth of the God of the Skies's domain, coalescing chaste air from the lofty peak of the Ushbah, which touched the foot of Sky's Throne itself. He exhaled, guiding thousands of pascals of aerial pressure into the flank of the flaming meteor with his outstretched hands.

The otherworldly rock thundered as it changed direction. It clipped the peak of the Lighthouse of Ellynon, spraying hundreds of Lysians with molten rock and killing at least half that number. The explosion of light and sound was nigh deafening to his ears, but it silenced the shadowy, enigmatic monstrosity climbing out of the harbor when it collided with its mishappen face. The colossal demon imploded, roared, and was swallowed by the sea.

Darius turned to rejoin Thyra. Her mouth formed words that never reached his ears, and her face brightened against the cataclysm falling behind him. The docks disintegrated underneath his feet. The sea swallowed him whole. Then…there came nothing but the darkness of the place from whence shadows crawl, a place where the darkest of souls are predestined to fall into a void inescapable and wholly forlorn.

The darkness at the heart of his mother's iron coffer encased Darius, and his mind numbed against the whispers of an elder demon king bound to three shattered souls.

CHAPTER ONE
THE BREAK OF DAWN

NORTHERN WINDS WERE CRUEL. MOUNTAINS buckled beneath their sting, and the winds of winter were no less frightening than the backs of the blizzards upon which they rode. A storm raged across the sky, lingering without lapse, howling through the night, and etching ice into flesh like patched leather on a worn vest. Even in death, Torlv battled Lord Jüte without thought of relenting. Even in death, it seemed gods and great men consumed her memories, her vision of the future, and the world surrounding Thyra.

Thyra Ehlrich's long blonde hair rippled against the same sky. Her pale, milky face—long bereft of a good tan—pierced the sleet and rain. Only the light spent from her taut, amber eyes broke the morning's darkness as she searched for her younger brother Ryurik, knowing he was not yet there. He marched beyond the storm in the west, and her gut clenched at the thought of him returning after spending five years away.

Thyra suddenly felt weak. Storms were vicious reminders of the family they left behind to die in the High East. Cataclysm rapt her mind when thundersnow split the sky. She trembled with the memory of Ellynon in ruins, her father despoiled, and her brother Darius plunging to the bottom of the sea. She so often yearned to succumb to the pain, yet when skies soured and storms roared, she suffered through them indiscriminately. Yielding to her doubts would only quash the sacrifices that had brought her family here and leave them at the mercy of the storm's whim.

A silver lark soared above Torlv's runic temple, catching Thyra's gaze. It ascended, leaving its home of pines, spruces, and honest white firs nestled against the Valheim like the loose folds of a snow-swept scarf. Then the wind whipped hard, and the lark was thrown against rocky slopes. Its sister larks sang beside a broader concert of tumult. They rang the morning's bell not far from where she stood, asking, "Why did she go?" Thyra did not know, only that the lark would die without its flock wholly alone.

Silver feathers fell from a dimly lit sky, having forgotten winter's most intimate edict. The weak perish; the strong survive. Lightning flashed overhead, striking the ground between Seer Dragoln and Seer Drurhelm's hovels. The lark's sister songbirds went silent, and from the Shrines of the Three Moons to the ritual hall where her sister Tanya weathered the storm, not a single sound answered its resonant call.

Bitter and cold, Thyra spun her gaze toward Stormguarde from atop the railed, stone ledge upon which she stood. The merchants of the market squares had draped their shops and stands in a surfeit of thatching to daunt the chilled rain. Farmers still drudged in their fields along the city's north-western edge, this late winter storm having failed to preclude the karlar from working their fields. Smoke stacked atop the hearths in the craftsmen's district over west central Stormguarde. Discarded thralls, slaves brought to Stormborne shores, shivered beside the sward-rooved homes which housed them and the poor. Below them, Stormguarde's harbor laved their tears. Above them, Thyra's Skjold—the Storm King's shield guard—stood guard outside their barracks as she had so rigorously trained them to. Waves crashed against the drakken longships and bardlen warships in harbor. Warriors rushed across the docks to tend to their ships, scurrying like maddened rats. In the adjacent shipyard, the men worked doubly hard to preclude the storm from dragging them underneath the waves. Knuth Svenson, commander of the Skjold and second only to Thyra, doubtlessly tended to his home amid this storm, but she was surprised she had not yet spotted the brawny man's fiery mane beside the ocean's murky maw. Perhaps Knuth was otherwise preoccupied, his face buried in his lover's loins.

The air settled with a haunting chill. A white haze thickened the sky, birthing a blizzard. The switch from sleet to snow gave her clear warning it was time to head inside. Thyra began to leave the ledge where she had stolen fresh air during the only calm the storm had shown in two days. Snow fell against Stormguarde city like a savage whip.

She maintained pace toward the heavy wooden door that led to warmth while coughing up white dust. Blizzards carried nothing but a wicked humor toward the suffering they dispensed. Still, Thyra appreciated the time they had shared. It succeeded in delaying her reunion with Ryurik and the jarls marching to Stormguarde, if only by bogging them down. She would meet them, play the role of her grandfather the Storm King's haunting guest, but it would not be an enchanting affair. Too much of hers and Ryurik's futures were at stake for Thyra to not break them, then bend them to her will.

Thyra took hold of the door's iron handle, then paused when something roguish croaked behind her. Hand on the pommel of her sword, she wildly turned. The beady eyes of a wild raven studied her, seeking refuge from the storm. This peculiar bird perched above the suffering below. Yet, even he was not safe from the storm, as the black bird's search for refuge and the lark's demise both proved.

Woeful thoughts were like droplets that left no ripples atop the pond. Thyra often filled her rainy days pondering them regardless. Her mind sought them out as fiercely as wolves sought prey at the scent of warm blood. Perhaps it was how she recalled all she had lost to this world of Eldaria. Family, her spirit, and Heaven's Halberd, that divine extension of her arm…some had been lost forever while others had simply been abstracted for too long. Some she believed she could recover while others she refused to believe were gone.

Thunder struck the sky as if the mountains had been ruptured, and thundersnow burned through the flurries like a torch lit a cavern. The Valkyrie etched against the oak door beckoned she return to the home she loathed, its eyes judging her a Lysian in disgust. The raven screeched and fled into the storm. Thyra pulled with all her weight to heave the door against the wind. She slipped beyond the threshold into a stiller world, and the oak slammed shut.

Battling boredom and the subtle feeling of entrapment, Thyra plunged onto a bench. The wood chilled her tight back, so she repositioned atop pillows instead. She curled her legs into her chest, sinking into the cushions in reflection. She was stuck in Stormguarde Keep with no desire to mingle with her grandfather, her mother, the Stormborne, or to engage with anyone from that turbulent half of her bloodline besides her brother. With Ryurik, there was the chance for change and a relief from the tedium of managing the Skjold through peace.

Perhaps it was the wilds which first taught man where the best refuge from winter lay. Theirs were the whispers of ancient times when men lived like them. Or had those ancient Jastorl and Styrleif peoples, predecessors to the modern Stormborne, found safe haven in the great halls of Frosthammer dwarves after dismissing the rambling of ravens? Once their mettle had been restored, did those ancient peoples wander the mountains to erect their own fortresses akin to those of the dwarves?

Some certainly had. They were now known as mountain lords. Yet, others returned to their roots and instead settled the fjords. Only the strongest would have survived so many nights with nothing but dwarven ale to dull their minds, especially when mead had been their first love. Now those Styrleif and Jastorl peoples lived as one, joined by the Jütenthrall folk from the far north. They had ruled over all the Stormlands since the time of Erun Runeheim, forefather of her mother's blood.

Survival was a timeless game of balance. Many accepted the challenge. More failed to reach its natural end—like Ellyan, like Darius, or like Ryurik had war with Ardent Avant not been as forgiving to him as it had. Yet, these were the Stormlands where those who witnessed their darkest hour knew the sun would shine brighter the coming day. Thyra half belonged to this land that climbed toward Halvalkyra as if to touch its bowed brim. She understood the sun and the moon rose higher than they ever descended.

Seven winters she had spent in Stormguarde since fleeing the High East, and unless she yielded to weakness, this one would not dampen her spirits. Mark her words, the Stormlands would learn to serve her brother once their grandfather was dead. They would bend to her will like the high country bent to the will of rangers, and Ryurik would be made Storm King.

A tear slid down her pallid cheek, burning at the thought of rangers, even though she had never known one herself. Much was lost to her because of the Stormlands, but so long as Thyra Ehlrich drew breath, there was vengeance she would one day dispense. Until this world returned her lost brothers, Ellynon, and her father's Lysian Empire, Thyra would bide her time. It was the break of dawn, and few first lights remained before she would reunite with her youngest brother. Ryurik was finally returning home, and from a war that was never meant to be his to own.

"It needs more wood, more cloth, something to keep it alive!" exclaimed Cadell as they shivered through the morning.

"We have nothing left to feed it!" Muiri laid more planks against his hovel to break the wind, stuffing undampened thatch into the cracks to hold in the scarce heat the fire gave them. "We need to insulate the walls, keep in the heat before the blizzard swipes it up."

"I can barely feel my fingers. What do you expect me to do after they fall off other than throwing them in?" groaned his closest and only friend Cadell.

Glancing around his mess of a home in the alley behind Durkil's shop, Muiri located more thatch the storm had not yet soaked. "The roof's holding strong. Not much water leaking in. Use half that stack for the fire and leave the other half to me." More than anything, Muiri wished he weren't forced to suffer the elements like a stray dog.

"You'll catch a sickness if you don't keep dry." While passing over the thatch, Cadell brushed against his soaked clothes. "Look, you mad Alterian! You're half soaked already!"

"You're right! I'm Alterian, Cadell, and we live damn near half our lives drenched in rain and sweat. Now hand me more of that thatch. The fire's roaring like a demon's hell." Life was grueling for thralls, but Muiri carved out contentedness in the little improvements that made it less so.

Muiri finished stuffing the planks. There wasn't much of an airway for smoke to escape, but the wind effectively drew it out whenever it howled. He shivered, furiously rubbing his arms as warmth returned in petite strides. Huddling closer to the fire, he giggled when Cadell shivered, which then caused him to shiver, which caused Cadell to shiver again.

His home was just one of the many shanties of Stormguarde. Thralls often slept between buildings and in ruts when their masters were unwilling to accommodate them indoors. War with the mainland had tripled their supply, and thralls were no longer valued like they once were. Muiri's master, the butcher Durkil, organized the cellars to maintain plenty of open space, but because of an archaic hatred of all Alterians, he refused permission for Muiri to sleep indoors. Durkil also feigned the fear that he might one day attempt to escape, even though there was no place for him to extricate. It was either die by Durkil's hand or as another man's slave. Muiri preferred suffering familiar pain.

Muiri did not mind the weather most nights. Like he told Cadell time and again, he was full-blooded Alterian. Only the wealthy lived comfortably in the Highlands, and Muiri had never been wealthy in his life. He and his mother survived on fish, hunting, fishing, and angling. In the Alterian Highlands, those were rather profitless trades, and Muiri had not forgotten how scarcely better life had been before here.

"It's working! I'm a little warmer than before," exclaimed Cadell as he handed Muiri one of their two dry blankets. "How you know these things, I will never understand myself."

Humored, Muiri explained, "It's because you've lived in the city your entire life. Comes with a different set of talents than those I boast, friend."

"What talents? How best to thieve, beg for food, or stay hidden and out of sight?"

Muiri cocked a brow and grinned. "Things I'm trying to improve on still."

"You aren't the most secretive man I have ever met. Too imperceptive to ever be as good a thief as I am." Cadell smirked before bolstering his body with bread and some damn radishes provided by none other than Muiri!

"I stole that bread you're munching on right now. That's the product of my theft you're enjoying as you slight me with a full mouth."

"But the Skjold caught you in the act! You would have failed if I had not distracted them with a well-timed slip, revealing the Helmyan pox plastered across my back."

"I would have outrun them, and they would have forgotten us in a moon-lit instant!"

Tenacious in his refutation, Cadell rebuked, "Would not! They would have eventually found you and stripped you of your hide." He nibbled at a half-eaten radish before offering Muiri the rest. "Who would be feeding me scraps then?"

Acquiescing defeat with a grudge, Muiri corrected, "No scraps tonight, Cadell. I won't risk inciting more of Durkil's questions about where I've been taking the trash."

"Tell him you bring them to the rats. That is technically what he thinks I am."

They laughed, and the storm drowned the echo of their conversation when Torlv's wrath cracked. Thundersnow struck the morning, brightening the clouded monotony as if the runic god of storm split the sky with his divine ax. Brightness receded to dreariness, reminding the lands that Jüte reigned supreme while Torlv no longer roamed free.

"Do you think Jüte and Torlv clash every time thundersnow strikes?" Muiri questioned.

"Torlv's bound to the Tempest Throne, and how would he cleave the sky with Ljósvásar the Stormcarver from a chair within the Valheim?"

"I reject the notion any runic god could be bound to a throne by a patch-work of dwarven runes. If they are real beings and if this is them battling for supremacy in Eldrahg's runic court, then they're no gods of mine—runic or otherwise."

"Of course not. You're Alterian! You worship Loretia's savory bush—"

The butchery's side door flung open against a gust of wind, which immediately slammed it shut. "What is that noiseee! Muiríoch, you weasel-rat, I better not catch you conspiring with street thralls on how to escape my shop."

"How in a moon-wrought hell did he hear us disparaging the runic gods but not laughing like fools before?" Cadell nervously chuckled.

"Cadell! You know he hates you even more than the other thralls. If he finds you near this butchery, he'll skin us both!" Muiri shoved Cadell toward the wet shirts and rags heaped into piles adjacent is thatch bed.

Cadell dove into Muiri's clothes, crawling half underneath the pile and half underneath his thatch cot. He looked like a mole with its butt sticking out of its burrow.

Muiri decided he would need to remind his friend never to lecture him on stealth again. Frantically, he shoved Cadell farther in and covered his butt with blankets. Emaciated as a result of years of starvation, Cadell blended in with the dirty clothes. It did help that his normal garments were as ragged as Muiri's inundated clothes. If Muiri could, he would lend his friend new ones. Durkil afforded him nothing, however, so he had nothing to spare. Muiri flung a few more garments over Cadell, kicked his rustling butt to tell him to be still, and pulled away to prepare for his master's advent.

The door flung open, and Durkil shambled in from the blizzard's freezing breath. The pudge-necked butcher, hulking like a Bjardja in full mail armor, seized Muiri by the throat like he were a squirming chicken.

"Who were you speaking with, you shit-spewing shite?! Speak over Torlv's thunder, or I swear I will beat the answer out of you and hang you like a bleeding hog," Durkil foisted.

"Must have heard Torlv's voice on the wind and mistook it for someone else. Nobody here but me master…just you and I and your nauseating breath."

Slapping him across the cheek, the butcher raged, "Breath it all up, boy, else it might flush out the weasel-rats you are hiding from this blizzard the runic god of frost sent to wheedle out the weakest of your kind."

"You'll need another thrall if I breathe anymore of that foul rancor oozing up from your guts."

Furious, Durkil exhaled a fresh wave of fatality.

If the runic gods could take him away and shove his face into a donkey's ass, Muiri would much prefer it to smelling Durkil's hideous breath. He wrestled away from his master's grip, then spun to avoid landing on the pile of rags.

After watching Muiri make a conscious effort to evade his clothes, Durkil rushed to them in a rage. "What are you hiding, weasel-rat?!"

Muiri did not know what overcame him. The iron will to retaliate against the butcher's torments filled him with blazing vigor, and he felt empowered for scarce seconds. As the butcher's hands tore at the piles of swampy garments, Muiri retrieved an iced over shirt and clouted Durkil across the face.

Rage bled from the butcher's face like sap from an oak tree.

His heart pumping like a wild stallion's in a chase, Muiri whipped the icy cloth to strike his master again. "What are you hiding in your saggy neck, Stormborne cur? Another scar from another thrall who tired of your beatings and insults?!"

Durkil began to beat him, jamming thick fists into his back.

Muiri curled into a ball, shielding his vitals as best he could.

Burly and muscular, the butcher's inexplicably saggy neck was the only fattening bit about him. That body's stringent force wailed on Muiri without remorse while Durkil cursed Alterians with every vulgarity he knew.

When Durkil's fists struck the tender flesh below Muiri's ribs, lightning pain surged through him. Muiri shrieked, kicked, and connected with the butcher's neck. Durkil yelped and then clouted Muiri with the back of his hairy hand. Muiri instinctively recoiled, but it was if his mind could not process anymore pain. His abdomen wrenched, Muiri clenched his oblique, and his whole body jerked violently, screaming out for an end.

Muiri writhed and twisted as Durkil crushed him underfoot. "They must've scurried off when they heard me coming. Right of them to do so," Durkil harkened while tending to his knuckles. "Won't be saving them from the blizzard in this condition. Better hurry inside to start tenderizing the meat before I decide to tenderize you some more."

"Who…in the sky-damned hell…is going to buy freshly cut meat in the middle of a blizzard?" Muiri croaked.

"This blizzard will be dead by tomorrow, and all the starving fools who did not ration for an ice storm of this length will come scrounging. Regardless, High Lady Valyria Runeheim has demanded that every butcher prepare to cater a Kingslag. Ryurik and the jarls are returning from victory at the Great Gates, and if I know anything of warriors and Bjardja…besides the taste of silver, they prefer the taste of meat and mead above all." Durkil plowed through his hovel to return to the butchery.

Planks fell from the wall, ripping away the thatch they'd spared to seal it. Before their efforts were torn apart, Muiri rushed to salvage the rest of the wall. The sudden movement shocked his entire body, which seized, plaguing him with violent torments, the aftereffect of every beating he had ever received from master Durkil.

Crying out, Muiri tripped, destroying more of his wall than Durkil had. Unrequited fury collapsed his throat. He touched a hand to his neck, recoiling at the surge of pain. He struggled against the wailing winds that now swept through the alley. Unable to stand, Muiri collapsed onto the mess of ruined hovel. Biting down on his inability to catch mercy, he scarcely realized his pain had morphed into tears.

Cadell, emerging from hiding, began to dry them with rags.

Shoving Cadell away, Muiri said, "You should dry yourself by the fire, then feed it so it's still breathing when I come back."

"You're bleeding! We need to dress your wounds first."

"No! I will be fine," Muiri lied, dreading the next abuse Durkil would bestow him as he did so. "Durkil will return once I've begun carving through his meats and the alley is clear of my guard. Do you have anywhere else to go?"

"I think I can reach the temple's hospice before dying to the cold. There might be an open cot, but even the floor beats freezing to death on the streets."

Grunting through every unbearably painful step, Muiri stumbled toward the butchery's side entrance. "Good luck, Cadell. Don't take a wrong turn, or I swear I'll follow you down to Drur's Abyss to scold you for leaving me to suffer this world alone."

CHAPTER TWO

SHADOWS OF THE FAR NORTH

RASHA STOOD AT THE FOOT of an enigmatic wall of stone. Its slabs were shuffled like the pieces of a puzzle carved into mindful disarray. The Witchqueen surveyed their every aching detail. A trollish warlord stared out with dull eyes, even though his face was scattered. Idling under the Altar of Garatha, Rasha would soon reassemble his visage, excluding a single stone slab lost to the Realms of Frostheim. Soon, she would complete a ritual for Garatha, the First Warlord, by splitting her soul for the mighty troll entombed in the altar.

The Altar of Garatha boasted the bulky, tiered design typical of all the Garathandi's illustrious spiritual sites. Instead of revering a Loa God, however, it eternalized the memory of her people's First Warlord. Massive labyrinths tunneled through frozen earth. Rasha stood at their lowest point, deeper than the old Stormborne ruins, in a room where privacy and seclusion ruled all. She inhaled the dusty air of her predecessor Witchqueens, who had stood here before her. She exhaled shivers with what needed to be done.

Ritualistic garbs dyed crimson and touched by frost chilled her fleeting nerves. The hair on her arms stood on end like bristles to teeth. She caressed them intently. Effervescent gray, her eyes never lapsed in their scrutiny of her body's unease. Deep as northern waters, they unnerved any who gazed in her direction. Severity was a trait Rasha fundamentally appreciated—it seemed inherent even in her missing reflection.

Rasha believed she boasted an aquiline look in general, quite contrary to the look of the vajdna spider which most Garathandi compared her to. Her eyebrows slanted toward the center of her face, gifting it a slight, ubiquitous scowl. Her ears stuck out from between the folds of fierce, crimson hair where they met at pointed ends. She had studded them with small silver. Her face was wrought in the shape of a heart, which rounded at her chin. Two blood-dyed tusks protruded from the corners of her quivering lips.

"If only you could see what's become of Gara-thandila, Everdark City where sleeps the night, mighty Warlord Garatha."

Rasha had arrived in the empire's snow-swept capital a day earlier. Gara-thandila was considerably large, considering how deep in the north it actually lied. Frozen soil where little grew might dissuade most creatures from settling so far north, but not the Garathandi trolls. Plenty of edible fungi grew in the depthless ravines of the Ralcrav. The Frallheim Timberlands boasted an abundance of wild game, enough to sustain seven trollish cities. Built deep into the Ralcrav and tall above the Frallheim, in its former glory, Gara-thandila had been a sight to behold.

Since pestilence wracked the Realms of the Frostheim, the capital and its northern allies had fallen into fleeting disrepair. Five years earlier to this day, the Garathandi began their consummation with a wicked plague. As the plague spread, it was christened the Crimson Curse, which was a grim reference to irrelated events that had ravaged her youth. She was uncertain which was more sickening: the plague that wracked the empire, or the extraneous name the Warlord Prince bastardized for it.

Pillars of smoke stacked atop piles of burning corpses. Their ashes left the air unclean, and Rasha barely drew breath when traveling the streets of Gara-thandila. Yet, it was not just fear of death that stayed the Witchqueen's breaths, rather the fear of how death befell those who were claimed by the plague. It swept through its victims quickly, drying their skin until it cracked like sourdough bread. Plagued blood soured until the body's vestiges pumped nothing but a vile, blackened syrup, seeping out like deathly molasses.

Grim times foresaw grim reactions, and so a revolution had been born in Rasha's city of Vel-thaka. It swept through to Gara-thandila, nearly enacting something momentous—an end to rule by iron hands that strangled the empire from within while the plague crippled throughout. Now with victory forsworn, the rebellion was being wiped clean from the scrolls of history, not much unlike the plague-ridden corpses of Gara-thandila's shattered streets.

Rasha had been informed Warlord Yel-jaraht's final assault on Warlord Prince Zun-jish's black-iron fortress had been little more than lambs gathering to be slaughtered. Within his first year, the warlord of Vel-thaka had nearly been victorious. His defeat now rung in the air with the bells that tolled for the plagued dead. His hordes were little more than fuel for plague fires.

"If only you saw the desecration which befalls our people, wise and reverent Witchqueen Vutuala."

Rasha's responsibility as the current Witchqueen was to preserve the empire and its culture through any means. In the privacy of her home city of Vel-thaka, she had shed tears upon hearing the news of Yel-jaraht's defeat. The caste of Voodandum had been left with one less ward against Zun-jish's insatiable avarice. Without the bulwark the Rebel Warlord provided, Zun-jish's demands would fall upon them and Yel-jaraht's allies again. With his forces summarily crippled and Vel-thaka exposed, Yel-jaraht had since gone into hiding deep within the Ralcrav. It was why Rasha had been summoned to Gara-thandila by the Warlord Prince. As she promised Yel-jaraht so many years ago, she bequeathed Zun-jish to call for a truce after five years of civil war. After extensive correspondence, Zun-jish eventually buckled to her request with a pique. Voodandum and the Loa would now guide the Garathandi into a bespoken peace, one which Rasha prayed would hold long enough for the empire and its people to replenish their former glory.

Before the plague, civil war, and Rasha's furtive role in the latter, seven trollish cities and five Loa Gods unswervingly bestowed their allegiance to the Warlord Prince. In those times, Zun-jish threw about his weight in matters of state more than the rest of the warlords combined. Rasha grimaced in a subtle rage over the injustice of it all. The Loa Gods and their chosen kin remained neutral through the entire civil war, regardless of how leaden a decision it surely must have been. Neutrality did not suit her, however, so in secrecy Voodandum leant their aid to Yel-jaraht's cause. What little good it had done. His rebellion had still been crushed.

"*Muthra.*" Mother was a name few had ever called her by before. "What be troubling you?" continued the warm and familiar voice.

Startled by the footsteps that followed, Rasha swirled her fingers over the palm of her hand until her tranquility returned. She spun to glimpse who'd spoken from the darkness. Her two acolytes, Sulja and Malith, hastily approached. She pressed her tongue against the inner edge of her lips to speak, lingering over a greeting before it actually came.

"Sulja, Malith, my children." Rasha then crossly added, "You should know betta than to disturb me. Speak, and let us hope it is worth my time."

Malith scratched the back of his head, falling in subtlety as was his usual tendency, and he tremulously replied, "We have nothing to ask. We were simply worried and thought to learn where you had gone."

"If you have nothing to ask, then why are you disturbing me?" Rasha questioned wholly annoyed.

"Because we were worried about ya, *muthra.*"

Rasha sighed, realizing she had fallen into a painfully familiar trap Malith had zero idea he had even set. "I made it abundantly clear I had important matters to attend to, alone, and still you decide to trifle me with nothing, hmm?"

"Yes, *muthra*, but—"

"No more!"

"Yes, *muthra*," he sulked.

"I left ya knowing full well I didn't wish ta be disturbed?"

"For sure," he confirmed.

Furious, she demanded, "Then why have you come to waste my time with questions you already have the answers for?"

"Because we was worried about ya, *muthra*," Malith blankly responded.

Daggers scratched at the back of her throat. "So you chose to disobey what I asked of you for no reason?!"

"This, I have no part of," interjected Sulja. "But we do have a good reason for why we've come. Malith! Will you just share it, you fool?"

"We were worried when we could not find you because we be bringing a message from Tyratus," Malith relayed so infuriating long after it was appropriate.

"And you didn't start with that? There's no place for pleasantry within this caste, but you decide to tell me thrice over you was worried before conveying anything of actual importance. Paontara strike the foolishness from your head before I do it myself," Rasha drawled.

Malith blundered at a complete loss of words.

Oh, Tyratus, why had she chosen this dull troll as her second acolyte?

As brilliant as he was when taking to his studies, Malith had no mind for the subtleties much less the fundamentals of trollish interactions.

"All of the Loa Gods have arrived, *muthra*. The Great White Owl sent us out to retrieve you before they begin the council," expounded Sulja.

"Have I taught you nothing either, girl? If you speak the name of da Loa, you speak their true name and nothing else. Such a blatant lack of respect," Rasha scoffed.

Malith summoned a most respectful composure. "*Muthra gundir!* Sulja meant nothing of it. Tyratus be requesting your company from da Hoary Perch. He never said why, but I know it be serious."

Hemorrhaging embarrassment, Sulja averted her gaze.

Rasha's bleatings echoed through the cavernous dark and rang against her silver studs before stinging her conscience, digging in like worms. Too harsh or not nearly enough? It was often too difficult to discern with Malith, but not so much with Sulja. Her mind felt quite numb, so Rasha presumed it had been a little too much.

Dabbling with her composure, Rasha replied, "Tyratus be the wisest creature in the far north. Of course he be serious about his summons, you damned fool. Now both of you leave me quickly and let him know I will be coming soon. You tread on hallowed ground disrespectfully, and I will not be continuing this ritual while you chatter on."

Malith sulked while choking down his apology. Sulja slapped his hands before Rasha could herself. What a brilliant display of dominance from the acolyte witch. The conquered sun itself beamed through Rasha's grin.

Rasha's acolytes then knelt and bowed their heads, offering Voodandum's parting when they stood. They touched their thumbs to their middle fingers in a loosely clasped hand, kissed the two, and swept them in a loose salute toward their mentor. Malith and Sulja hastily departed, and Rasha was left idling between peace and anxiety once again.

Rasha had grown fond of Malith, a miracle considering she reserved little love for men, but she grew tired of him as well. He was a brutally clueless acolyte priest, male, and in her experiences, men cared for nothing other than war, ruin, and sex. Furthermore, she would bless no troll's ascension to a role of significance within Voodandum until she purged them of those vices. Miraculously, Malith strove for better things, but his head was still harder than the rocks that formed the Fulklar Foothills. Malith's particular blend of mental sluggishness as well as the challenges that came with training him were both unique.

Rasha meant no harm to Sulja either. The girl had been in her tutelage since infancy—abandoned to the streets until Rasha had adopted her into Voodandum. Sulja became Rasha's most polished disciple, a spitting image of the determination Rasha commanded at her age. Sulja did not know it yet either, but she was also to be the successor to Rasha's title. Sulja's intuitions often surpassed her own, but they still required the occasional refinement. Consequently, Rasha could never allow such silly mistakes to pass without reprimand.

Long after their return to the world above, her acolytes were a potent distraction, but she needed to discard her thoughts of them. Rasha still owed the First Warlord tribute. Even in death, Garatha was unaccustomed to waiting. Witchqueens were required to offer a tribute to the First Warlord several times throughout their lifetimes. Her first was long overdue.

Her breath dispensed her apprehensions into the chasmic abyss, and Rasha began to whisper an ancient chant. The weight of her words strained stone. Dust sifted off the patterned wall. She quickened, sharpening her voice and focus, and the chamber grew more clamorous. Shrill tones crawled over hallowed dark as Rasha chanted on. The slabs shifted and twisted and adjusted by the measure of her spirit as it bled through her words. Awe gripped Rasha's neck at the sight of her own power. She tensed against its inhibition, reticent to fail in her sacred task.

A purplish glow began to emanate from the runes outlining the wall. The troll carved into the shifting slabs began to faintly glow. A tremor shook the entire altar. Its strength matched the rigor of Rasha's chant. It rose and fell beside her voice like an auric seer's shout. Her voice straining and cracking, she concluded the chant. Garatha settled in lithic splendor, standing guard over his own eternity with Rul-Thraze the Thrasher in hand.

Duty distilled a broad sense of purpose. It either bestowed equanimity unto its wielder, shattered their bonds until they turned apart from passion, or caused them to buckle underneath its tremendous weight. Duty never changed. It derived itself from emotion, and while turbulent, all emotions were grounded the same. One's destiny might evolve, but never their sense of duty. The spirit might flicker and waver, but a mortal's soul remained unchanged.

Having found her sense of purpose in Voodandum, Rasha took hold of the knife hidden in her robes. She rolled it over her three fingers, danced it between both hands, and admired the ornate artistry of the blade while she recovered her breath. With a resolute flick, she opened the palm of her hand to draw a crimson pool, then nicked a finger to draw tinier droplets of blood. She approached the stone carving of the First Warlord and smeared blood across Garatha's divine blade. She dabbed the teardrop holes that speckled the sword's edge as well. She fed each teardrop twice, satiating the stone carving's eternal hunger, and the stone slurped it up. Her cuts rapidly healed after the stone absorbed the last drops of her blood. She studied her fresh scars, bewildered by the complexities of voodooistic druidism and how little of it she fully understood.

The altar trembled, and a slab at the foot of the wall dropped from its socket.

Rasha knelt, shoving aside the heavy stone. From the hollow within, the Witchqueen withdrew an iron-braced trunk. She pressed a finger against the insignia sealing it. Moments passed like wildfire as she concentrated her spirit, forcing it into the seal. The trunk persisted in its defiance, and Rasha awaited the runes to pulse with the same purplish glow as the carving had before.

The lid flung open to uncover a small vial bearing a purplish, vaporous fluid.

Rasha withdrew the vial with painstaking care, swirling its mystical contents over the palm of her hand. She briefly thought she saw the minuscule mark of life flowing alongside the swirls. She examined the fluid more closely. It appeared to subside as if reacting to her attention. The vessel shimmered, then dulled. She sojourned, and the fluid began swirling around the vial of its own mystical accord. Her usual composure abandoned her, taking to the dark like the flicker of torchlight. Her heart began to race like wild fraycrest oxen amidst a stampede. As if registering the slimmest alterations in her mood, the fluid churned. The rent souls of past Witchqueens, predecessors to the legacy she humbly carried, swirled above her sweaty palm.

Rasha set down the vial when its top began to wiggle. It sprung, bouncing around until disappearing completely. Nearly half of the purple fluid splashed out like foaming waves before dissipating into thin air. Rasha choked the vial. Gradually, the fluid's agitation receded. She clenched her hand to bring the fluid under her rigid control. An iciness enveloped her body, the soul solution's mechanism of defense against her intrusion upon its sanctities. She outstretched her arm and drew together her fingers like she was gently tugging strings from her throat, disregarding its resistance. A shiver shot down her spine. Rasha sustained the pull, and a tenebrous gloom befell the chamber as if the world had gone forlorn for the imminent parting of her own soul.

Willfully, Rasha strove for the ritual's swiftest end. Her soul stirred within the depths of her being, wracked with anxiety and unease. An indescribable agitation swelled as if something irreplaceable was being torn away. It most certainly was, but it was the sacrifice all Witchqueens made. Rasha would be no different. She would not break traditions that had held since the time of Witchqueen Moudula and Garatha himself. Fear did not belong with the Witchqueen of Voodandum, so she discarded it like the misplaced emotion it was.

Rasha continued plucking the air, even while the rest of her body began to thrash. Her throat tightened against her mythical command, and an invisible hand lurched her head back. Startled, she nearly screamed, but her throat closed to preclude her the chance. Her face opened against the ceiling. She began levitating above the floor as if her body were lighter than the dust shaken from the stones. Her mouth bled a warm mist. Her eyes veiled. The tempered glow of olive, the mark of a uniform soul bound by wisdom and peace, glowed harmoniously with crimson. A pale perspiration beset her body. All color bled from her face, draining her of her quality to guide and protect. Her confidence and courage soured, and she briefly yielded to her fear of failure.

Latching onto that severance in her nerves, a wispy stream escaped her body, untethered from all it had ever known. The fragment of her soul abandoned her anguished face. It bounded in torment and confusion, dashing about the room to elude empty air. Darkness tailed the wisp. The two leaped about the chamber. One danced in reckless terror and the other in glee. The fragment fretfully condensed, purveying the strange impression it had found a new master who streamed it into the vial as if by invisible hands. It writhed, slinking through the air, screaming bitter reluctance. Its nature to struggle, to fight, and to live were extinguished before her very eyes. Olive tinged with crimson soured to violet, and the ritual was made complete.

The vial's plug sprung up in a furious arc before jamming into the vial's neck. Encased by a veil of smoky shadow, the vial leaped off the floor, then plummeted into the trunk. The clasp wriggled shut, and the runic insignia reemitted its ever-present purple glow. The trunk slid into the wall and then the unfastened slab smashed into its socket, clenching against the dark hollow.

Freed from the invisible hands and drained of nearly all her strength, Rasha collapsed to the ground with a shriek. Her heart and dignity diminished as she struggled to suck in air. Pain pinned her against the floor where dust dirtied her cheek. While smiling sadistically, Garatha's visage tore itself into a hundred pieces. His gaze persevered after the wall's rearrangement, and he leered over her as she sprawled in inert pain.

Flames burst from their torches as they were freed from the shadows of the far north. Like snowfall in early autumn, the flecks dusted the floor and then swirled into a sinister silhouette. Darkness, complete and utter darkness, swept through the room. Two blood red eyes stared out of the abyss with nothing to accompany them but a crude smile. They had been satiated by the offering of her soul, if only for a short while.

—⟨◆⟩—

Rasha strolled the altar's upper stratum with a forcedly stern expression. She unnerved those who passed her by, but what they failed to realize was that she was mightily unnerved herself. Her ever sharp expression masked the genuine discomfort ravaging her mind. She strode silently, silent as the dead, because the dead had claimed some part of her. She wished to speak with no one but Tyratus, wisest of the five Loa, a trusted advisor, and her friend. After replenishing her strength off nuts stashed within her robes, Rasha reached the Altar of Garatha's upper floors.

She recalled her first days with Voodandum, when she was a whelp at the ripe age of thirteen. Nothing but a lowly slave before then, she'd believed servitude was her ultimate fate. Then came the day it had changed forever, when wise, sagacious Tyratus bat a curious eye her way. Before then, Rasha had not known kindness in her entire life. For no other reason than a destiny he drew from her eyes, Tyratus took pity on a worthless slave and saved her life.

Rasha recalled the first time she'd walked onto the Hoary Perch. Garathandila, Everdark City where sleeps the night, had appeared vast and oh so magnificent from the Great White Owl's perch. Then came the memory of her second visit when Tyratus and Witchqueen Moudula had informed her she would become the next Witchqueen. Rasha had found immeasurable pride in that emotionally charged moment, and it was the first time she'd felt anything like it.

"*Muthra gundir*, we were unsure when you would be finishing up your work," spoke Malith, groveling for attention while prodding into her affairs as was his usual tendency.

"Shortly, was the answer I gave you earlier, Malith. It took me less than that to arrive."

"A ritual gone well then, *muthra*?" he said without mulling for a single second.

Rasha snapped back at Malith with such alacrity that he flinched like a squirrel darting from the sound of rustling leaves. "You will know regret more than you ever have if you keep forcing yourself into matters that be of no concern of yours."

"*Muthra gundir*, I won't let it happen again. Just uh, a minor slip," he apologized.

"Oh, Malith, my clueless acolyte voodoo priest." Rasha livened, riddled with a levity nobody else yet understood.

Stricken aghast by the mere fact she was smiling, her acolytes froze.

Their confusion offered her a little something to genuinely smile over. Rasha dismissed the other trolls flanking Sulja and Malith. They scurried off without so much as a word, their sandals paddling the ground as they left.

Pleased, Rasha informed, "You claim you will do something now or that you be doing it later, but I cannot believe you, Malith. I look at you, see your blank gaze, and realize no matter what you promise, you'll always be making the same mistakes. You're like the lemming who, while mindlessly trailing a thousand lemmings like it, strolls off the Ralcrav, survives the lofty fall, and turns around to walk off that same cliff with a smile plastered behind your tusks."

A sudden burst of mirth escaped Sulja, but she suppressed it quickly.

Malith turned from Rasha to shoot his companion an angry glare. His feelings of betrayal only contrived her struggle more because they distracted him from the point.

Rasha demanded his attention with a growl, abandoning the excitement she wore so well before. "I fool myself each time, thinking soon the little lemming might choose to nibble at the grains I feed it instead of brushing them off my hand so he can run with the rest of his friends."

Malith paused before asking, "What be the grains?"

"The grains are the knowledge I be failing to instill into your thick head!"

Sulja sharply exclaimed, "Witchqueen!" A terse pause followed while the acolyte witch awaited Rasha's attention. "Malith's mistakes can be reprimanded another time. More important matters be at hand. All seven of da warlords and da council of da Loa have arrived for the truce. All but Hulvassa, which we came to relay."

"I see. Da Red Claw keeps council at bay once again. Perhaps, we should bend time to his will to better fit his demanding schedule," Rasha scathed.

Sulja nervously shifted and in a soft whisper frivolously asked, "I thought you taught we should only speak da true names of the Loa to show our respect?"

Sulja was correct, especially considering Rasha only recently enforced the rule, but as with every rule, there were bound to be exceptions. "I misspoke. Remember this. Not all are so deserving of our respect—even a Loa, should he flounder in his place. If you don't earn respect, there is no respect to be given." Swiveling to Malith, Rasha soundly added, "But for your sake, speak with nothing but respect since ya don't know any betta than to ruin it for yourself."

"*Muthra gundir*, please forgive Malith. I know he can be dense at times, but he means nothing but the best," Sulja woefully defended.

Harsh words came more easily to Rasha than kind ones, albeit Malith forever expanded the boundaries in which her harshest words were appropriate. She bowed as if to implore Sulja's reprieve before stating, "Don't be worried, my child. I see that you are right."

"*I pray you do not reserve such scathing language for our Tyratus when other Loa are so easily belittled."* The voice gently pecked itself into her mind.

Rasha sweltered through the connection both forged by and tethered to a Loa God. She pivoted to receive the great horned owl humbly hovering before her. Lifted by dusky wings, Tyratus's servant lifted her fatigued spirit with its whimsical grin. Had it not been for Malith's gaping stare, she might have completely forgotten his earlier mistakes.

"Tyratus's flock should know that truth betta than anyone," Rasha replied in the confines of her mind, soaking in the euphoria as she did.

"Forgiveness should prevail, lest we never glimpse what lies ahead out of fear of what happened in the past," hooted the owl.

Rasha stipulated, "Wise words, my friend. I expect nothing less from one who spends so great a time with wise Tyratus."

The owl accentuated its more mirthful hoots. "To be servant to Tyratus is good, otherwise I would be unable to speak my mind. Tyratus wishes to see you now. I will escort you to him, if it pleases the Witchqueen."

Rasha locked eyes with her two apprentices before insisting, "Malith, wait for me here after you have gathered and prepared Drukkabi and Jalcha for the meeting. Sulja, engage with the council in the meantime. Prove yourself a worthy acolyte witch until I return."

Both of her acolytes betrayed pensive joy, filling her with immense pride. Too eager, and she would have questioned their actual preparedness for the tasks. Too indifferent, and she would have reconsidered the roles they would eventually take in Voodandum. An even, balanced mind was the greatest trait a troll could obtain, and realistic expectations of the challenges one would face was the first sign it lived within one's mind.

Malith paced away in a hurry, and Sulja bowed humbly before rushing after her friend. Rasha returned to the whimsical creature hovering beside her. Beady eyes as wide as the Bright Moon on a cloudless night greeted her. With a smooth swipe of the left wing, the great horned owl motioned for her to follow.

Rasha stepped onto the widest berth of the Hoary Perch, a sweeping arch marked by the Crescent Lady's eternal dance. Built against the altar's uppermost outcropping, the crescent arch swept from corner to corner. The ledges were rimmed in limestone, a material uncommon to the Realms of Frostheim and most likely procured from the Seas de Cielos. A massive buttress on the altar's northern side reinforced the Hoary Perch. Close-knit columns enclosed the perch, touched by the sun's flicker and the derision of countless winters.

Here Tyratus perched and stared out over a frosty sky. His leaden plumage rustled in the high breeze, and he blended into the clouded skyline seamlessly. Tyratus most closely resembled a snowy owl. He bore distant relation to the hawk owl, features that revealed themselves in his rugged talons and sharp, curved beak. He was as magnificent as the antecedent owl Loa he drew lineage from, refined as elves who knew not what incivility was, reticent as the monk who spoke only when the spirits bade him to, and stoic as the wolf who only howled toward an aloof moon.

Rasha unveiled her deference when her entire body shivered within its grip. She paused before assuming the pleasure of speaking with the wisest being she knew. Having completed the ritual of souls, only the forthcoming summit of truce rapt her thoughts. She wondered if a Loa as ancient as Tyratus pondered the future like her, or if the Great White Owl instead peered into a future of augury like the Goddess of the Moon.

"My respects, *Faia ma fua* Tyratus. It is good to see you."

"I was beginning to wonder if the Witchqueen of Voodandum had tired of my counsel or if you were simply too ravaged of spirit to visit." Tyratus spoke in a low tone, his voice echoing crisp and clear. "Do you know why your order is feared yet loved, why the name Voodandum is whispered only in the bower of evergreens by the fearful flock that are our Garathandi?"

Rasha had considered the question before. She had also conceived her own notions for why the empire, which owed Voodandum so much, despised it so greatly. She held her tongue under the impression Tyratus wished her to ponder his words rather than speak at all.

"The power you and your caste possess, the mysteries of voodoo magic, gives you and Voodandum great influence over the empire and a sway in its affairs. You and many a member holds the power to heal, to harm, to mend, and to maim. The Garathandi fear what they do not understand and what they themselves cannot control. They fear the mystery that shrouds your caste and the domination your powers bestow you over the empire and its trolls."

Rasha rolled her shoulders, but it did little to make the tension disappear. "So you understand the roots of my anger. Ill-bred be the warlords who flaunt positions of power they did not acquire on their own. They pretend they be high and mighty but are no better than weasels who gamble with fate by betting the lives of those beneath them."

Gray eyes streaked with blue stared at the Witchqueen, and Tyratus spoke, "It is in their nature, young one. Power, wealth, and posterity. These are the envy of all trolls with strength in their hearts. Envy ensures even the brightest of lights extinguish themselves in the dark."

"It is no mystery the empire is collapsing. After so many millennia, it shames me to live through its fall, fail the legacy of my predecessors, and dishonor the lines of the Loa Gods."

"All empires inevitably fall, but once they have fallen into such piteous debility, they are no better than the ground they were built upon, though they can be reborn with a vitality that shadows their former selves." Tyratus gazed across a frost-bitten sky with a taciturn, plaintive expression. "It is the cycle of all great things, the rise and fall of empires. Perhaps it is the Garathandi's time to follow in the Lysian's footsteps."

"I do not wish to see Voodandum fall along with the froth of the Garathandi! I will that when the time comes, we will be the ones to rebuild the empire, restore its glory, preserve our history, and prevail against all odds."

"You speak of forsaking your people with such ease and fervor. I remember not long ago when a young acolyte witch thought herself no different than the trolls she speaks so ill of now," said Tyratus with an aura of concern.

"I see no need in serving a people who spit at my feet, disregard their heritage, and would kill their own blood if it suited their immediate needs."

"Duty and faith dictate anyone who joins Voodandum to preserve it. Without order, the foundations of civilization crumbles, and the empire ceases to exist—millennia of growth and prosperity lost in the folds of time—and yours and your ancestors efforts all become for naught. The empire might collapse, but the people's foundations must hold or else the wind and waves will sweep everything into memories as old as those of the elves."

"Duty does not account for Zun-jish. As long as that tyrant sits upon the Throne of the Riven Moon, the empire is doomed to dissolve into nothingness," Rasha retorted, retaining her anger at the very thought of the Warlord Prince, but forcing it under her control.

Tyratus chortled as only an owl would. "Eldaria is resolute, and we all have our parts to play in the endless cycle. Zun-jish is envious of legends greater than him. If the pieces fall where they should, then in time he will be extinguished like every envious being must and we will find the burning of his legacy to be just as bright if not brighter than those which came before him."

"For Zun-jish to wield legend would be for the Warlord Prince to forsake the ruin he has brought upon our people."

"Not all myths are forces of good. Many, even our own, were bridled with doubt and burdened by evil deeds. What they all share in common is how they brought us into a time in which legend remembers them as they wished to be but not as they actually were."

"And what of me and my legacy once this plague absconds and passing peace returns?"

"You, young Witchqueen, hold the threads of destiny in your hands, and you must wield them wisely. Never let them slip through the cracks. If ever I had known then of what I think to know of now, I do not know if I would have burdened you. I doubt I would have weighted you with such tremendous responsibility."

"I promise you, Tyratus, I will hold to everything I am. This plague of mythic proportion, this civil war that has swept over the empire, the waning grace of the Garathandi troll who has endured much worse many times before, they will not stifle my faith. I swear that everything you fear is to come will never break my spirits or keep me from doing good," she promised with such overwhelming resolve that it felt as if her word had already been made good.

"It gladdens me every time we meet that I may still gift you some novel wisdom."

"Your wisdom is vast, but when must words cease and action begin? Why speak of our empire's fall when instead we can cease to suffer the injustices that plague our people?"

"Wisdom is our greatest asset. The greatest font of wisdom is attained with experience. Experience gifts us the insight, intuition, and instinct for when it is time to act and for when we must stay our hands. We are, therefore, gifted a choice. When to fight our battles, when to turn away, when to take a life, and when to spare them to their own fates."

Rasha contemplated Tyratus for a long while, absorbing his words to style an appropriate response. "Then I choose to fight my battle today, even if I cannot wage it with force, because it must be waged and won for my people's sake. I refuse to tolerate this civil war any longer."

Tyratus nodded before concluding, "Tread carefully, Rasha. I know not what today will bring. You and your order should prepare themselves as such. Times are more grievous than we would like to let ourselves believe. Even in the southern Frallheim and upon the eastern edge of the Fulklar Foothills the Garathandi whisper of the Crimson Curse. As vitriol as this truth might be to your ears, it is one you must never underestimate."

The Great White Owl unfolded his plumage, striking Rasha with awe. His wings had lain too still for too long, beckoning to feel the renewed rush of the sky through their feathered tips. Tyratus sliced through chill, northern air. His departure let loose swirling gusts that dissipated like smoke off a kettle's lid. Tyratus soared from the Hoary Perch, vanishing behind limestone pillars and disappearing into clouds of milky gray complexion.

Rasha looked to where her mentor and friend had just been, then ruefully whispered, "Better hope you don't let your tongue get the betta of you today, Warlord Prince."

CHAPTER THREE

THE CABIN'S CREAK

THE NIGHT LINGERED AS FRIGHTFULLY as a stag's legs beneath the leer of a king's longbow, yet such anticipation was a normality for the ranger. Long winters had come after long summer's past, then were always brushed away by the renewing winds of the west. The sky glistened with starlight and the moon shone bright without the cover of clouds to douse its luster. The young ranger's mind, peacefully slumbering, wandered through the alpine lands.

Pines whispered the forest's secrets with the wind above them. The scurry of squirrels, the whistles of thrushes, and the chirps of purple martins transcended his stroll through the spirit realm. Bedding owls hooted their discontent, bidding the rest to keep quiet. They did not heed the ominous creatures' demands.

The ranger respected their wishes, but the forest's chatter drew him into the depthless space where consciousness and dreams both dwelt. He dreamt of his livelihood, of hides and hunting, and of his arrows buried in the eyes of wild things. From the comfort of his self-built cabin, the ranger wondered if the storm would be gone when he roused.

Modest, if not diminutive in stature, his cabin stood atop a hill in a discreet mountain glade. Timber uprights wedged into a cobbled foundation, the subtle façade of snowskin pine and blue-spruce firs held firm against the season's cyclic derision. The roof depressed ever so slightly under the weight of hefty snowfall like the pines it was neighbor to. Three windows peered out into the world, the largest beside a thick oak door. The second, a small squarish porthole, huddled in the corner of his cabin home and overlooked a vast wilderness of ash, pine, and brush. That particular window enticed nature's creatures to spare him occasional visits. For that alone, the ranger enjoyed it the most. A long, checkered window peered over his still-water pond, providing the widest view of his world.

Winter's fangs encroached on the edges of the pond, despite a glimmering sun rising behind it. Wondrous rays of golden yellow danced over crystal waters, and light's festive flickers filled the glade for the first time in three days. Two streams of hearkening snowmelt nourished the pond from a receding glacier. The pond trickled downhill in turn, swilling through the forest to pass through an open meadow where it joined a bulkier flow.

The ranger rustled when light peeked through the third window and fell unto his eyelids. He opened them with measured speed. Light gingerly soaked his tumultuous irises. They bore a chaotic green as opulent as the lush Verdant Forest. Thin lines of azure splendor stretched from their centers like depthless ravines. A nigh imperceptible scar split his right cheek as if it were a vessel for his soul's chaotic sea. He peeled away layers of blankets and leaped from bed. Thick black hair draped his back, a trimmed beard hugged his jaw and chin, and a silver necklace hung languidly around his neck. A small key dangled at the necklace's end, one which never left his neck. The ranger gripped it to confirm its existence, then let it fall over his muscular physique.

As swift as the elk's stampede when departing the wolves' company, he moved like it was any other day. It was. It had been. It would be. The ranger had been without company for many years. Without company there was nothing but trifling routine. Routine jaded most men, but his promise and love of family had forced him to acclimate in the end.

He knelt by his wooden nightstand, opened the upper compartment, and searched for the skinning knife or the gutting blade that should be lying beside it. He fumbled around the drawer, finding nothing but his steel-forged hunting knife and silver-tipped dagger. He had not expected a single, three day storm to break his routine so quickly, but it absolutely had.

He opened the lower cabinet to retrieve the day's attire. Comprised within was a pair of burnished leather boots, a flecked girdle, a hooded vest tinted a greenish-brown color, buckskin leggings, woolier leggings whose color matched his vest's, fur-trimmed leather bracers, and a plain cotton undershirt. He reached in farther, fumbling until he seized a pair of foot furs, pushed in his feet, then strung them up his calves. The ranger quickly donned the rest and cloaked his head before striding toward the door.

He paused to inspect the shelves on the wall beside the door. A bronze, maple-leaf clasp, various accessories, a torn washcloth, and a coarse bar of soap sat undisturbed. Two hooks were affixed to the bottom. One supported a leather vest trimmed with wool, mud-slathered leggings, and a mottled, hooded cape. An olive skin girdle and a bundled cord of rope hung on the second hook. A smaller shelf sat beside the first where he found the two knives he'd searched for before. A small iron coffer lazed beside them, his most prized but loathed possession.

Without hesitation, the ranger grabbed the bundled cord of rope, left, and closed the door behind him. He hustled down a cobblestone path, pausing where the moss met a wooden dock when an unfamiliar noise disturbed him. He searched the nearby vicinity for signs of an intruder. When nothing transpired, he continued on to the dock.

Kneeling beside a metal pail filled to the brim with minnow, he peered into the pond. A pool of salmon swum about, chasing smaller fry. The elder spawn scurried at the sight of slight movement above their aqua prison. Were the salmon anything more than skittish fish, he would have frightened them regardless. Ranger's carried ominous auras wherever they went, which benefited this one's call to seclusion.

The ranger retrieved the metal pail, brushed aside the grime lining its rim, and sprawled over the wood planks. He began sorting through the minnows, setting them aside into two distinct piles. The first comprised the gashed and rotten fish that were worthless for the task at hand. The other comprised those fresh enough to be mistaken as living. He discarded the half frozen minnows whose stench repulsed him into their own foul pile. Once done, he steadily fed the frigid waters with the freshest of the minnows. Salmon jumped in delight as they gulped down the lifeless fry. He abandoned them to their frenzy and seized hold of a rope looped around the nearest upright post. He heaved back with fearsome speed until a net broke through the pond's floor, engulfed the salmon, and muddled the pond.

As the salmon were raised into an airborne cradle, a few flopped free and speedily swam away. He leaned in to entwine the netting, tying it off with the extra rope he'd brought from inside. He then lowered their new prison back into the murky pond.

The salmon dashed about, desperate to escape, but accomplished little more than bumping heads. They palliated, then gradually began to float in aimless defeat. While they were simply unlucky to have crossed the ranger's path and pond, there was one inherent truth to their struggle. Eventually, a bigger fish always swam along to disturb those it crossed.

The ranger distributed the rotten minnows around the edges of the pond, hoping they would dissuade any ambitious predators from wandering too close. After some time, the waters stilled, the mud settled, and the salmon huddled together like sleeping children. The ranger sat, shifted, and stared out over the icy waters.

At three days' end, it seemed the storm had not stifled him much at all. This catch nearly completed his current order for the villagers of Skraelg. He counted twenty salmon, and he'd already gathered the requisite supply of venison. The meat chilled in a cellar beneath his cabin's creak, where he had stored enough to satisfy those he called his neighbors and to feed himself for months too. The silver-streaked hide of a dire wolf would finish out this order. Then, the ranger would be left to his peace until the next came along.

Leaves rustled within the heated sprint of someone light, nimble, and swift. He left the salmon to slovenly whisk and sprinted up the cobblestone path where sound escaped the glade. Andurial be damned. Why were they there and what did they take?

The ranger rushed into his cabin, scrutinizing his every belonging in no particular order. Everything seemed intact at first glance. His bed and kitchen were unviolated, and his cabinets and trunks were undisturbed. Even the wood panel that led to his cellar remained closed.

He rushed to his nightstand, shuffling through its contents madly at the thought of lost coin. He did not particularly care for money, nor did he hoard riches. Much of his work was done for charity, however, and what coin was left from Lysian, he absolutely needed. After confirming his coin caches remained intact, he checked underneath his bed. Finding nothing amiss, he staggered back. There were no signs of thievery afoot, odd as it might seem.

Perhaps his imagination had hurled him toward suspicion. He had been without company for so long. The contents of his iron coffer did enjoy tormenting him by laying shadows on the edges of his sanity and sight. Were his senses betraying him out of spite? Maybe the sound had simply been the bustle of a critter skittering about.

An epiphany struck, and he glanced to his shelves. Andurial damn him for convincing himself otherwise. The high country never ceased reaffirming even the most uncanny of fears, regardless of the burdens he carried and locked away. His knives remained, but the iron coffer was nowhere to be seen. Aggravation snapped his neck to the paper left in its wake. The ranger grabbed a folded note inscribed in black ink. "Good morning from A.I.D."

"She is damned devoted to her vow," he admitted before crumpling the note and tossing it to the ground.

Without delay, he exchanged his vest for the one trimmed in thicker wool, affixed his hooded cape to his shoulders, and retrieved his steel-forged hunting knife and silver-tipped dagger, clasping them both to his belt. Transitioning away from the door, he reached underneath his bedstead to retrieve two black wool casings. He speedily unraveled both to unveil his juniper bow and a collection of spruce arrows packaged into three bundles of nine. He loaded two bundles into his quiver and slung it across his back before latching on his bow.

Throwing open the panel to his cellar, he descended below. From the racks on his right, he seized bundles of rationed food, rootless supplies, and deerskin flasks filled with icy cold water. He threw each into a satchel tied taut to his hip, then hurried up the steps to return to the perfidious world above. He sprinted from his cabin toward the woods, momentarily forgetting to close much less lock the door. Miffed, he backtracked to lock the door, then prayed the rotten minnows would keep the high country's hungriest inhabitants at bay. Ehlaru Sidrich departed his humble forest abode at last, upon the trail of his surreptitious thief.

Ehlaru had unintentionally gifted his thief ample opportunity to pull away. Regardless, the ranger believed he could make up lost time, at least quicker than she could manage to fully escape. Agneta was his student, after all. Everything she knew of being a ranger she had learned from him. That alone gifted him an advantage since he was inherently tracking himself.

Moss imprinted with petite footprints crossed his gaze. Ehlaru followed the impressions until the moss dwindled into needle covered dirt. From there it was rather easy to follow her trail over broken twigs and trodden snow. He paced himself to reserve his energy for a burst chase. It was effortless, and at this speed he could honestly run forever. He had acclimated to the high country many years ago. Life at this elevation made him stronger than he ever believed possible. Before escaping Lysian's fall, he had been a skilled soldier, sorcerer, and commander of men, believing himself already perfect in most every aspect.

Ehlaru jogged for a solid hour through a day well underway. Birds scouted the forest for food. He even caught wind of a fox chasing a startled hare. In due time he would be no different than the fox feasting on its morning meal. His prize, however, was to simply capture Agneta, or rather to take back that which was rightfully his.

He paused when an elk and its calf sprinted across his path before stopping directly in front of him. Both panted, and steam sloughed off their hairy backs. Had they been fleeing a predator, Ehlaru assumed they would have ignored him and continued to sprint. More likely they were searching for running water buried beneath the layers of snow. The path they were on would eventually intersect the streams, which fed his stillwater pond.

Agneta's trail led directly through them, and Ehlaru needed to press on. Fortunately, he spotted no more elk in the surrounding forest and could safely startle these two without inviting a stampede. He approached while dispensing a commotion. Mother and son bolted, and Ehlaru proceeded after his thief.

He ran for another quarter hour through bramble and brush. Bushes rustled, and he slowed to a leisured jog. Having closed in, he walked her broken path to keep quiet until the trail bled away, then halted near the rustling bushes that had since gone still. He knelt, examined the ground, but discerned no footprints. He rose to go around, the bushes shook, and a neigh leaped in from the other side. By the God of the Skies, he had done it. He had caught up with his thief.

Ehlaru lowered his shoulder, covered his head, and tore through the thicket like a wild man. Twigs slit his cheeks. Thorns ripped through his clothes. He wiped away the poison before it could bother him anymore. Brushing off the twigs plastered to his face and plucking the thorns from his hands, he stumbled into an open meadow. Scarce patches of dead grass peeked through melting snow over which his thief and her steed ran away.

He waded through the loose snowpack at the meadow's edge, sprinting until better ground materialized beneath his feet.

As if hearing him break into chase, Agneta gathered speed, pulled on the saddle, and kicked her leg up and over her horse's rear. Pulling her weight forward, she slid into a better position, tied down her offhand, and kicked her horse into a full gallop. She looked back to smirk and wave, sparing him a fleeting glance of her blissful face.

Realizing Agneta was too far off to catch on foot, Ehlaru unslung his juniper bow. He flicked the bowstring to test its strength. It quivered alongside a violent twang. He retrieved the arrow that would be its fleeting mate and knocked the shaft into place. He drew until the string touched the flesh of his cheek, took aim at the fleeing thief, and closed his left eye. The sun shone too bright for him to properly use it. He focused with the right until he measured the speed at which they strode and the distance they had already traveled. He found the angle at which the meadow rose, felt the lick of the morning breeze, and adjusted for them both. Pressure was nonexistent, the air hung thin, and he could taste his lips as he drew a final breath.

Ehlaru waited, wavered, and sucked at dry air, watching as both the girl and his stolen iron coffer sped farther and farther away. He waited until his thief cleared the montane meadow and galloped beyond his bow's reach. Then, without the realization he'd meant to, Ehlaru sighed. He lowered his bow with dissatisfied angst. Somewhere on her person or in one of the satchels draping her horse's flanks, Agneta had hidden his last keepsake while she selfishly rode away.

Snow wet the linings of his boots, biting his ankles. He realized he had not properly dressed before pursuing his thief. Fittingly, he now paid the price for his earlier hastiness. The ranger re-slung his bow and tossed aside the arrow that was never meant to have been drawn. After dusting the white powder from his ankles, he stuffed his leggings inside his boots, pulled the thicker wool layer over the top, and sighed with warmth's return.

Agneta adored disturbing his seclusion, upsetting his routines, tormenting him with her heavenly physique. Black hair dawdled with the breeze like the loose ends of cloth banners upon the ramparts of a mountain keep. Hair rippling skyward, it revealed a pale perspired neck that curved into soft shoulders; a slender, muscular back; and a tight rear. Her ranger's cloak fluttered like an escort's veil, taunting the mind to lose itself within the beauty underneath. She had been so graceful in her flight, in withholding her iniquitous prize, knowing he would chase her to the ends of the Nordland for the chance to have them both, even if he could only surrender to one.

Ehlaru retrieved the unspent arrow from the snow. Trailing his fingers down the buffed shaft, he compared it to every other he'd ever drawn but never loosed. He strode through the meadow until reaching its obvious center, then dropped to one knee. Like so many times before, he drove the arrow deep into frozen grass to mark the spot.

It was their unsullied tradition. On every occasion Ehlaru drew his bow against Agneta, whether while training her or in the time thereafter, even if he never took the shot, even for as infuriating as she often was, he would drive the unspent arrow into dirt to forever mark the spot. Their little game of cat and mouse speckled the high country with his arrows. The sight of them reminded Ehlaru of her stubbornness, a trait he admittedly liked, and of the strength of his own resolve. He had always been fond of her, but to deny their love was better for them both.

Ehlaru rose like the rising sun and strode toward the meadow's western edge. Agneta had ridden in a different direction, but he knew she ultimately headed to Dekryl and her horse would probably not make the entire trip. She would need to cross the Hünderhelm, a river too swift and too deep for a horse to wade, and the closest bridge lay to the south in Skraelg. He intended to cut her off at the river or in the village should he fail. Regardless, Ehlaru could not let her reach the Godrulheim Divide, or he would be hard pressed to keep sight of her trail.

Reaching the meadow's edge and the base of hulking pines, the ranger paused to witness the day. The length of the journey ahead of him knew no legitimate bounds. With a grunt, Ehlaru shrouded his head with his motley hood and began his marathon run.

CHAPTER FOUR

SHROUDS OF DUST

SEVEN TROLLISH WARLORDS, FOUR LOA Gods, a congregation of Voodandum's elites, and the strident Witchqueen herself encircled a massive, rectangular amphitheater of stone in the shadow of Zun-jish's black-iron fortress. They had gathered for a summit of truce, yet each stood on discordant pillars and thought to break the others. A theme could be placed upon them all, one which exemplified them perfectly. Rasha recounted the disputatious story that was their ode to bitter strife and brutal civil war, wishing she had not agreed to Yel-jaraht's plans so long ago, wishing it had not gone wrong.

Warlord Yel-jaraht, who once ruled the city of Vel-thaka, took his station upon the first pivotal locus in their empire's broken trifecta. He bore an average build and stood at an average height. His thin black hair, coal-colored skin, and ruddy tusks sheltered a sullen face sunken in from years spent ahead a vain insurrection.

To his left stood Warlord Kindril. Kindril's lank hair, muscular body, and curled tusks were wrung in the rustic umbers hidden under the Frallheim's frost. He and his cleaver's edge were as ever sharp as Hulvassa's claws, but his wit was more refined than the carcajou Loa's. Domildin's warlord hid his attributes well beneath a poised grace as strong as his spear arm.

To Yel-jaraht's right towered the massive troll who ruled the southern city of Bul-karat. Gekas retained a slim resemblance to the ancient tawny appearance the Garathandi boasted in the time before their exodus. He was a relatively brutish troll. Fierce in battle but slow in speech, he relied heavily on the judgment of his cousin Kindril in regard to the finer dealings of his city.

Beyond the three warlords' greater ensemble lazed the elder, Behemoth Loa who roamed the Endless Wastes. Mammotte and his chosen consort lay in each other's downy comfort. The Woolly Mammoth had not betrothed an alliance with the rebels' cause, but his lofty placement behind them at this somber gathering served as a looming reminder of the rebellion's just heart.

Warlord Prince Zun-jish's syndicate gathered athwart the dissident warlords. Gara-thandila's warlord glowered indignantly over the assembly he'd summoned at Rasha's behest. Boldly thick and muscular, he was born from the stock of trolls whose blood had been scoured by carcajou blood. The Warlord Prince was as savage and cruel as the Red Claw. Zun-jish was, likewise, a loathsome reminder of the horrid results that came from mixing the blood of the Loa with the blood of the troll. His once stone-spruce skin had been reddened by Hulvassa's fiery blood. Zun-jish was also quite hairy for a troll. It was a well sought after side effect of mixed Loa blood. However, those who reaped the curse that came with bearing mixed Loa blood could never live without it again.

Warlord's Ruh'rehm and Rhak-jan—rulers of Gara-thandila's neighboring cities of Malakal and Damari to the west—flanked Zun-jish like faithful dogs restrained by their master's chains. They were average trolls who possessed stone-spruce skin, black hair, and burned umber tusks. Ruh'rehm was a half-hand taller than his counterpart, but Rhak-jan stood out amongst any of his fellow trolls. The Red Claw had once marred the warlord's face. Rhak-jan had since cinched the savage gash with small iron rings. Once healed, it resulted in a dark, grisly mien. Ruh'rehm simply studded his lips with rings instead.

Rasha positioned herself and Voodandum as the meeting's third pillar. She stood at the head of an alliance wrought in the cold embers of neutrality smoldering within the fires of hot avarice. Warlord Beh'kliar stood beside her. He was a warlord wiser than most. The ashen troll had become Rasha's closest ally since the onset of her Crimson Curse and the dawn of the civil war. He alone understood her most enigmatic pangs because of all he was privy to.

Tyratus perched high above the Witchqueen's throng and the dissident warlords' milieu. Leopard of Snow Paontara and her current mate lounged on the amphitheater's steps below. She chose that distant stone for the warmth the sun bestowed it, and Tyratus and his flock overlooked its glow. Ursala, Bear of Winter, concluded their alliance. Ursala hailed from a silent stock, and he seemed simply content to ravage his meal while waiting.

Rasha stepped before all those who had gathered. A few thousand trolls, their warlords, and four of the Garathandi's Loa Gods were enough to warrant she begin. Hulvassa dishonored the summit of truce with his unwarranted delay, so the Witchqueen would dishonor him. Rasha did not much care. She neither enjoyed the company of the Red Claw or his sizzling quips.

"As tongue to the Dreamwalker Loretia whose spirit rules over ours in death, as speaker for the lunar realm which forever dresses Monomua in her shifting shrouds, I address you, Garathandi. You have been summoned by our Warlord Prince, who calls for an end to the strife between us. He has been answered by the Rebel Warlord, who sues on behalf of the trolls without the breath to stand before you now. You have been gathered above rivers of blood each troll has drawn from his enemies throughout this civil war. Glory you have attained, and now glory is begotten. Each day we fail to cull this bloodshed, we belay the return of glory to our two goddesses, the Garathandi Empire, and our Warlord Prince." She paused to gauge the crowds.

There was a relatively even split in opinion between the three regimes. The line lay between those who thirsted for further bloodshed and those who craved an end to the wanton death. Her task was a magnanimous one indeed. Convince trolls born in war's fierce womb to pursue peace in the stead of violence. It was a daunting task that fundamentally opposed the innately trollish erudition that prosperity and power came only from conquest. Yet, if she urged the right players in the right direction, most would have no need to consider the day's quarrels at all, which would be all for the better.

Conferring the mantle of speaker, Rasha addressed Zun-jish. "I leave the stage for you now, Warlord Prince. Speak, so we can honor a promised peace."

"To promise peace is to promise defeat, and I have made no promises to any troll here. You betray your true self before my assembly by claiming otherwise!" Zun-jish snarled gruffly.

Furious with his snide accusations, Rasha moved to speak, but wisdom demanded that she not. Hers was the power to mend as well as the power to harm, so she stayed her tongue. She would defend herself and rebuke his subtle divisions, but it would be wiser to first permit Zun-jish the opportunity to expound upon his opening remark.

"I never promise what I cannot give. I offer da subjects of my empire da simple prospect of peace. It be da traitors who be making promises they cannot keep," he finished, and a savage grin spread over half of his jawline.

After suppressing her irritation, Rasha plainly answered, "A generous proposition, one I never considered you capable of giving. But this be no battle, Warlord Prince, and we have not yet reached the point of settling this armistice."

"You do not decide, and have I not already done my part?! I opened my doors, welcomed these rebels into my home, and chose not to spear them on my gates when they arrived."

"Yes, Zun-jish," Paontara drawled afront a long and candid yawn. "You have taken the first steps toward negotiating a truce. I congratulate you for your astuteness…"

"Do not mock me, Leopard of Snow. I might have welcomed these ungrateful dogs back to the crate, but I cannot make them choose to stay."

"I am no dog!" rumbled Warlord Gekas sonorous and low. "I am aspected of Ursala, and you are like a weasel-bear who squirms beneath my mighty foot."

With his massive great-axe in hand, Gekas stretched his arms wide to survey the crowds. Many roared in answer, chanting his name in fierce repetition. Gekas turned to face the Warlord Prince, grinning as only a lump-brained clod could.

"You dishonor the carcajou Loa with your thick tongue! Does Voodandum accept insults against the Loa Gods too?" the Warlord Prince accused.

"I do not speak to how you rule, yet you expect to speak for mine? Bury your hypocrisy before you dishonor da legacy of da First Warlord," Rasha faulted furiously.

"I expected da Witchqueen of Voodandum to demand that respect be given to each Loa and warlord here! Did ya beg for me to send these summons so you can proclaim this civil war now lies on two fronts?" Zun-jish spewed, his temper overblown and volcanic.

"We have reserved our judgment since the beginning of this civil war.

Voodandum and the Loa Gods have taken no sides. Nothing has come to pass which warrants we alter our stance, so we remain neutral in the hope it might meet a natural end," Tyratus pensively interjected.

"I would not speak for Hulvassa. Our brother has been scarce of late, and the Warlord Prince has always been his favored, mortal friend," Paontara snarled.

Rasha gently refuted, "No, Hulvassa is merely sly by nature. I do not pretend to know where he might be, but I know he holds his oath as sacred as we hold ours."

"Perhaps," the Leopard of Snow yawned. "Do not pretend there is not one who knows where he is. Where is the Red Claw, Zun-jish? Why does he dishonor your call to pursue peace with his absence?"

"No carcajou spawn has ever dishonored me, but it be clear to every troll here that your words and da actions of da other Loa are meant to despoil my rule. All except da Bear of Winter have made it clear whose throats they mean to rend!"

Bewildered by it all, Ursala flayed an entire flank clean off his caribou's bones. The bear Loa consumed the meal whole and then expelled his lungs of air with a forceful cough that rose from deep in his throat. Ursala raised himself to all fours before he settled on the other side of his meal's corpse.

Rasha slid with the rush of wind that swirled when his paws hit the floor.

"No further disrespect will come to you, Warlord Prince. I expect you will offer the rebel camp the same respect, or I will lose my patience," Ursala pledged.

Zun-jish bowed in accordance with Ursula's undeniable request. He struck the flat of his ax against his chest, holding it there with respect.

Rasha tensed with the utmost severity until Ursala returned to his meal.

Drifting from his stance of deference, Zun-jish gifted a mock smile to Paontara and her seasonal mate.

The silent Loa's mate snarled and fixed its gaze on Zun-jish.

"Come now, Zun-jish. You make yourself seem like a tasty meal looking at me like that," Paontara sardonically proclaimed as she readied herself to pounce.

Ursala rose to two legs, extending to his full height. The snowy hair on his neck bristled. His muscles rippled across a frightening physique as if droves of salmon swam beneath his skin. Ursala roared, and every trollish warrior and warlord across the arena cowered in fear.

"Did I not speak my mind?" Ursala rasped before he grounded himself onto four massive paws and clawed at the ground.

Paontara growled frustration, but she did not openly challenge the bear. She kicked her legs to the side, poising herself in faux relaxation.

Rasha suddenly realized she was holding her breath and expelled it to her lung's great relief.

Unfortunately, Paontara's slighter mate did not follow in hers or his mistress's example, and he growled at Zun-jish again.

Then arose the unmistakable snarls of the carcajou Loa descending the arena's steps to lurk behind Zun-jish. Blood dripped from his mouth. Flesh from a misfortunate meal still clung to Hulvassa's teeth. Trolls skittered like frightened mice from the red claws on his feet. Like lightning flung from above by the Stormborne's favorite runic god, Hulvassa darted toward Paontara. After closing half the distance, Hulvassa abandoned the effort and returned to the side of his mortal pawn. Falling for the Red Claw's trick, Paontara's mate whimpered like a frightened cub. Paontara openly dejected him for his show of weakness by snapping her jaws at his throat. The mate scurried off, and Rasha expected she would never see him again.

"You are late, fierce Hulvassa, but you have been sorely missed. I would have hated to finish this meeting without a friend by my side," Zun-jish ingratiated.

Hulvassa clattered his teeth and replied in a shrill voice, "I had many matters to attend to, although I think I might have missed all the fun."

"The fun has only just begun. Eat with mighty Ursala while Rasha tells us all how peace and plagues be formed," Zun-jish crudely joked.

Zun-jish and the Red Claw might both pretend to be more clever than the Stormborne's trickster god, but in actuality they were duller than the brain matter staining Hulvassa's fur. Wisdom and patience drown beneath the ice shelves that lined Vel-thaka's port. Rasha had tolerated enough of their disparagement and stalling. The two could incite their base as much as they like, but Rasha intended to speak to every troll. She would force the truth to be heard after their insults were doubly returned.

"Was your business with your stomach, great carcajou Loa? How comely. You must be feeding a litter of unborn cubs."

"Hello, Rasha. Did you miss me? I do not see it in your eyes if so, but I missed you and your snideness both," swaggered the Red Claw.

"I thought you did not care to join us. Forgive me for commencing Zun-jish's meeting of truce without you, carcajou Loa."

"As I said," Hulvassa drawled on the edge of a second snarl, "I was exceedingly hungry, so I took my fill before joining your summit of truce."

"Zun-jish's summit of truce," Rasha staunchly rebuked. "If this truce prolongs as I think it will, then we should share dinner after it ends."

"What need? You have done a marvelous job without me. Besides, I love food, and we are not all so willing to concede that which is most important to us..."

Rasha froze so her face could not warp into the grimace it so desperately desired to. She bit her tongue until her teeth drew bitter blood as red as the Crimson Curse. She knew her words would melt her veil of amity like magma devoured mulched soil. She must be wise like Tyratus expected because she had found herself within the confines of an eminent test of her will.

After a tense moment, she moved to speak. "I know passion like yours. I would never endeavor to steal it away."

Hulvassa cackled madly but gave her no further grief. He licked his teeth to taunt her, cleaning them of their stains.

Her bleeding tongue stung her tastebuds, leaving behind an iron grit. Rasha untensed her jaw to offer a smile. She kept her lips shut, however, because she did not wish for the carcajou Loa to see what she had done to hold back her tongue.

Swallowing bitterness, Rasha said, "The Warlord Prince has spoken to his whim, and he has shared why we are summoned."

"Aye ya," Zun-jish bellowed. "I be extending my hand to Warlord Yel-jaraht. I give you"—Zun-jish pointed—"this one chance to surrender and reenter my fold!"

Yel-jaraht, who had sat silent through the entirety of the meeting thus far, rose. "What be the conditions of your invitation. I know da offer does not come without rueful terms."

"You will receive no vices from me, only what punishments your crimes deserve," Zun-jish responded.

Gekas growled beneath his breath, yet the boom was audible to every troll in audience. Yel-jaraht bade the juggernaut to calm, and he reluctantly obliged. Donning a fulgent visage like the one Rasha suppressed, the warlord spun away from Zun-jish. It was a remarkably effective gambit that effectively culled their quarrel before it could begin.

"Do you deny my offer for peace and forsake da trolls who live in Bulkarat? What of your wives and your spawn? Do you think my armies will spare dem when we tear the rebels in your camp apart?" Zun-jish inquired.

"Zun-jish! I have promised you as you have promised me. Do you dishonor your oath and me?" Ursala rumbled between gulps of caribou.

Zun-jish averted his eyes and lowered his head in repudiation. Warlord Gekas, of all the trolls, had misled the Warlord Prince into a trap to which he was none the wiser. Old Yel-jaraht briefly smiled before urging his ally to turn back around. Zun-jish twitched like a skittish insect.

Had it not been for the tension still lining her jaw, Rasha might have giggled like a little girl.

"I count my terms then, Yel-jaraht. We all know da way should you refuse, so I'll be sparing you the gruesome details. I will accept ya surrender. In return, I be offering two choices. Disband your hordes to the cities of their birth and return to rule as daunt of the Endless Wastes. Once you reclaim your mantle, my hordes will occupy Vel-thaka, Domildin, and Bulkarat. You will be taxed until the empire's coffers are refilled and da debts of ya insurrection be fully paid. Only den will I give my hordes da order to leave," recounted Zun-jish boldly.

Enraged, the rebel camp descended into anarchy. Let them riot for all she cared! Taxes had been the primary cause of Yel-jaraht's insurrection. When plague struck the north, Zun-jish reaped the south of their gold, swine, and crops. His taxation of those regions least affected had not been erroneous in the slightest, but Zun-jish taxed more than was needed under the guise of administering aid to the afflicted. For Zun-jish to so blaringly call for the same taxes that had sparked the civil war spoke to both the smallness of his mind and his rule.

Zun-jish spared no efforts to conceal the truth, believing himself both untouchable and above every troll. Yel-Jaraht then traveled to the capital with half of his hordes on behalf of Vel-thaka, Domildin, and Bul-karat. He neglected the Warlord Prince's summons upon arrival, seeded the truth through the Everdark City, and the common trolls rebelled. Yel-jaraht rebelled alongside them, seized Gara-thandila, and diverted the remainder of his hordes to engage Rhak-jan's forces after the warlord marched out of Damari to reinforce Zun-jish. Thus began the civil war that had torn the empire apart, one it appeared Zun-jish wished to prolong.

Yel-jaraht raised a single hand and closed it into an iron fist, and those rallied behind him hushed. "And what be your second offer, Warlord Prince?" he grievously asked.

"Surrender yourself to me, and I will allow your armies to leave. You will become my prisoner until the day you die, although I think that day be fast approaching. I won't be taxing your cities and my armies won't occupy them either, but I'll be the one to choose Vel-thaka's next warlord in a time I see most fit."

Zun-jish sought to trade one savage offer for another. Both were violations of her city's right to self-governance and a mockery of Voodandum's intermediary rule. Within days of the beginning of his rebellion, Yel-jaraht emptied Vel-thaka of its hordes. For five years thereafter, Rasha managed Vel-thaka in his absence without sending a single troll to support his cause. She administered aid to the injured on both fronts and supplied the poor so they did not starve, all while Voodandum was engrossed with cracking a cure for his Crimson Curse. Zun-jish did not seek an end to the civil war. He sought only power and ways to bring Vel-thaka under his direct rule.

Rasha surged to speak out against his avaricious offers until Tyratus calmly whispered, *"Patience, young Witchqueen,"* in the confines of her raging mind.

Yel-jaraht turned to witness his warriors as well as those from Domildin and Bul-karat. He exacted quiet with such vigor that one who heard him from afar would have thought he were a drastically younger troll. Yel-jaraht's shoulders heaved until his breaths found a steady beat and his coughing ceased.

Rasha's heart plunged upon seeing her great friend traipse through such a fragile state of health.

Yel-jaraht swiveled to confer with Kindril and Gekas. The three spoke at length, casting their gloom between Rasha, Zun-jish, and the Loa amidst their discussions. The trio parted from their heated conference. Gekas snarled near the end, but he yielded to his cousin's judgment as he always did.

Kindril stepped forth to speak, and with vigilance, the umber-tusked warlord of Domildin hailed Zun-jish. "We believe an agreement can be reached with da terms of your second offer, but we'll be making our own amendments before a deal can be struck."

"I didn't invite ya to be extending your own offers, and I won't be listening to more of your frosty jütengolk shit! Did I summon these crippled dogs to offer our surrender?" Zun-jish asked spastically.

"No, Warlord Prince. You summoned these dogs to bring them to heel," Rhak-jan barked to the exclaim of the trolls behind him.

"It is a negotiation, Zun-jish!" Rasha thundered with knocked hostility. "They can make their every offer, and you must hear them before passing your judgment."

Zun-jish scowled, eyes seething like steam off a hot bath. Neck flexing robustly, his lips split to dispute her.

Rasha bared her teeth and flexed her tusks, betraying every sliver of patience for the rage bottled down. Her eyes forbade him from stepping any further down that ill-advised path, and the steely webs that laced her eyes stifled the rise of his nonsense. Without so much as a single word, Rasha had silenced the Warlord Prince.

"*Baf galut* this affliction you seed with your presence," Rhak-jan mumbled after spitting something foul and smearing it over the ground.

Rasha jeered, "Speak louder if you have something ya wish to say."

"You be wasting our time! We either accept his demands, or we'll be finding ourselves slaughtering dogs in da streets before they spread more plague."

Rasha savaged, "The only troll who be wasting time we could be spending elsewhere be you, Rhak-jan. What reason do you have to challenge the right of each party present to offer their terms in this negotiation?"

"Da same right a deceitful whore be having in leading these rebels!" Rhak-jan shouted with a swell of indignation.

"Ya bark like a big dog, Rhak-jan, but shake like a little mouse. Scuttle between ya master's legs before squeaking again," Gekas mocked.

Knowing there were some she could control, Rasha demanded, "That be enough! Present ya party's offer or state your peace with theirs, but do not waste our time again!"

Gekas grunted as if he had been crossed, but her severity forbade anymore noise from sliding off his tusks. She did not heed Rhak-jan's disrespect either. He was not worth the effort. She did look upon him, however. To her diffident surprise, the warlord had nothing else to say. He received her gaze unyielding, a challenge in itself. She admitted he had balls for that.

"There will be no occupations. There will be no new levies. Domildin and Bul-karat will return to your fold. Our power will be unquestionable, but so too will our service to da Throne of the Riven Moon. Our allegiance will be renewed as if we had never rebelled," Kindril specified.

A raucous tinged with a mixture of excitement and confusion arose from the opposition. Even the Loa Gods stirred at the boldness with which Kindril exacted the rebel's demands. The warlord inexorably continued, striding as if nothing of import had arisen from what he'd said.

"Vel-thaka's next warlord will rise when the time is right, but he will not be yours to choose. The city will not be made your mutt. Its ruler will be no dog who fears your rule. Vel-thaka be Voodandum's prime dwelling, so it will be Voodandum who selects their city's next warlord."

Zun-jish's hordes howled like starving mongrels, and Rasha could scarcely fathom the boldness of the offer herself. Gekas and Kindril were no friends of hers, yet they would entrust the selection of Vel-thaka's next warlord to her and her order alone. What did they intend to exchange to justify the vagaries they placed upon Zun-jish's initial offer? Even now, Yel-jaraht plotted without leverage, thinking himself cleverer than them all.

"In exchange for da terms we offer, Yel-jaraht will surrender his head to ensure the death of his rebellion," Kindril apathetically concluded.

Disorder descended into bedlam. Zun-jish roused with the bearings of shocked intrigue. Rasha shivered with malevolent fury, wishing for nothing more than to place a curse upon him, Kindril, and every troll who deigned to believe their woes could possibly end with Yel-jaraht's decapitation. Resentment did not bleed like sweat. It simmered until it grew so great it burst with unparalleled vigor. If not Kindril, Gekas, and Vel-thaka's next warlord, then one of the tens of thousands of other trolls would rise to lead the southern city's hordes against the hands wrapped around their throats.

"Kindril? You have betrayed your wicked cause and those foolish enough to have ever followed it. Would ya have me cut off the hydra's head to reveal the true spine of your roguish rebellion?" Zun-jish exhumed with curious exultation.

"I betray nothing," Kindril staunchly refuted. "Will ya now be spreading lies you declaim to be da truth because you cannot see the reason behind what we offer?"

"I speak no lies here. My word is law! I only share da bitter truths my subjects deserve ta hear, and you can see it in her every actions. The Witchqueen sympathizes with your cause and might be an ally to it, too. My mistake was trusting an ancient order of witches, warlocks, and priests to serve my empire in good faith."

"You will not smear Voodandum's reputation! What proof do ya have to support these vindictive claims? You have nothing!" she screamed. "So you distract from the matter at hand."

"The proof lies with you. It has always lied with you," cackled Hulvassa from behind a pair of jagged fangs.

Rasha requited, "Share your proof or begone with your lies and heresies!"

"You defile the empire with wicked words and smear its Warlord Prince's name. You move every rebel motion forward and in the same stroke of your hand, murder words of loyalty. You curse the Garathandi, poison your people's blood, and now that your motives have been exposed, your savage fear makes your guilt excessively clear."

Warlord Beh'kliar roused to defend, "The Crimson Curse is your and Zun-jish's lie. Even Loa Gods must substantiate their claims, and you have never spent a shred of truth to confirm your filthy fearmongering."

"Silence, whelp!" Hulvassa shrieked. "I will take no spite from the coward who sits when battle thrives around him. You disgust me, but not enough that I could not eat you whole."

"You are a savage hidden in the proud line of carcajou Loa. You could do better to hide that fact, Red Claw," Warlord Beh'kliar rebutted.

"I am savage. It means I have a keen scent for blood. It is how I know Rasha beset Gara-thandila and its allies with her Crimson Curse," Hulvassa cooed to Zun-jish's hordes as if they were his own cherished young.

"Voodandum has pored over every ritual, lent every shred of its aid, and toiled through every labor to find an end to this vile plague. Why would we waste all of our efforts if I cursed the Garathandi troll? It be freakishly absurd!" Rasha roared.

"You wish to make them feel your pain—the pain you're always hiding.

You wish to make them wear your shame—the shame that makes you question if you deserve to be Witchqueen," Hulvassa growled with a sudden surge of intensity.

"I wear no shame because of the failings of other trolls! I carry that burden like a cloak of wool furs, and it warms my soul knowing I survived it. I am the Garathandi's Witchqueen as much as I will always be yours!" Rasha resounded in defiance, not permitting Hulvassa to vilify her anymore.

"When then will I be presented with the queen of the empire's soul?! If you are truly my Witchqueen, then when shall the ritual be drawn?"

Rasha stammered for an answer. She was caught completely unaware by this foreboding interrogation. She had not prepared for such an event, expecting an open scuffle to devolve long before anything of this nature developed. How could Rasha have expected Hulvassa to disregard everything at hand in favor of revisiting one of their pettiest feuds?

"How does this bear any relevance to the negotiations at hand?" Ursala roared, urging the Red Claw to swiftly answer by spreading his jaws.

"Paontara, Tyratus, and even you have been honored in this sacred way, but I have gone without this blessing because she denies my every request."

"But to what end do you call for the ritual now?" Ursala prompted.

"What better way for the Witchqueen to prove her innocence than to draw the ritual of souls here in Gara-thandila, where all Loa and trolls can bear witness," Hulvassa responded, the words surging off his tongue like geese migrating south for winter.

"I have not yet received the ritual of souls, yet I do not complain," bellowed Mammotte, the behemoth Loa. The roamer of the Endless Wastes shook the snow from his coat, then faulted, "Patience would suit you better than this savage display of unrestrained passion, Brother Loa."

Rasha swallowed her pride and peaceably replied, "When the time is right, you too will be honored, Hulvassa, but it is not something which can be done on a whim."

Hulvassa interrupted her quicker than she could finish, passionately shouting, "I have no patience for disrespect! The time is not yours for the choosing. It be mine to demand!"

"My soul be mine alone to relinquish, and I will not heel to your churlish demands. This be irrelevant to the peace nearly at hand."

"Do you not wish to see peace in your time? Do you not wish to satisfy a Loa God and bring an end to your curse?" Hulvassa chattered alongside the murmured agreement of several deluded trolls. "You will not deny me this sacred right any longer. I will see ya soul! I will be offered a piece!"

"Your actions ordain otherwise. You are not worthy of such an honor when you stand to shame me in the heart of Gara-thandila!" defied the Witchqueen.

Hulvassa spat in vile disgust. His eyes narrowed like the slits embedded in a Helmyan horse lord's hood of war. He then licked icy callous from his lips as if a fevered chill had overtaken his impassioned soul. Before the hairs of his back could settle, the heat of his heart retook him like the raging carcajou he truly was.

"I am the fiercest Loa of them all! I will claim this gift since you deny me, even if I must rip it from your heart and split your body from your soul."

"Hulvassa! Be reasonable!" she implored.

Rasha gasped in disbelief as Hulvassa charged toward her headlong. She frantically cast a lunar circle and muttered an ancient call to the Dark Moon, enwreathing her hands in shadowy moonlight. Even though they stood amid Monomua's waxing cycle, she had been drained of too much energy to summon anything more than a feeble flicker. Regardless of circumstance, Rasha had little choice but to settle for what diminutive power she could draw to defend herself against Hulvassa and his pride.

She glanced to find Sulja and Malith following in her lead. Warlord Beh'kliar and his host immediately blocked the path between her and the Red Claw. The warlord handled his axes and his warriors their spears for what would soon be utter carnage. Even Paontara roused from her sprawl to stand in Rasha's defense. They were like the uncemented backing of a thin brick wall, but the hammer soon to befall them would test the true strength of their enduring forms.

Beh'kliar ground in his feet, aligned his phalanx for battle, and roared, "Step no farther, Hulvassa. You be far out of line!"

"Another meal for me? You and your black-iron will be mighty crunchy," cackled the carcajou Loa.

Before Red Claw could lunge at Beh'kliar and his host, a shadow descended from above to thwart his bellicosity. The Great White Owl spread his wings and dipped his beak low. Tyratus poised afront a frightful caw, obstructing the path by which Hulvassa would have struck at Beh'kliar. The carcajou Loa leaped back to hastily reposition, batting aside a few trolls with his energetic claws. Hulvassa paced in a futile effort to flank Tyratus, who surrendered no ground to his fellow Loa God.

"Do not stand between me and the patrimony the Witchqueen owes. You will not defend her refutations any longer," Hulvassa hissed with scornful ferocity.

"She does not deny your entitlement out of spite but out of irrefutable necessity. The time was far overdue for Rasha to satisfy Voodandum's tribute to Garatha, and so I bade her complete the ritual prior to this summit of truce. Rasha does not have the strength nor the stamina to split her soul again, not at least for another cycle of the moon."

"Lies. Filthy lies from the hooting bird. The Witchqueen never mentioned such things, so I do not believe you!" An acrid steam suppurated from the carcajou Loa's nostrils. It smelled of deathly char.

Rasha had never come this close to Hulvassa, nor had they faced each other like this before. That truth utterly frightened her, even in the protective shadow of Tyratus's wings. She struggled not to exhale its sour verity, even as it scorched her lungs.

"What chance had she to share this knowledge?" Tyratus ardently inquired. "This was not the reason we were gathered, and it should not be the reason we leave without resolving this truce."

"Excuses never-ending. Obscene lies! This offspring of the Garathandi offends me with her blatant disrespect. I will give her reason to revere the Loa—*all* of the Loa—and you won't keep me from teaching her how she might reclaim lost grace."

The two reached their argument's peak. Confrontation appeared imminent. Paontara reviled her brother Loa when she drew beside Tyratus. The silent Loa bared her fangs to spare Hulvassa a vicious snarl, which the carcajou Loa matched in kind.

"Stand yourselves down!" Rasha shouted, surrendering her hand's flickering moonlight to restore it to the Goddess of the Moon. "If you will permit me one final request, I will draw the ritual and we will conduct it here and now."

The Red Claw staggered between cackles and light growls. "Give me your terms, Rasha, and perhaps we might strike a deal."

Rasha vociferously shouted for all to hear, "If you think it be so obvious I side with the rebel camp, then it be equally obvious you side with the Warlord Prince. You will return to the Warlord Prince's side, and Zun-jish will settle with Kindril's and Yel-jaraht's terms. Then, and only then, will I grant you the honor of presenting you with my soul."

"It is done! Foolish Witchqueen," Hulvassa barked, "you demand an agreement that would have eventually been settled upon."

"Rasha," Tyratus whispered as he folded in his plumage and gently swept her under his wing. "I cannot allow you to follow through on that rash promise. It will devastate your soul's bindings. Your body cannot sustain the damage."

"I am strong enough to manage it once more." She faced him before stoutly reinforcing, "I was strong enough to split my soul for the First Warlord, climb my way to the Hoary Perch, and lead this summit for Zun-jish. I am strong enough to present Hulvassa my soul, and we can be done with his captious vacillations and the lies he likes to spread."

"This will not bring peace. It is an extension of a bitter truce, which will crumble to dust when pressure is first applied," Paontara snubbed.

"Peace is what we make of it, Paontara," Rasha staunchly corrected. She turned into the silent Loa before proclaiming an oath, "I will always strive for peace until my soul is spent and my lungs draw life no more."

Hulvassa regrouped with Zun-jish's regime, and his temper flared as he spat, "Accept the Rebel Warlord's offer. Ya strife will be at an end, and you will acquire everything for which you hunger, and I will find my peace."

His peace? What role did her soul have in delivering Hulvassa his peace? She considered the carcajou Loa's comment. Hulvassa could not possibly have placed such tremendous value on the ritual he had not yet received, could he? Did the Loa who had defiled her reputation with the Crimson Curse value her that much? Rasha studied the bloody lines of greed and gluttony that streaked his eyes. No. She decided it was nothing more than a slip of his tongue.

Zun-jish spoke, "I will not concede my ground after I have fought this long to seize the upper hand. What benefit does dis—"

"I will see it come to pass, or do you wish to defy me? You would not betray me...not when there is so much for us to accomplish. Not when there is so much life in you left."

Trolls around the Red Claw shriveled like infant spawn. Zun-jish stood tall, eight feet in all, but even he was unnerved by Hulvassa's feral ferocity. The Warlord Prince sought to speak out in defiance, but when Hulvassa bumped his fangs against his tusks, Zun-jish instantaneously decided against it.

"No, Hulvassa, I was mistaken. They offer me everything I covet and more…" Zun-jish reluctantly conceded, his voice trailing off into a softening string of laments.

All those gathered trembled in stunned silence. Hulvassa triumphantly danced away. Rasha watched as the blood drained from Zun-jish's face until his skin turned white as winter snow. She touched a hand to her cheek to confirm her blood had been drained also. Zun-jish shuddered, and like a yawn through a flock of sheep, it induced shivers in her.

"We accept your terms, Yel-jaraht," Zun-jish beckoned to his rival. The Warlord Prince then howled, "Clear space for this ritual of souls and thank the carcajou Loa! Once the deed is done, we will debate the details in my unbreakable fortress!"

With little more than hateful claims, Hulvassa steered the Garathandi into believing a ritual of souls would banish their Crimson Curse. They wholly believed it, their cries speaking to its undying fervor, but they were mistaken, of course. The two bore no relation, but amid the ashes of death arisen from war and plague, the sham eased their dull minds. They clung to its specious richness, and Rasha to her heart still aching from the morning's ritual of souls.

Rasha allotted Tyratus, Beh'kliar, and the priests, witches, and warlocks of Voodandum no time to dissuade her. She sauntered down the amphitheater steps with tragic grace, believing herself defeated due to her own rashness. Tyratus had given everything she needed to avoid this outcome, or at least anything remotely like it. Instead, she allowed her passion to overcome her, and wisdom died in its place.

A chorus rose as Rasha ambled. Its spirit was filled with curiosity and animosity alike. Trolls teemed the edges of the amphitheater to overlook the arena below. They would witness a ritual that a thousand of their generations had, perhaps, never seen before.

She shivered when her feet touched cold dirt. She might become the first Witchqueen to ever break the lines of tradition that had existed since the Garathandi came to the far north. And for what? To cull infighting, a civil war, and a plague she was falsely blamed for?

No laws forbade Garathandi trolls from witnessing the parting of a witch from her soul. Voodandum simply preserved its mysticism by disallowing its secrets to be so easily exhumed. A Witchqueen typically performed the ritual of souls on several occasions for Garatha and once each for the five Loa Gods. Rasha had followed in Witchqueen Moudula's footsteps closely by only performing the ritual in a Loa's sanctuary for them and their loyal followers alone.

Morbidly forlorn, she strode to the arena's center. Dusty slabs fashioned a shattered dais several steps above the dirt. She ascended the neglected dais, turning to witness every face watching her from above. Rasha looked away, the pressure too much for her to bear. Her heart ravaged her veins, and her blood pulsed hot as molten iron.

Rasha drove her knees into the ground atop the dais, splayed her palms, and began to recite the ritual's first chant in the olden tongue of the Garathandi. The voices surrounding her grew quiet, and trolls watched in awe. She caressed her hand into a tightened fist. With shaky fingers, she plucked at the air escaping her throat. She felt no fear, only heat rising within her. Tension no longer wrought her physique. Unlike the variant of ritual she had performed for the First Warlord, this one gifted a forbidden warmth.

Rasha lost control of her facets, and the ritual mostly completed itself. Her head lurched back, her face opened, and her arms spread wide as if presenting angelic wings to the carcajou demon looming above her. She was lifted above the stone platform. Her face sweat profusely, and its every orifice bled auras of olive pain. They sprung like beams of moonlight, dashing into the sky above, and a hollow pale befell her face as her crimson soul was ripped apart from her body's soft allure. She shrieked in pain, then toppled to the ground.

"Crimson? Yes, it would be crimson, but what is this other color it seeds?" Hulvassa yapped confoundedly.

"It is green," Zun-jish exclaimed from far away. "It is the green from the trees that grew in our ancient homeland."

The fragment of her soul whipped about lithely. With every instance of its passing, her heart skipped a beat. She raised her head, a simple task that had become utterly daunting. Her eyes instantly fell out of focus. A coat of gloss distorted her vision. Tears rolled down her tender cheeks. Her face's vapid heat burned them away, shrouding her vision in a mist of her own pain.

Through the haze, Rasha pieced together Hulvassa, who towered above her a mere arm's length away. She raised her own arm, muscles straining when she did so. She bade the fragment of her soul to lift before Hulvassa. The carcajou Loa studied it with a curiosity that frightened her to the core. She crumbled in the face of the Loa God whose hatred for her burned pure.

"I don't care where the green came from. I will take it all for myself," Hulvassa cooed.

Rasha feebly rasped, "It is not yours to take."

Hulvassa lifted a paw and swiped Rasha to the ground. He began flirting with her soul fragment like a cub would with its mother's tail. He bounced it between his paws and streamed it between the blood dripping from his teeth. The Red Claw seemed content to continue playing as if her soul fragment were a toy and nothing else. He nipped at its wispy tail, and she relinquished a blood-curdling, violent screech.

Rasha collapsed. Her head struck stone, blurring her vision further. Her mind numbed, but she watched Hulvassa cower in the shadow of something massive. Incapable of discerning what it was, she rolled into a more comfortable position. Whoever cast the shadow wrought Hulvassa with terror, and that observation replaced the pain with something more joyous.

Hulvassa relinquished the fragment of her soul as the shadow began to stomp. The wisp flew down her throat where the riven halves refused. Her body vigorously shook underneath the massive beast again, and again, and again. Her eyes flickered against the rising shrouds of dust until she closed them.

Peace rapt her head, peaceful as the promise of treatise that had seized the day. It was her victory, one which she had gifted to her people accordingly. She slept with confounded joy upon that cold, solemn fact for which she would receive no thanks. Rasha slept, and without the knowledge of which side of Death the Reaper's Arch she might awake.

CHAPTER FIVE
TRAIL OF A THIEF

AGNETA HAD GIVEN EHLARU AN easy path to follow. Initially, it led him far enough away from home that he abandoned the thought of returning to retrieve his yoked, draught-fjord horse from wherever it currently roamed. He pursued her on foot, falling behind as a result. Their footfalls echoed across the Valdhaz like lovers quarreling in the dark, or like two wolves escaping their hearts by pursuing their moons.

Ehlaru Sidrich ran for an entire late winter day, trekking the landscape until he reached the lower slopes of the west Valdhaz. He crossed two burbling streams rebirthed from winter's thawing, then engaged in a free hand climb to overcome a stout ridgeline and save himself hours on the journey. He relocated her trail shortly after. It swung west toward the setting sun. He utilized shallow mountain descents to close distance as he continued in hot pursuit.

He took rest in the timberline for a short respite, bundling brush and broken saplings to construct a shelter. The night was calm and surprisingly warm. Not a single cloud blotted out the sky. Ithilia and her infinite stars glowed with immeasurable splendor. Monomua's moonlight persisted like a dying beacon beside them. The Crescent Lady was nearing the end of her waning cycle, waxing toward the dark to the doom of moonlight's prism. Soon, there would be nothing left but her most dour visage—her recollection of an ancient pain unknown to the world below.

Ehlaru awoke to the magnificence of the celestial realm and utilized its shining starlight to recommence his chase. His calves became enflamed as he ruthlessly pressed on. His muscles twitched contemptuously, but he did not relent. Soon, he caught the faint gush of rushing water off in the distance ahead. He was close, so very close to the landmark by which he could possibly cut her off. The Hünderhelm was before him, a river that could not be easily crossed.

The Hünderhelm was the largest river between Stormguarde in the east and the Range of Tjorden to the west. While it would not have overwelled, the river would be too turbulent for her to wade across on horseback. Agneta would be left with two options. Travel south to the nearest village of Skraelg and cross by bridge, or quest north in search of a natural crossing that might sustain her horse's weight.

The Hünderhelm grew more garrulous as Ehlaru drew near. Splashing water traveled beside the wind through the foliage before him, carrying a robust, frothy weight. His earlier conclusion might have been rash. He did not yet see the rushing waters, but they sounded quite substantial. The river ran heavy for both this primitive age of the year and the altitude at which he traveled as well.

He caught the cries of the fae folk in the river's whip. They sang of its lithe wonder, of its descent into the Wrathgorne where its destruction would spread, of drowning humans, and of the joy that potential solemnity afforded them. There might have been some truth to their malevolent choruses. Winter was shedding her full coat. If any of the Stormlands' mightiest rivers engulfed their dams, there would be massive floods.

The fae folk's songs grew brassier as he approached. River sprites were a particularly wily lot, well known for drowning hapless travelers caught unaware in their spiritual spheres. Truthfully, Ehlaru despised dealing with the fae and their trickeries, even if it was expected of rangers. They were tricksy creatures, Eldrahg's inspiration for the runic god Lok, and Ehlaru took no delight in Lok's variety of wickedness—not for a lifetime at least.

Ehlaru deferred their meeting to gather some intelligence from afar. Two river sprites frolicked through a lighthearted quarrel in an elongated meander. Beside them, a crimson faerie sprawled atop a bed of prickly roses growing beside the river's banks. She must have envisioned herself pretty, because she had drawn her form in the natural world as utterly ravishing. Fae folk enjoyed depicting themselves in the colors of their strongest attributes. It helped them compose their tricks, but to a clever mind, it also exposed the ruse of their ways.

Ehlaru approached measuredly, ensuring he made little noise so as to not be noticed too quickly. The ranger was as equally cautious not to accost them unexpectedly. Anything more and anything less might anger the three fae.

The crimson faery regarded him the instant he entered their spiritual sphere. She grinned enthusiastically but made no motion to alert her companions. Instead, the little winged faerie cursed the air and fell atop her roses in an accentuated display of despair.

The demurer of the two river sprites gently sung, "You cannot steal my love because you share my gritty realm, brother! This faery's heart belongs to I, and it will be my children who call her mother!"

When he could hold his tongue no longer, the excitable brother who was doubtless the far younger, uproariously bellowed, "Nayyy!"

"Can you not refute my claim? Thus, I have won the day!"

"Nay. Nay. Nay, you win the day!" the cheeky brother repeated to the elder who appeared heated.

"So you agree with my fabulous claim!" the elder cloyingly slaked.

"Nayyy! You have no claim, and I shall make you rue this day!"

"I do have claim, with one whose heart will receive it, so what is there for me to rue this fine day?"

"Your claim!"

"Nayyyyy," the elder sprite exclaimed.

"Boys, boys, behave. If you will not for me, at least try for my company!" the crimson faery boldly beckoned, to which the sprites' shenanigans subsided.

In the quiet moment after the faery's plea, the three fae spun as one to regard him, donning unique masks for the occasion. The faery shed her reds to reveal gold locks draped over a milky face, then discarded her costume as quickly as she had betrothed it. She redressed herself with crimson cheeks, hair as black as midnight, and long bangs that veiled her emerald eyes.

He squinted, confused by the shifting shades of her eyes.

The emeralds withered into sapphires as if a hopeless future were consuming a tragic past. The faery must have read his mind.

The excitable sprite dipped into the water before bursting free. He imagined himself as a man who either hailed from the mainland or the Kingdom of Helmya. Blond hair curled above a face bleached like ocean sand. A square-cut face followed a strong jawline and rounded beside a prominent chin. Blue eyes twinkled like a font of mystic magic enwreathed in celestial starlight.

The elder river sprite was far less innovative in his design. He dressed himself inside a turbulent ball of water. After dispersing his aqua shield, he edified the finer details of Ehlaru's own face with pellets of rabbit shit. The sprite's attention to detail was impeccable, but Ehlaru would have utilized phoenix droppings instead.

Ehlaru discovered the faintest traces of hoofprints in the grass beside the roses where a horse had trotted beside its human. They carried away from the stale, punctuating meander toward the heart of the Hünderhelm. While ignoring the fae, Ehlaru began to follow the apparent trail.

"'Tis not kind of the mountain's stranger to depart without a farewell. Does he know not how to treat a lady? Does he know not how to show the faery her worth?" hummed the crimson faery as she skirted the edge of her thorny vale.

Ehlaru gazed over the riverbed where ended his thief's trail. Narrow, shallow pockets flanked the river's roaring center. Agneta had given her mare time to rest and replenish before moving on, but there were no indications she had ever withdrawn. There were also no signs she sallied the river and led her mare within. His chief question was left without a clear answer. In which direction had she disappeared?

Ehlaru needed time to consider his options. It did not matter whether he searched for a natural crossing or traveled south to cross by bridge if his trail diverged from hers. Perhaps he should humor these three fae while he pondered the dilemma further. Perhaps they might hold some knowledge as to which direction his thief escaped.

"Forgive me, my crimson darling, for I have been too long deprived of a lady's touch. I would know not how to honor your beauty without leaving a smudge."

"A gentleman I see, or roguish is he? I suppose I care not as long as you continue to lavish me," intoned the crimson faery.

Ehlaru opened his mouth to speak. Before he could form any words, it was filled to the brim by the river. The sprites splashed him without surcease while laughing maniacally betwixt themselves. Ehlaru spat out a broken twig. He considered igniting them as unexpectedly as they had accosted him but decided to outwit them instead.

75

"You betray yourself, little sprite, for you do not know me well. Begone with your tricks before the forest hears your knell."

"What is a knell, big brother?" the younger sprite innocently questioned.

"For the death of another when tolls the bell, the ring one hears is that of the knell…" answered the elder sprite before he struck Ehlaru with a spiteful gaze.

The young sprite shivered as he came to understand the implications of the threat. With perplexed distrust, he then climbed behind his elder brother. Contemptuously, the elder sprite proceeded to splash more water in Ehlaru's vague direction. They drenched the crimson faery more than him, a fact with which the lady was none too pleased.

"Keep thine troubles to yourselves! I do not wish to dry beneath a sky-damned hell," the crimson faery lashed, vindictive and begrudging.

Marking her the easiest target, Ehlaru piped in, "Do not blush, my exquisite friend. I will turn my back while these matters you attend."

The faery surrendered a blush, and a frivolous smile spread across her cheeks. "My suitor is so kind to me that my heart bursts full of glee. If only now my friends could see the benefits of quelling their juvenile sprees."

"He would not do you well for a lover. His heart unmistakably pursues another," accused the elder sprite maliciously.

Upon hearing his accusation, the crimson faery seethed like an ember spent in a dwarven furnace. She wrung the water from her miniature form. Gone was Agneta's midnight hair. Gone were the lustful eyes of desire. In their place she revealed her truest form, and her rose petal face metamorphosed into a wreath of thorns.

Both river sprites cringed amid the revelation, dropping into the water so nothing but their eyes peered above.

The crimson faery turned to berate Ehlaru, demanding, "Does your heart truly lust after another? Have you then stricken me with this ugly pother?"

Ehlaru licked his lips as he amassed the proper words with which he might conciliate this feisty faery of faux roses and earnest thorns. Upon acquiring them, he replied, "My heart remains bereft of vows, but a thief has driven me here and now…"

The river sprites gurgled water, spitting bubbles into the air above their meander. In slow, methodical succession each bubble popped and their troublesome voices harmonized, "A thief to which he would endow, his line's inordinately handsome brows!"

Having had enough of their taunts and trespasses, the faery shot them with a beam of rose petals bound by thorns. Quaint, but the manifestation was a fraction of the magic a fully-fledged druid could harness. Wilting petals slapped the sprites, who retreated underwater. Once they rose again, they made the clear gesture of sealing their lips shut.

"Do not mind my spritely friends, they know not how to quit while ahead."

Ehlaru pinched his nose amid mild contemplation. He agreed with the river sprites in one regard. He did have handsome brows. They were keen, if little else.

"They were little bother. My vigil keeps, but I now have questions for which you might have answers, if you still wish to speak with me."

The crimson faery eyed him suspiciously. "What questions, stranger?"

Ehlaru offered an exaggerated bow. "Was there another before I who infringed upon your domain this fine morning?"

"Perhaps there was a woman. Is this of whom you speak?"

"It is indeed, and the woman is my thief," he answered correspondingly.

"And what has the woman stolen?"

"An iron coffer."

"What does the coffer contain for which you have pursued her all this way?"

With considerable effort, he confessed, "A trinket valuable only to me."

"Strange thing to cherish. You would risk to perish by retrieving it so irresponsibly?"

"It means more than you know," he answered plainly.

"Then journey forth no farther. For you I replace the trinket begone from your grip, and so wonderous I shall take its place," she incanted with a desolate face.

"If that which you offer is so wonderous, why so easily give it away?" he rejoined to her unmissable disdain.

"I was mistaken about you, stranger. You are nothing more than a rude and silly ranger!" she screamed.

"How do you know I am a ranger?" he questioned smugly. "Perhaps, I am a no more than a lone wanderer or a rogue in hiding."

"There are no others who look like you in the high country. Let down your blasted hood, and you will prove my point!" she lashed.

Ehlaru refuted, "Yours has grown unappealing and lost all of its lithe. Temper yourself, faery, and I might oblige."

The thorn's enwreathing the faery's face tightened until they her pierced skin. She twirled in sweltering anguish until he believed she was on the verge of imploding. The river sprites doused their crimson crush with streams of water. They were astoundingly successful in cooling off her temper. Her heart shaped face pulsated in cold imitation of its earlier splendor.

Ehlaru peered beyond her joyous facsimile to only find his own regret. He'd almost certainly ruined any chance he had of gathering useful information on his thief.

"Is this more pleasing to my love? A crimson face, with a voice like the songs of doves," the crimson faery blithely rejoined.

Ehlaru peaceably conceded, "Forgive me, for I spoke out of turn. Do not appease me, my crimson love, because that is a right I have not yet earned."

"I forgive you, but you will receive no help from me!" she stoutly intoned.

"Then you would steal away the truth? This makes you as nefarious as my thief!"

"Hmmm?" she hummed. She spoke no further, but the smugness of her smile reaffirmed her pestering resolve.

"Who then must I speak with to obtain the answers for which I've come?"

Rising from the idle meander, the young river sprite exclaimed, "Yes! The queen you must speak with, ranger. Lok's favorite daughter, our Liminal Queen of Tongues!"

"True, we steal away every lie from the world," the mellower river sprite purled.

"So nothing is left for her but truth's born to be sung," the crimson faerie intoned with a melody befitting the ears of a lustrous elven king.

Ehlaru laughed, charmed by their quick-witted lyrical display. "I have only the present to meet this queen of tongues. Summon her from the ether, and if this you promise to do, then here I will wait till her song is sung true."

Heckling Ehlaru's arm, the mellower sprite spoke, "Not her song, fake ranger. Yours!"

Ehlaru swat away the sprite. It spat on him with icy contempt. From pale blue it morphed into a profound flake of snow. The river sprite then brooded atop the meander's peace, glaring at him with each passing word that was not its own.

"She shall lay upon the ranger's ears fates which hang by threads. A fate which should never be unfurled, a fate we cannot coherald. A destiny she shall impart before those you love are most fraught with peril!" quoth the faery with a sullied crimson heart.

Morbid severity stung the crimson faery's tongue, and by Andurial had she delivered it with outstanding poise. Ehlaru mulled the fae as they bustled in eager anticipation and then decided he would allot them one final opportunity to speak their peace.

"Indeed, I am a ranger, whose undue haste has wrought his journey with danger. So why am I unworthy to meet your liminal queen and hear her fateful song? You share dreadful tidings, yet we dance around the meeting in melody and delay without resolve!"

"We guide you, Ehlaru Sidrich. We guide you to your first truth."

"I guide myself to my own truths, forge my own path, and you will delay my journey no longer," he abruptly resolved, disliking how this faery knew his false name without him having ever given it to her.

"Not a journey, but the beginning of your quest. From one quest rises another until many have met their end. Then arises the ultimate quest by the strength and weight they each lend!"

"Then I shall depart from this place to save us both the trouble of babbling nonsense."

"Go then, silly stranger. You're no fun anyway!" cried the young river sprite whose face had soured into a snowflake at winter's end.

Ehlaru dismissed the sprite's drivel, making it clear he detested him the most. The sprite appeared too astonished to muster any words to delay him further. The last Ehlaru saw, the river sprite dove head first into the river's icy blue. He did not glance back again. He carried himself north along the river's eastern bank, resolute to play one last trick on the group.

"Alas, mighty ranger, do not walk too far in the wrong direction!" the crimson faery cried out in a mocking shout.

Long, decisive strides carried him forward faster than before. Ehlaru knew little of the fae, but he was quite familiar with one of their chief mischiefs. When loss loomed over one of their heads, their hearts turned to vile anger and they stooped to spreading lies. Trickery betrayed veracity for anyone clever enough to look beyond its shade. The crimson faery had unwittingly assured Ehlaru he was heading in the right direction.

Ehlaru transitioned into a run. With good luck, he would find her point of crossing soon enough. Doubtful Agneta would have discovered a shallow or a fallen log wide enough for her horse to cross. He would either find the mare without its master, or he would find them both. He repeated the promise with each step, and it fueled his fast pumping heart.

It was the hour in which the conquered sun climbed its highest when Ehlaru found a mare lounging above a knoll beside the river without a care. He approached cautiously at first, then decisively when the mare seemingly motioned for him to come and stroke her mane. He laid a gentle hand against her neck, and she brushed against him as if they were age old friends.

She was a handsome horse, whose white freckles and mottled dun coat gifted her a cheerful look. A draught-fjord, she was relatively short but incredibly powerful and agile. Her breed was evolved for mountainous terrain. A draught-fjord horse could survive the wild on its own, but this mare's absolute carelessness toward strangers suggested she once belonged to a mountain hold where danger did not. She had no chance without a master and a proper home.

Ehlaru urged the mare to stand and guided her in the direction from whence he'd run. She initially resisted, so he soothed her into an impermanent calm with soft words of guidance. Once certain she innately understood the path he wished for her to take, he firmly slapped her rear.

The mare trotted on by herself, neighing of her disgrace. Better she detest him now than later, after night descended and danger crossed her path. She would reach the village of Skraelg in about a day. There, she would find herself in Draven's Dominion, if she finished the journey before dire wolves, ursa bears, or Soudland mountain cats claimed her as a snack.

Ehlaru spun to address his own concerns. Pines felled by a late winter storm spanned the Hünderhelm like outstretched cats connected at the paw. Their roots remained partially lodged in the river's stone banks. The crossing was reliably solid. He would have chosen it as well.

He refilled his emptied deerskin flasks with pellucid water before taking a shallow swig. Freshness spread from his heaving chest to his fingertips. He succumbed to the desire to take another swig. Crisp snowmelt revitalized his breaths. He returned the flasks to his satchel, climbed onto the first log, and swiftly paced to where the overturned trees joined.

The Valdhaz was buried beneath a blanket of snow. The fae were right in their songs. Once spring reclaimed the world, the Hünderhelm and every river like it would pour over the Thunder Falls and flood the Wrathgorne. Ehlaru did not envy the Stormborne beneath the falls. Torrential floods succeeding war's end was an ill omen for the Stormlands, and he gave thanks to the runic gods that he lived above them both.

⎯⎯⎯⎯⟨◇⟩⎯⎯⎯⎯

Salted perspiration drenched her skin, her muscles juddered like a frightened lamb's, and her bones ached like fragile glass. The day had barely begun, and Agneta felt she could walk no farther. Pain was in the mind, however, which meant it could be overcome. One foot in front of the other and she would eventually arrive in Dekryl. Mental fortitude would help her reach her goal, but by no measure was the journey enjoyable. In fact, she decided it was the worst she'd ever undertook—second only to her ascent into the Soudland high country some five years ago.

Desperate to embrace civilization, Agneta hiked through the entire night. Three satchels were latched to her hip, and two hung from her back. Five satchels of meat, furs, and bones was a respectable draw for a late winter hunt, but, runic gods, had it been easier to carry with the help of a horse. Why again had she turned north at the river instead of south?

That blizzard which had bogged her down in Skraelg started it all. She'd spent more time there than she cared to admit, but she'd also had little choice. Snowfall had been heavy, and her horse had jumped the stable fence to wander off recklessly and freeze to death. She recoiled at the thought of her Frida dying alone in the cold. Frida had been her faithful companion since the beginning of her pithy tenure as a ranger. It would have been suicide setting out to retrieve her, but it had been devastatingly difficult to abandon her to that storm.

The blizzard had devastated more than just her though. Thundersnow destroyed a farmstead on the outskirts of Skraelg and obliterated three of

81

the rancher's sheep. Agneta had chatted with the rancher in the local tavern the night before it happened. Otto was his name, and he had been excited having just purchased a mare from Draveskeld to service his little ranch. She'd felt contrite for his situation, although there was nothing she could do to remedy his misfortune. Secrecy was a blanket she need wrap around herself twice over whenever she came close to Draven's Dominion, so she'd done just that. Donning her hood, she'd walked right past the rancher while he tended to his barn's ashes and then borrowed his mare. The horse had just been meandering in his fields, digging through snow in search of grub until she'd stolen it away, and Otto had no idea.

Hopefully, Ehlaru trekked north after passing those fae. Knowing him, he likely irked them without acquiring decent directions instead. Runic gods forgive her. She had doomed that horse to certain death. Regardless, Ehlaru at least knew where she was headed. Where else did one take a hunt's plunder? Either a village to sell off a portion or home, of course!

Agneta had convinced herself Ehlaru would be out hunting as well. It should have been the reason her heist succeeded. While stuck in that damned tavern, she'd overheard that her fellow ranger was fulfilling an order for the villagers of Skraelg. She assumed he would actually be out hunting, not idling in his cabin during the blizzard. Weather hardly affected him, and she swore he could keep warm in the depths of Drur's Abyss.

Agneta wiped the sweat from her brows. She must have legitimately lost an entire layer of insulation on this hike alone. She looked great, which wasn't particularly preferable in the high country where food was scarce. Then again, the reason she'd left home was to gather food for her wolfhound pups. They were worth the effort, no matter how exhausting the journey currently was. They ogled her as if she were their mother, and their exultant love soothed her soul.

"All for you my precious little scamps," she mused.

She sighed as her journey approached its respite, then stepped onto the village's eastern trail and entered Dekryl at dawn's first light. There were only twenty individuals, maybe twenty-five, who lived within or around Dekryl, and only a few were up and out. Anyone else would be a ranger like herself or a band of Bjardja, mercenaries who commanded lunar magic molded by the runic gods, resting through the winter until the war with the Ardent Avant reignited in Tjorden's Reach.

Dekryl was quite small, but it maintained a mead house like all Storm-borne villages. It also boasted stables. Hopefully, it held horses in reserve. Agneta couldn't borrow one this time, especially since someone might recognize her from Skraelg. She needed to purchase a legitimate replacement instead. Considering it was ridiculously early, she decided that task could wait.

Agneta made haste to the mead house at the village's center. It would be the best place to procure lye and a warm bath to wash her clothes and herself. She had eaten some salted pork and cracked oats before finishing the journey, so she could do without another meal till dusk. If the hostess offered one out of pity, however, who was she to deny? It had been years since she'd last passed through Dekryl. If the mead house were managed by the same unbearable lady, however, she would receive no charity. Agneta opened the doors.

As expected, Grunda Helida, lived and breathed. The plump woman also seemed displeased to have received a guest. "If you're looking for a drink, lady ranger, you better leave and come back this evening. If you're looking for food and a room, we might have reason to talk."

"No mead, ma'am. I was hoping to buy a bath and claim a room for half the day. I won't fill either for long."

"Why bathe if you're only staying for half the day? Means you'll be leaving after half the day is done. Means you'll look like a sweaty meat pie again before nightfall."

Agneta swallowed her anger at Grunda's insult. "True. I'll leave before the sun peaks, but I loathe traveling in filth as much as I loathe sleeping in it."

"Chose a strange profession if you don't like filth, but I suppose we don't always have a choice in where we end up now, do we, Lady Ranger?"

"No, ma'am. I expect most of us do not."

"I'll heat a few tubs of water if you buy some food as well. Won't waste the warm water otherwise." Grunda lightly slapped the closest bar top. "You could use some meat too. Maybe save more of your kills for yourself instead of selling it all to grungy fools!"

"Normally do," Agneta responded as placidly as her temper could manage. "Ran it all off after leaving my mare on the other side of the Hünderhelm."

"You abandoned your horse? Are you mad?!"

Agneta coldly replied, "Couldn't afford the delay of a day's ride south to Skraelg and another two day's ride here. Left her with a friend. I'll retrieve her when I return."

"Strange girl. To walk all this way with all those trappings just to save a measly day or two." Grunda shook her head in baffled disapproval. "Three copper for the meal and hot water and a silver coin for the room."

Agneta counteroffered, "I'll give you six copper, if it will buy me some lye, and a silver and a half, if you'll wake me an hour before noon."

Grunda huffed in disbelief. She did not verbally fuss, but she made certain her discontent was well known.

Agneta pleaded with a smile, a humble gesture that enticed the mead matron to oblige.

"I'll draw your bath. Come back in an hour. I'll have it ready with your room. You'll even have the chance to throw more meat on those ragged bones. You're going to live like the Lord Son of Draveskeld this morning, and you better tell every other ranger about it too!"

Agneta swiftly responded, "Thank you..." while trailing off to allow the mead matron to fill the void like she had all those years ago.

"Grundalav Helida. Just call me Grunda, and we won't have problems."

"Of course! Grunda it will be," Agneta resolved with a gauzy grin, and she paid half the money owed before leaving her things to the mead matron and hastily departing.

"Damn girl. Asking for my name without giving hers. Don't like the lot of them...except for maybe this one," whispered Grunda poorly. "Did you mean to leave your bags, girl?"

Agneta chortled and masked it with a hasty cough. She had mistakenly given her name to Grunda upon first entering Dekryl and now thanked the Draconic Father and Lok it had not been remembered. Soon, she would become as unrecognizable as Ehlaru himself. After thinking on it a little further, she realized that would never be the case. Ehlaru was a damned ghost when he needed to be. He adored living in isolation beneath the shadow of his motley hood. He wasn't Stormborne either, or at least she didn't think he was. He only had half the look. The other half was more elegantly imperious than anything a jarl or their lords could boast.

The door swung shut after she nimbly passed through, closing with a racking swoosh. Not much time had passed since she first arrived in Dekryl. A few more villagers were now awake. Agneta ignored them and strode directly to the stable house. To her excitement she found a few unmarked horses. She lulled over the slim selection, deciding which would best fulfill her needs. She would have preferred more time to bond with each before settling on any. Having none, she would rely on her gut's first instinct instead.

A dusky gray beauty lightly whinnied, catching her attention. The horse was stunningly gorgeous, and Agneta checked to discover it was a mare. A foot taller, a touch slenderer, but as stocky as a full-blooded draught-fjord, and the mare admired Agneta as much as she admired her. Perhaps her decision would not be so difficult after all.

"Beautiful, isn't she?" posed a voice from a fair distance off.

Agneta regarded the freshly awakened stable owner attending to his equine collection and the many duties that came alongside it. The gray-haired man tread cautiously. Her ranger's garbs afforded him that right. His sleeves were rolled past the elbows, so she regarded his arm's inked scars. The runes sung of Drur, Torlv, and Helti, runic gods of death, storm, and war. They were the unmistakable markings of a Bjardja, making Agneta now wary of the man too.

Lowering her hood to shed her indulgence, Agneta diffusively warned, "Careful, friend. Right as you might be, speak of me like that again and you're liable to lose your tongue."

"Didn't realize you were a woman. No harm. Take your time in admiring my stock."

"I have. I like what I see, and I have a favor to ask."

"Bolveig Svenson, but you may call me Boll."

"Of course. Boll is a handsome name, and I like saying it," she innocently flirted.

"What of this favor then, lass? Don't prod an old man's heart, then leave it to rot."

"How much for the dusky mare?"

Without hesitation, Boll replied, "Not for sale! Can't ride her because of my broken back, but she's mine, and she always will be."

Agneta persisted, "I will take good care of her. Been around horses my entire life. Well, at least in the life before this one."

"I believe you, lass, but her heart belongs to me and mine to hers. I will not part with her."

"Aye, but is it fair to the dusky mare to never pierce tumultuous winds again? She'll find the most joy in this life with a rider at her back and a destination days away."

"She's done enough in her life. Ridden through Helmyan gales, a fae's nightmare, and against Garathandi wolfhounds as well."

"So she wasn't born in the Stormlands?" Agneta asked without truly needing an answer, to which Boll shook his head. "Guessed as much," she muttered.

Boll approached the dusky mare and began stroking her neck. "She's half draught-fjord and half-Helmyan mare. I took her off a Helmyan knight whom I killed when they first sieged the Great Gates. She's been my faithful companion ever since."

There was a softness in his eyes behind the gale of war's ruin, and Agneta liked this old, misplaced Son of Sven. She allotted him the proper room to reminisce, not wanting to witlessly challenge him. There was obviously too much history between them. Shame though. She was a fine mare.

"Aye," Boll steadily continued, "Solveig saved me from the Ardent Avant and Helmyans on several occasions. Outran the Light's Champion once. I barely believed it until I looked back to find my fellow Bjardja crumbling into ash."

"She's incredible, isn't she?" Agneta admitted after discarding that awful image and thanking Drur and Freyja for sparing the mare.

"Aye, lady ranger, but don't sucker up to me too much. I still have another horse that will serve you well."

"Can I meet her? I would like to see if we're a proper match, even though I'm honestly a little short on time."

Boll eyed her curiously. "Something have you running? Haven't seen you here in Dekryl before, which means you've only just arrived."

"Nothing in particular. I'm tired, desperately wish to sleep in my own bed, and have a hunt I need to haul home," Agneta lied, if only partially. Her bed did sound quite nice.

"Aye," Boll conceded. "I have a horse for you. He's not the fastest, nor is he a warrior's steed, but this draught-fjord can carry across the high country with relative ease."

"That will suffice indeed!"

She retrieved a handful of coins from a hidden pouch, then counted out twenty pieces of silver. She approached, grabbed his left hand, and relinquished the pay before she stepped away.

Boll counted the coin for himself. Upon finishing, he nodded with his thanks then led her to where the horses slept. He woke the beast tenderly by soothing its anxious neighs. It attempted to immediately lick her face, to which she humbly consented. A dun gray coat brushed against her cheek. He was a tad dory for her tastes, but Agneta forgave it. No animal chose what traits it was born with, only how it handled itself and spread its seed.

"I will pay double if you mark him for me," she stipulated.

"No need. You've already paid me more than Greyjka is worth, and I am no thief."

She cringed at the remark.

He shed her another peculiar look. "I'll change his irons, prepare his saddle, and have him marked for you an hour after noon."

"How about an hour before for a ranger with a destiny pitilessly calling her north?"

Boll grunted. "Aye. That's something I can do. I'll have Greyjka ready for you before noon."

Agneta smiled at the irony in her new horse's name. "Greyjka? Not quite as original as Solveig."

"It suits him, he answers to it, and you would do well to remember that," Boll countered.

Her triviality having failed her, Agneta smirked.

Boll returned to stoicism, dismissing her jubilance with another grunt.

Agneta assuaged a brow but did not comment on the sudden change in his demeanor. She guessed further flippancy would dissuade him from liking her even more. Did he dislike her? That was a silly thought. He was giving her a discounted horse! She said, "Thank you, Boll."

They shook to seal their arrangement. His grip tightened around hers until she felt the callouses of a man who had spent his entire life climbing through the furnace of war. She held firm, unwilling to look weak before the aged Bjardja lord. Boll smirked, appreciative of her resolve. Agneta thanked him with a satisfied nod.

Agneta left the Son of Sven, donned her hood, and strode toward the mead house. More villagers had awoken since, although Dekryl boasted few to begin with. The village ambled on whimsically as if she weren't even there. It had a certain charm, but quaint captivation would never entice her to settle in such a boorish place herself. Agneta preferred grandeur, whether of the natural world or manmade she did not care so long as it was grandeur surrounding her every step and every day.

She digressed. The ranger's lifestyle oft weighted her with sullen thoughts. Isolation played dirty tricks on the mind. With good Frida gone, her only companions now were Greyjka, two Garathandi wolfhounds, and the amalgamation of fae who delimited her home. They scarcely even counted as real company, but they were at least more engaging than Ehlaru amid one of his nastier moods.

Agneta took pause to trade a satchel of wolf hides for meats, frozen milk, and additional rations. A local thoroughly enjoyed their look, so she humored him with a selfish deal. The man declared he could stitch together a rug from the shaggy skins. His loss. They were exceptionally average skins. Had they come from a dire wolf… Well then, they might have warranted her price. After farewelling the giddy man, she burst through the entrance of the mead house.

"There's the lady ranger. Good timing," Grunda remarked from behind her bar.

"A touch early, but hopefully no more than a touch?"

Grunda puffed her nose before replying, "Exactly on time. Must be in your blood."

Agneta gave no response. She was a touch perplexed by the inn keeper's rather aimless intonation. She lowered her hood to test whether the mead matron actually remembered her.

Grunda puffed her nose, softly sighed, but deceived no recognition of who Agneta was. "I drew the bath and placed its trimmings beside your bed. Through the back door there!" She pointed toward the open door to the right of her bar. "Second on the right, and try not to ruin the wood by getting it wet!"

"I won't!" Agneta brusquely replied. She paid the second half of what was owed, then added another half silver coin.

Grunda counted the coins before staring baffled at the extra silver in her palm. She looked up, searching for sign of why it was there.

Agneta did not flinch against her toxic scrutinization but instead met her gaze with placid indifference.

"What's the extra silver for?" Grunda stammered. "Do you think I need your charity, or do you not know how to count?!"

"I was hoping to buy the heat off your stove to dry my clothes once I finish the wash."

"Humph," Grunda snorted before licking at something between her front teeth. "Would have been included, but I'll take the silver since you don't ask the right questions."

"Fair enough!" Agneta moved past the counter, toward her room.

"Do you want your meal now or later, Lady Ranger?"

"I'll trade it for my clothes," Agneta answered without breaking stride.

Agneta entered the bedroom and swiftly shut the door. Speaking with Grunda was no better now than before, and she wouldn't bear anymore of her insults. She relinquished her weapons to the floor, stretched, then cracked her back after dropping the last of her possessions next to the satchels beside her bed. She felt like she had been reborn like Helti on Freyja's birthday. Well, only partially reborn. Her body still ached, but at least only from the strain of its own weight.

The room was modest, but Grunda kept it quite clean. Agneta scarcely cared to admit it, but she could quite possibly refine the art of cleanliness by befriending this server of mead. The linens were fresh, and not a speck of dust traipsed the room. She closed the furs draping the window. They too were free of dust and even smelled aromatic, like lavenders with a hint of honey and something earthy at its core. Drur be damned. The mead matron was good.

Two baths sat before her: one for her clothes and one, she presumed, for her. She touched two fingers to the farthest. The water had been heated to an agreeable temperature and brimmed the edge of the tub. She dipped the same two fingers into the next tub to find it much hotter than the first. Lok be damned too. Had Grunda always been so smart?

Agneta dropped her clothes to the floor and began scrubbing them against the washboard. It took a while since she was thorough, but she eventually got through. She then wrung them one by one and hung them over the edge of the tub to dry. She climbed into the second bath. Having cooled to a reasonable temperature, it beckoned her to sink into its divine waters. She did so with an exhalation of bliss.

Agneta had not washed outside of Nordland fjords in a very long time. She enjoyed the feeling that came when everything was rinsed clean, leaving behind fresh skin. The heat soothed her soul also. She lay within its warmth longer than she should have, but she hardly cared. It was a gift sent by Halvalkyra, and she only wished this fleeting comfort could last an entire lifetime, or at least until she reached home.

The pleasantness vanished as the temperature dropped when she rose to dry her toned, vestal form. Pulling a spare set of clothes from one of her satchels, she redressed, gathered her washed clothes, and exited the room.

Upon reentering the bar, Agneta discovered a plate of bread and a bowl of skause awaiting her return. She searched the nearby vicinity for Grunda. After failing to find the charming mead matron, Agneta snatched her food, dashed from the room, and left behind her clothes.

Tender beef protruded from her bowl of skause. She chuckled at the thought of Grundalav Helida heaping on an extra portion in the puerile hope that the "lady ranger" might gain some weight from the meal. White carrots, an onion, and something unrecognizably green floated in the stew. The green mystery's structure might have dissolved in the pot while sitting for the past few days, but its lovely taste still remained.

Agneta bit into sourdough birch-bark bread. Freyja be blessed. Bread was nature's finest gift. Slathered with some skyr, a delicacy lying somewhere between thick yogurt and soft cheese, the slice of bread was supremely perfect. The meal was more than she'd expected it would be.

In self-confession, she wished she had paid for more. Too late now. She would lose face with Grunda asking for a second portion after refusing the first. Agneta Ilesha Dravendottir would not lose face with Grundalav Helida over anything, much less a second bowl of skause.

With a clean body and a full belly, Agneta turned to sleep since Ehlaru would grant her little time to do so. The ranger was undoubtedly closing the distance between them even now. Her mentor had probably been running through the majority of the night. It was nothing she could control, so she let those sagging thoughts fade to nothingness as she plummeted into her thatch cot. Quicker than arrows could fly, she drifted into sleep with the man on the move on her mind.

Dawn delivered fresh dew to the trimmings of his boots as Ehlaru consumed the last of his rations. He ate beside the fire at which he'd cooked the morning's meal. Around him lay an assortment of broken flint, empty satchels, and logs that had been too wet to set aflame. He would leave the pit and unused branches for the next ranger who made camp beneath this birch. The spot was exceptional, he was finished with it himself, and he was not fond of making waste.

Ehlaru studied his general location while chewing through peppery strips of beef and kicking dirt over the dying flames. He had crossed the Hünderhelm before noon on the prior day and driven hard down the Valdhaz thereafter, like a boulder rolling fast and free. Dekryl lay before him about a half day away. There, he would acquire a horse to free his feet from the burden of carrying him. With fresh supplies, he would then recapture his thief, or at least regain her trail.

Andurial! He was the man who had molded Agneta into the ranger she was. Her skills in hunting, tracking, fighting, and survival were the products of his training, not of the frightened girl who'd lost herself in the woods after rashly departing Dekryl. He did not judge the decisions which inevitably led her to him, only her execution of the skills that he'd instilled. As of this moment, the woman was performing infuriatingly well.

Agneta was noble and, thus, willful and strong, but in the heart of the high country five years ago, she had been nothing but a lost, frightened girl. He had found her hopelessly alone on the brink of death and chosen to save her life without regard to his own. They'd nearly died escaping that winter storm, but at night's end, Torlv had decided their mettle was worth his mercy. By the time the conquered sun rose over one of her distant sons, Ehlaru had taken the girl home.

In the years thereafter, Ehlaru had taught her all she would need to survive this world. In return, she'd aspired to live beside him, her savior, with whom she'd fallen in love. That was a pleasure he could never afford to indulge, so with prodigious regret he'd refused her, heart and soul. From there on, their paths should have forever parted. Being willful and strong, Agneta did not care at all. As the days of this marathon run were witness, his rejection had only stoked the passion submerged in her heart.

The woman's incessant intrusions upon his isolation were becoming boundless. He once enjoyed the high country, its reticent seclusion high in the heart of the Stormlands, and the peace and tranquility they both proffered. No longer. Ehlaru was stripped of a companion he could not pine, a solitary life whose hand was severed from his by a deprived love's knife.

Ehlaru devoured the last of his skewered beef. Flecks of pepper taunted his tongue—the byproduct of a scarcity in available seasonings. He wiped the gristle from his lips and dusted his butt. The fire smoldered, so he piled on more snow. He retrieved his hooded cape and latched it to his vest, then gathered a few more accessories to clear his camp.

Ehlaru expected to reach Dekryl before the sun peaked the sky, although enervation was creeping in. No force of will would keep it at bay much longer. Not even the strength of Lysian could carry him much farther. Regardless, once his food settled, he would drive himself toward Dekryl like a horse to see what his wit and coin might procure. He would reach Dekryl on foot, of course. He just wasn't certain if he could make it out without a horse.

<hr />

Listlessly, Agneta caught wind of a conversation between Grunda and an unfamiliar voice. Startling herself awake, she tore to the window, parted the drapes, and looked to the sun. Breathing in relief, she thanked the runic gods that the sun had not yet ticked to noon. She had time still to outpace Ehlaru, but a touch behind schedule, she needed to move.

She spun around to find most of the preparations had been auspiciously completed for her. The baths had been emptied, her dishes removed, and her clothes were folded. Grunda had accomplished it all without stirring her awake.

Agneta donned the accoutrements that completed her ranger's attire, strapped four of her satchels to her hips, and slung the final one over her back. She latched her bow and quiver to her cape and summarily left.

Striding into the main room with her head turned down, Agneta found Grunda speaking with a man about his ranch. The old rancher regarded her warily, and Grunda spun to regard her as well. Agneta lifted her chin amidst a sigh. She had no time for a fresh conversation, but she owed Grunda a proper goodbye.

"Good morning. Sleep well?" Grunda cooed while shedding a wry grin.

Agneta confessed, "Aye, ma'am, was a good sleep...and a fantastic meal as well."

"Aye, my grub is the greatest!" Grunda jubilantly announced. She swung about to call to the rancher, "You wouldn't believe this lady ranger, Okrel. Fresh off a winter hunt and she walks in a wilting mess after traveling for days on foot, and when I offer her a warm meal, she refuses! I mean look at her. She doesn't need to be skipping meals."

"Careful, Grunda," Okrel cautioned. "These rangers are an entirely unpredictable lot. I wouldn't advise speaking ill of omens unless you know them well."

Grunda socked Okrel's arm. "You know I'm a proper judge of character! Besides, there's no need to fear this one. The lady ranger's no Lok, more like a daughter of the moon. She's good at killing wild game, but she hasn't harmed a man in all of her short little life."

"Aye, she might be a lady, but that doesn't mean she can be trusted. There's danger hidden in everyone. Why, I was stuck in Skraelg through that blizzard when a lady ranger stole a rancher's horse right after thunders- now demolished his barn." Okrel cast her a dark, studious look.

Agneta subtly shifted away.

Perturbed, Okrel leaned in to gather a better look and nearly slipped off his seat.

Disconcerted by the rancher's curiosity, Agneta adjusted her stance until the hood of her cloak shrouded her entire face.

"When did you say she entered town again?" Okrel asked.

Agneta tightened her nerves and slid her hand to the knives beside her hip.

Grunda glanced between them. A fire could be ignited from the nervousness oozing off the mead matron's face, and Agneta simply awaited the decision the mead matron needed to make. Grunda uncharacteristically chose not to speak. Agneta had no idea why. Grunda had no reason to protect her from this man or even deny his accusation.

Grunda diffusively chuckled, "You leery fool! This one's been with me since the blizzard began. She came off her hunt from the other side of the Hünderhelm, and I already told you she's been traveling on foot! Do you even listen, old man?" She slapped the back of Okrel's head.

"Aye! Doesn't mean she didn't steal the horse."

"Aye! It does!" Grunda slapped him again. "Stop hassling my good customers with your suspicious nonsense. I knew I shouldn't have given you that second cup of mead!"

"Don't you threaten me like that, Grunda! I am a paying customer too," Okrel wailed.

Grunda slapped his head once more for the road. "It's about time you return to bartering your wool. You have only the rest of today to sell."

Okrel grumbled with bitter discontent, but he offered no arguments with Grunda's toxic will. He downed the last of his mead and settled his due, then rose, glancing at Agneta once more.

Agneta withdrew her hand from her hip and settled it on the counter to deny him the view. Eyeing Grunda while the rancher begrudgingly departed, she shed her tenseness like rancher's sheep shed their sheared coats. Once the front door slammed shut, she lowered her hood. "What a suspicious man. Don't much like him. I thought you didn't serve mead until after the sun sets?" she dryly questioned.

"Never to you rangers, especially one as young as yourself! It's exactly how you lonely fools develop bad habits. Then I have to hear how one ranger found the bones of another because they were probably too drunk to defend themselves during a hunt gone awry."

"That's endearing of you, ma'am. I didn't think you capable of such an emotion."

"You don't know which emotions I'm capable of imparting," Grunda piped back. "What I don't understand is why one as young, beautiful, and, dare I say, witty as yourself is living life as a discarded ranger. You could be a lady to a lord or jarl instead of a Drur-damned omen if you so pleased."

Agneta savagely rebuked, "I need no lord to rule over me. I may not know the first thing about you, Grunda, but you also don't know the first thing about me!"

"Fine…not a lord or a jarl, but at least a man. Most of them are shite, but the right one makes the days go by quicker and warms the bed at night."

"I wasn't expecting a real meal, skause with meat no less. Thank you."

"A little appreciation for my cooking. I was wondering when it might show!" she barked.

Her temper boiling on the tip of her tongue, Agneta asked, "How will you manage not to waste it all with so few travelers coming through?"

Crudely, Grunda commented, "You ate the last of the pot."

"How came that to be, for me to be your last 'fortunate' customer?"

Licking her lips in a state of confusion, Grunda whispered, "The Lord Son of Langreklif and some of his sworn swords took rest here in Dekryl three—no, actually four—days ago. Traveling to Stormguarde, he said."

"How do you know it was the Lord Son of Langreklif?"

"I've seen his father, the jarl of the Nordland!" she exclaimed. "The boy wore the same matted mohawk as Baelgrant, only had it drawn into a ponytail at the back of his head."

"Traveling by land and not sea?" Agneta continued, striving to acquire information of actual import rather than teasing her adversary.

"Aye. I asked myself the same question. Said they were in no rush, would prefer to tour the country. Tour the damned high country, of all the damned places. There's nothing but antiquated farmers, ranchers, and you damn rangers idling up here. Maybe a mountain troll or two…"

"And the fae, Grunda. Do not forget the fae."

"You keep the damned fae away from me, lady ranger, and I'll keep you fed for eternity," the mead matron jested with a hint of fear.

"Did they speak to why they are traveling?" Agneta asked.

"The lord let slip in an overturned stupor that he is to be his father's representative at Ryurik's Kingslag."

"The prince from Lysian? I thought he and Eljak—" Agneta stumbled, her words decaying like autumn leaves before she recovered and steered them in an unbeaten stride. "I thought the prince and the jarls were commanding the defense of the Great Gates of Tjorden."

"Oh, I don't blame you for not knowing," the mead matron replied in a manner befitting of her mortified prying. "The war is over. The Ardent Avant has gone."

Agneta indignantly fumed, "This is *good* news for the Stormlands. The best of news for some. Goodbye, Grunda!"

Agneta donned her hood, stormed out, and tore into the daylight without sparing Grunda another word. She acknowledged no one as she strode headlong to the stables. She found herself upon Greyjka's stall in a few bitter heartbeats. The draught-fjord was nowhere to be seen, so she moved to the adjacent field. Greyjka roamed unattended in blissful glee. Agneta approached the gate to find it barred. Jostling the chain, she cursed the additional delay.

"You're late, Ranger," startled Boll from behind.

"I got distracted while preparing for the journey and lost track of the sun."

"Doesn't bother me. You're the one with a tight schedule."

"That I am," Agneta casually answered while setting down her many satchels. "Would you mind if I rode him first, before we're on our way?"

"No, so long as you don't take too long. I have a nap I would like to soon take."

Agneta stepped back, and Boll unlocked the gate. Stepping onto the snowy field, she casually approached Greyjka. The draught-fjord whinnied and pranced away. What idyllic lives domesticated horses lived. To them life was nothing more than chasing feed, striding with the wind, and teasing their owners like whimsical fae. After following Greyjka into a long sweep of shade, she gently stroked his mane. Then, with a mother's tenderness, she pressed her face against his. She wanted to establish familiarity, which, truthfully, would take half of the horse's lifetime to amass. Unfortunately, she did not have half of Greyjka's lifetime, only half an hour before she needed to be gone.

Still, it was only fair to Greyjka and herself that they learn who each other was before they rode off together. Thus, they first needed to reach a basic level of trust. Agneta also did not much enjoy the thought of being bucked off in front of Boll, especially after her earlier proclamation of her deep familiarity with horses. That would be an embarrassment she could not easily dust off.

Agneta caressed her horse's neck while whispering into his ear, "Come, Greyjka. Show me how you ride these hills."

A gentle tug led them away from the shade. Agneta began to jog thereafter, leisurely at first, then quicker as Greyjka gained confidence in her ability to lead. Once they reached the upper edge of the field, Agneta led him in a tight circle downhill. Greyjka felt her fervor, heart beating like the crack of thunder, and he broke into a full gallop. She heaved herself into the saddle, and together they soared with the wind.

Returning to the stable while Boll watched her with wide eyes, Agneta complimented, "Runic gods, you trained him well."

Boll gave no answer besides a soft grin.

She relished the moment by completing a few circuits around the snowy field. Greyjka beat Dwolv's good earth with furious hooves. She held to him like ice to the mouth of a cave. She rode Greyjka to the birch-wood gate where they slid to a halt. Agneta dismounted to walk Greyjka through while the horse happily shook his mane.

"Wish I were the horse," Boll flippantly joked.

Before Agneta could chastise his rough tongue, Boll handed her the first of her satchels. She ripped them away while lending him a disapproving smirk. Anger did not cross streams with her blush. Since she was choking on her own tongue, she knew no other way to disapprove of his frisky comments and flirtatious gaze.

Temptation lured the Bjardja in, and Boll brushed against her while tying off the rest of her satchels to Greyjka's flanks. After ensuring each was secure, she shoved the lord away. Boll laughed before tossing her a sixth bag. Perplexed with the unsolicited gift, Agneta peeked inside to find it was filled with feed. Boll chuckled, striking her with embarrassment.

Flustered, Agneta remounted Greyjka with the elegance of a swan to feign indifference with his tease. Greyjka was not nearly as impressive as Solveig, but the draught-fjord horse and its master had duly charmed her. She would never admit it to the overfamiliar bastard, but his flirtations were rather refreshing. It felt nice to be desired back.

"If I visit you, Bjardja, if I care for you in your old age, would you leave me your Solveig after you pass through the Arch of Death?" she asked.

"Maybe, but probably not. I know your love would push me over that edge faster than I would like," Boll mischievously admitted, winking as he joined in on her sultry jest.

"It wouldn't be intentional, but I'm not gentle with men."

"Nor I with my woman," Boll added as a matter of fact.

Their eyes met through the shadow of her hood, and she vaguely blushed. She enjoyed the snarky Bjardja lord. Even if there was nothing there but passing flirtation, he gave her good laughs. It was fun to tease, and she needed the occasional reminder of what conversations were like among those who responded with more than a neigh or a gruff bark.

Agneta waved goodbye before riding from Bolveig Svenson's stable, cantering through the heart of Dekryl, and exiting along the north road that led to the Godrulheim Divide. She sojourned a fair distance on the village outskirts and swung toward the east with the ominous impression that she was being watched.

On the nearest hillside stood a solitary man, caped and shrouded beneath his motley, green hood. Ehlaru, twenty-seven years old and in the prime of his life, lowered his hood and casually smirked. The ranger had caught up on foot alone, and she hadn't even covered half the distance home!

Agneta spun in a blistering fury and rode Greyjka toward the heart of the high country. Taunt her as much as he might like, she would make him work to recover his iron coffer. She had plans for her friend and mentor, and they all involved helping her. Once they reached the Godrulheim Divide, she would afford him the chance to talk.

<hr />

Ehlaru overlooked the exceedingly small village of Dekryl. In truth, Dekryl was little more than a trading post set between the Nordland and the Soudland. Contained within was a mead house, ranches, and a stables laid against a meadow. A well had been dug at the village's center where two men chatted with a rye-fattened woman. Three roads led within.

The plump woman sighted him from afar and scoffed as if he were the child of Lok and Drur, then angrily waved him off. Fine by him. Ehlaru sighted a far greater prize by ignoring her outlandish tantrum. A ranger bogged by the weight of several satchels wrestled with the gate to the stable's field. Ehlaru waited, watched, and caught his breath in favor of rushing in. He was too fatigued to sprint the rest of the way. Even after almost catching his thief, circumstances placed her just beyond his reach.

Agneta spoke to the stable's owner, rode his draught-fjord around his field, then spoke with him a little while longer. She departed thereafter, leaving Dekryl altogether by way of an old trail leading north toward the Godrulheim Divide. As if stricken by premonition, she paused and turned to glance upon where he stood. Ehlaru dropped his hood to grin, expecting it would be enough to taunt her. It did. Agneta rode north, and damned quickly as well.

Exhausted, Ehlaru slogged into Dekryl looking absolutely ragged, and he honestly felt it true. He refused to relent so close to his catch, so he planned to make his stay brief. Since most of the Stormborne believed rangers were like Eldrahg's blacked-beak messengers—ominous to a fault—they would probably appreciate his haste. They might even lend their aid to further hasten his departure from their village.

Dashing his hopes, the blonde-haired pig immediately squealed as he passed by the village well. He refused to acknowledge her or the other villagers, a ranger's custom with which they all were likely familiar. Instead, he strode directly toward the stables, using the gusts from her tirade to swiften his steps. He reached the stables rather quickly, happening upon the owner while he tended to his three steeds. Two draught-fjord horses neighed while a magnificent half-breed mare gazed quietly in his direction. The strength of a draught-fjord native to the Stormlands and the speed of a stallion from Helmya on the other side of the Great Gates pumped through the mare's veins. How such a fine beast came to dwell in the Soudland, he genuinely wished to know.

"Greetings, stable man," Ehlaru said, signaling he meant no foul.

"Greetings, ranger. I did not notice your approach," the man answered unperturbed.

"I did not care to let you," Ehlaru returned.

The man's stare hardened before he relinquished some concern. "Just finished dealing with another of your ilk not too long ago. I must admit she was less mysterious than you, so I took to her with a kinder tone. I see you are no novice at your craft, so I suggest we do not traipse each other's nerves."

"I commend your intellect—"

"I need it not," the man rebuked.

Ehlaru studied the graying stable man. The skin of his neck had been resewn beside his jugular from a wound that had assuredly befell him in battle. His silver hair was trimmed sleek so he looked more like a Lysian. His sleeves were rolled loose about his wrists, and his arms bore the inked markings of a Bjardja.

Ehlaru liked Bjardja. They were mostly reasonable men and fierce warriors in battle. He decided to adjust his temperament, hoping the Bjardja might do the same. He lowered his hood and shed his scowl in favor of a softer face.

"What go you by, Bjardja?" he asked.

"You mean these?" The Bjardja paused in his work, smirked, and rolled up his sleeves to reveal his whole arm. "Antiques from a former life. I've not used them for some time. Suppose I should have commended your intellect too, Ranger."

"If I were truly an intelligent man," Ehlaru indulged, "I would not be a ranger."

The Bjardja chuckled. "Well, friend, that and your strange eyes lead me to believe you are as clever as the fae."

Ehlaru fibbed, "A seeress's curse, and I seldom deal with fae. I will admit I recently engaged with a crimson faery and her two admirers in a lyrical bout. Neither of us parted as well endowed with each other as either of us would have liked. I may have crushed two river sprite's chances at ever finding love."

"Curse the river sprites!" exclaimed the Bjardja. "They're the damned worst of all the fae. Lake sprites might dunk your head underwater in a malicious jest, but the bastards won't murder you in cold blood like a river sprite will if given the chance."

Ehlaru confessed, "Never knew they were so murderous. I suppose I should have tread more carefully while I stole their lady's heart."

"Can't blame the little lass. Even a faery would find comfort in your arms!" he hollered. Ehlaru cocked a startled brow, to which the Bjardja stated, "Don't worry. I don't fancy rangers, not even the gorgeous lady ranger who was here before you."

"Nor I a fine-looking stable man like you."

"I'm no stable man. I am Bolveig Svenson, second son to Sven Agulbarg, the Wardunwyrm of Riven Hold. I was a Bjardja during much of the war with the Helmyans and the Ardent Avant. Took leave a few years before its glorious end, after I busted my damn back. Can't even ride my horses anymore. Poor Solveig, my half-breed beauty, thinks less of me for it, I'm sure."

"And what was the name of the girl who broke the back of the mighty Bolveig Svenson?"

"Ulda Verengadottir," Bolveig thundered in an uproar. "Damn finest woman I've ever slept with. Fancied my singing voice too. That's when you'll know she's a keeper…when she smiles and laughs through your drivel, even if it's nothing short of shit."

Ehlaru chuckled. "I'll remember that. It might help me dig up the gems buried beside the coals of Dwolv's molten heart."

"Aye, but it's the coals which fuel the fires which birth the gems. We need ourselves a few uglies if we're ever to appreciate Freyja for what she is."

"Which of us is the clever man again?"

Bolveig chuckled. "So what then brings you to me, Ranger?"

"A thief's trail, after which I have traveled since the blizzard's death."

"On foot?" Bolveig posed for clarity.

"Aye. A horse's path would have crippled my chase. I chose the harder route in crossing the Hünderhelm, in the failed effort to cut her off here."

"What of the thief?"

The pain of pines swept through their needles. The leaves of those tortured spirits shifted restlessly amidst their flight. The withered grass over Bolveig's field swayed like an ocean's rising tide. The mountains themselves seemed to breathe with tree-walker life.

"I would never betray a fellow ranger's name, but I fear you have already met her."

"I met your thief this morning. She wore the aura of a hare fleeing the fox's clutches, but I did not realize the hare was also a thief."

Ehlaru smiled at the analogy, which hearkened to one so similar he had drawn himself. "She's the reason why I've come to Dekryl, but not why I come to you now. I need a horse to carry me through the Godrulheim. I fear my legs won't make the journey by themselves."

"I could lend you a horse," Bolveig roughly conceded. "But I need an assurance you'll return her after you've caught your thief."

Ehlaru nodded in agreement, then rifled through the inner pockets of his wool-trimmed, leather vest, digging until he found the secreted pouch containing his coin cache. He grabbed a light handful, siphoning each back into the pouch until only three remained. Determining his insurance was not enough, he unlatched the necklace dangling from his neck, then tossed the coins and his key to the lord patiently awaiting his guarantee.

"What need have I of your key?" asked the Bjardja lord.

Ehlaru calmly answered, "None, but without it I can never open the iron coffer stolen by my thief. I'd like to borrow the dusky half-breed. She is utterly magnificent, and I know she'll carry me swiftly wherever I go."

"Hmmm. For this coin, and because you bear the aura of nobility at a bare minimum, I'll allow you to borrow my Solveig."

Bolveig admired the gold Koelecks, turning them over his fingers to watch the sunlight dance over each to glorious effect. After beaming with satisfaction, he pocketed the coins and began untying Solveig from her stall.

The mare was both taller and slenderer than any draught-fjord Ehlaru had ever seen. Solveig was a fitting name, and Ehlaru was supremely pleased with the result of his sincerest efforts. He tossed the lord another troika of gold Koeleck's while taking Solveig's reins. "A fair trade, if by some ill fate I should fail to return."

Bolveig tossed back the coins in a humble rejection. "No need. If I do not see Solveig's face by spring's sprightly end, I will find you for dead myself."

The Bjardja filled another satchel full of oats and feed, then latched it to Solveig's left flank. Solveig stamped twice in protest that nothing was presented for her to eat. Bolveig relinquished a handful of carrots to ameliorate her distress. She snorted satisfaction, shoving through his hands in search of more, and Bolveig relented a second handful before Solveig was fully done.

"Aye, Lord Bolveig. I will see you by spring's end, or you will learn we have ridden to the morbid side of the Arch of Death. Don't pursue me thereon, for when I transcend the necrotic realm, neither the Halls of Halvalkyra nor Drur's Abyss will receive me. Ascend Halvalkyra, and there your Solveig will wait." Ehlaru mounted the dusky mare at his oath's somber end.

She carried him as swiftly as the winds off the Range of Valdhaz, and Ehlaru reached the well that marked Dekryl's center in an instant. The village's mead matron, the same griping woman who only earlier had cursed every ranger's name, stepped outside her establishment to shoo him away. His silent refusal infuriated her, and she charged him like a bear. Silence beset the whole of Dekryl when Ehlaru stood his ground. Ranchers and villagers alike dropped conversation to witness the standoff between their matriarch and the ranger.

"I don't want any more Drur-damned rangers bustling through my village. Off with you, tongue-less, soulless man," demanded the woman alongside a flurry of unfavorable gestures.

"I would speak with one who'll sell me food and supplies before I depart your wretched company," Ehlaru declared without betraying a sense of emotion.

"I am no wretch, you shadow walker. First my little lady ranger, and now this one who tries to hide the fact that he was once a pampered lord. What business do you have robbing my village of its supplies?!"

Ignoring her entirely, Ehlaru vexed, "Does this woman speak for every man here, or should I check you each for a tongue with which you might answer me in her stead?"

"Eldrahg damn you, ranger! Monomua as well!"

"Grunda! You're making a scene of yourself," a half-drunken rancher cried out.

"I'm making no scene, Okrel. This ranger is defiling me with his foul tongue!" Grunda huffed in wild disbelief.

"Nay, he is riling you, Grunda, and that is all." With timidity, Okrel spun to declare, "I'll take your offer, ranger. I have milk, honey, goat's cheese, skyr, vegetable preserves, and a little flint and tinder for a good price."

"Any meat?"

"No, ranger. I have no meats that would last until you reach wherever you're going."

"Do you presume I am going far, Okrel?"

"Aye," Okrel answered simply.

"Why is that?" Ehlaru posed.

"Because I've never seen you here before, and I can tell I'll never see you here again."

"Astute observation," Ehlaru conceded plainly.

Ehlaru nudged Solveig beside Okrel to leer down at the man. The rancher's shaggy beard and handled mustache trembled in the shadow of the dusky mare. Finding Okrel terrified enough, he relieved one of the satchels strapped to Solveig's flanks and dropped it at the man's feet. He withdrew two pairs of silver coins, studied them, then motioned for Okrel to open the palm of his hand. After due hesitation, Okrel obliged and Ehlaru relinquished the four silver Koelecks.

"Fill this satchel to the brim with your wares, or to whatever height my coin is worth."

"This be rare coin. I've never seen this mark before…"

"The silver is purer than any to be found within the Stormlands. When next you find yourself in Draveskeld, take it to its smithy to be melted down. He'll recompense you twice the value you think to see before you now."

"Aye, ranger, I will certainly do that."

Okrel eagerly scurried off to complete his allotted tasks, and Ehlaru returned to the mead matron to discover another brave rancher had beguiled her into a transitory calm. Disliking her more than the fae folk, Ehlaru spread a sly smirk to the same width of the piteous woman's hips. With that single, admittedly uncommendable gesture, he shattered the rancher's hard-fought work and Grunda's rage was reborn.

"What are you smiling at?!" she reeled.

"It is my requisite hope that we can end this quandary so I might acquire some salted meats for the length of the journey ahead me."

"Piss over your fancy language," Grunda shouted as fire surged through her plump cheeks to leave her ears as fumes.

Ehlaru dispensed a pair of silver Koelecks into the mead matron's hands. "Reconsider, if you care to keep them."

Grunda studied the coins at length, eyes widening and narrowing upon him until, at last, she grumpily probed, "To where will I bring it then, Ranger?"

Ehlaru handed her his second satchel, specifying, "Wrap it in a blanket that will warm this fine horse through the night, then bring it to where I stand."

Under fumes rising like volcanic ash, the mead matron scampered off.

Chuckling underneath his breath, Ehlaru dismounted Solveig and stood beside the mare motionless while the remaining villagers eyed him suspiciously. None dared to approach him, although Grunda had been somewhat successful in stirring their moods. They spared no effort to hide their glares, but Ehlaru enjoyed the attention. He could feel every pair of piercing eyes, and so he knew exactly where they were.

Okrel and Grunda returned at the same moment. Ehlaru swiftly retrieved his satchels and relatched them to Solveig's side in a rush. Once tightly secured, he remounted the dusky mare. Solveig kicked dirt into the air, signaling she too was done with Dekryl and its affairs.

Ehlaru did not speak, give thanks, or extend a single goodbye. The ranger simply left Dekryl in stark silence, riding along the north trail toward the Godrulheim Divide. He would either catch his thief within the next few nights or lose her trail to the vastness of the Nordland. Should the latter transpire, he might find himself as much a hare as Agneta, only with a Bjardja lord and his wrath instead of a fox at his back.

A few days had gone by since Ehlaru departed Dekryl. He now approached the squalid foot of the Valdhaz that formed the Godrulheim Divide. There was nothing exceptional about the vast patchwork of mountains. Little distinguished it from the rest strewn throughout the Stormlands either. The Godrulheim Divide was, simply put, the most easily traversable chain in the Range of Valdhaz and a point of connection between the Nordland and the Soudland.

Even now, his thief strove to carry his iron coffer to the other side. Blinded by her senseless triflings, Agneta could not possibly realize her mistake. Regardless of how she might justify her actions, she still stole his most prized possession and his one connection to his past life. He needed to recover his iron coffer, if not for his own sanity then at least to preclude its contents from devouring Agneta's. He owed both her and his mother at least that much.

He had not divulged much of his life during the years he'd trained her, but of one thing he had made brutally certain Agneta knew. He loathed thieves. Those who were once closest to him and then betrayed his trust, he loathed most of all. Why Agneta would ever believe leading him on this wild chase might change his mind on the matters of his heart baffled him. Runic gods! If anything, it only succeeded in pushing them farther apart. Moreover, she had abandoned her past life just like him. It was unforgivably hypocritical for her to punish him for forbidding himself from indulging in another. It had never been his choice to abandon his name and all it upheld, only his to lay faith in his mother when taking on her charge. What renown lay in abandoning one's family to claim another's by planting his seed in a father's daughter after she'd fled him like rivers fled the mountains in the spring.

Tired of carrying his weight, Solveig hopped and neighed. Withdrawing from thought struck him with the realization that he too was weary of riding. Perhaps it was why his nerves had grown so tense. Brooding had always been his greatest gift, even in the days of the Black Prince.

Ehlaru studied his surroundings to determine the best location to set up camp. They had not yet ascended the lower slopes of the Godrulheim. Plenty of solid ground stretched beside the trail, but it was all too open to satisfy him. He saw nothing with a backing where they could rest safely through the night. Too much open ground would expose them to wild predators or rogues patrolling the mountain trails. He urged Solveig forward, and they strolled far above a sharp outcropping in an eastern mountain passage that overhung an open enclave and appeared free of snowmelt. A dense grove of spruce trees provided suitable coverage to the south. It appeared the clearing had been carved as a staging post for travelers to rest.

Solveig bustled forward on her own accord. Ehlaru tacked his tongue, gladdened that she was pleased. The dusky mare carried them off the trail and plopped down beneath the overhang with a grateful neigh. Ehlaru dismounted, removed her saddle and his bags, and she whinnied with glee. He stroked the mare until she hushed. Once she agreed, he offered her a handful of white carrots, teasing her with every single one. Solveig stood and followed him step by step until they bumped into the trees. He tied her off to the thickest pine before draping her back with Grunda's blanket to keep her warm through the night. Solveig casually shoved him off, whether to find time alone or push him back to work, Ehlaru did not know.

He began gathering firewood from the surrounding forest, ensuring he did not travel too far. He would not sequester Solveig before he constructed a fire with which he could test the wild's resolve. He returned, then began constructing a stone circle. Interlacing the branches into an orcish tipi, he shoved broken twigs within. He retrieved the rancher's flint and tinder and struck them together, igniting a fire like a mage. Sparks flew from the cracked stones like rubble from a trebuchet, striking the kindling and setting his fire ablaze. He adjusted the logs and supplied the flames additional kindling. Solveig edged closer in appreciation of their warmth. Distrustful of exactly what they were, she paused. Ehlaru gave her a bowl of feed to calm her nerves. Solveig disregarded the flickering flames and shoved her nose straight into the bowl.

Brushing back the loose strands of his sweaty hair, Ehlaru reclused through the forest like a spider in the shadow of its web. Damp leaves rustled, and furry paws ripped through the dead of night. He stalled, withdrew his bow, knocked an arrow, and marked the place where the noise had arisen. He caught sight of a rabbit before it reconciled its misfortune. His arrow sped through black night, piercing its heart. Ehlaru beheld his surroundings, ensured nothing stalked him in the darkness, restrung his bow, and retrieved his dinner.

A slight incision under the rabbit's throat punctured its still heart, and Ehlaru drained it of its blood. Sable red blood trickled into the snow until the rabbit bled no more. The ranger removed the organs his stomach would surely refuse, burying them beneath snow. Hibernation had treated the critter well, and now the fruits of its long slumber would benefit him.

Ehlaru returned to camp with his hare in hand to find Solveig snoozing beside her bowl. He retrieved his skinning knife, peeled away skin and fur, snapped the rabbit's bones, and ripped it into two. Grabbing the nearest branch, he skewered the two halves. He drove four more branches into the ground before tying them off in pairs, laid the skewered meat over the crackling fire, and began cooking the gamey flesh amidst a refreshing silence.

Soon he devoured the hare, discarding the bones once he was satisfied and finished. Sizzling embers devoured its remains. Bones cracked and gummy fat imploded until all was ash while he watched them melt away. He spread splintered wood to the edges of the stone circle and overlaid it with a thin layer of brush. Once assured the fire would breathe deep into the night, he rolled against Solveig to join her slumber. The half-Helmyan mare flicked his face with her tail but thankfully did not kick him away, and he thanked her for her matchless grace.

When the coals eventually subsided and cold nipped at his sleeping form, he would wake to rekindle its warmth. He preferred those nights when his sleep was disturbed. Restlessness gifted him a brief escape from the nightmares with which he was eternally cursed. Or would they even come? The ranger could scarcely remember whether they were his mind's own constructs or purely torments elicited from the contents of his iron coffer.

He soon drifted into the ether of dreams, wondering when they would turn to malice.

———————————— ◄◆► ————————————

Ehlaru awoke beneath the gleam of a midnight moon fallen farther within its cloak of shadow. The night was expectedly dark. He split the crust of his eyes to find clouds concealed the stars. He dusted the crumbs from his ranger's cloak. Darkness surrounded the sliver of the Crescent Lady, and the fire burned timidly bright.

Solveig leaped to her feet, heaving with tremendous fright, and neighed toward the spruces. Her fear gravely palpable, the half-Helmyan mare shied as far back as the slack in her harness permitted.

Ehlaru seized his bow and leaped around the fire so he might see their enemy the same as she. When his eyes adjusted to that distant gloom and the terrors hidden within it, he discerned the outline of something feral, too large to belong to a Soudland mountain cat but too quiet to belong to a grizzled ursa bear. He crouched so the fire shielded his right flank, and his shadow sprawled toward the shadow of the beast. The creature crawled the forest's veil, awaiting a sign of weakness. Ehlaru knocked an arrow against the bristled movement at the thicket's edge.

Looming on the edge of worrisome unknown, Ehlaru's eyes dilated beneath Monomua's darkest shroud. Streaks of silver slicked through the beast's grisly mane. A dire wolf approached him without a pack, a mate, or an answer to its lonely howl, pacing with the reckless temerity that it had found easy prey. Let it come like skis down the mountains' shadows soon after Dwolv repulsed the savage assaults of Jüte. Ehlaru would drive its misplaced confidence through Death's solemn Arch with cold hands and nothing more.

The beast regarded Solveig ravenously, lips dripping with the aridness of countless missed meals. It circled closer to the frightened mare, so Ehlaru circled against it. Caught in a deadly sky dance with the feral beast, he countered its every subsequent step. Remarkably measured, the dire wolf sought to pincer him against the crag and maraud the dusky mare. Missing the beast's intentions, he fatally overstepped, exchanging the fire's refuge for the cold of night's abyss.

Terrified, Solveig reared to the height of spruce saplings. The silver-streaked monstrosity leaped. Ehlaru placed his first arrow into the beast's lower throat. The head stuck firm, but it only dampened its voracious pace. Ehlaru loosed two more toward its hemorrhaging throat, but the wolf pivoted to avoid both. The arrows pierced the wolf's front flank. As blood gushed from the wounds, the beast relinquished a frenzied growl. The dire wolf took no time to lick its wounds and charged him directly. Ehlaru exploited the direct angle to align two more shots with the beast's throat. As quick and true as the arrows flew and connected with their mark, the dire wolf endured in its relentless charge.

Hands colder than runeforged steel plunged into innocent hearts gripped his knives. They might never again feel the warmth of the conquered sun or fling fire toward her sky. Solar sorcery could not shield him from the dire wolf. He had none stored within himself to spare, so he had no choice but to fight in melee. He flung his bow through the pillar of smoke billowing off his disregarded friend. Hope forgotten, Ehlaru would fight until Death the Reaper selected her prize between the two of them. He would not die to some brooding wolf, Eldaria's twisted visage of himself should he ever buckle before Agneta's wish. It was an oath he mouthed to his feral foe, who alone bore witness to sustain it. Grinding his feet into the ground, he inhaled the fresh death of gales and prepared to meet his foe.

An arrow soared off unknown wings when the dire wolf leaped. It met meager resistance, pierced the dire wolf's eye, and ruptured its skull. The dire wolf collapsed atop him in a bundle of taut muscle, sinking onto both of his knives. The impact expelled all air from his lungs, and a shockwave like a crack of thunder broke the mountain's calm.

Ehlaru struggled to breathe through the beast's matted fur. He heaved, summoning his own dire strength to toss off the wolf. Lungs gasping for air, his breaths ragged and uneven, and his mind hazed, he hunched over without regard to the world while he regained his senses. Ripping through cold dirt with the ends of his fingers, he focused on the bloody, dirty blades with an intensity akin to the fright of his borrowed mare. His heart pumped wildly, but he retained his focus. Somewhere in the shadow of the thicket stood a new threat, who had not yet given him their name.

Slyly glancing about, Ehlaru located his juniper bow. If he could only cover the distance, retrieve any wielder of sky magic's second greatest armament, he might level the ground upon which he and this unseen stranger stood. Embers cracked, sparks sprung, and they fluttered lazily next to the arched, shapened wood. He leaped out to retrieve it, but his hand was beaten back by the whirr of sundered air. Another arrow pierced the ground between him and his bow. He froze, furious with the one who had loosed it his way.

"Will you not thank me before recovering your bow?"

Irked by her arrogance, Ehlaru flouted, "I wouldn't have been here if not for you. What thanks is there for me to give for that?"

"The one which pertains to your life...?" she expatiated with an impatient sigh.

Ehlaru lowered his hood to reveal his dissatisfaction with Agneta and the world. "Thank you for saving my life," he then groaned.

"You're welcome, friend," she sung with peculiar lament. "My apologies for how I brought you here."

"Whatever the reason, whatever your excuse...the answer is no."

Agneta rolled her sapphire soul before wryly admonishing, "You haven't heard me. You cannot deny a request I never gave without allowing me the chance to explain myself first."

"I would rather be left to the wilds without my hands than indulge your requests," Ehlaru insulted flatly.

"You'll only survive for so long fighting life resentful and alone. We've seen it come to pass for many rangers before and beyond us both."

"I'll take my chances with the dire wolves."

"I'm not asking for you, you half-wit. I am asking for your help by offering my own."

"I am susceptible to admit I no longer have the will to help you."

"I think you enjoyed having a reason to branch out on a whim," she countered amusedly.

Ehlaru bluntly rebuked, "I'll admit I'm fresh out of joy too. I ran it into the ground these past few days. You cannot steal more."

"I would have doubled back for the horse, had I been you," she replied with a smirk.

Ehlaru cocked a brow, astonished by the hubris with which she mocked him. She'd always enjoyed teasing him to the bitter ends of his patience, but her insults were currently procuring an entirely unique reaction. Consternation shrouded his thoughts, not entirely reserved for her but mostly for himself. Had he not played some part in enticing the Fates Three to weave this brutal abound by staying his hand when she first rode away?

Disenchanted, he mumbled, "It's not your decision to make."

"Come again?" she asked.

"Your trials are not mine to suffer. You cannot make them thus. I have already given you all you need to survive. You've proven it, so why do you keep coming back to break my solace?"

"Survival isn't the reason why you have come," she pestered.

His temper flexing like the mouth of a clam, Ehlaru lashed, "Survival is the only thing I care for any longer! I choose to pursue nothing else for the remainder of this life because I must. You cannot change that."

"Except for your box," Agneta censured before wistfully continuing. "Your furtive little iron coffer." She paused, giving him time to reconsider, but before Ehlaru could demand answers, she interjected, "Are you any good at raising pups?"

"Dogs?" he prodded through the utmost confusion.

"Yes, dogs! Specifically Garathandi wolfhounds."

"Aye, I'm unfamiliar with the breed, but I'm generally feigned with dogs. Conquered sun blister my eyes, do not tell me this is why…"

"Aye, and you've finally stumbled upon the point," she noted in wispy delight.

"I cannot believe this damned fictitious nonsense!"

Settling to test his speed against hers, Ehlaru reached for his bow. Failure mocked him unrelenting as she delivered another arrow between them in an instant. She nocked and locked another onto his groin, not unlike the torrential exhalation of wind heralding a squall's demise.

"Not yet, or the next goes straight through your thigh!"

"You're not aiming for my thigh, and you'll miss regardless," he buffeted.

"No, I won't. I was trained by someone who never misses. How possibly could I?"

"Archdemons take me again, can I retrieve my bow?!"

"No, because you're liable to lose your cool. Did you not teach me grand gestures require grand responses? Hmm?"

Well, that did sound exactly like something he would say. "Could you have not just asked for my help?" he deliberated.

"Because you think everything is some exalted play of Fate's Weave. Because your head is so thoroughly lodged up your ass, only divine intervention could pull it back out! Ingenuity and sheer will is all I have left to move you, friend."

"I suppose the dire wolf is what makes this chase of ours so grand," he acknowledged in an ode of departure from strife's gripping hand.

Agneta abruptly laughed before pointing to the wolf's corpse. "This was never a part of my plan," she admitted with a self-censorious grace.

"Ill fate, I suppose. Now can I reclaim my sky-damned bow?"

"If you promise to remain friendly."

"We're still friends...whether I like it or not." After some defensible hesitation, Ehlaru safely seized his bow. "If you help dress this kill, I'll lend you what experience I have in raising pups."

"That would work," she settled. "If only it were your wolf to dress."

An irregularity latched itself onto his façade.

Agneta returned a smug, indulged look of her own. It struck him, then came the sky-damned epiphany that shattered his leverage. She glimpsed it in his face, and her smile broadened before she quickly stuffed it away.

"Mine was the arrow that felled the beast. It is mine, but I will help you dress it since we are friends," Agneta sardonically agreed. Her elation was strikingly clear, her rationale perdured, and she gave him ample pause to think before specifying, "If you return to my home and show me all you know. I'll learn better that way, I assume my wolfhounds will thank us both, and that's when I will return your iron coffer. After the deal is done."

Ehlaru reared to his full height as he considered his options. There he lingered on, openly baffled by the predicament she triggered. He meant to corner her in this wretched divide or even in the Nordland on the other side. No such luck befell him, and he was legitimately left without an option other than accepting the one laid within this trap. Worse yet, he knew this would not be the last. Her success here would only endow her with the vigor to keep coming back. Even more problematic was the dire wolf bleeding out by his fire. Its hide would fulfill the villagers of Skraelg's open order. If he denied her offer, his hand would be ripped from the single silver lining hidden in this inglorious chase. She would leave, and with her would depart his iron coffer, into the realm ruled by Jarl Baelgrant Trollsbane.

"I'll dress it myself," he replied.

"It's only a favor in return for the favor you're granting me—"

"There are no favors here. This dire wolf's hide is the final piece of Skraelg's most recent order, and you've miraculously found a way to extort me of it with something you stole."

"Then think of it as a gift!" she shouted. "And your iron coffer as your oath's payment!"

"So be it! You have my oath, and I have yours!" he shouted back.

"I'll leave this to you," she conceded with a sigh. "I'll join you here again in the morning, and from there you will join me till our deal is done." In rhythm with her final breath, she leaped beyond looming dusk, returning to the forest's fold.

"At the light before dawn, or I will find you again and be all the less fucking forgiving," Ehlaru cursed as he watched her midnight tresses whip through the bower of the Dark Moon.

CHAPTER SIX
STORMGUARDE'S SOUR

The day was young, but in Thyra's heart it reigned supreme. A dormant sky unrestrained by the command of tempestuous winds gave rise to a discordant cadenza. Excitement overtook Stormguarde, one which its denizens had not known for many years. Prince Ryurik and the jarls were returning home, and with them marched nearly every defender who had manned the Great Gates of Tjorden. Their arrival heralded the fresh potential for Thyra to change her stars.

The Ardent Avant's siege had since lingered for ten winters, five by the time Thyra and her family first arrived in the Stormlands. Like all other exiled Ehlrichs before him, besides herself, Ryurik forsook his name and, on the sixth year of the siege, departed for the Great Gates. He sought to earn their grandfather's favor by proceeding with the only strategy he had ever really known—their elder brother's strategy to dash toward deathly winds where he thought he might best preserve his providence.

The Storm King, Grandfather Lothair Runeheim, spared little thought toward Ryurik's return. Thyra had come to understand there was little that moved the man. Lothair's heartless thrusts were precisely what led her little brother to strike his banner and ride to the Great Gates. Ryurik had only been fifteen when he left, and he would return a man by Stormborne standards. Oh, how inescapably time elapsed without a chance for mortals to cherish all it held.

"What troubles you so greatly that you look so grim? It's the eve of Ryurik's return. This should be a joyous occasion, not one you need to mellow with a nasty visage," came the pleasant voice of Tanya, her younger sister of seventeen.

Thyra received her sister's concern. Amber eyes laid against a fair face and bound by a tender jaw strained against her hardened brows. Her little sister searched for a reason behind her grimness, for without it theirs was a reflection marred only by the sharpness of their cheekbones and the time they had each been alive. Tanya's hair was tied in marriage to the Runic Faith. Such was the custom for its priestesses when leaving their runic temple. The frost of these lands might have ripped all mirth from Thyra's cheeks, but they only made Tanya's rosier.

"Bitter thoughts," she admitted, trailing her fingers over the gilded phoenix necklace her sister always wore. "Ones I won't divulge because you are right. They would ruin the occasion."

"I can handle your most sour thoughts. It would do you well to feign the same," Tanya muttered, laying a hand over hers to shroud her cloying offense.

Thyra squeezed her sister's hand before tucking the necklace within her robes where it could neither be questioned nor seen. "They don't weigh me. I wear this face as a ruse, so I can never be genuinely read."

"You overestimate how much thought these people put toward us," her sister reconciled with a disillusioned grin.

"I never engage the mindless unless it is needed. I reserve my suspicions for a select few upon whom my sight does not waiver."

"Waiver for a day then, Thyra, for Ryurik's sake. None would question you taking joy in his return. I, for one, would love to see it myself."

Thyra chuckled at her sister's sarcasm, then left it to simmer like skause at the end of the week.

Flustered by her casual dismissal of a valid concern bundled into a joke, Tanya jostled her away.

Without the need to dwell over spilled emotions, Thyra lightened her leer. It eased vexations just enough to free her from their draining obligations, so she returned to observing the day.

Thyra sighted their grandfather at the height of the stone steps that led to Stormguarde Keep. Skjold—shield guard to the Storm King and the Erunheim—flanked their hoary king. Knotted hair draped his shoulders, splitting at their ends. His beard was thickly bundled beneath his chin. Lothair's hardened brow peered out from behind the mesh of hair. A sleuth forthwith to where his blue eyes glazed, so Thyra faced hers away before he noticed them.

"At times I might waiver, but I will never fully relent," she promised.

"Just smile once for Ryurik and attempt it a few more times for Mother. Give her a reason not to betray happiness for sorrow when the day is done, and give Ryurik reason to be happy he is returning home," Tanya pleaded stubbornly.

Humored by her sister's relentless charm, she cupped Tanya's head in her hands. Gentle as the hands that urged a dove onwards afront the eyes of Sky's Throne, Thyra held her still. Thyra smirked in playful jest, an obvious tease, and Tanya rolled her eyes. Her little sister was pleased with her tacit acquiescence, and it drew forth a clement warmth from Thyra's own chest.

"You are the one who should be practicing her smile." Thyra withdrew her hands to pinch her sister's elbow, then whispered drolly, "Think of the suitors Mother's gathered in one place for you to meet. I fear with mead in their bellies, you will be overwhelmed by them all."

"Stop it!" Tanya hushed. "Mother made this day for Ryurik, and think of yourself before consigning me to that nonsense."

Grinning, Thyra mockingly exclaimed, "I've consigned you to nothing. I'm simply too grim and obdurate for these men's tastes, so they'll look for someone else to seduce and entertain."

"So this is why you walk so sour? Perhaps she conspires to promise you off before that look sticks like butter!" Tanya snapped.

"The day might light itself for Ryurik, but the night is promised to us. Should I share how I know, little sister? It's quite simple to be honest."

"Oh, pray tell," Tanya mumbled behind an injured frown.

"Because I think like Mother once did, which is where I learned to always strike forth off an observation as undeniably true as the fact that she'll immediately request you let down your hair when she sees you next."

The gate to the mountain fortress cracked, revealing the soft-tempered bracing that drove through its stout frame. Valyria, their mother, stepped into the open day and directed her accompanying thralls to service the nearby seers. Dragoln and Drurhelm stood to Lothair's left halfway up the stone steps. Valyria exchanged pleasantries with Dragoln, the runic father of Torlv's runic temple, then she spoke with Drurhelm at length.

Drurhelm's gaze inevitably crept toward Tanya, and he whispered something foul into their mother's ear. Valyria's compulsory smile brought Thyra to gag. Her cordiality was in good show, of course, but it sickened Thyra deeply. Their mother once warned of all the Stormlands' perils, designating Drurhelm the chief. Thyra feared no runic seer, but she did loathe Drurhelm's prurient hunger for the attention of girls no less than a third his age.

A closer inspection lead Thyra to believe her mother feigned none of her glee, not with Drurhelm specifically but with the Kingslag and life itself. Valyria had begun the preparations for this Kingslag the moment they received word of Ryurik's forthcoming return. The news bestowed the estranged empress of Lysian reinvigorated purpose. Even now it overwhelmed the revulsion she must surely feel toward the noxious waste pouring from Drurhelm's mouth.

Valyria Ehlrich—reclaimed by the line of Runeheim—was forsworn her married name with her homecoming to the Stormlands. Her home of Lysian had vanished alongside her grief with the life it forced its empress to lead. Her eldest sons forsaken to the High East's fall and her third drifting as a limp carcass at the bottom of Lysian seas, the High Lady of Stormguarde had been consigned little love by Fate's Weave.

Her change, however, was nigh uncanny. Clinging to the fortune of her surviving son, she handled the task of drawing his Kingslag in full. Valyria had composed the many summons, instructing all of the Stormlands to travel to Stormguarde before its mighty host. Forests were felled, camps were drawn, time was made, and a king's reaping was called. Her mother was then left with the necessary means to draw together a Kingslag in storm. Karlar did not care a ram's horn what brought mead to their lips, but Thyra still felt their tantalized hunger as they awaited the arrival of the celebration's spark.

Departing the auric scum, Valyria joined them both. "Your welcome is strong as always, and your faith so beautiful, my love. I am pleased Ryurik will return to sisters unchanged. Tanya, let down your hair so he might recognize who you are."

Tanya visibly shuddered, but the clutches of Thyra's earlier intuitions were pithily lived. A mirror image in mind and body both, Tanya recollected herself, unbreakably resolute. It did not transpire smoothly, but her sister did banish the discomfort with shrugging Mother off.

"If Ryurik has grown wise while defending the Great Gates, he will rejoice to be returning to something candid," Thyra interjected to save her sister's skin.

"This is a good day, Thyra. Don't start by spoiling it! Your strife can wait for tomorrow, but your brother needs you today. Tanya! Did you not speak with your sister like I asked?"

"I have, but she won't buckle to one girl's piping…nor would I, in her position. Oh, and my hair remains the way it is. Unlike Thyra, I only enjoy the tender caress of a breeze on my neck."

Pride ripped through Thyra like the prows of a jarl's drakken longships through shelves of ice. The indignation that came from being teased as a whore might sting a more sensitive soul. Her satisfaction in Tanya taking to snark to outwit their mother certainly did not. Thyra spent an uncertain amount of will to suppress her smirk, but whatever replaced it only riled Mother more.

"I don't demand much, but promise me just this day, Thyra, and tomorrow I'll cull the oath," Valyria requested, electing to ignore Tanya's rebuff.

"One day, then tomorrow Tanya can join me in splitting the toads from the wyrms."

Tanya burst into a giggle. "Only if Siv and Ella can join!"

"The seers will not tolerate you igniting doubts in her faith. Thyra, your obstinance will force them to part the two of you like chaff from the grains," her mother chastened.

Thyra provoked, "My obstinance precludes a seer of toads from gulping down Freyja's innocence like it were a ripe worm. Better I instill wisdom for her to share with the girls before the toad lashes the flock with its false tongue."

"Better I make the most of this day for Tanya instead. She will be confined to Torlv's runic temple forever, should you surrender those opinions to the seers."

"Or so they might believe," Thyra mumbled so only her sister could hear.

"Say nothing else, please," Tanya plead.

Nettled, Valyria asked, "Why are you laughing while she puckers like a squid? Have you switched bodies for the day?"

"No," Thyra answered in a soft chuckle. "I was just recalling something of our brother before he changed his familial name. I'm wholly uncertain what ails our little piper."

Instability consumed the crowd's mood. Horns sounded, grumbling low at first blow before rising toward a triumphant repertoire. A song played, though no words were sung. It was one that rung of the might of the Stormborne, the valor of Bjardja, and of victory over the mainlanders at large. A relatively pleasing tune, the hum of woodwind paired well against the punitive blows of horns. Somewhere in the background there beat a giant drum, but she did not know from where. A skald galloped ahead of his brethren and seized the wings of welcome to sing an ode to their march's close.

Ryurik thwarts Rune's end
Raise your mead to praise high
Jarl's jaunt glory's herald
Join forth and drink, soigné heir

Scorned sky, moon awaken
Swift sword, our thane's slain lull
Oath of strife who loathes runes
Our Prince of Storm did cull

Thyra's guard slackened, for the skald's lavish, poetic tale failed to depict the awe with which she witnessed her little brother. It was an ode worthy of future kings, but Ryurik returned no elegant, foreign boy. Bereft of youth's stake, he had grown years beyond his age. Tall like all the children of Edvuard Ehlrich, he poised like those around him were insignificant bugs. His hair had grown significantly longer. Gone was his tight, eastern shave. Long, golden strands curled against his neck and shoulders. Hardened lines pulled against his jaw on an oval face. Stoic, amber eyes gazed out like a toughened man's. There was debt buried beneath those eyes, debts which bespoke a life abandoned and of the life he now possessed. A dense beard hugged Ryurik's chin, giving him the look of a Stormborne variant of their brother Ellyan. Even for all his newfound luster, Ryurik was nothing like the charismatic giant who buffeted legions thrice his numbers, then reconquered the mighty fortress of Attal. Try Thyra believed her brother still should to wield a legacy as grand as Ellyan's, even if it was for a lesser cause.

Ryurik deserved better. Her brother deserved better than serving as hand to a shattered sovereign whose own were frail and weak. Lothair did not care for an heir, only for assuring his rule sustained until the Valkyrie claimed him and carried him to Halvalkyra for accomplishing nothing at all. Lothair was a shade of the man whose songs were once sung with fervor. Ryurik deserved better than the shadows his failures drew.

Where would Lothair's legacy leave her brother should he choose to inherit all it was worth? Begotten of his pride like so many incapable of succeeding the seats of their fathers, Ryurik would ride into more dangerous conflicts. He would fight until his worth was weighted in silver and Stormguarde became the envy of any dragon. Ryurik sought Lothair's approval no different than Darius had sought their father's, riding headlong toward his tragic demise. By time's repeal, Thyra's sole surviving brother would lie dead, gouged in the back by strife's crippling knife or scorched to ashen char by the breath of draconic nightmares.

Left the eldest of the Ehlrichs in the wake of their new lives, Thyra took whatever actions were necessary to ensure the full breadth of their lives. It had been Ellyan's responsibility first. When he rode forth from Ellynon to repulse a rebellion's encroachment upon their eastern front, it befell Darius and her. Then upon Ellynon's end, with one brother forsaken to vile spirit, the other trapped without escape between rebellious and demonic fronts, and the third propelled through Death's forlorn Arch, the task was left to her and her alone.

Tanya had always been simple. Ryurik never was—not before…and most certainly not now. Maladaptively dreamy, his magnanimous aspirations encroached upon absurdity, but Thyra also did not know how war had changed him. She'd only visited him once in the opening annuum of his tenure. He was unchanged then, untested also, but he seemed to be every bit a different man now. What other changes wracked her brother's heart and wreaked havoc on his formative mind?

Ryurik's face wrinkled as he strode to the foot of Stormguarde Keep. The Valheim's aerie peak struck above a cloudy sky. Slivers of light peeked through to illuminate the ground. Ryurik stepped into a firm, stoic stance in front of Johan Lodinson—true commander of the Erunheim's sworn swords.

There he waited, sword strapped to his left hip while a tanned, leather bag sagged from the other side. Then Ryurik dismissed the commander with an indecipherable murmur.

Standing six feet and a half-hand tall, Johan was bulkier than most other Stormborne. As commander of the Erunheim's warriors, he maintained an unexpectedly clean shave and an orderly weave of locks. Johan leered over her brother. His eyes were not dangerous—most likely either recalcitrant over being pushed aside or perceptive of the world to which they returned. One was understandable. The other was commendable. Both were malleable motives she believed she could make use of if given enough time with the hulking warrior of at least fifty years or more.

Jarl Eljak Draven came to stand at Ryurik's right hand. An embittered sun had scorched the hair from his head, so the Lord of Draveskeld had responded by growing himself a rugged black beard. A forest covered his baritone chest. His ragged blue eyes held to Ryurik's like a bear's to the falls when salmon were rushing in from the sea. Because Jarl Eljak Draven was a reputably ill-tempered man, Thyra did not enjoy the familiarity he and Ryurik so visibly shared.

Jarl Harald Gormrik, who ruled the many towns of Breidjal by the Helmyan Sea, approached with his warrior cousin, the shield-maiden Hela. The two were a fascinatingly close pair. Lady Hela's father, Lord Haneul Gormrikson, gifted his daughter's youth to Harald's mother when his own wife had died giving birth. It was said they were raised together, learned to ride together, explored the Stormlands together, and learned to fight and to fuck their conquests as if they belonged to the same soul. They adhered to the words of the runic seers with a practical fervor. Had they not been born noble Stormborne, they would have most certainly been forged into mercenary Bjardja warriors who would happily sell their potent swords.

Valyria turned an inquisitive eye in Thyra's direction. "They say the Breidjal Bakari is the strongest fleet the Stormborne have mustered since that forgotten time when our Jastorl, Styrleif, and Jütenthrall ancestors set sail to oceans unexplored. Our peoples might have disseminated the Realms of Frostheim, northern Emrysia, southern Helmya, and the High East's Pentland coasts, but it is the Gormriks they fear when their seas howl in the dark."

Harald came to stand a fair distance off Ryurik's left so he faced her directly. His beard was short, well kempt, and dipped behind his stout chin. He had tied his sideburns into two forks, weaving them along his jawline, and his muddy blond hair dangled loosely over the left side of his head. His head was shaven around the right ear. The bald patch revealed an inked scar, one which he openly reveled as if it were the antique symbol of his Jastorl line. Skin embossed with the sigils of Helti and Eldrahg gifted him the strength of a bellicose Bjardja. Deep-set cerulean eyes glistened. Long, thick eyebrows finalized his descendance from Breidjal eagles—a karlar claim Thyra found mildly hilarious. Harald was handsome, but it was an impression Thyra would never betray. Vainglorious minds never needed lavishment where crops grew in abundance, even if they bore a seed of truth.

Hela Gormrikdottir stepped beside her cousin. Her stance entrenched her like the mountains upon which Frosthammer dwarves roamed. Small copper rings drew her blonde hair into thin cornrows, which caressed the sides of her head two inches above her ears. Rebel strands of hair fled the rings, and the shield-maiden pulled them into the ponytail that caressed the back of her neck. Her bangs were pulled away as well. Two axes hung above wide, sumptuous hips. The handles pulled with her long, muscled thighs. At her back she scabbarded a short sword inlaid with lapis lazuli along the handle. It was claimed she only relented its sting once she found an opponent she deemed worthy. An uncanny air of poise rapt the chief shield-maiden of Breidjal, tense like the talons of eagles.

The Jarl of Breidjal by the Helmyan Sea honored the High Lady of Stormguarde, offering her a ring. Quickly, Valyria bid him to rise and inspected the gilded ruby. Her mother's show of amusement bore the candor of intrigue, and Valyria flashed both it and the ring for Thyra to see.

The ruby glowered an indignant light, twinkling as if conscious of its theft. The setting was of poor craftsmanship. The gold was wrought in wide, twisted rings without a resolute shape, but there was some beauty in it. An etching of a dragon wrestled an eagle atop a hill across the ring's setting. Strange for there to be so much detail inlaid upon such an otherwise forgettable ring.

"If the High Lady permits it," Harald relished, "I offer the slain Lord Durward's family signet to the fairest lady in Stormguarde, who is unsurpassed in her mystique."

Entertained by the gesture but mostly unmoved, Valyria replied, "Pretty, but I do not speak for my daughter." She returned the ring to Harald's hand.

Stepping back, Harald imparted, "Then truly she is a daughter of Runeheim, as you have been and always will be."

Valyria smiled, finding scarce comfort in the duality of his praise.

Thyra ignored his irritable show. It worked against her, seemingly enhancing his vigilance toward seducing both her and her mystique.

Hela then joined her cousin, impassively whispering something into his ear. The two rejoined Ryurik, stepping away from Thyra's regime.

As with all the jarls, Thyra recognized that theirs was a relationship only beginning. Harald would likely reoffer her his rubbish ring when he thought her severity was at its weakest. Then, Thyra would need to decide how to properly receive it, so as to find a use for him.

Jarl Dulmir Svenson of Riven Hold and his two sons, Lord's Bjarni and Mielni Svenson, were the last to join Ryurik. Dulmir was the first Son of Sven Agulbarg, an incredibly venerated man. Sven's life had ended a few years after Thyra's began. Thyra pinned that irreversible incidence over which she had no control as her life's greatest regret. Sven's three sons, Dulmir, Bolveig, and Knuth, were each worthy of carrying on his name, but none compared to the Wardunwyrm of Riven Hold himself.

Dulmir's hair was tied into a silver bun. The jarl's sons mimicked him with half buns of their own. Their brows overhung their eyes like rigid lines of granite. Each boasted sharp noses that had been broken in disparate fashions. Bjarni squinted through a pugnacious glare. Mielni stood in a tenor as if on the verge of equanimity's collapse. One of Dulmir's eyes shone a faded hue of green, yet the other five shared between them were blue. Thyra could not recall him boasting that particular attribute when they'd first met in Stormguarde seven years prior, and she wondered if it was an advent of the war.

From her periphery, Thyra caught sight of Lothair raising an unhurried hand. It was calm, measured, and the Storm King forced it upon the crowds with an immovable glare. Warriors quit shuffling and grew quiet as their Storm King prepared to speak. Most hushed, except for the blends of karlar vying for better views.

Lothair lowered his arm, inviting Drurhelm to tread forward. "How long since our great jarls last graced Stormguarde?" The seer did not permit the question to linger. "Since foreigners marched to the Great Gates of Tjorden to challenge the Draconic Father's court and the Runic Faith! God of the Skies sought to end the line of Runeheim, like he has tried many times before. How fitting, then, that one who was once his own flesh and blood rode as herald to his defeat!" Drurhelm incited excitement by spreading his arms, whereupon he paused, beckoned for an answer, and with uproarious shouts and curses, was obliged. "The runic gods breathe easy this day, for Monomua, Goddess of the Moon, was not forsaken like so many of her sisters. Thanks be to the brave warriors who bled death at the Great Gates of Tjorden, for the Storm King, for Prince Ryurik, and for the jarls of Torlv's thunderous realms. Eldrahg rejoices in your victory, Drur rejoices atop the corpses of our foes, all while the babe of winds weeps from the height of Sky's crib!" he roared, hands spiraling skyward as he slyly cursed Andurial's aerial demesne.

Drurhelm's recount of the Stormborne's victory vivified the people, but Thyra found it dishonest. The most surprising aspect of the Stormlands' victory, in truth, was that victory came at all. The Stormborne were a militant people but conditioned for skirmishes rather than overt warfare. A people accustomed to raiding and pillaging their neighbor's coasts had miraculously held against an endless blow from Sky's Throne. Hundreds of thousands had crashed against the Stormlands' western wall, and the Stormborne held against them all. The Ardent Avant and its vassal kingdoms' expurgation of the Runic Faith was already floundering when Ryurik bolstered the Great Gates, yet some portion of their victory did belong to him. How she wished it were a victory they could have shared.

Thyra could manage the many styles of politics, but she far preferred engaging in their zest with military might. With that taken from her, commanding not but two thousand Skjold, she was no more than an estranged princess in a foreign court overtly forced to observe war instead of leading conquests like her father had raised her to.

"Drur smiles for the sky's dogs our warriors delivered through Death the Reaper's Arch! Eldrahg smiles for the warriors Valvítr has brought him, who now eat and drink within his halls. Speak the prince who left us a boy, returned the son of Runeheim, returned a thundering son of storm!" Drurhelm adjured in a rampant close.

The crowds gradually quieted until the seer's exigence was made complete.

Hand lain against the pommel of his sword, Ryurik scanned the keep's ascent. He nodded in appreciation of Drurhelm's welcome, skipped acknowledging their grandfather, and pinned his gaze to Thyra, whereupon they conducted a battle of durative stares. He dissected her demeanor, searching for feelings she would never divulge. Thyra tendered him a slight grin before returning to cold iron, then motioning him to face Lothair.

You've not needed me or my insight for this long. Do not falter in this critical show of yourself now, Thyra thought to herself.

Thyra said nothing, but Ryurik read her sentiment true. Neither displeased nor satisfied, he did appear ostensibly annoyed. Her lack of engagement evidently bewildered him, so Ryurik regarded their grandfather as he should. He marched forward, his feet trudging over cobble as if he were preparing himself to vindicate the pine bestowed through Seer Drurhelm's inspirational words. As if striving to speak to Ryurik over the future of trade in this stormy world, throngs of Imrahli traders shoved against the lines of Skjold blocking off the market squares to the north of the keep.

"No doubt word has reached you of our victory at the Great Gates and of its formidable besieger's defeat," Ryurik inferred.

Lothair swallowed cool air and descended two steps toward the cobbled path connecting his fortress to the cloudy world he seemed to resent. "I heard the tale on raven's wings, a crow that our enemies have tasted defeat. Recount it for me. Old minds grow stale. I have already forgotten the black-beaked omen's tale."

Ryurik repurposed his stance, and the crowds vying for a view from the main road two dozen paces behind the arc of unyielding Stormborne nobles excitedly shifted with him. "Helmya grew tired of the sting of Torlv's ax. Their lord's drained of their silver, their land reaped of livestock and grains, and their people's lives forfeit, they fled. The Alterians, being none the braver, turned tail and ran, leaving the Light's dimmed Champion and his Avantian soldiers to die to ours."

Ryurik savaged Urien Aylard's superlative title with the faintest trace of personal qualms. Whatever engagement he might have endured with the Light's Champion doubtfully was not one he wished to remember, nor one he should divulge. The Paladin Supreme was, quite likely, the most powerful practitioner of solar sorcery Eldaria had ever known. He boasted formidable sky magic too. Thyra thanked the Draconic Father, if only this once, that the Light's Champion had not been her brother's death and defeat in the war.

"Five fortnights ago on Torlv's day, the Helmyan's abandoned their allies' siege. Their supply lines cut off and their forces afflicted by hunger and dysentery, the armies of the Ardent Avant made a hasty, impulsive retreat. Jarl Eljak and I devised we harrow their retreat through every pass of the Alterian Highlands we controlled. Seven thousand were slain in Helti's name, and so we have delivered them all to the realm of Drur."

Striding forth to scowl into Eljak's face from five paces away, Harald Gormrik interjected, "Seven hundred of ours and a handful more have also passed through Death's Arch. The glory belongs to them the most."

"Thousands more died in the years before. They do not resent the day. Their glory is clearly known," Eljak rebuffed in a ravening tone, stepping past Harald as if to shield Ryurik from his fellow jarl's remark.

"Would you claim their glory as your own then, Eljak?" Hela goaded as she moved to spite Eljak directly beside her cousin. "I do not recall you ahead of the first, nor the second, nor any harrowing charge. I only recall your tongue as the one that relegated the battle's strategy so you could watch us slay the mainlanders from afar."

"We all agreed to the strategy, Hela. Prince Ryurik led the charge well, and those valiant souls who died stand tall in the Halls of Halvalkyra," cracked Lord Bjarni Svenson.

Eljak grated his throat before he spun around to bark back, "We've claimed ten mainlander heads for every one Stormborne lost. Their blood made for good mortar for Jarl Ulfruk's walls."

Hela slowly tread forward with a patronizing grin and her arms loosely spread. "There is no glory in escaping death, Eljak. Only shame for the warrior who evades it."

"Better to serve as death's deliverer than to stand on her knife's receiving edge. You are courageous, shield-maiden, more than Eljak could hope to be, but your youth blinds you to a long life's richness," Lothair commentated dryly from the air above their squabble.

"I will die an old man and leave my sons to the next war's glory. Death is delivered as Drur wishes, but glory comes from delivering his death," Eljak furiously chided.

"Those men died by their swords for the Stormlands. There's glory enough in the victory we achieved from their deaths. Even now," Ryurik declared, raising his voice for all to hear. "Our dead take seat in the Halls of Halvalkyra, watching over us all while feasting above, and that," he concluded sharply, "is an honor worthy of death and more."

Thyra grinned, valuing Ryurik's defusal of the situation. His friendship with the rancorous Lord of Draveskeld, however, peeved her still. The whole affair was horridly redolent of the relationship Lothair and Eljak were said to have held before war drove a scythe between them. Eljak clung to his side so tightly in the effort to spite Lothair, Thyra feared that even a scythe would fail to slice a wedge between them.

Hela obviously despised Eljak. Her demeanor made it more clear than Jüte's mood on a frost-bitten day. But Thyra was yet uncertain of Harald's position. By the binding principle of honor, he most likely shared his cousin Hela's opinion. The Gormrik cousins were aligned to the Runic Faith, which served the Storm King above all, but it did not necessarily guarantee their loyalty to the successor to the Tempest Throne.

"I will make their sacrifice worthy," Ryurik laconically drawled. He stepped out of Eljak's shadow to approach Lothair upon the steps which climbed toward Stormguarde Keep. "Thus, I bring you all a token from the seven thousand who spent their lives in Tjorden's Reach upon our swords."

Ryurik dropped his hand to the loose leather sack hanging at his right hip and untied the knots about its mouth in long draws, then stared down at his prize. His eyes hardened for an uncertain length of time. Huffing, he paused, portraying doubts for his fastidiously built scene. He soon discarded his hesitation and overturned the sack. A skull, which preserved half of the bearer's putrefied flesh, plummeted to the ground. The smell was disagreeable, although it had been cleaned well enough that it was not totally unbearable.

Tanya gasped and clenched her stomach in revolt. Thyra bolstered her sister's nerves by clasping her hand, reminding her for as repulsive as the sight was, this was Ryurik's day.

Ryurik picked up the atrophied head by the strands of its withered, blood-matted hair and flung the skull to Lothair's feet. Languidly, the head rolled down a few steps before gumming to a halt. It tilted askew, facing the runic seers. Dragoln chuckled as if it was a common occurrence. Drurhelm scrunched his face in marvel, revealing grotesque, yellowed teeth.

"Lord Gefre, right hand of King Averick who hails from the Valley of the Three Kings. He commanded the Ardent Avant's rearguard during their retreat. I bring you what remains of him as proof to our victory beyond the Great Gates," said Ryurik.

Lothair visibly mused a chuckle but did not follow through in its execution. He studied the rotten skull with heightened curiosity. The spectacle's thrill was not lost upon him, although he did not share in the karlar's more energetic fascinations. Instead, their grandfather regarded it as an obligatory token for which he cared little. Thyra concealed her disgust with his demeanor by tugging Tanya up a few steps until they were comfortably out of his sight.

"Brother to Lord Derrick whom Lord Bolveig Svenson killed. You have traveled far to show me this man's fouled skull," Lothair noted.

With a wry grin, Ryurik resolved, "It might have been a better flaunt had you met us halfway at Riven Hold, but I do not question your ravens' caws."

Thyra's insides twisted like writhing worms. She enjoyed deploring their grandfather more than anyone else, but this was such an inopportune moment to do so. Why would Ryurik choose to taint the taste of victory by slighting the man for whom he fought? Lothair Runeheim was a wizened coward, but he was the unchallenged Storm King and Ryurik's sole gateway to inheriting the Tempest Throne.

"I would have preferred to witness from Tjorden atop Jarl Ulfruk's Great Gates," Lothair grated in a brunt, gruff admission. "My old bones do not warrant travel, so a less moldered token would have sufficed," he concluded with an amused grin.

"I will remember it," Ryurik acknowledged in sly countermeasure.

Lothair descended the keep's steps to meet Ryurik face to face. "Very good, my grandson. Exceptional indeed. You may be a worthy heir to the Tempest Throne yet."

"I eagerly walk the path which leads me there." Ryurik's hands trembled like autumn's air against the thunder's whip. "Should you one day deem me worthy of taking your place."

"And I will not forsake you like your father of old," the Storm King goaded, embracing Ryurik as mightily as his frame allowed.

"Storm King," Drurhelm impeded as he weaseled his way to Lothair's side. "If this gift does not suit your tastes, perhaps I can make better use of it. The runic gods thirst for offerings of their children's play in this world. Drur the Absconding, Delas to the Goddess of Death. Helti borne of war's boon and forge. Torlv who once ruled storm. Even the Draconic Father Eldrahg would take pride in our reception of this lord's putrescent skull."

"I have heard enough!" Lothair snapped. "Take your leave, draw it into whichever ritual you see fit, and impart the summons once it has been prepared."

Lothair waived away the seer of death, who scurried to recover the moldering skull. He swaddled it with sheets of cloth as delicately as a mother would her newborn son. Drurhelm then invited Dragoln to join him, indiscriminately reveling when he was refused. In a vivacious flurry, Drurhelm shoved through the crowds in the direction of Torlv's runic temple to the northwest.

Tethering Ryurik with his grip, Lothair veered him around so together they faced those who were gathered. "I revel in knowing it was my blood, Ryurik Runeheim, who crippled the Ardent Avant. His hand buffeted by our warriors, even now, Andurial trembles in fury from the height of Sky's Throne!" After offering the crowd ample time to relish that ironic truth, he continued, "Tomorrow we will divide their spoils. Look now at Eldrahg's supreme, for tonight this is for whom we eat and drink at Kingslag!"

Lothair glanced back at Thyra, urging her to commence the event. It was mildly degrading, although Lothair was too unrefined to understand why she viewed it as thus. Opening the gates to Stormguarde Keep was her sole responsibility in this Kingslag besides maintaining order with her Skjold. Lothair often discarded her to lesser things. It occupied her mind through the dullness of exile at least, and she'd thought this distinct 'honor' would never come.

Thyra relinquished her hold of Tanya's hand, offering it the warmth of their mother's instead. She summoned two Skjold, and together they opened the gates to Stormguarde Keep. Thyra withdrew more Skjold from inside the fortress, then lined them along the entrance to the keep. With a crushed smile, she rejoined her grandfather closer than he normally allowed.

"Your doors are open, Grandfather. Let your…*Kingslag* commence."

"It is your brother's, girl. Do not spite his merited celebration before it has even begun because there is no place in it for you," Lothair ruefully whispered.

"I never spite family," she perjured. "Besides, I find this Kingslag too garish to be worthy of everything Ryurik has accomplished for your rule."

Dismal with the exchange, Lothair swatted aside her contempt and addressed her brother instead. "Come then, Ryurik, tell me more of what you have learned from war, so I know what wisdom there is left for me to impart."

"Aye," Ryurik acknowledged, his attention briefly fleeing to her. "There's knowledge I believe I can now share with you."

"Let us find the truth in that together," Lothair replied aside prudent laughter, and the two trudged into Stormguarde Keep.

Eljak was the first to approach the gates after summoning his eldest son to his side. The Lord Son of Draveskeld Byron Dravenson stooped into view. His midnight hair was looped into a bun which sat atop cleanly shaven flanks. The rear of his head was pointed while his face was rigidly square. His nostrils flared as if they were constantly engaged by some foul smell. Long, stocky brows brooded over his marginally inset eyes. His lips were thick but tight, and his ears mirrored those qualities. Truly, his visage was what the runic seers saw in faces of the moon, for while he was neither unsightly nor traditionally handsome, his face was wholly unique.

"What a fine hour to begin drinking mead. Enter with me to the halls of the Storm King, and when there is no room left, drink with me in Stormguarde's streets!" Eljak called to his warriors before father and son wended alongside the many.

Thyra stepped beside the procession to return to her sister. "I wager I could outdrink any of them, especially Eljak Draven," she said.

Mother's eyes were unkind, but Thyra expected no less of a stringent response. "I would not goad your grandfather any further, lest you incur a change in today's mood," Valyria chided.

"What have you heard that warrants such an accusation?" Thyra cynically questioned.

"It is seldom what you say, Daughter, but how you choose to intone it."

Thyra repentantly rejoined, "Cheer, Mother. It's Ryurik's day. Whether

Grandfather and I clash or not, you've done a swell job in preparing us a worthy stage."

Valyria glared.

"But I will not," Thyra yielded, "as promised. Not today…and not till first light on the morrow."

Valyria scoffed, settling for her cheeky answer before departing to join the men. Silver strands dangled between bright blondes that glistened in the rare daylight. With a youthful vigor she thought her mother had resiled long ago, Valyria entered Stormguarde Keep beside Dulmir Svenson, eldest son to a man she had known well long ago. The Gormriks soon became her sole remaining company, and they too were not long to be gone.

Hela Gormrikdottir reproached her cousin, "Lothair would stoop to partition our plunders for a war in which he did not partake!"

"He means to strengthen the boy's claim. He is old, from the era of Sven Agulbarg before Dulmir Svenson ruled Riven Hold. If Ryurik seeks to take the Tempest Throne, our first question should be if we will submit to the foreign fool," said Harald.

Hela replied, "That boy knows nothing of war or this place, much less anything of what it means to rule. He has lived in exile too long to belong to Lysian, but he is no son of storm."

"You are no son of storm either, Hela. Does this mean you could never rule?" Harald asked.

Socking her cousin's shoulder, Hela stated, "I would be its sovereign queen and daughter, and the lash of my sword would be twice as deadly as yours. Besides, your next conquest would be the preferable ruler."

Thyra trembled, suspicious of who they were referring to as a conquest.

Harald yielded his own smile and made for an injured escape. Hela pursued, unrelenting in her string of cunning insults. The Gormriks and their Bjardja and sworn swords wended through city streets in the direction of the Sea of Storm. How befitting of those who ruled over Sjógurn's deepest fjord.

Tanya giggled beneath her breath. For whatever reason it arose, Thyra expected it to last a few seconds and no more, especially considering the day's already bitter mood. After her little sister failed to suppress her bizarre mirth and it mounted into something more, Thyra began to wonder what exactly she was laughing at.

Thyra asked, "Has something unexpected unfurled? I must admit while the day has only just begun, already it is magnificent compared to most."

"Nothing in particular. I always assume Mother will fret and you will find a reason to quarrel with Grandfather," Tanya finished with a simple shrug.

"You seem concerned…"

Tanya swung around as if she had been cherishing the arrival of this precise moment. "I am simply pleased that in being pursued, I will no longer stand through tonight alone!"

Teasing her own exasperation, Thyra stated, "I hope you're prepared, because if you are truly my sister, you will find most of the pursuants to be dreadfully dull."

"So we will see, my ruby rose," Tanya enthusiastically mocked before leaving her to join in the Kingslag's fun.

Thyra scoffed, "If I must smile through this whole sky-damned occasion for the sake of my mother, I at least hope he does not start by offering that odious ruby ring afront his little…"

⎯⎯⎯◄◆►⎯⎯⎯

Pausing for breath while towing master Durkil's meat-wagon, Muiri angrily groaned, "Dwolv spare my feet from this bushing burden. I want to be home."

"Why doesn't Durkil just purchase a mule to cut down the time it takes to haul around this wagon?" Cadell questioned from behind his leather mask.

Muiri gritted his teeth. "I yielded on one single occasion, towing the wagon after his old ox perished in its sleep. He's exploited me as a workable replacement ever since."

They heaved the wagon's wheels over an exposed rock in the middle of the market road. Cadell offered little help in his languished state, so Muiri bore the brunt of it himself. The wagon dramatically wobbled, and they almost lost a few cuts of meat to the dirt. Fortunately, Cadell caught them in the nick of time.

The straps they used to tow the wagon went slack when Cadell gasped for breath. He said, "Valvítr's mercy is righteous, Muiri. Besides, we're almost there!"

"Could you build up your appetite and earn your Kingslag feast by pulling a little harder, Cadell?"

"Runic gods, I bet they've laid hundreds of honeyed chickens over several dozens of pots of white carrot and salted cabbage."

Baffled by Cadell's eccentric account of this labor's worth, Muiri exclaimed, "So that's what you get out of this, the chance to gnaw on some salted cabbage?"

"You're an uncultured ass!" Cadell laughed as he returned to finishing the haul. "Stewing the cabbage with a little salt gives it the best flavor. You should try it when we're done."

"Then we must make it to the very place where they are cooking the cabbage, so I might try these mystical leaves you condone!" he shouted while finishing the struggle to reach the steps of Stormguarde Keep.

Muiri collapsed at the foot of their destination, squealing pitilessly while Cadell chortled. They were received by the lines of Skjold guarding the gates. Most laughed at Muiri's eccentric display. The remainder cracked wide grins. Muiri inhaled deeply, exhaling relief that this was the end of the road. Let the Skjold take it the rest of the way, for all he cared. All he needed was final payment, so he might pacify his brutish master with silver's glorious return.

"Thrall boy, why's the thin one wearing a mask? What have you brought to the gates of Stormguarde Keep?" exacted the group's leader.

Muiri had forced Cadell to mask his face for this precise reason, to dodge the misplaced fear that arose when men noticed scars of a childhood illness that had long since abandoned his flesh. Yet, in predictable Stormborne fashion, the mystery enticed their attention. What to do, and quickly. Muiri could not risk exposing Cadell's face. His back could not afford Durkil's delivery being spurned on account of Cadell's pox-ridden lips.

"Lord, he is," Muiri cried out to elevate the Skjold's ego. "The most hideous man you would ever see in your life. I would spare your eyes from the horror, if you do not mind."

The Skjold's leader stammered, "Drur's Abyss. What ails him?" before leaping back as if the two carried the plague.

"He is cursed! A seeress cursed this hapless wretch for defiling Freyja's runic temple in old Aidelgard!" Muiri exclaimed.

"They fuck everything in Aidelgard! They say the Kennings even take their women rooftop because the dragon's lapis soaks the first bleed."

With a hefty chuckle, another Skjold asked. "Why punish a man for upholding the common law among the hogs?!"

Muiri slyly grinned. "Because he is poor, Lord! He is not noble like you."

"I am no lord, but I am also no thrall," spit the same Skjold.

The first man rejoined swiftly, ruling, "I don't care if his face is uglier than Kazbel's ass, have him remove the mask or there is no going farther."

Well, there was no stepping aback from this ruse. "I wouldn't recommend it! The seeress who wove this curse bequeathed that any who dare look upon his grotesqueness would bleed beauty themselves. She believed it would keep him from bedding more of Freyja's priestesses, but in one thing you're right. They'll fuck anything in Aidelgard. They would have their way with a snake if they could hold its head and bar its bite!"

Cadell stepped beside Muiri amid the resulting uproar and, through the muffled folds of his mask, garnered their full attention. "It's true, Skjold to the Storm King. I fled Aidelgard after my ugly pother turned their women into hideous ældrik. This thrall was once Stormborne like you, but after gazing upon my visage, he became the Alterian goat you see before you now!"

"Eldrahg guard us from this curse. What in Freyja's name has Seeress Dalla done?!"

"Wrap another mask around the funny one's face before entering, thrall."

Damn Cadell for savaging him so justly. Damn Cadell for completing a ruse where he could not. Muiri assumed if he could look upon his own face now, it would appear as if the same seeress had cursed him to float his tongue without touching anything inside his mouth. Perhaps if he failed, he might suffer a fate like the one Cadell described.

The Skjold did not cease in their laughter for a ridiculously long while. Eventually, two more joined the cluster, and the rest hushed. The newcomers motioned for the others' attention, heralding some news. Next, they planted themselves in front of Muiri, Cadell, and the gathered crowds who wished to enter Stormguarde Keep.

"Orders from Commander Thyra and the High Lady of Stormguarde. None are allowed enter unless half of those within clear out."

"Eldrahg scorch my hair..." Muiri cursed. "Just let me deliver this meat."

"Too late, thrall. You heard as well as me. Nobody's allowed in, not even Durkil's delivery boy or your funny friend," remarked the most sociable Skjold of the group.

Muiri piped back, "We are here to deliver an order the High Lady made herself. Valvítr have mercy on everyone within! Why would anyone want to enter Stormguarde Keep if there isn't any cooked meat to wash down with ale?"

"Weren't the cooks short on food when last you checked, Ulf?"

"Got my fill already, Halvor. Don't care about the rest."

"I've been on guard all day. I want there to be food left when I eat," Halvor complained.

"I won't disobey the commander. I enjoy my life and pay. Ignore her orders yourselves," Ulf announced with a wide-eyed stare.

"Too little too late," came the same Skjold again. "Orders are orders. The Lysian always has her way."

"I judge Thyra Ehlrich would be more dissatisfied if our brother's Kingslag ran out of meat because two thralls were prevented from entering the keep with their delivery," commented a girl from behind the throngs of karlar.

"Princess..." several Skjold muttered.

Striding in from the city accompanied by two Skjold, a youthful, blonde-haired priestess of perhaps eighteen spoke up to Ulf, Halvor, and the remainder of the shield guard. She was tall for a woman, her shoulders rounded as if they were delicately plated pastries, and her eyes shone like amber stars. Supple cheeks stretched over sharp cheekbones, a soft jaw hung half agape, and she licked her sumptuous lips in jest.

Muiri caught himself gawking. Terrified, he shook himself of his infatuation, praying none of the Stormborne had seen.

"I am as much a princess as you are a lord," she chided.

Monomua's moon-wrought grace struck Muiri as he wondered who the girl was.

"Tanya," readdressed the warrior. "The commander, your sister, will not abide their entry into the Storm King's halls."

"I know my sister's mind better than you, Gaur. I also know she permits you all to adjust her orders whenever situations demand you should. And this is your food!" she exclaimed. "Damn I would help the thralls carry their master's meat to the kitchens myself, if I were you!"

"Aye," stammered a few while the rest began to slowly nod.

Halvor beamed. "I think I'll have the cooks cut me something special!"

Runic gods shield their Storm King from all harm destined to soar his way. It was always the idiots who ascended to leadership, even in the Storm King's Skjold.

Cadell swiftly added, "Might I suggest some honeyed chicken served over salted cabbage."

Muiri shot him a derisive glance, and Cadell drove an elbow into his flank.

"I like that suggestion!" the princess priestess resounded. "Do bring me a plate when the chicken is done."

"I like salted cabbage as well!" Muiri resounded, and Cadell shot him a foul glare as well.

Giggling, she added, "Leave the thralls with one plate each, and make sure they are properly paid before they leave. I wouldn't wish for my mother to be perceived as a thief." The priestess softly smiled before entering the keep.

Muiri swore she'd blushed before departing. Moments later, as they were transporting their delivery to the kitchens with the Skjold's assistance, he came to understand why the commander had forbidden all entrance into the keep. They scarcely had room to move toward the kitchen, let alone force their way back out. Luckily, the crowds despoiled none of the honeyed chicken he or Cadell ate, nor the generous pay Muiri received on his master's behalf.

<hr>

Despite herself, Thyra had enjoyed the Kingslag's commencement. The subtle bindings of Drurhelm's words unraveled clear as day. The seer was bound to the Delas of Death, and so death and its execution were his life's passions. The Stormborne may not have realized it, but they too were bound to Drur's ruin. Death, the solemn Reaper cared naught for any soul's pride. Dranur and her Delas claimed everything in the end—an understanding Thyra and the seer both shared.

Drur, Delas of Death, long ago took his place amongst the runic gods beside Eldrahg, Delas of the Moon. Drur was the sole member of Eldrahg's court who had not been forged by the moon-wrought grace of the greater Goddess of the Moon. Those who sought glory by the sword were most assured to meet at face with Drur, if they were deemed unworthy and if the Valkyrie did not carry their souls to the Halls of Halvalkyra. Fate intertwined itself in such vacant, ironic manners. Life gave the journey meaning, whereas death was truly the road's abysmal end.

Ignited from a speech heralding mead and meat, the Kingslag began as Thyra expected. Not long after the gates to the keep were unbarred, the great hall of Stormguarde was filled to the brim. An open brawl had erupted at the gates between throngs of drunken karlar distraught they had lost the opportunity to drink free mead. The Skjold had summarily dispersed them, although similar mindless incidents recurred frequently since.

It was not until the Crescent Lady's splintered rise that Thyra was finally relieved of duty. Enough of the karlar fell unconscious that she could comfortably abscond her Skjold. Fortuitously, it arose when her stomach first began to yield to hunger's yearn too.

By fireside Thyra sat in the keep's dominant bailey amongst other Skjold and Ryurik's warriors. Chicken legs and rashers of ham were generously portioned to every plate. The keep's cooks delivered a whirlwind of slaughter to the gluttonous pigsties and coops of uncouth fowl to her partial benefit. Famished from skipping meals since the early morning, Thyra tilled the food on her plate. The jugs of mead she drank accentuated the ham's tender taste. Buzzed like a bride fresh to the taste of her husband's lips, Thyra thoroughly enjoyed the meal.

"I enjoy fighting as much as any other man," Audun excitedly claimed. "But I never want to fight by the sides of Bjardja."

"By Helti, why wouldn't you, Audun!? One good Bjardja on either side and there will be few enemies left to meet you," countered the Skjold's second commander, Knuth Svenson.

"It's no challenge, or those battles are riddled with the assurance of death. When I strike with the vanguard beside a jarl's contingent of Bjardja, my ax never cuts anybody down! Then I reach a predicament. If I drive forward to engage what few foes are left, I'll die without earning my place in the Halls of Halvalkyra! I prefer fighting beside regular warriors, so at least I'll wet my blade before I'm slain and give the Valkyrie a reason to carry me away."

"That's a subtle way to admit your cowardice!" barked Barul. The Skjold captain sloshed his mug toward Audun while striking the accusation, spilling some ale. "Look at ya, you son of a bitch…making me waste good ale."

"How is dying in an apposite fight dishonorable? Don't spite me when you are too drunk to even stand." Audun wiped the ale from his face and shook it into the fire.

"I'm no more drunk than the commander," Barul declared, feigning personal injury. "Am I not, Thyra? I would wager there's another five jugs we can easily manage between us."

"More likely I finish your five after I've finished five of my own," she replied with droll humor.

Barul's eyes widened at the challenge latent in her jest.

Knuth quacked through laughter, "I think the commander just said you've had enough."

"I've had enough of patrolling this dreary keep! Not in ten years has an assassin reached Stormguarde. We should have kept this coward here, so I could fight for the Stormlands!" Barul pointed to Audun to assure everyone knew of who he spoke.

Reaching a low-walled threshold, Audun rose to demand, "Then stand with Helti's honor as he stood for his Einvígi Dauðan with Baelric the Black Sword. I doubt your legs will even let you, Barul."

"Bastard!" With an agitated roar, Barul met Audun's challenge, charging through the fire to drive him off his chair and into the dirt.

Thyra yelled after them, "With your damned hands only, fools!"

The two wrestled for a time—heads butting, arms weaving, and legs interlocking like bitter Alderian lovers. Cheering in excitement, nearby warriors surrounded them, throwing out bets on the fight. Barul won with a smothering pin drawn across Audun's outstretched left arm. Weight and size were his lone advantages, for when he rose in glistened triumph, the blond bear abruptly vomited into the ground.

Plainly, Knuth commented, "You're quiet, Thyra. I have not yet seen you speak with your brother. Is this the reason why?"

Regarding him with mock appreciation, Thyra answered in kind, "No, Knuth, it is not. He'll come to me in his own time, and until then, I will keep vigil over his Kingslag's peace."

Indifferently, Knuth forced his cup of mead into her hands. "Take a few more swigs of this. It will carry you through your vigil."

Knuth left to engage Barul in a surprise second bout, for which the blond bear was wholly unprepared. Tackling the leather clad warrior like a cornered boar, Knuth lifted Barul into the sky, then dropped him like a sack of flour. Barul chopped Knuth's legs on the descent, bringing down the Son of Sven with him. They rolled over level ground where neither man fought with much advantage.

Setting aside Knuth's mead, Thyra chuckled at their foolery and pondered the reason for her cascade toward silence. Her successes and failures were well known across Stormguarde's court. Having employed experience attained from her time spent as Joint Commander of Ellynon's Guard, she'd first established a rigid structure to replace the irregularity and unpredictability amongst the Skjold. Her talents were many, her achievements considered great, and they were instilled unto her Skjold with a combative fervor, and eventually she had been accepted by her new contingents, albeit not without resistance.

The Skjold submitted to each other's wills when essential and always to hers. Their fierce opposition to new order eventually melted into mutual acceptance of the lives they led together. Warriors preferred the company of other warriors, and the Skjold was publicly considered more of a police force than an army. The Stormborne craved freedom, and their warriors yearned for its tender touch like a young man yearned for the sweetness a woman's legs forgave when he showered her with flowery words. Thyra left her Skjold unaffected by most of the Stormlands' political drivel as best she could—beyond her final edict that they forever serve her and her family first.

Perhaps there was a sliver of truth to those vice opinions, but she believed they were mostly incorrect. The seers believed her an enemy to the runic gods who meant to bring Andurial into the heart of Monomua's rule. The jarls supposed she intended to establish her own holdings in the Stormlands. All she ever took from them both, however, were those who were displaced by grievances yet still worthy of joining her Skjold.

The Stormlands were brimming with resolute people the land occasionally broke. When broken, they were often discarded like unwanted thralls. Thyra collected them each like injured doves washed upon the shore after a frightful storm. In diligently mending their spirits and then renewing them with purpose, she had cultivated herself a slight military core.

Knuth Svenson had been her supreme dove. Finely attuned to war, when the Son of Sven was ousted from the Breidjal Bakari, he had come to her. Through Knuth and those like him, Thyra fashioned a new Skjold. Unity would be their eventual calling, and it was something she wished to speak of with Ryurik whenever he finally approached her. All of this was known. How came the loss of the divine extension of her hand was the only story left to her alone. That was a sore topic, one which she had spoken of to no one besides Lothair, a magnificent mistake on her part.

Thyra departed the bailey and strode through the golden gable of the great hall. Doors opened underneath the warrior-maidens who guarded them. Behind the great hall lay an atrium, which conjoined with the bastion's bosom where lived and worked the thralls. Two stairwells climbed each side of the entrance, leading to a hefty balcony that encircled the ground floor. Two dwarven bastions could be reached thereon, winding through the dusky mountain that was their impenetrable hold. The Storm King's personal quarters stretched inland with the first. The offices, workplaces, and chambers of his trusted counsel filled the second.

She scanned the crowds of bumbling warriors along the Storm King's tables that lined the great hall's posterior wall. Behind it whipped a roaring fire. Lothair sat at center with her mother. Drurhelm sat upon his right. Tanya sat at the table's left end. Dragoln stood behind her. Behind him stood a pair of Skjold. Several Agulbargs and a few of Dulmir's sworn swords surrounded the two. The jarl's younger son, Mielni, took a seat beside Tanya and began to intrusively flirt. There came her next task, presenting itself on foolish wings like an ursa bear's sweetened snout to the bumblebee's vengeful sting.

Thyra quickly shoved her way through the crowds, bumping ale from a few cups before expending mock, apologetic smiles to appease those she'd accidentally disturbed. In the mess of ambling bodies, she bumped into

Hela Gormrikdottir. The shield-maiden of Breidjal appeared drunker than Thyra, yet miraculously unhampered by its pull.

"Princess Thyra. Well...from that sweet scowl you seem to have misplaced, I guess you prefer the title Commander."

Thyra regarded the shield-maiden without guilt for lost decorum. She had been caught in her displeasure open handed, so she did not relinquish its hold. "Quick mind, shield-maiden. You are correct in that assumption."

"Quicker eyes too. Did I frighten you, or do you always grip your sword when you first meet strangers?"

Abandoning her sword's grip, Thyra relaxed her sword hand and waved the second in a slight, dismissive gesture. "Said it yourself. The Skjold's commander should have plenty of reasons to keep wary of strangers."

"No need to fear me, Commander." Unjaded, Hela gripped her shoulder, slugging them to sit at a nearby table. "Take a drink and lighten your nerves. War is over for a time, and I would like to speak to someone with enough of a mind that it will be worth my time."

"Thank you?" Thyra posed in bewildered gratitude. "But I do not have time to idle—"

Forcing a cup of ale into her hand, the shield-maiden interrupted, "Your sister will be fine. Ryurik might be absolutely worthless, but he is a smart enough man to never allow it. Better if she gets good practice disappointing her suitors in the open, unlike him."

Perturbed by Hela's callous indifference, Thyra begrudgingly accepted the invitation. She was curious of Hela's motivations, even if her outward remits portrayed otherwise. She studied the shield-maiden. Hela's left eye was inked like a hawk, her neck bore azure talons, and her lips were as starkly red as a freshly wilting rose. Being a veteran to war, she looked younger than Thyra, and by Lysian standards, Thyra was relatively young.

"How did my brother fare against the Ardent Avant? I am reticent to admit I know little other than the outcome."

Hela dodged the question. "He is alive, is he not?"

"Lothair buried all news from Tjorden." Swigging her ale, Thyra confessed, "I know little, so if we are to share ale, Hela Gormrikdottir, let it be worth both of our time."

"Too much fire in his belly, but well enough for a..." Hela paused, finding complacency in a swig of ale too. Ceremoniously, she concluded, "Foreigner. You understand the Stormborne rue rule which is not their own."

"Fair point, but one which can be easily trounced and conquered."

"So each of Valyria Runeheim's children searches for their own way to achieve this same lofty goal."

"Do tell me how you have come to see us," Thyra mistakenly taunted.

Astoundingly observant, Hela conferred, "The youngest daughter abides the runic seer's zeal to cleverly disguise herself as one of them. The errant prince without purpose rides to seize glory from his patron's war, where he found shelter beneath a stray jarl's wing. Then comes you, Commander, strictly holding to that which you know—power—bending the Skjold and others to your whim. I would guess it's as if you never even fled the High East."

Irked by the shield-maiden's chasmic scrutiny of their lives' accords, Thyra loosed her response with winged fervor. "Not in the slightest! Ryurik would have done well to learn by me before departing. A victory claimed through another man's sleuth is no victory of yours."

"I tell Harald this whenever he allows me to lead our charge or take point in our shield wall," Hela replied.

"Does the Jarl of Breidjal by the Helmyan Sea send you charging at me now?"

"I come on his behalf as much as my own. You find these petty rivalries now returned to Lothair's court strange and diminishing, do you not?"

"I have found them, and that is all I care to share."

Brows arching like a Breidjal eagle's when it descried a feebler bird, Hela said, "Then know we find the ones to which we have returned as equally disturbing."

"Should we delve into such subjects further?" Thyra asked.

"Not here and not now. Not until adequate privacy can be found."

In amiable contrast to her earlier blunted admission, Thyra aptly confessed, "You are smart, Hela. Clever enough to realize these things with no one's guidance but your own. But why then share them with an admitted stranger to whom you owe no shred of trust?"

"It's dangerous to fight alone, whether in war or beyond it. We Gormriks have long been accosted on the fields of battle. My cousin and I think we recognize your motives better than the rest. You wish to see us united, through conquest if that is the only way. Unity festers within you Lysians. It's painted all over your faces." Hela hushed to a graven whisper and continued, "You have yet to fashion allies for you and your Skjold, so we offer to be your first. Our armies and our swords, when the time comes for your wit and knowledge to rule Lothair's court. A fair trade for a time until the old man passes and, I hope, beyond."

Thyra openly ridiculed, "You misplace my motives to think I would ever strike out against my brother."

Hela solemnly corrected, "I do not misplace you, Commander, but others, however, do. I'll never swear to that boy directly, but should you desire it, then he might use us through you."

"Why bind myself to the Gormriks when Ryurik has others? He has Ulfruk Dulfang and Eljak Draven, as I now know."

Hela sardonically chuckled before banishing the mirth to atone, "Every Storm King since Erun Runeheim has withheld Tjorden's allegiance. Their line is as damned old as yours. As for the jarl of Draven's Dominion. Well, he is just one among many, his swords are fewer than ours, and his ships number nearly none."

"Do you think Jarl Eljak incapable of rallying further support from within the confines of his realm?"

"That is a truth I'll leave to you to discover for yourself."

Begrudgingly, Thyra prodded, "Do you seek to seal this alliance in blood?"

"I do not. Harald might, but should you deny him, I doubt he would rescind our offer."

"Is that your guarantee?" Thyra provoked, searching for a calcifying answer.

"I can guarantee he would pursue you through any alliance."

"I don't like your cousin," Thyra responded in partial truth. "I won't surrender my Skjold or myself to your coalition if my bed is to be accosted by him."

After slogging most of her drink, Hela stated, "My cousin is an, undeniably, hot-willed whore, who I still love greatly. If he wants to bed you, then he will eventually succeed."

Stricken aghast by her claim, Thyra reproached, "So the Jarl of Breidjal wishes to violate me against my will?"

"How would he accomplish that, Commander?" Hela smiled against the ale's lingering taste, licking those damned sumptuous lips. "He never sleeps with a woman who does not also wish to violate him."

"Then you would do well to inform him I am not his woman. I prefer a much different kind of man."

"I will not, but only because I see you lie. Then again, maybe I should, if only because I think you and I would make a finer pair."

Thyra spurned, "I have heard enough. You know well what I want. Return with it to your cousin or another raving table. I do not care which."

Having finished her cup, Hela rose to leave. Halting before she walked in any direction leading away from Thyra, she summarily concluded, "I will drink a little more before I find a man with a tough bone to slough. That's my reward, but to you I would suggest throwing that insufferable man-child off your sister before he sticks like skyr."

True to her word, the shield-maiden of Breidjal drifted two tables over into the company of her and her cousin's sworn swords.

Thyra swiveled to find her sister trapped in conversation with Jarl Dulmir's younger son. Lord Mielni's cheeks burned bright red like the hearth. He had since unfurled his half bun, so his ruddy hair hung high above his shoulders. Laying his hands on Tanya's shoulder, his fingers slid where they should not. Shoving through a half dozen Agulbarg men, Thyra reached the torrid whelp before he even noticed she was there.

———◆———

Tanya strained through annoyance as Mielni Svenson gripped her shoulder. She forced a smile, laughing sparingly throughout the rhythmic tales of his raids on Helmyan supply lines. In truth, she hardly registered them at all. As soon as he'd laid those unswerving, beady eyes on her, she'd known how uncomfortable the conversation would become. He failed to comprehend her disinterest. How right her damned sister was, claiming this night would be thrust upon her as much as Ryurik, her mother's sole surviving son.

Tanya still kept the hope that Darius and Ellyan had survived the High East's fall. With each passing year she spent trapped in Torlv's runic temple, however, it declined. She clutched at the golden necklace where hung Lysian's jeweled phoenix. It was a gift to her brother from a High Lord of Lysian's daughter whose heart he had stolen by mistake, a gift then passed to her before a ship carried her to haven, and a relic by which she still held him close. If passage through the Arch were the culmination of Darius's sacrifice to see Ellynon's evacuees saved, she prayed her brother had been swept to the Fields of Elysium by such valorous wings as he deserved.

Taxed as she was, Thyra tried her best to fill their brother's shoes, but she had her own goals. They utterly consumed her. Tanya understood them, respected them, and even urged her sister toward reclaiming pride from something other than the Skjold. Even more so, Tanya thought to gain freedom from Thyra through the push, but she genuinely gained none. She only exchanged Thyra's rule with that of the Runic Faith and its seers of old.

Tanya did not necessarily care for religion. Like most faiths, they were bound to known truths, but they too were often plagued in fiction and wicked guiles. Between the Ardent Faith beholden to the mainland and Lysian and the Runic Faith that served Monomua and her Delas Eldrahg, Tanya preferred the latter, if only slightly. The runic seer's teachings and tales were, at a minimum, heroic and inspiring, whereas those depicting Andurial, Eshkalah, and their eternal adversaries were chill, sour, and disturbing.

Mostly, however, the Runic Faith offered her protection from the brutal uncertainty of life as a Stormborne princess. Drurhelm took too kindly to her, but he was a feeble minded toad she hardly feared. It bothered her less after fashioning a novel father in his fellow seer. She meant no disrespect to Lothair, but he was a distant man who rarely showed affection to anyone besides her mother, and rarely at that.

"Two years before this moon's reign, they claimed my warrior's raid over autumn shipments of Helmyan grains saved my brother Bjarni's forces. The mere chance of his armies' starvation through winter forced the Light's Champion to withdraw, and it saw us hold strong."

Face resting upon bored, slothful hands, Tanya piped back with a scarce hint of sarcasm, "How, heroic, my lord. Your father must be proud."

"Grandfather Sven Agulbarg himself would have reveled in the victory Mielni Svenson brought to our family and the Stormlands."

"That is a bold claim, Mielni," Dragoln croaked. The seer gripped young Mielni's arm to tentatively request that the lord face him. "I do admit it is a good foundation, should you begin a quest to exceed your grandfather's greatness."

"And begun I have! You can attest even Eldrahg now favors this second son of Dulmir Svenson!" Mielni proclaimed for all men to hear.

Tanya rolled her eyes at the young lord's ramblings.

Mielni then shook Dragoln's hands in gratitude for a claim he'd bestowed himself! Oh, how the boy's face brightened like a child's as he considered how to proceed. Inside, Tanya shed tears of self-pity. She knew there was no easy way in denying a man who drank himself into the stupor of a spoiled brat.

"Child!" Dragoln exclaimed. "I make no claims for the Draconic Father without casting runes atop his sigil. Do not disrespect his name again."

"Then let us draw a runic circle and ask him. We will have the time once Seer Drurhelm offers that lord's skull to his own runic god," Mielni chimed back with drunken enthusiasm. Wavering, he gracelessly took a seat with the obvious purpose of settling beside her and pulled his chair close so his muck breath overwhelmed hers.

Tanya faced away and shut her nostrils. If not for the tender insults the boy chucked against Dragoln, eldest seer of the Runic Faith, then the scandal he sought to lay upon the Storm King's granddaughter would soon sting sorely upon his cherry face.

In the precise moment Mielni Svenson reached out to touch her, rapt by lust's allure, Thyra announced her arrival in a style wholly resemblant of their father's eldest daughter. She stooped low to drive her shoulder into Mielni's and swung into the startled lord, dragging him back to his feet. Mielni stumbled, and a few of his swords took notice when Thyra thrust him into the wall adjacent to the raging hearth. Waiting until he recovered, Thyra dusted her hands, flaunting the ease with which she'd discarded him with a subtle grin.

Thyra disregarded the Agulbarg's retaliatory concern to observe, "My lord, you must have drunk too much to have so carelessly misplaced your strength of arm."

"What right do you have to injure me in the middle of my conversation?!" Mielni howled while he aimlessly adjusted his attire.

"I have the right to protect my sister from being violated by a lord hammered senseless," Thyra answered dashingly, unafraid of the eyes now beset upon them both.

Beginning in a murmur that rose into another yell, Mielni erroneously claimed, "What violation, you vile woman? I've done nothing to deserve your fist!"

Thyra mockingly acknowledged, "I gave you nothing more than a shove, Lord." She then asked of Tanya's two Skjold, "Was it not clear as day beside this hearth in your Storm King's open hall? Am I mistaken?"

"It was wayward," the Skjold woman answered. "But the lord did lay his hands on her."

Mielni seized one of his men as he barked like a famished dog, "What does the word of one bitch count for another?"

Dragoln chided, "Come now, Lord, before you insult her further. Thyra exaggerates what occurred, but do not claim what I witnessed as false."

Ignoring Seer Dragoln, Mielni persisted, "What would the Storm King say to you striking one of his favored lords in court!?"

"I doubt my grandfather would be fond of some faux pup of war attempting to lay his way into the house of Runeheim!" Thyra roared.

Eyes widening and pupils narrowing to points, Mielni bumbled, "Rotten bitch," before he swung his fist forward.

Thyra laid her own into his nose before the young lord finished his first step. The thin rings of Lysian steel around her fingers did the most harm to his face. Two of Dulmir's sworn swords lifted him by his shoulders before he completely sagged. A half-hand of the Agulbarg's warriors confronted Thyra and her Skjold while the lord regained his senses. Tanya gasped, frightened of the brawl surely to come.

"Step back, all of you!" Jarl Dulmir Svenson thundered while he cleared a path through the commotion with his eldest son.

Lord Bjarni strode to the side of his younger brother and grinned upon inspecting his busted nose. "Not as mighty as he would like to think."

Jarl Dulmir rumbled low, "Do not provoke them further!" before his gaze vexed Thyra.

Tanya observed the jarl corner Thyra, even though she yielded him no ground. The two whispered their grievances, but they were cordial enough to keep their qualms hidden between themselves. She looked beyond to where their mother hurried off, presuming she flew to fetch Ryurik. She genuinely prayed Mother might find him. Ryurik had been strangely absent through the evening. Tanya only wanted to regale so late for the chance that they might reunite and talk.

"Where is she? Where is the commander of the Skjold?!" Mielni stammered as he shook himself awake.

Humored by his brother's mulish outrage, Bjarni mocked, "Whom, brother? What woman shames your name?"

"Do not scorn me, Bjarni. She shames *our* name, and thus rues *yours* too!"

"I fear no woman's sting, and I don't invite it as callously as you've invited hers," Bjarni replied in firm, sardonic form.

Bjarni's comment was well received, and laughter drove his brother further into anger's embrace. The young lord shoved him off, so Bjarni slammed him against the wall and pinned him there with his forearm. The sudden change in composure shocked her, and she noted to never cross the man herself.

Jarl Dulmir held no such reservations, and the first Son of Sven departed Thyra to address his son Mielni in her wake. "Why do you insist on stirring up trouble. You're meek when sober, and descend into a fool's garb when you drink, assailing the Storm King's granddaughter." Dulmir raised a hand to slap his son. "Do not embarrass me again!"

"It is all right, Dulmir. We are meant to engage," Lothair impassively dismissed from the comfort of his chair.

"Your forgiveness aside, Storm King," Dulmir growled. "I will not allow a Son of Sven to smear my father's name in this way."

Lothair ripped charred meat from a fowl's flank, swallowing the poultry while Jarl Dulmir impatiently awaited a response. "It is a Kingslag, Dulmir. It would be disgraceful if we did not occasionally spar aside our warriors at such an event."

Jarl Dulmir grudgingly conceded before withdrawing from his son's mistake.

"Why do you trouble my court, girl?" came Lothair unexpectedly once the jarl's men had stepped away.

"Excuse me?" Thyra replied.

Finishing another bite of his haunch, Lothair solemnly expounded, "Why would you not speak with the lord before you moved to strike him? What ill temperament so overtakes you that you must always rile my court?"

"None," Thyra grated, withholding the fires of Lysian ire that bled behind her tone. "I do my utmost to enact what I think to be your will."

"You think it my will to injure my own lords and jarls?"

"No, Grandfather."

"King, girl! I am your Storm King! You my unwanted and unlikable guest. We are no longer without company, so do not further test my patience."

"Aye, Storm King," Thyra grumbled. Her eyes hardened upon her grandfather as her neck tautened into rings.

The sight brought her shivers, but Tanya knew of nothing to alleviate the stress. Thyra stepped gently past her and shoved through the Agulbargs, flanking Jarl Dulmir. She slapped a hand contritely against Mielni's shoulder, and Bjarni forced his brother to make peace. Thyra reclused well before that moment came to pass, sparing a few words to her Skjold and little for anyone else.

Tanya did not catch sight of where her sister wended off but reasoned it was far outside of Stormguarde Keep. She wanted to follow, but pursuing would likely be seen as a deliberate split from her grandfather's company. Outings from the runic temple were a rarity for its priestesses. Even a short, unspoken divergence from her caretakers would be unwise.

Dragoln laid a mollifying hand upon her head, giving peace to her discomfort. His eyes bade her to keep her peace also. With a single whip of his hand, Eldrahg's seer compelled Drurhelm to assume his place. They passed one another in mild disconcertion, whereupon Dragoln reengaged Lothair in conversation. She recognized the astounding effect of Dragoln's sedative wit and smiled at how easily it softened Lothair's rigid mien.

"Too long in the company of young men has tarnished your bliss, my acolyte priestess," Drurhelm drawled soft and concernedly. "I knew you should have rescinded your reunion with your brother once the conquered sun fell."

"I do not control the tempers of those around me," she shallowly admitted as an unforced countenance of indifference beset her face.

"You induce fervor and nudge passions, even without knowing you have engaged or been engaged. This is the curse all young woman bear. It is no fault of yours. It derives itself from the runic goddess Freyja, so we must respect it in the end."

"Of course it would be derived from the runic goddess of beauty, fertility, and life, but was Freyja not gifted those traits by our greater Goddess

Monomua, and some say Ithilia too? It's said she was born to save a man—the runic god of war, was it not?"

"It is not the only reason behind the brilliant birth of Freyja, Hearth of Life, although it is perhaps her highest calling," Drurhelm mumbled, confused.

"Born beyond Helti's catharsis from war's grip on the fifth day in our week as a gift from the Goddess of the Moon and a crucible through which the runic god of war would one day be freed. Freyja is an epitome of the lives we women can nourish within ourselves. It is a gift more than a curse, and hardly reason for chastisement. Would you not agree, Seer Drurhelm?"

Drurhelm spurned, "Those truths belong to the Bjardja. There is no place for passion toward men for a priestess of the Runic Faith. We fulfill our roles by serving the runic gods and the Crescent Lady. Do not fear your place." Drurhelm whispered unnervingly low, "I find it far more aspiring than the depravities of Bjardja battle whores enthralled by Valvítr's shadow." Giggling repulsively, Drurhelm instructed, "Come. I've spoken to Dragoln. We shall draw a runic circle to Helti this night for his warriors returned home."

"Of course, it would be an honor," Tanya lied behind an artifice of calm, knowing no such conversation of the likes had taken place. "Return me to the temple, and I will gather those we will need to see the draft complete."

Taking the seer's wrinkled hand, Tanya joined him in walking from Stormguarde Keep. She sighed upon passing a level of celebratory noise sufficient enough to mask it. Where in all of Eldaria was Ryurik? Where was her brother on his own damn day, and why did their grandfather not even care that his grandson was nowhere to be seen? To see him alive and well, to speak with him again…it was all Tanya had wanted from this King-slag. She felt subtly betrayed.

You have always baffled me, Ryurik—no differently than the rest of our brothers—and I have always questioned yet still found reasons to accept your rash and unpredictable ways. But know it is Thyra's heart you have broken. Mother forsakes herself as Lothair's sour shadow each and every day, and so you injure the true keeper of this family who rose in her shattered place. Tanya was utterly dissatisfied with this day's reprieve.

Thyra slammed another cup of ale as she insulted Mielni Svenson. The Stormborne's camp tasted much sweeter than Stormguarde's sour, so she rejoined her prior party, befriended new faces, and irreverently claimed them as hers. They were hesitant to share her company at first, her reputation obviously proceeding her, but Thyra broke bread by speaking to the hearts and minds of all soldiers. Insult and offense, and their insolence flew unhindered athwart every name imaginable. Knowing the camp disliked Lord Mielni exulted her. Speak ill of his boyish name she had, and it effortlessly became the topic they reviled and reveled in the same.

Thyra gleefully insulted, "The brazen fool looks like an unsheared wolfhound. His matted hair knotted by his smug, complacent master."

"He sniff's his father's ass like one too, sniveling every time the good jarl spanks him," said Ulbrack, who wheezed through broken speech and could barely be heard above the group's flippant laughter.

Audun threw his voice into the mix, exclaiming, "He's unrelenting once he's gotten a whiff. How many times did Dulmir smack that child to only find him caked to his butt like an unwiped turd?"

Ulbrack boomed in laughter before massaging his cheeks. After some effort, he replied, "The lad will say damn near anything to impress his father."

"Then why does he shame his grandfather again and again?" Thyra asked, the sincerity of the question oozing off her buzzed breath.

Knuth announced, "It is because he is young. Been fighting the Alterians and Helmyans and taking their woman for himself for too long. I don't blame little Mielni for wanting to partake in something more Stormborne."

Thyra feigned no appreciation for the manner in which he'd spoken of her sister. Frowning, so her grievances were well known, she punched his arm. It was a pointless gesture that would surely make her righteous grandfather proud, but the steam had already swelled and she needed to let it out.

"I never meant to disrespect your sister," Knuth growled. "You two are just an eclectic pair of women the lord has no place pursuing."

"Aye," she admitted. "I'll accept it. I suggest you spend less time thinking on the little lord, or you will end the day as bereft of a brain as him!" They particularly enjoyed that last jest, so Thyra satisfactorily lounged to enjoy another swig of dwarven ale.

"Lucky I was not there," Ulbrack proclaimed, face widening like the eye of a summer storm on the verge of bursting forth.

"Why?" she growled in curiosity.

"Because I would have taught the boy a lesson, bent him over the table and done to him everything he thought to do to her. No quicker way to burn away lustful fire from little men."

Her laugh suddenly burst. Squinting, she moved to cover her face. She could hardly look at the man. She was not used to so much laughter, and its unfamiliarity startled her. Few appeared to take notice, however. They were preoccupied expunging the foul image from their own heads while cackling as well. Too bad for the rest then. She enjoyed Ulbrack's humor and repartee and would partake in more before the night's end.

"You're mistaken to think you could manage him, Ulbrack. He would buck you off like a horse and leave you broken like its saddle," arose a voice from outside of their ring. Harald Gormrik hovered afront two of his sworn swords. A bemused grin stretched to the corners of his mouth. His hair dangled in dense clumps. He tilted his head so the runic tattoos on the shaven half glimmered above the fire.

Ulbrack rebuffed the jarl with his lack of interest.

The jarl received his disinterest as provocation. "You should stick to men who come in sizes more to your liking. Or a woman, like most of us prefer," he ordained with an incendiary humor.

"Do not confuse your desires with mine on account of a fireside joke," Ulbrack spoke.

"How can I confuse what I have heard," Harald responded smooth and droll.

Ulbrack spit into the fire, then tossed in his mead to watch the flames roar.

Thyra eyed him, wondering how he meant to answer after that clear fit of pique. He caught her glance and cocked an assuaged brow at the attention she inquisitively shed his way. Curiosity engrossed her, and she presumed that was exactly what Ulbrack wished.

Turning his stump to face the Jarl of Breidjal by the Helmyan Sea, Ulbrack allayed, "Test me over the fire, and we will see whose strength is to be most feared."

"Where's the joy in embarrassing you by myself," Harald confessed without refusing his offer. Shorn of looking away, the jarl commanded, "Find cousin Hela and my uncle Haneul and summon them here."

"So you accept then?" Thyra questioned, her voice fluttering near the end.

"I'll not deny any man's challenge. Will you be joining my side then, Commander?"

Pleased with the reception, Thyra said, "I would rather stand athwart the embers to watch you slip," wondering how those words had even escaped her lips.

Motioning to Knuth, Audun, and three other men, Thyra designated them as her team in this tug of war. The scales were slowly shifting, and she liked the way they tipped. She beamed in answer to Ulbrack's sudden chuckle, believing the contest favored them.

"Good," Harald retorted. "Then it will be a fair challenge after all." He dismissed his other sword to fetch rope and retrieve allies from Breidjal. "Don't carry the group too much."

Thyra quipped, "I would offer you your own advice, but I fear it would go unheeded."

"There are many things you can offer me, Thyra, and I would gladly accept them all."

Her mead abruptly betrayed her, and she blushed. Her cheeks reddened like ripened apples. She scrunched her forehead and clenched her teeth to drive off the color, then exhumed her frustrations with her body's infidelity, transitioning back to an angry scowl.

"It is good you sent for your cousin. The wait will be worthwhile for Hela to watch you burn your feet," Ulbrack bantered smugly.

Ulbrack was much larger than Harald and obviously wished to show it. His curly, russet hair tumbled over his broad shoulders. Thyra struggled to see around them. He boasted a clean figure, one too large for longevity in life. Palpably unimpressed, Harald yawned in response. Even more surprising was when the jarl stepped against Ulbrack unconcerned.

Humming low, Harald asserted, "It is good you've drafted the Lysian. A real warrior now pulls beside you," he finished, tapping Ulbrack on the chest.

Knuth Svenson pulled Ulbrack back before the presumptively perfect moment. As Ulbrack relaxed his nerves, Harald's own tightened. Knuth never spoke of how he was ousted from the Breidjal Bakari, and they never spoke of how an unblooded warrior who sailed the Aidel River, Sea of Storm, and Helmyan Sea came to join the fleet at all. Yet, from Harald's emotive betrayal upon seeing her second, Thyra recognized that history stung them both.

Harald's sword returned with his lord uncle and cousin. Hela smirked upon rejoining Thyra, and Lord Haneul did not.

"What is so important that you choose to break your uncle's sleep?" scathed Lord Haneul Gormrikson.

"With the Lysian prince absent, his sister and her friends have put forth a challenge in his stead. You are required to witness, Uncle. Your rest can wait for the day."

"This one?" Haneul lashed while pointing at Thyra. "I'm to answer to this one, who just this evening has begun a fresh vendetta against lords and old men! Do not rile me from slumber for this nonsense again."

Dropping pleasantries, Harald irrefutably instructed, "You will humor us, Lord Uncle, but I do not expect you to take an active role."

"Bring me some damned mead if I'm to be made to stay awake through this Drur-damned nonsense," grumbled the lord to the warrior who had ruefully awakened him. Haneul turned to speak with his daughter, utilizing her as the primary inheritor of his reprimand. "Your cousin is insufferable. Had you been born a boy, I would've died long ago to see you as Breidjal's jarl."

"You honor me with your bitterness, Father, and there's still time to enact this dream if we sleep less and fight more."

Venting indignantly, Lord Haneul brought himself to sit by the coals. Sullen and slow, the warrior returned with his mead. He accepted and vigorously drank, scrunching his eyes through each gulp. The warrior took advantage to extricate his lord by darting into a far friendlier crowd. Thyra envied him, but she envied Haneul Gormrikson more, who had since discarded his spent mug to flutter into sleep's reprieve once more.

Thyra joined her line opposite of the embers from Harald, Hela, and their men. She had observed the game enough times to know what to expect. Challengers faced off over a run of hot coals, pulling against each other on a long rope. The first to yield was sent running through the embers to scorch their soles. It was good fun to watch, but should she lose, Thyra knew the fun would be hers to rue.

Harald's second warrior returned with a handful more men. The jarl picked them until his count matched theirs. Hela took second. Harald joined front and center. With grit as tempered as quenched steel, the Gormrik cousins dismissed the rest to the gathering crowd. Harald tossed the rope across the fire. Knuth received it, handing it down the line. Thyra took the front at Knuth's behest. Audun and two more of Ryurik's men took up positions behind her. Knuth circled around to take next, then Ulbrack drew up the line's conclusion.

Ulbrack—a man from Ulfruk's personal regiment—was far gone from the Great Gates. Regardless of the distance set between the sword and his jarl, she understood why he had been chosen to man the back. The muscles ascending his arms rippled when he clenched the rope. He was brutishly strong, mildly handsome, and she was allured by his honest tongue. He took notice of her gaze again and lasciviously smiled. Thyra responded in kind, shying away so he would not see it. Better those thoughts remain her secret than escape into the open where they could be used against her when the conquered sun rose.

"Now we show you what it means to have Gormrik strength," Harald shouted once the lines were complete.

"And on whose count do we begin?" Ulbrack shouted back.

"On my father's count," Hela shouted, averting her gaze to discover the lord had fallen fast asleep.

"As my uncle calls it," Harald confirmed.

"The lord's lulled himself to sleep. How in Drur's Abyss is he meant to count?!" Ulbrack angrily spouted.

"Then we begin on account of his yell!" Harald yelled.

Resigning the rope, Harald jogged to a nearby tent. He borrowed a bucket of water from within and returned with desultory haste. With a grin plastered from cheek to cheek, he splashed the water directly into his uncle's face. Haneul choked and coughed, and upon clearing his lungs roared in anger. Harald reclaimed his position, seized advantage of the ensuing confusion, and heaved in unison with Hela and his men.

Thyra was still laughing as the rope tore forward. She planted her legs like anchors and pulled back hard. They regained sparse ground but failed to pull any farther, and the two parties found themselves locked in the dirt. Arms bent, she dug in her feet and strained to pull away, but found no success. She altered her tactics, locking her elbows and pushing with her legs instead. Others followed suit, and Harald gained no more ground. The everlasting pull improved, and she breathed with ease again.

"Ease," Ulbrack, then quietly commanded.

Thyra did not grasp why the man would cede the ground they'd gained, but she chose to trust in his decision anyway. Her feet neared the edge of the coals, and flickering embers singed her toes. She curled them in and dug in her heels more.

Ulbrack roared they heave together, and, concordantly, they answered. The unexpected tug brought the rope heavily into their favor.

Reticent to lose the bout, Harald grunted through every single breath like a bird clicking its beak to a beat. Inch by subtle inch, breath by labored breath, they regained a nigh uncontested advantage as the jarl's line pulled as one.

Thyra's arms grew tired. She glanced back to realize the rest were faltering as well. She stumbled forward, her feet racing over the burning embers. Having drank so much she briefly forgot she was the descendant daughter of the vengeful sky and the conquered sun, it surprised her when the coals were not particularly hot. Mind numbed from mead and fatigue, she tripped over her own foot. With a soft grunt, she stumbled through the next few steps until she escaped the run of coals. Then she relented in the spectacled effort and prepared to fall face first into the dirt. A hand reached underneath her shoulder, pulling her to her feet. She rose into Jarl Harald's chest in a single, smooth arc as if that had been his only intent. He beamed like a kid.

"Ask," Harald implored while dusting off her clothes, "and I will leave your name out of this story."

Thyra regained her footing and spryly leaped away. "And enflame your ego more? Where be the sense in that?"

Harald rescinded his offer with a bemused grin that seemingly en-wreathed his whole face. His teeth shone with the moonlight, far whiter than most. It was nigh mystifying how the runes shimmered upon his head as his teeth shimmered within his mouth. It was nigh mystifying how Thyra momentarily lost her focus within their radiance.

The name, chant, and call of the Draconic Father were embossed in black cerulean upon his shaven temple. They wrapped around his earlobe where they clawed at his scalp. Helti's runes pierced through Eldrahg's claws, drawn in thick globules of ritualistically dried blood. There was surly beauty tattooed into this man's skin, and Thyra only saw its scant beginnings. She assumed seeing anything else would indicate she had fallen into his bed, and she had no need for that.

"Then I have been accepted?" Harald prodded while stepping into her.

"I have considered your offer," Thyra replied while sweeping him aside. "I accept neither it nor you."

"It is good to know my offer was at least heard, but probably not understood."

"I have heard Hela. I assure you that your cousin's words came as if they were spewed as your own," she replied with deadly tranquility.

Harald considered his cousin, observing her tend to his uncle's waning temper from afar. "Doubtful," he casually confessed.

"You don't believe me?"

"Do not expect me to believe you think my cousin is without a mind of her own."

"That is good. Then I can trust you will respect that I too bear a will of my own."

"So I have been accepted," he returned with a reinvigorated emphasis.

Unyieldingly, Thyra corrected, "Not yet. I will have my assurances. I will have yours."

"Your price?"

"Is that I am to have none. No gifts. No silver. No pursuits of passion. This is to be a martial contract and nothing more."

"What is there left to bind me to it then?" Harald sordidly replied.

"Your honor. Your oath. Your word. You will swear it by your gods or my two. I do not care so long as it is sworn."

"Did you not like my gift then?"

Taken aback, Thyra professed, "I found it crude and garish in the same stride."

"Then I will offer it to you again in a much simpler fashion." He retrieved the ruby ring from his pocket, presenting it with pride. In a leisured tempo, he explained, "I have studied this ring and thought upon its seal during a long march. I think no other bearer is worthy, so I wish to ensure it lands upon a finger where it belongs."

"No gifts. No more praise to fall off that sly tongue," Thyra rebuffed while failing to hide her blush.

Cocking an eyebrow and stepping in unopposed, Harald commented, "Your tongue tells me to come no farther, but your face betrays your heart. I'll admit it is a simple token, but you must admit you like its glow."

"I reckon the lord from whom it was stolen would value it immeasurably more. Such a 'token' would fetch a hefty sum of silver otherwise."

Harald snickered in excitement, "I will never return it, even for a price. I have balanced Eldaria by claiming this mainlander lord's ring."

"Pray tell how you have better balanced Eldaria by thieving the ring of a lord who you did not slay?!" she laughed.

Decisively quick, Harald ruled, "He was unfit to wear a ring boasting an eagle, much less the dragon carved beside it."

"How so?" Thyra prodded.

"Did his ancestors slay either? Why else should the lord pay homage to their strife?"

"There are both dragons and eagles on the mainland," Thyra chuckled while wiping a tear of laughter from the corner of her eye. "Dragons reside in the mountainous realms of dwarves, if you did not know."

"Eh," Harald grunted. "No mainlanders have slain a dragon in centuries, whether human, dwarven, gnomel, fae, or centauri."

"Have you, Harald? Have you slain a dragon to warrant wearing that lord's absent ring?"

"My ancestors warred with Elder Wyrms. So have yours. This gives me right enough to offer it to a better owner like you."

"So you think I've killed a dragon, Jarl? I have faced one, yes, and not of my own accord. I nearly died while doing so." Thyra faked laughter to conceal the morose the encounter fused to her soul while the jarl considered if she spoke the truth. "The Draconic Father stole from me the second greatest treasure I have ever owned. Look where I stand because of it."

Harald tilted in as he beguiled her in a whisper, "Next to a striking man who wishes to share your greatest treasure as his own."

Thyra did not pull away. Strangely, she enjoyed his pursuit. There was some pleasure in having this jarl's acute attention, though his arrogance admittedly repelled her. Stricken with the recognition of who Harald thought she was, Thyra ultimately rebuffed his advance. She gently pushed him off while asserting his assumptions were wrong. "You mistake thinking I am my own greatest treasure. Your offer would be tempting, I admit, if I were partial to doling out my sister like she was some common whore from a nearby village."

Amused, Harald persisted, "Your sister is too virtuous for me. Besides, what else is a life's promise to another than the sweetest union of their blood?"

"A temporary measure for attaining greater power," Thyra answered dryly as her grin swung, then sunk. "Do not think your charm eludes me, Jarl. It is cute, but I want no more."

Harald regarded the rend between them with wide, studious eyes. "This ring was made for you," he contemplated while tenderly fondling the ruby. "Like dragons hunger for treasures that are not their own, your passion drives you to stand high within Eldrahg's mortal court. I expect nothing in return but the promise you'll speak with me again when I need you to," he concluded before flicking the ring into her hand.

She did not entirely desire to, but Thyra instinctively caught his gift. "Do not fail me," she professed. "Heed me should I request it as well, and that is a promise I will keep."

The jeweled ring clammed in her hand. Thyra swore she could feel its pulse, or perhaps that of the man.

Harald departed, smiling dissolutely.

For the first time since their conversation had begun, Thyra realized she was flustered. Red flourished through her cheeks unrepentant. She cursed the mead for betraying her mind. Harald was soon gone, and, absurdly, she rued his departure.

Thyra had learned much of the budding strife in Ryurik's court in the short time they spoke. If Harald were any less flamboyant or if she were any less averse to his cunning, she might have pushed for something more. She thanked Andurial she had not. Their's were appetites insatiable. Her enduring ambitions would rend anything borne of it. She had pushed too far in her drunken state already, and regrettably, lamented that some of their conversation's pleasure might actually have been real.

CHAPTER SEVEN
TJORDEN'S REAPINGS

E RE THE DAWN'S RISING, THERE was a stir within the air that smelled and tasted of silver. Not the metallic savor when pressed against one's lips but of man's rapacious sweat. Driven livid by its scent, their bodies trailed in writhing shambles, but to what ends did they strive? Coin slipped between their fingers when they tired of their hoards, and they set off to pursue another's in vehemence. Peace and sleep only just finished drinking their fill of the Stormborne men and a scarce few women whom Thyra sensed were rising with that insatiable hunger born anew.

Her nose twitching when it caught the scent, Thyra softly lulled herself awake. Darkness abounded. Ulbrack slept flat on his back, one arm atop his belly and another curled behind her neck. She lifted herself to sit beside him and studied his naked body. Curled hair twirled down his chest and feathered across his torso like a gnarled forest of black pine. Stocky but untoned, Ulbrack was physically unappealing to her eye, but then again, few Stormborne were appealing.

Thyra cracked her neck, and the noise rustled Ulbrack from his slumber. He swallowed hard at something the night left him, then hemmed his throat clear of the rest. Catching sight of her stretching in the darkness, he endeavored to rise. She did not allow it. She grabbed a knife beside the cot, threw one leg over his chest to ride him, and squeezed tightly while pressing the knife against his neck. His eyes opened wide.

"Good morning," Thyra whispered. "I hope you found good sleep too."

Smiling disconcertedly, Ulbrack replied, "I could use reason to rest a little while longer." He lifted himself against the knife's slack.

She forced him down with the cool blade. She would not see him rile the camp. She could not permit him to think in that particular manner. What had happened between them must die with the night.

"That cannot happen," Thyra responded while softly shaking her head. "And it *will not* happen again."

"How are we to know—"

Thyra flipped her hair behind her neck, covered his mouth with her off-hand, and in a cold tongue demanded, "You will repeat what I say, and our oath will be forever sealed."

"Not forever," Ulbrack jested in candor.

"Forever," she repeated while pressing the knife tighter against his neck. She awaited the precise moment she was certain he understood her. "I'll dream of this night till Halvalkyra..."

Having gone silent, she compelled him with an urging nudge, to which Ulbrack sorely responded, "I'll dream of this night until Halvalkyra."

She continued, "But be silent until the Halls receive me, lest the Valkyrie banish me to Drur's Abyss."

"But keep quiet until the Halls receive me, or they will banish me to Drur's Abyss," the burly lover echoed.

Thyra dug a fingernail into the palm of Ulbrack's hand, then wiped the blood against his lips. She flicked her own thumb to draw another diminutive pool of blood. Discarding the knife, she smeared the red across her lips and pressed them against his, consigning their oath in the union of their blooded kiss.

Perplexed, Ulbrack fumbled as she withdrew. Her execution of an antique runic tradition befuddled the man, who balked before she soothed his nerves with a slight, tender caress. He lightened but did not look at her the same.

Good. Thyra was pleased.

Thyra dismounted Ulbrack's chest, moving to recover her discarded clothes. She spared his leering eyes the sight of her breasts and clad herself quickly, adorning each cloth garment, studded leather trimming, and the plates that overhung them all. Her head seized at the task's completion. Too much mead and an early rise from bed banished pleasantness from her morning. She massaged away the discomfort in quick, willful circles.

There were few others whom Thyra had taken to bed before Ulbrack. Such indulgences did not suit the First Princess of Lysian. Her responsibilities routinely overwhelmed her. She had little time to fulfill her lust, even if it was the stress of her responsibilities that gave her reason to engage in the sin. She did not find sex particularly sinful, but most Lysians did. One advantage of living in the Stormlands, she was no longer beset by the empire's sacrosanct scrutiny.

Three lovers counting, and Thyra had taken the other two long before this. The second had been wild, unreasonable, and free-willed. Had it not been for Darius conscripting the man into his legions, his tongue would have betrayed her. Darius had never ceased in reminding her how less forgiving Lysians were to women than men. Thyra had always dismissed his concerns with a laugh, rolling over the prospect of the Ardent Avant attempting to force her to repent.

"You're content with this and nothing else? You would rather decamp into the night than walk tall when the sun rises?"

Pondering Ulbrack's injure, Thyra grinned and bit her lower lip. "I'm always contented, though I did enjoy you while it lasted. Forever, and never again," she firmly concluded, wiping away the remnants of blood from her finger unto her puffed lips and leaving him one final kiss.

Thyra departed, peeking through the tent's flaps to ensure there were no patrols before she crept into the night. She did not believe in runic oaths and curses. She had never witnessed one hold true. As long as Ulbrack believed in them though, the ruse was worth the work. Two could hold a secret if one were bound to death should they croak, and Thyra had sold the mock assurance that Drur himself now held their oath.

<hr />

Thyra directed her Skjold into formation across the runic fields adjacent to Torlv's runic temple. Four lines stretched at center, and she tripled those numbers at the flanks. The reserves waited in the rear, and she threw the remainder into an opposing phalanx. Tjorden's plunders made this training day possible, and their morning was well underway.

Five hundred strong, only twenty of the Skjold were recruits. Five hundred outweighed the one hundred Stormguarde typically withheld. Five hundred constituted a small raider's army and, when properly trained, could control a fortified city. Five hundred could shadow a larger force, which was exactly how Thyra meant to use them.

Five hundred gifted Thyra the capacity to enlarge the scope of their training. The Skjold numbered two thousand in all, but never had they gathered in the same place at once. If five hundred were made auspiciously aware of their strengths through rigorous training, five hundred could direct and inspire two thousand. Ever the visionary, Thyra ascertained these next few days would transform her Skjold even more.

The purpose of the day's training was twofold. Five hundred Skjold would first learn to surmount feint warfare—the antique art of martial deception. Such maneuvers required keen execution alongside latent courage since they directly contradicted traditional Stormborne military tactics. The Stormborne valued their harrowing raids, shield walls, and a furious charge above all else, whereas most of Thyra's strategies were complex and imperial by nature.

If a force commenced a feigned retreat and failed to execute it to completion, they would expose themselves and cede their position of strength to no lasting avail. The Stormborne neither cared for nor appreciated tactics that were not headstrong. Her task was to convince the Skjold there was sometimes honor in ebbing ground.

Second, Thyra sought to deceive the jarls by manipulating their perceptions of her Skjold. Rigid detainment to the defense of the Great Gates and Tjorden's Reach obliviated them to the advancements the Skjold had undergone. No longer the diminutive shield guard to the Storm King alone, the Skjold now bore an affinity to a standing army.

'Dishonored' warriors, karlar forsaken to debt, and the occasional thrall augmented her Skjold. Their bodies were sharpened to succeed its challenges. Their minds were sharpened to enact its will. Their souls were bound to their brethren in martial resolve. She did not care what their beginnings were so long as they fought and bled for the Skjold. Thyra would also prefer if the jarls continually underestimated her and her Skjold.

"Commander," Knuth called as he jogged in from a distance.

"Aye?" she returned.

"Every available Skjold has been called to count. We begin on your command."

Thyra bestrode the birches separating the city from the runic fields.

Knuth followed in close proximity of her ear.

She halted in the bower of a towering elm, holding far enough back so onlookers could not eavesdrop on their conversation. "Excellent," she commented. "Let them idle a little longer."

Cackles echoed loudly. Thyra glanced to her peripheries. A pair of untamed ravens clattered their beaks as if mocking her mien, caught in deep laughter or comedically weeping. She hardly appreciated their derisive adulation. She sneered, not fully comprehending why the ravens so vehemently peeved her. Eldrahg's black-winged messengers. Was there a truth to that echoed myth? Did the Delas send these birds to mock her with reminders of his theft, or had the ravens merely distinguished her an easily riled target?

"How many have come to witness?" Thyra asked of Knuth. Having lost him to the cackling circus, she garnered his attention with a light shove.

"No more than thirty, no less than twenty-five."

"Good. Does anyone of import stand among them?"

"Mielni seems to have dug himself up from Drur's Abyss to brood smugly."

Taking her turn to grunt in speculation, Thyra replied, "I would have expected his brother to grace us before him."

"His brother stands beside his wife and son in Torlv's runic temple. Bjarni might well be watching with your sister from above."

"I doubt that," Thyra chuckled. "Having Seer Dragoln exalt his second blooded son, or so I have heard."

Knuth mused aloud, "Too long after the boy blooded his sword to be worth a damn."

"The only one who would watch from above is Drurhelm. He loathes that Dragoln allows us usage of these fields in exchange for safeguarding temple grounds."

"He is too old, fat, timid, and abnormal to ever challenge us. We should till Drur's runes in the fields before we abscond but leave them with a few errors to drive the seer mad!"

Thyra chuckled. "Don't go making more work for my sister and the priestesses simply to rile the seer of toads."

"Commander!" Knuth abruptly hissed.

"Aye?" she returned.

"It appears your new friends have arrived."

"Ryurik and some of his men?" Thyra's heart thumped against her chest. Indolently twisting her head, she realized they were neither Ryurik nor his men.

"Harald, Hela, and a small contingent of their men. Some Bjardja from Breidjal stand among them as well."

"Better than the Agulbargs, I suppose. Let's see if our new friends are actually clever or if their wits are as repressed as Lord Mielni's." Shifting her tone into that of his commander, she firmly instructed, "Shield wall. Have the phalanx advance at full speed."

"Shield wall!" Knuth roared over the withered field.

Her order echoed thrice over as it carried through each detachment. The defenders flayed their flanks, and their center withdrew to form a mild trough. The first line drove their likstadt shields into the ground. The second shuffled forward and locked together their shields at chest height. The third drew in from behind and interlocked their round, wooden likstadt's high. The final row served as the reinforcing buffer that would fill the gaps abandoned by those stricken down and strike those who engaged their shield wall.

"Phalanx charge!" Knuth mightily roared.

The Skjold positioned across the battlefield brandished their weapons and roared. They charged, swarming the defenders' shield wall in a disheveled, disorganized mass. Not the charge she was particularly hoping for, but it would suffice. The two collided, and the defenders buckled on impact. The aggressors fought like unrefined warriors, and the defenders would give them the better answer that would hold against the runic gods if executed right.

The shield wall braced. Shields clasped together in white-knuckled grips. Thyra's Skjold engaged at the field's center—a faux horde of Garathandi belligerents against a modified shield wall that was the Stormborne's martial heritage. Heavily reinforced flanks held strong, and the center began to bulge. The attackers recognized the point of weakness, so they concentrated their efforts there.

Thyra swiped her hand, her second read the signal, and in a slow rise, Knuth resounded, "Ease together!"

The defenders eased, retreating in half steps over dead, sodden grass. A warrior at the center slipped and tripped over his back foot. He scrambled to retrieve his shield and reclaim his position in the shield wall but was too late for a seamless recoup. His position was quickly filled by a woman from the fourth line who bashed back the man. The defenders ceded ground until their trough was definitively pronounced. The right flank slowed as their rear backed into a knoll and higher ground. The left flank pulled ahead of the center as the maneuver demanded. Steadily, the shield wall morphed into the shape of an iron horseshoe in need of a few more strikes from the smith's hammer.

"Break lines!" Knuth bellowed strong.

Thyra vamoosed to join the more favorable group of spectators. Knuth joined the left flank, forcefully assuming command from the mind-boggled Barul whose head was reeling from the night before. They scuffled, as was their undeniable custom. Thyra mutely laughed. She had no idea why the two felt the need to compete so fiercely, only that she enjoyed the results.

The shield wall rounded into a semicircle until the left flank clipped the field's edge. The right flank aimed to match the left, but instead they pushed against the attackers to cede the knoll. Thyra spit, disdainful of the tactical error displayed by their leader Brynjar. This show of bravery in practice constituted nothing but foolishness in battle. Should his decision go unreprimanded, he and all his charge would inevitably lie dead upon Helti's veritable fields of battle.

Captain Oddall, whom Thyra recalled from the village of Húsavik in the Erunheim, led the center's forthright retreat. The shield wall buckled, but the captain exacted they hold against the onslaught in a firm, united front. Staggered resistance gave the defenders ample opportunity to break ranks, turn, then retreat. The attackers not harrowing the encircled flanks gave chase and pursued Oddall's contingent to the terminus of the runic fields.

Driving her heels into the ground before the Gormrik cousins in an acrimonious display of dominance, Thyra exalted, "Welcome, Harald and Hela." She glanced to Mielni, who blankly squinted over the drills. "I'm relieved the morning gave me some worthwhile company while I watch my Skjold train."

"Do not rile the Agulbarg boy too much, Commander. We don't want him running off to tell tales to his father," Hela stated wryly.

"Especially not of this horse's shit," Harald reviled with a confounded, derisive flare. "I am beginning to question Hela's judgment as I watch you train your guard to turn tale and flee when a real battle bares its fangs."

Hela openly snickered, "It was your judgment as well. Don't be so quick to deride the commander because you do not understand her ways."

"I only agreed because it suited my drunken tastes. Explain to me what I am witnessing, Hela, and it might remind me why I agreed."

"Did Seer Dragoln not make a show of piety last evening? I won't give you reasons I do not have. Thyra is no fool. Time will tell why the Skjold drill the way they do."

Unamused with his cousin's response, Harald shook his shoulders and bitterly inquired of Thyra, "What am I watching then, Commander?"

"Ask me again in a moment, my"—Thyra searched for the correct word with which to scathe Breidjal's jarl—"newfound friend."

Her tact worked wonderfully. The face Harald made was not much unlike that of a little boy who had pricked the webs of his fingers while splintering wood. Hela smiled, shying it away from her cousin. Harald chose not to incite them any further. Instead, he observed the conclusion of the drill, straining in unembellished judgment of her Skjold's every move-ment.

Thyra disregarded his malcontent, observing her Skjold for any signs of lax form or weak will that required eradication. Oddall called for the fleeing center to shift tactics at the field's edge. They leveled into two columns of five divided by a horse's breast. With shields raised and weapons in hand, the defenders advanced while the emptiness between them carried the ideal of a fully manned counterattack. The opposing sides clashed until Knuth called for the drill to be drawn to its conclusion. The turtled flanks flayed to surround and collapse upon the attackers. They sparred until the last of the aggressors were left without heart but to contemporarily resist the tides of a triumphant defense.

Thyra forgave Harald no chance to pose further questions, making it pallidly clear where authority between them stood. "You just witnessed the most common of feigned retreats, an ancient pyrrhic tactic first developed by Bairam in the Deserts of Rhavi. Stay longer, and you may watch us drill through another faux dozen, if you wish."

Harald's sleuth crumpled. "Training? You force your warriors to repeat retreats rather than holding a stronger line of defense?"

Thyra exhaled displeasure. "The first line of defense is almost never the most favorable."

"Then fight to make it favorable! Tighten your flanks and reinforce your center. Instead, you leave your men surrounded when the enemy breaks your shield wall."

Standing steadfast against his admonition, Thyra gave her own irreverent response. "In some circumstances, you might be right, but only if this was the full strength of my Skjold. Look to what isn't here but remains at my disposal. Perhaps then your leer might lighten enough to speak of tactics with me."

"Well then." Peering across the far reaches of the runic field, Harald gave a scathing show of his incredulity. "Where be the unseen Skjold come to reinforce your broken center?"

"Guarding the Erunheim until they are called upon to engage a real enemy. I train, I teach, and I tire every member of my Skjold until they know their rightful place in every sky-forsaken situation. See them not now. Fear them all the more later. You show me how little you know, Harald Gormrik."

Harald's sanctimonious, vulnerable eyes narrowed in a fit of ire, and the Jarl of Breidjal strained his neck as he cocked his head to belittle her. Thyra returned the same undiminished rebuke, and the two sapped all life from the surrounding air. Amused with them both, Hela gripped Harald's shoulder to alleviate a touch of the tension. Thyra did not yield, and although Harald did lighten, she knew it was by no means an admission of defeat. This man she called her newfound friend was irrevocably proud, but Thyra was, perhaps, more obstinate than him.

Harald grinned in a peculiar motion. "You're a strong-willed woman, Thyra Ehlrich. You've more blazoned blood in your body than your brother ever will."

Hela leaped onto Thyra's relaxation. "Who do you view as the real enemy? Have mine blood and I not already slain them by their thousands outside of Jarl Ulfruk's Great Gates?"

Thyra solemnly exacted, "That is entirely left for us to decide. I think we can agree it is yet ambiguous upon which side of the Great Gates they actually lie."

A horn blasted from the center of Stormguarde, rippling with a repetitive, bombastic fervor. The cries of intrigue spoke to the arrival of one smug in their greatness. Finished restructuring the Skjold's lines, Knuth took note of the booming horn and left his post to join Thyra.

"Commander," Knuth stated, "That horn sounds the arrival of another jarl."

Thyra replied, "Probably the Bane of Trolls since Denurl Kenning thinks his Storm King is not worth the visit. Repeat that last maneuver before you proceed, cut to an end an hour before nightfall, and report back to me on the outcome of the day's training."

"Aye," Knuth affirmed as he left to reengage the milling Skjold.

"Wait, wait!" Thyra yelled out in quick succession before he strode too far. "Tell Brynjar that if he cedes the high ground again, he is to personally inform me, and that he need not wait for an enemy to break his legs."

"Aye," Knuth reaffirmed with a nigh imperceptible smirk.

Knuth crossed the runic fields, wading through shallow snow, and halted where Brynjar reformed the right flank. The two spoke at length. Brynjar cringed before glancing to her. His cynical visage reaffirmed her disappointment. Better he learn from his mistake here than when battle demanded an answer and he had naught but the wrong one to give.

Mielni interrupted Thyra's concentration like a young buck displaying its antlers. "Do you hear those horns, Thyra? That is the call of a true warden come to claim his share of our war's benumbed glory."

Thyra snubbed, "You should run along and learn something from this valiant soul you aspire to be."

"You should join me." Lord Mielni gritted his teeth. "To see the toll a real commander incurs while defending the Stormlands."

"My lord." Harald laid a savage hand around Mielni's neck and shoulder, then rigidly squeezed. "Leave the commander to her drills, so her Skjold might move beyond these retreats. We will welcome my friend Baelgrant together, then we will see how tough you are when you come to face the Bane of Trolls."

Shaking himself free of Harald's pinch, Mielni snorted, gathered his men, spat disgusted, and stormed off toward the center of town.

Eyeing Thyra concertedly, Harald gathered all of his sworn swords except for two. Aquiline sigils had been pinned to their leather lamellar tunics in a vibrant display that they were sworn of sword to Jarl Harald of Breidjal by the Helmyan Sea.

Azure fury gathered in a whirlpool as the jarl stepped into Thyra's space.

"I'll see you at Ryurik's council. Make sure your brother wakes for it in time, else our Storm King might retract his good graces." Harald's rumbling voice fell to a fleeting mutter by the time he finished.

The jarl wisped back into the circle of his Bjardja and sworn swords before they powerfully strode away. He left two to Hela, who stepped into the far edge of Thyra's shadow. The warriors withheld an iron grit in their broken teeth and scars, but the shield-maiden's own grit outshone them both. It bade they maintain a healthful distance from her and Thyra both.

Thyra poised against Knuth's resounding roars, and to Hela she stated, "I am beginning to think you lied to me, Hela."

"I have never lied to a friend before. What makes you question my word's worth?"

Thyra locked eyes with the shield-maiden. "You did not actually speak for your cousin last night, did you?"

Ostensibly humored, Hela confessed, "No, I did not. He was quite drunk, in an entirely different state of mind. Just as your flush betrays you now, you know his goals were different than mine. I speak for the both of us now, however. That should count for plenty."

"If I am to take your hand in this alliance, should I simply entrust all of my ambitions to your word?"

Straightening to slowly unfurl a sardonic grin, Hela answered, "We're both women who have found ourselves ruling over some odd number of men. Who is to deny us taking advantage of their stifled minds for ourselves when the opportunities present themselves?"

Thyra betrayed a genuine smile to counter Hela's smirk. The two turned apart, both finding answers aplenty in that which was left unsaid and, thus, unheard.

Happening upon her Skjold's second iteration of Bairam's feigned retreat, Thyra observed their improvements. Old Oddall prepared to disengage the shield wall's center, and Brynjar rescinded far up the knoll. Overall, the repeat maneuver developed superbly in comparison to a not too terrible first.

"Harald was not just teasing you when he left to join Baelgrant," interjected Hela. "Follow me and Ingvar while our men still have your brother and the farmhouse secluded."

Recalling Harald's quip with a sudden, austere fury, Thyra recalled the pervading issue perturbing her.

Again, Hela beckoned her to follow.

Thyra eagerly obliged.

Hela Gormrikdottir enjoyed burying truth beneath biting mire. The shield-maiden knew the whereabouts of Thyra's little brother, who she had not seen since the Kingslag's rise.

A half hour after leaving her Skjold in the capable hands of Knuth to follow Lady Hela and her accompanying men, Thyra was nearing her patience's end. Elden ash and yews still stripped of their leaves by winter's haunting crossed the rugged terrain of the farmers' reach. Annoyed, Thyra rumbled in the silence proffered by Hela and her men upon their hike. She knew only that they were leading her toward Ryurik, and in realizing she did not even know that for sure, her dissatisfaction dissolved into an ire more befitting of her father's vision of her and her family's blood. She drew breath to speak, but failed to formulate the demand before another spoke first.

"You must forgive my cousin," Hela commented idly. "His skull is thick, his head small, and there is little room to push in anything new. I am thankful there's little he does not already know, so I did not need to take my father's gripes more seriously."

Ignoring her appeal to conversation, Thyra demanded, "How much farther until we reach Ryurik?"

Hela sighed. "One farmstead remains before we reach the one where he was found."

"How did you even come to find him? Your camps are set beside the Sea of Storm, and we have trekked through nothing but farmsteads braced against the Valdhaz."

"My camps are set against the slopes. I've always preferred the warmth of Hælla Dwolv to the raging uncertainty of Sjógurn." Hela tapered her breath through her unabashed slight of the Ravager, the runic god whose salted dominion was the lifeblood of Breidjal.

Thyra peered beyond the florid squelch, where she construed an air of indifference. Halting, she decided to hold her ground until her qualms were quashed like a moist sponge. Some threat must have befallen Ryurik for Hela to dismiss her, and that recognition only worried her further.

"If you viewed this as anything less than vital, you would fetch my brother and bring him to me. What has happened to Ryurik? Why am I being brought to the outskirts of the city?"

Motioning for one of her warriors to step into the light of the conversation, Hela exhaled, "Ingvar, tell the commander of how you found Ryurik while taking your morning piss."

"Woke up later than I like to. Mead had my head rolling like that dead lord's skull. I eventually wandered out, looking for a good tree to water. That is when I heard him screaming at a farmer like he usually does. The farmer had him tied against a fencepost and was whipping his back raw." Ingvar began to chuckle, and Thyra's nostrils exhumed flames. "Farmer had no idea who he even was, but I recognized Ryurik. I have seen the prince like that a dozen times since he first stumbled into Tjorden."

Thyra struggled to quell her alarm. "Did you at least take him down?!"

"No," the bastard Ingvar laughed. "The farmer's dogs wouldn't let us anywhere near. When last I was there, we had at least convinced him to quit beating your brother senseless."

"You son of a bitch!" Thyra snatched the man's shirt and barked, "Why in a sky-damned hell was Ryurik even there?"

Hela hushed Ingvar before he could mutter a word. "You'll learn that for yourself. I ordered my warriors to clear the farm and not harm the man or his hounds. We should hurry though. Who knows when his patience will break and he decides to whack your brother with more sticks."

Thyra suppressed her colic with the shield-maiden's joke. With a groan, she released Ingvar and strode on. The similarities between the two cousins grew more apparent with every passing moment. She began to understand why they were often referred to as twins rather than cousins at all.

Hela consigned a wry grin as she drew beside Thyra, and the two marched on in obdurate silence. Frozen dew dwindled off bladed grass, and the morning's mists lifted the Valheim. In the two's departure, peppered sunlight split through puffy clouds. The scene flexed against the Stormlands' typically dour skies. Thyra overstepped two creeks that had never flowed there before. Born aside a myriad of chilled, virgin flows, they rushed toward the Sea of Storm.

When spring reared its head over winter's shoulder, the Stormlands would be scoured. War with the Ardent Avant might have drawn to a close, but in its place an older conflict would rise. Strife would be reborn beside the people's grudges. Blood would be spilled since it was the land's heritage, and that blood would be entirely drawn by the denizens of the Stormlands.

It was for this exact reason that Thyra needed Ryurik. The Gormriks portrayed themselves as honest, but she did not yet understand their cause. Eljak strangled Ryurik with the promise of a lost daughter, hoping to turn his line royal. Hers and her brother's alliances would be shattered and re-forged in this violent crucible of storm. Her fledgling bond to the Gormriks and Ryurik's alliance with Eljak might need to be destroyed to ensure their lasting futures.

They had been friends long ago, Lothair and Eljak Draven, but her grandfather blamed Eljak for the death of his son Lætsven during the earliest years of the war with the Ardent Avant. In a disreputable response, Lothair stripped Eljak of some massive wealth during a time he could not dispute it. Eljak's sole aims now were vengeance, her brother undoubtedly being his pawn, and seating his descendants upon the Tempest Throne.

Thyra intended to form a stronger coalition around her brother until his succession was ensured. Once stripped of all their ill alliances, they would be prepared for when each of the jarls' immiscible motives conjoined in a brutal explosion. Every day Lothair's life waned was one nearer to an uncertain future. The only ostensive fact within his line's succession was that Lothair's last male heir was the Fourth Prince of Lysian, son to a once bitter adversary Lothair vehemently loathed and of a people all Stormborne loathed.

"I swear by the line of Runeheim I'll have my men eviscerate your balls and obliterate your home if you touch me with that branch again!" Ryurik's cries resonated beyond the trifling hill that rose before the nearing farm.

Thyra saw little more than the sward-roofed hovel beside the heads of Gormrik archers tethered to its front door. She switched to a jog, verging upon a full run, and the skip of her armor alerted those ahead. They made no effort to obstruct her as she climbed the hill's zenith. She witnessed as two women, mother and daughter, tussled with the warriors holding them inside their home.

Thyra forgave no patience for their zeal and barked while jogging by, "Get inside, and don't come back out!"

The blonde-haired, button-nosed beauty Thyra guessed was the older woman's daughter mouthed a sly curse. Thyra ignored it, but the mother certainly did not. The woman ripped her senseless girl inside and slammed the door shut without muttering a word. At least one sky-damned Stormborne soul was astute enough not to poke at her ferocious mood.

Hela and her warriors followed in Thyra's footsteps closely. The shield-maiden's other contingent had established a loose perimeter around the farm's hog den, barn, and rocky fields. Most meandered alongside the fence where stood the farmer with his dogs. The mutts flanked her brother, rapt with impatient zeal.

The farmer's blond hair and ruffled sideburns hung like untrimmed weeds. He was as thick and dumpy as feral hogs taken refuge in a grain silo and wielded a branch in his right hand, which was assuredly the same one he'd beat her brother with until he'd cried out his chagrin. It took an extensive lump of willpower for Thyra to not fling flames the farmer's way.

Thyra slackened her pace when she drew close. Disinterested, the farmer merely grunted. She slipped through the fencepost into a fenced ring adjacent to the barn and hog den, laid her hand against the hilt of her sword, then stopped. Bared teeth and barks were a clear sign she was not welcome any closer.

Furious, Thyra beseeched, "Do you know who I am? Do you know the man you've tied to that post and beaten?"

The farmer swiveled, his face expounding clear recognition. "Commander Thyra! Have you come to judge the swine who aimed to defile my daughter?"

Thyra disregarded the farmer to exert her focus on Ryurik instead. Face fraught with anger, his eyes pled for an escape. She returned her brother nothing but a hint of an embittered glare.

Ryurik scowled and shied away. Years apart could never strip them of the consequences of sharing parents. He shrank to her admonition no different than when he was scolded by Mother as a child. His trepidations also confirmed her formerly facetious suspicions. Ryurik trailed the shadows of three brothers, and she prayed he favored the right one.

"I have come to retrieve Prince Ryurik. Untie and return him to me, and I will pass judgment not to repay his beating in the same."

"I will not!" chided the farmer, bewildered she'd even deigned to relay the demand.

"Listen closely," Hela warned with snide and pitiless intent. "You have no friends here. You will do as you are bade or die by one of my warrior's blades."

Lifting a hand to snuff her, Thyra scolded, "Thank you for fetching me, shield-maiden, but the rest is mine to correct."

Hela scrunched her eyes, then undulated her brows in steady, inquisitive waves. "By all means…correct the boy's mistakes. I know I'm tired of trying, and Eljak will thank you too."

"We're overruled by law, even here in the Stormlands." Thyra motioned to Ryurik. "Take down your prince. If your claim to injury is veracious, then I'll spare your family the hardship of losing you."

The farmer jostled his haunches. His hounds recognized the altercation in his stance and stood tall to match his anger. Thyra gripped the pommel of her sword as she awaited the farmer's response. The man made no further motions and chose not to speak at all. The hounds seemingly understood their master, pacing to service his unspoken word. Displeased with Thyra, the larger mutt strode between them, and the second bared its teeth at Ryurik.

Ryurik began cursing the beast.

Thyra seized the opportunity the distraction provided to examine the true extent of her brother's beating. His lip had been split, his back wore several welts, and his right shoulder was heavily bruised. She strove to suppress the fury that marred her face but was unsuccessful. She held no desire to slay the dogs or the aggrieved farmer, but she would see no further pain come Ryurik's way unless it came by her hand.

"I will not be your judge." Thyra proposed, "You have my word no harm will come to you, your family, or your farm, and I will deliver you to the althing of Stormguarde, whereupon that communal, karlar jury will judge whether you have broken Stormborne law."

Mistrustful of her intentions, the farmer furiously refused. "I know the punishment for striking royal blood. You will have my head detached and laid on a spike while these Gormrik seal fuckers claim my wife and daughter!"

Grittily, Thyra avowed, "I am commander of the Skjold, and my word will bend that law if I so desire it to."

"And I am still your prince, you scraggly bastard. Untie me and fight me like a man to save everybody the trouble of killing you themselves."

"Careful, Ryurik. You are in a poor position to threaten the man. We won't let the dogs kill you, but I cannot guarantee they'll be downed before they rip away at your more...exposed bits." Hela gestured to her crotch, then to the scraps of fabric barely covering Ryurik's genitals.

Anxious uncertainty abounding, the farmer shook his finger at Hela while inquiring of Thyra, "Do you speak for this Bjardja and her warriors? I did not go out seeking your brother! He chose to squirm into my daughter's bed!"

Without fidelity for his well-being, Ryurik bantered, "I was invited, old man."

Without hesitation, Ingvar sarcastically muttered, "Farmer's right. Ryurik's a weasel. I have never seen a woman welcome his company before he flashed them coin myself."

"I demand assurance!" the farmer roared, unsettling his mutts.

Thyra hastily replied, "Since my brother so idiotically admits to his own offense, I offer you this instead. No trial. No judgment. I will see to it that he is reminded why he should never wander near your farmstead again."

"The same Drur-damned promise he shat after waking to find himself tied to my fence like a bundle of sloppy logs. You Runeheim's are all the same. How long will it take until my dogs prove you too are a liar?"

Thyra communed her final, heartfelt plea. "I am only half Runeheim, and we both know not a shred of it shows compared to my brother. My words are bound by Andurial, and because of that, they can never be construed as false."

Spitting before licking his gums, the farmer conjectured options. He spared an unsavory glance for Ryurik, who insanely returned his own. The farmer shifted, drawing in his dogs but bidding they maintain their guards. He struggled, his pride and anger clouding his judgment. Thyra understood how embedded the pangs of her brother's incursion must surely have been to stomach. Emotion was the bane of compromise, and she worried the farmer's emotions were already too far gone. The farmer looked to Thyra last, face softening ever so imperceptibly upon receiving a suppliance she rarely spared. She softened, reminding him how sorely he needed her aid. She abhorred the farmer's hands for striking her brother, but she abhorred Ryurik more for what he had done to incur the farmer's wrath. In some cruel fashion, Thyra conjectured Ryurik deserved all he righteously got.

Without warning, the farmer approached Ryurik. His dogs flexed like trees against the wind, the hairs on their necks standing on end. Pugnaciously, they followed the farmer. Her stomach wrenched, and Thyra gradually began to draw her sword, regretful toward what was to come.

The farmer kicked aside his dogs, and they obligatorily scurried off. "Back off, you Drur-damned mutts. Go bark at squirrels you'll never catch and leave the prince alone."

"Thank you," Thyra disbelievingly called.

Gruffly, the farmer beckoned her to his side, then continued trudging forward. She reached them both simultaneously, ascertaining the farmer was much shorter than she first realized, but confirming most of the other observations she'd made. His hair was more knotted up close. Like most Stormborne, the man was surprisingly clean, but his breath smelled of fouled goat's cheese, or perhaps a skyr that's culture had been infected by fungus that clung to the stock of wheat.

"Do you love your brother, Thyra of the Skjold?"

"Of course. Even when I rue him for pretending to be someone I hardly know."

"I understand the feeling." The farmer slacked his jaw like a disappointed mule. "I know my Astrid probably invited him into her bed. I did beat him knowing who he was, because I love my daughter. Even though she has nearly grown into a full woman, I still see her as my little girl."

Thyra found his attempt at bonding comically touching, but she outright refused to joke over an embittered father's admission to aggrieved love. "You were within your rights. You must one day choose her a husband to protect her health, prosperity, and your farm."

After releasing Ryurik, the farmer coughed, "Bagh! This is no fertile, desirable land we live on, girl. Hælla Dwolv's arse is either too rocky or sandy for much to grow. I have nothing to give her once my wife and I are gone, nothing to offer any decent man who would bind his hand to hers. Not off this shite land we were all born to."

She smirked, and the farmer aptly responded, "Most all of us, I suppose."

"There's little left for us Lysians in this world anymore," Thyra spoke true.

Having hastily dressed, Ryurik now chose to speak out of turn. "Shitty folk deserve shitty lives and lands. You sacked your family's one chance at seizing greatness when you pulled me from between your daughter's legs."

Thyra swung about to face him, and Ryurik stammered back, "It's great to reunite with you, sister."

Thyra swept aside her little brother's meager defense to drive her knee into his ale-softened stomach. He keeled over from the force of impact, then quickly strove to straighten in a show of strength. The overcorrection stressed his clenched stomach, and he hunched over the fence. His guts did not spill handsomely, and his cheeks retained much of the remains.

Thyra removed herself from her brother's nauseating side. "You are lucky to have only acquainted this one brother of mine. The first would have killed the girl when he was done. You would have only caught the second when he chose to visit for the tenth time, and the third would have left her ensorcelled for an eternity, oblivious of what he had done."

Wedged between an amalgamate of amusement and disdain, the farmer questioned, "Was every one of your Drur-damned brothers left unwiped like Kazbel's swollen arse?"

"Only the first," Thyra replied with a somber, defeated sigh. "Forgive me, but I am only one Ehlrich, perhaps a Runeheim, though I think not. It's impossible to manage more than one shitty brother at a time, much less the far cry this one has become," she lied.

The farmer loosed a harsh, indescribable jumble of jargon before contenting himself with the most inexplicably peaceable reply. "Just this once, and if I see the boy around my farm again, I will whip him until I've drawn blood no matter how much he begs I stop!"

Concertation was a veil she seldom wore, so Thyra spared an equivalent assurance that they had reached a concord. "You will not."

"He will see my sword shoved through his throat before this day ends," came the ill-tempered voice of her brother after he summarily finished draining his guts.

Swinging an arm over his shoulder to support him, Thyra lodged her fist into her brother's sternum to send him reeling into the abyss again. "Again," she promised, "you will not see him lest he wishes to lose every meal."

Chuckling through another string of absurd noises, the farmer grabbed his own stomach in a feigned show of fright. "Aye, Commander. If only the High Lady gave Lysian less sons and more daughters. Perhaps then I would have seen my own son return home from the Great Gates of Tjorden."

Exasperated, Thyra replied, "You hardly see it in this one now, but I swear the High Lady gave Eldaria all but one wicked son." She shoved Ryurik aside to where he stumbled, lulled his head, and regurgitated sordid air, and with a sobriety arisen from the poignant appreciation of someone she never expected to, Thyra added, "Your son feasts in the Halls of Halvalkyra, where he will drink mead beside our greatest Bjardja, jarls, and Storm Kings forgone to time. You've a daughter who lives. Focus on her instead."

"Damn girl hasn't listened to me since her brother left for the Great Gates. Listened to him as if his words were drizzled with wisdom from the Draconic Father himself. He's the one who taught her how to fight and be better help about the farm. My wife and I, we're too old to handle the shite she pulls. The war stole nearly every decent man from Stormguarde, and I am tired of shoveling up after human swine once I've finished cleaning the sty."

Thyra joked, "You must think I command a small portion of those men you curse."

The farmer's eyes widened as if he discerned some solution to the woes his daughter's self-vitiations imposed. His mouth hung agape, as if Thyra had become the misplaced component to his daughter's salvation.

Thyra stepped back under the weight of his ingratiating stare.

His face brightened, but the farmer only dabbled with the premise of sharing his thought. After struggling through a string of wispy and wispier breaths, he succeeded in wheezing, "If you were to take my Astrid into the Skjold, there would be hope for her. She has little clout, but she has tremendous heart."

Considering him for show, Thyra rebuffed, "The Skjold will receive anyone—man or woman—worth receiving my benediction, but I will not drag a lost pup into our fold if she does not choose to come of her own accord. She will walk to us if and when she is ready, and I will not smear my slate with cracked chaff before then."

"Lady!" the farmer exclaimed in an unfinished protest.

Grabbing Ryurik by his wrist, Thyra blunted, "Quit with what you have already gained. You reaped more from what you sowed than you would have if anyone other than I had come."

Having acquired her contemptible little brother, she left the farmer as Ryurik mocked, "Just, but merciful to the core. You have not changed at all."

Thyra scoffed. "You *have* changed, Ryurik. You're no longer the little brother I once knew. Grown into an ill-tempered man-whore, or maybe you simply grew into the man you were fated to become."

"Ellyan is still alive. His is a decent enough destiny that I am happily willing to succeed," Ryurik jeered.

"Fate's Weave is nonsense, Ryurik. Ellyan never believed in it, and you sour his memory by justifying yourself with his name. Only a child cannot control indulging their desires. Perhaps you haven't matured at all."

Thyra wrung Ryurik to where she joined with Hela outside the farmer's home. Hela wore an arrogance about her but made no effort to engage with her. Instead, the shield-maiden aggravated Ryurik with a smirk. Ryurik sneered in bitter contempt. Thyra would confront Hela under more favorable circumstances. She would not tolerate Hela's tendency to bestow aloof truths bereft of clarity's embrace if they were to ever be lasting friends.

Today, Thyra needed to prepare her disheveled brother for the task he must soon face. Alacrity toward the responsibility of managing Tjorden's plunders eluded her little brother, but Lothair would force it upon him all the same. With the advent of Baelgrant Trollsbane, their grandfather would expect the event to commence. Lothair would not be pleased with a delay.

Thyra had not been invited to join herself, but she knew the debates were due to begin. Ryurik's lascivious delights had left him stranded and ill-prepared. The treasures of victory would need to be divided in a manner befitting all. War with the Ardent Avant had come to its end. This did not entail another war would not begin. One, terminal misstep, and Ryurik would reignite internal strife in the Ardent Avant's absence, whereupon the Stormlands' and their own futures became infinitely more grim.

A commotion sprung from inside the farmer's home, and Thyra wondered why the door was reopened. Slipping free of her mother's grip and bolting through the door, the farmer's daughter sprinted toward Ryurik before Hela's warriors stopped her. She made the paltry effort at leaping through the two in a majestic profession of love. Thyra balked at the farmer's earlier suggestion that she take any part in this twiddled fool.

"Ryurik, don't leave me! You promised to make me your Storm Queen!" the farmer's daughter shouted.

"He promised nothing more than to make you his whore, girl," Hela jeered.

"Don't spite me for wanting something you'll never have!" the daughter snapped.

"A horse-shit promise from a weaselly man to spread my legs?" Hela laughed.

"Let me go! Ryurik, let me walk with you hand in hand through Stormguarde to the gates of Stormguarde Keep," the daughter plead.

Thrusting her brother in the direction that led directly away from this, Thyra brutally insisted, "Forget her. We all have higher callings than listening to this girl howl her nonsense."

Dismayed she was being wholly ignored, the farmer's daughter shouted to Thyra, "You cannot keep us apart. I will find my way to him!"

Thyra physically dismissed Hela's warriors to handle the senseless whelp herself. "Do you honestly think anyone here believes you? You are witless to think you were anything more to my brother than a warm hole for his cock. I could easily disregard my promise to your father, claim you attacked these men, and punish the offense to be rid of you." She took the girl's chin into her hand, twisted up, and soberly instructed, "Look around you. Everything you see here is worth more than you deserve, my brother's insult to you most of all." Thyra released the girl, whose eyes widened in trepidation of her perjury of the law.

"What did I ever do to deserve your abuse?" the daughter sobbed.

"Keep apart from my brother, or I will find reason to toss you into the Sea of Storm."

Thyra departed the broken-hearted girl, joined Ryurik, and forcibly propelled him forward. Hela and her warriors smugly followed. Once gone from sight completely, Ryurik divulged his anger by growling underneath his breath. Thyra wrinkled with malcontent while considering the disparate ways with which she might smack some sense into her brother's thick head.

Quietly, she demanded, "How much did you leave behind at that farm that I will need to send my Skjold to retrieve?"

"Some leather armor I stowed beneath her bed, my pants, and a fair bit of coin with them. You should leave her the coin, no? It will be the best draw of their year, better than any harvest that old bastard could reap," Ryurik derided, his haughty indifference miring his every word.

Thyra inhaled deeply, summoning the strength with which she might reply by words alone. After considerable consternation, she imbibed her brother's soured drizzle and remained silent instead. No wisdom, fortitude, or kindness would ever be shared between them in this fraught state as long as her brother drooled this crass idiocy. Ryurik's spectacled arrogance and sordid tongue elucidated the changes he had undergone while absent from her enfold. It was clear his truculence would burden her heavily in the future, and it was quite unlikely to dwindle before it grew. Ryurik, so desperate to fill the void left by the brothers who came before him, seemingly boasted the worst qualities of them all.

They skirted Stormguarde, purposefully parted with the Gormriks, and then returned to the fields where trained her Skjold. Cross with the day, she conveyed nothing but silent displeasure when they reached the birch row. She had neither the will to impart nor him to receive anything but clean clothes and a suit of Skjold armor.

She dissembled disinterest with his attempt at striking conversation, masked her anguish behind an insincere face, and strained like the wilting rose when autumn sleet came. Ryurik angrily departed, grumbling like an embittered mountain troll. Thyra's sole consolation of five years became the little brother returned home she no longer knew, so she buried herself within the drills of her Skjold.

Ryurik wended the market squares toward Stormguarde Keep with a fair bit of hustle. The people hardly recognized him. He seldom frequented the city before departing for the Great Gates, but he still expected a better reception.

Perhaps the shawl of Skjold armor disguised him too well, or maybe he looked different from when he'd last tread these streets.

For each man who did recognize Ryurik Runeheim, a world of frivolous chatter arose. The karlar whispered insults differently than Ellynon's common folk, who cheerfully murmured under vibrant spires so their thoughts were theirs alone. The Stormborne blustered their words. They enjoyed their voices being heard. Some sought after Ryurik's name. Others simply cried out his titles. "Ryurik Runeheim, Ryurik Ehlrich, Fourth Prince of the Lysian Empire." A fair multitude cried out, "There walks the blistering whore."

Ryurik did not humor them with a response while he walked on. Their insolence certainly irked him, but he chose to feign indifference toward the insults they spewed. They would die with names unsung. Regardless of his current diminution, he would see his name gifted hundreds of songs by the skalds. His blood was twice royal, and theirs was from the stock of raped thralls, peasant wives, and common whores.

They mostly commented on his choice of attire. Ryurik would not have chosen it himself, but he had been in no position to refuse his sister's gift. He would have preferred collecting his personal belongings after slaying the farmer. Incurring Thyra's wrath, however, would have been utter folly. She was furious enough with him already.

Thyra seldom tinkered with demure, yet had employed it quite well to mollify the farmer and his hounds. That particular demeanor did not suit her. Ryurik understood Thyra would renunciate anything for her family. Hela, clever bitch that she was, ascertained that trait perfectly as well.

He swore he would have preferred anyone else finding him as Hela had. Of course, Hela, who infuriated him the most, would be the first to find him. The shield-maiden of Breidjal had led his sister right to him, deducing his predicament to be the perfect catalyst to exploit to rend them apart. It had been as easy as splitting dry wood for Hela Gormrikdottir. Ryurik cursed the woman for seizing the opportunity like the visceral hawk she was.

Ryurik frowned, frustrated he could not retaliate. The Gormriks served too key a role in the defense of the Great Gates. Ryurik, Eljak, Ulfruk Dulfang, and even old Dulmir Svenson would downplay Harald's impact on land, but the Jarl of Breidjal's victories against Urien Aylard on the Helmyan Sea were undeniably massive. There was reason to why the

Paladin Supreme never attempted bypassing the Range of Tjorden by sea after the opening years of the war. That reason devastated Avantian fleets as ferociously as Sjógurn, and it was named Breidjal Bakari. Victory would never have been achieved without the Gormriks.

Ryurik suspected Harald would place a larger claim unto Tjorden's plunders than his provisions warranted. Battle after battle, the jarl reminded how his was the strongest fleet ever assembled in the Stormlands. Drunkenly, Harald would jest how he should receive the coastal fjords of Tjorden's Reach to grow his fleet further. That land fell within Jarl Ulfruk's dominion, where the Range of Tjorden frayed within the Helmyan Sea. In essence, they were Lothair's lands since the Dulfangs were permanently bound to the Runeheims by old blood and runic oath. While all the Stormlands technically belonged to the Storm King, much of it was administered by his jarls. Only the Erunheim and Tjorden's Reach were directly overruled. Ryurik would one day inherit those dominions, and he intended to retain them in full.

He turned the corner unto a cart of soft cheese, fermented milk, and skyr and a thrall arguing with another thrall on behalf of his master merchant. A short, verbal scuffle ended in a small loss for the thrall procuring the disposable goods.

Walking on, Ryurik caught sight of Jarl Harald embracing a youthful visage of Baelgrant Trollsbane. He'd once met the Bane of Trolls. Baelgrant wore a ferocious mohawk that swept from his forehead to his nape, bludgeoning the air in two. This apparent friend to Harald boasted a mohawk also, but it was shorter and had been woven into locks that dangled behind his head. He presumed the man was Bolvark, eldest son of the Bane of Trolls, heir to the fjord fortress of Langreklif, and protector of the Nordland's fjords.

Ryurik cleared his throat, and Harald looked up at the sound. The jarl immediately smirked after lacing it with infuriating smugness. Bolvark studied him without concern. The two stood beside a large, caged wagon draped in several layers of furs.

"Ryurik, where did you slink off during your Kingslag? Hela guessed a whore slew you out of spite for your cock, but I assured my cousin you've had too much practice handling their disappointment to fall to one of their cuts," Harald mocked, as was his predictable convention.

Years of fighting alongside the jarl had taught Ryurik that the key to curbing his affronts was to simply play along, so he plainly replied, "Did you find no bed to sleep in? There's no shame in admitting you slept alone through the night."

Chuckling, Harald countered, "You should have joined me in the great hall or in our camps after. I would have enjoyed meeting the girl you promised to marry before your sister pulled me into her bed."

"I have just returned from speaking with my sister. I am pleased to inform you were wholly disappointing. She hardly noticed you were there and regrets not taking Hela's cock rather than that runt you call your own," Ryurik deflected, knowing Harald's lust for his sister was rivaled only by his overgrown ego.

Drollness dripped from Bolvark's smirk as the lord casually commented, "The prince must not care much for his sister to speak of her so poorly."

Bolvark Trollsbaneson stood as every bit his father. He bore a smidgeon of a vibe of a better-mannered man and wore the look to which trolls cowered well. His ears were small, their lobes studded, and his shave untouched by ink. He knotted his brown hair into dreadlocks he then bound together behind his head. His beard hung the length of his nose beneath his chin and the length of his eyebrows everywhere else. Tall and relatively broad in stature, Bolvark's stance imposed his iron will. The Lord Son of Langreklif wore light trappings that bestowed him an image of deadly skill.

Ryurik saw within Bolvark the unblemished image of Baelgrant before time had torn his life asunder. He also discovered the bellicose yet tempered grace of an ally. He would choose his next words wisely, for he spoke as much to Lord Bolvark as to Jarl Harald Gormrik of Breidjal by the Helmyan Sea and Jarl Baelgrant Trollsbane of mighty Langreklif atop the Jüteheln Sea.

"Only a fool would believe a rumor that the First Princess of Lysian ever settled for Harald Gormrik. I would not dwell over his claim. My sister will remain unwed and un-promised until she reaps a far stronger man than him."

Amused and intrigued, Bolvark equalized his focus between Ryurik and Jarl Harald. "Ryurik thinks me better than you, Harald. My mother will remain the Lady of Langreklif until my father dies, but perhaps I've found myself a wife to replace her once his body burns atop the Jüteheln's winter shelves."

Cynicism burgeoned at the corners of Harald's mouth. "You would leave your sister to young Trollsbane like that whore you just departed with the promise of a crown?"

Deflecting the jarl's question, Ryurik asserted, "You will know if ever you earn Thyra. She will walk to you if that is what she desires. Until then, you are better off sticking your cock into the ground."

Harald turned, squaring his body against Ryurik's, and stepped in to brush him with his broad shoulders. "You are right, Lysian. I have not known the pleasure of your sister's touch, but slight me again and I'll be sure to share her with Baelgrant before you wed her to his son."

Swallowing his tension in swift, secreted drafts, Ryurik stepped against Harald. "You stand alone. Baelgrant sends his eldest son because you're no longer worth his own visit. Slither however you like, but he will still serve the line of Runeheim and the next Storm King." He teetered on the edge of insanity when he mocked the jarl with a whisper befitting a child. "Walk with Thyra tonight in your dreams, and lust over everything you will never touch."

Harald leaped in to seize his shoulders and whisper into his ear, "They will set our corpses ablaze as we drift beside each other over Sjógurn's beard. Don't worry, Ryurik. I'll make sure your body drifts to the Pentland coasts before you are buried beside your brothers, unless you would prefer to drown like your favorite one." He shoved Ryurik hard at the end of his insult.

Ryurik staggered back enraged, then regained his footing and narrowed his sights like a fjord tiger setting upon its prey. He gnashed his teeth, letting no sound bleed out from between them.

Harald laughed, Bolvark laughed with him, and their warriors snickered too.

Irate and overflowed with volatile ruminations, Ryurik walked forward to engage the jarl where he stood.

"That is enough posturing, lords. Petty vilifications will not lay leverage to your claims," said Seer Dragoln from the gates of Stormguarde Keep.

Both Harald and Bolvark's warriors parted to gift the seer space to descend. One offered a hand to assist him. Dragoln rejected his offer and staunchly waved him away.

"I have heard your prescience is both prodigious and vast. How do you know the claims we think? We never shared them. Does Eldrahg's seer read minds as well?" Bolvark splayed his arms, inviting Dragoln to read his in a mocking jest, and yet the lord's voice still bled complete respect.

Indifferent to trivialization, Dragoln chastised, "That is a wicked power long outlawed and not seen since the first wars with the Garathandi. Does your father no longer uphold the laws of his Storm King from Langreklif? Does Erun Runeheim's legacy mean nothing in the distant Nordland?"

Defiantly, the Lord Son of Langreklif avowed, "My father has always obeyed the Storm King's judgment, even when it belittles his worth."

"But questions it greatly," Dragoln quipped.

"My father is well within his rights as jarl to impose his concerns!" Adjusting his faculties, Bolvark continued with a better canter. "Baelgrant has never failed to enforce the Storm King's rule, no matter the insults we've accrued."

Stepping between the two men, Harald remarked, "There's a piece of the treasure for us all. You and Baelgrant still have time to make more glorious conquests."

Speaking to Harald directly, Bolvark disclosed, "And that is why he remains north of the Godrulheim Divide as instructed and reaves the coasts of the Garathandi in preparation for the Storm King's next war."

Dragoln scuttled between the jarl and lord but gripped Ryurik as if he spoke to him alone. "War, wealth, and power. Draconic Father bear witness in your wisdom, for what else could it be. I have never had need to read the minds of young men because there are but five things of which you ever think."

The elder's notion triggered a curiosity in Ryurik, and he duly inquired, "So what be the final two incentives you claim move the heart of man?"

Ogling Ryurik as if he had been asked a question which need not be asked, Dragoln shook his head. "Impetuses you think you know well but over which you have no grasp." Harald grinned to supplement Dragoln's quip, but Dragoln summarily silenced him. "Save your breath for the division of Tjorden's plunder. While Lothair expected to receive your father with your arrival, Lord Bolvark, we are adequately represented. The rest have already gathered. Follow me so deliberations can begin."

Dragoln gazed upon them, imparting a unique measure for each glance. He began with Bolvark, toward whom his blood inexplicably boiled. While they did not necessarily lie while slighting each other, Ryurik was uncertain why the seer appeared to distrust the lord. Dragoln discharged the Lord Son of Langreklif and regarded Harald next. The frailty that came with age did not tenderize Dragoln's iron core, and the two locked eyes—each incapable of fearing the other's scorn. Dragoln wasted no time in scrutinizing Ryurik. Confounded, impressed, and disappointed all at once, his eyes trailed the Skjold armor Ryurik reluctantly wore.

Ryurik shuffled by Lord Bolvark, Harald, and Seer Dragoln to enter Stormguarde Keep and arrived in the great hall shortly after. The thralls had positioned the tables to form a rigid circle around the hall's center where rose mounds of treasure. Only a portion of Tjorden's plunder rose before the assembly—a majority portion, but a portion nevertheless. Lothair had instructed a third remain with Jarl Ulfruk in Tjorden's Reach. It was his reward for long withstanding the siege and Tjorden's compensation to finance the restoration of their devastated lands.

Lothair headed the engagement. His hearth flickered, casting a shadow over his folded hands. Sunlight streamed through the open doors to streak lines across his face. He maintained a lengthy knot of silver hair that languished against his back, but he had sheared his beard and exchanged it with a far more focused fade. The Storm King otherwise appeared livelier than Ryurik had ever seen him before. Rejuvenated faith in the future of his kingdom could be the sole explanation for his grandfather's change in mood. Ryurik smiled for the trust merited by his victory at the Great Gates. He wiped away his grin, realizing he withheld Dragoln's full attention and the weight that burden entailed.

His mother, the High Lady of Stormguarde, Valyria Runeheim, stood intensively beside his grandfather. Ryurik had not taken the time to speak with her since returning to Stormguarde. She looked panged, but that particular look's overuse and triteness sorely dampened its effect. Exile and exodus altered her mood into something eternally dour. He witnessed his mother's current distress and compared it the sanguinity she'd shed upon his return. He arrived at the conclusion that it was transitory instead. Still,

Ryurik did return from war—the sole son of four who'd ever accomplished that feat. Was that not enough to lift her spirits?

Eljak seated the table to Lothair's immediate right where he convened with his eldest son. House Agulbarg claimed the next few tables. Dulmir Svenson's collection of sons, nephews, and cousins was far larger than most other families in attendance. Harald toiled with impatience at the head of the left tables with his lord uncle. Hela was nowhere to be found. The two were nigh inseparable, so the shield-maiden's absence perplexed him. Bolvark seated himself afront half his guard at the horseshoe's leftmost end. Ryurik assumed the rest stood guard over his caged wagon and its mysterious contents.

Ryurik bestrode the unclaimed seat beside his brooding mother. Pressing through her discontent, he embraced her with outspread arms. Reluctant at first, her body tightened as she strained away, but she inevitably relented and squeezed back. He stepped back and let his hands trail down her arms until she caught them in hers. She clasped them tightly, unwilling to release, and he did not resist. Her eyes danced across him before brightening with a thought.

"I see you've spoken with your sister and spent time aside her as well. I must admit I am envious I could not steal your company first," she said with jubilance and a shred of snark grace.

"We spoke a fair deal of the morning. After misplacing my armor, we agreed the Skjold's would serve as a fine substitute," he lied.

Scanning the great hall for sign of his sister, his mother frowned when she could not be found. "I presume you were unable to convince her to join us."

"She's left us Skjold enough to quell any of the heightened passions of the jarls. Thyra believes I can handle this day alone." Ryurik slipped his hands from hers to invite Eljak Draven to stand. "Eljak Draven will be there to fight beside us if it were ever called to such." His eyes adhered to his mother, but he spoke to his grandfather most. "The years we've spent at war afar have not led us to forget our loyalties to the Tempest Throne."

"You have a working memory and a silver tongue."

Ryurik assuaged a befuddled brow, exacerbating his grandfather's nerves.

"You have also not forgotten your pledge to that slippery girl?" Lothair asked perturbed.

Grievous disdain befell Eljak Draven at Lothair's sleazy mention of his lost daughter. The knotting of their hands and souls never came to pass, but technically, Ryurik and Agneta were still engaged. Agneta had slipped through Eljak's fingers to escape her marriage to him. To where exactly, nobody really knew.

Her disappearance came shortly after Ryurik had first met her while riding out to reinforce the Great Gates with supplementary forces from Stormguarde. He did not care who the girl was. He simply understood the importance of tying together the jarl's allegiances. It was why Ryurik accepted Eljak's offer of his daughter the precise moment it had come.

Eljak interrupted his table's derisive chatter and resoundingly stated, "War might leave us, but our victory remains. The full force of my army will return to Draven's Dominion when our time here draws to its close. I never abandoned the search for my daughter, but now it truly begins. I will deliver on my promise to you."

Standing, the Storm King boomed, "You fought for years beside my grandson against the Ardent Avant. A day after he returns, and already I hear of rumors of his wandering cock." The Storm King bestowed him brief rage, and Ryurik cringed until it returned to Eljak. "Do not feign ignorance," Lothair savagely continued. "Why do you promise a daughter you no longer hold to a boy who has clearly moved on?"

Eljak bellowed back, "I feign nothing for you! I will find my daughter, they will be wed, and my promise will then fulfilled. Ryurik is a young man. I do not care if he uses another woman to relieve himself before he's married. I encourage my sons to do the same."

Harald chuckled, his laughter echoing nigh as loudly as Eljak's rage. "Excuse my insolence, Storm King, but I do not understand the problem with a prince who likes to fuck. It was war, and the desire is there in at least half his blood."

Valyria rose to counter the jarl, exclaiming, "Because Runeheims should not behave like a band of unsworn warriors, or whores, least of all."

Entertained with her response, Harald persisted, "Nor should a jarl once his hands are bound to his intended's. Ryurik's a free man. He's made that brutishly clear." He smirked. "Perhaps the boy can look to his sister for advice on maintaining better discretion."

Valyria adorned fake pleasantries, and Ryurik watched as his mother summoned the fires beholden to her estranged husband's blood. "You speak highly of the daughter who scorned your advances afront us all. Recasting her belittlement onto her brother is no way to win her heart."

Lothair suppressed his anger, then reclaimed his seat. Dismissing Valyria's concerns, he instructed her to retake hers as well. She did, vigorously glaring over the Jarl of Breidjal by the Helmyan Sea the whole way. Lothair motioned to Harald Gormrik, making clear from thereon that the jarl would answer to him alone.

"Then there is truth to these rumors?" Lothair instructed, "Speak to what you know."

"I know nothing," Harald clearly lied, though Ryurik did not understand why. "Until I have heard it from Hela or seen it myself, I assume them to be the ramblings of drunken men."

Lothair pivoted to confront Ryurik directly, clenching his hands into mild fists as they beat against the table. "What have you to say then, boy? Let my hall hear it from you."

Ryurik summoned his cheekiest perjure. "Do rangers dismiss their motley hoods when in the company of stranger things?"

Even his mother betrayed a smile at the cleverness of his response, albeit it did not last.

Bemused, Lothair pondered the thought for a long moment. "No, I suppose they do not. I suppose it doesn't matter at all. You may have left me a shallow child, but you were under no obligation to return to me unchanged and ungrown."

Ryurik replied, "Karlar and our thralls believe whatever stories they're told, particularly if the implications are undesirable. Why bother addressing them at all?" he posed.

Lothair's mouth drooped in unspoken agreement.

Relief overcame Ryurik.

Contented with the answer he'd received, Lothair beset Lord Bolvark with his focus. "I am pleased you have come to partake in Tjorden's plunder, but where be your father?"

Bolvark bowed in deference toward Lothair's mention, then straightened. "My father extends his regret for missing this outstanding reunion. Currently, Baelgrant reaves coasts controlled by the Garathandi on his drakken longship with five of his swiftest bardlen warships. The northern trolls have been strangely quiet as of recent. He set sail to discover the reason why while also scouting where we might march our forces next."

"A bold assumption of my motives, as always. The High Lady and I have discussed what comes next for the Stormlands at length. That option never presented itself. I suppose Baelgrant seeks to deliver us all into the one that presented itself to no one but himself," Lothair openly confessed.

Laughter abounded from the right side of the great hall. Even the characteristically stern and studious Dulmir Svenson chuckled amid the uproar. The jarls quieted once Ryurik's grandfather raised a stern but shaky hand. Their mirth's end was as abrupt as its commencement.

A fire lit in Bolvark's eyes, and a fervor overtook his voice. "The Garathandi are weak. Their raids on Nordland fjords grew less frequent each year the mainland's siege endured. Their raids have all but dwindled to a halt, and all my father and I could wonder was why recluse when our defenses were never feebler? Why not strike when the Nordland stood alone?"

Unreserved absolution scarred Lothair's voice when he said, "Because they are trolls, young Trollsbaneson. Their advantage comes from their height, strength, and ferocity when they corner a kill. They are not intelligent creatures."

Bolvark maintained an inexorable determination to deliver his full tale. "I never claimed this recent voyage to be our first. Thrice we have landed on Garathandi shores, and we will land them many more. Their coasts lie undefended by their juggernaut vessels. Entire cities and villages lie unprotected. Their silver stores are ripe for plunder, their wives and babes ripe for seizure. Now is the time to slaughter these barbaric invaders who robbed our forefathers of our ancestral land!"

Ryurik indulged in the mounting curiosity. He, like every other intelligent man here, fairly believed Jarl Baelgrant elected to disregard Valyria's summons out of spite for his omission from the defense of the Great Gates. Yet, if Baelgrant did clash with Garathandi trolls thousands of leagues from the Nordland, who else but his lord son would travel to Stormguarde in his place. If Baelgrant did remain in the Nordland and, if he did simply wish to break from his Storm King, the jarl would have sent no one in his stead.

In a bold challenge to Lord Bolvark's call to arms, Lord Mielni piped, "Let me speak for every warrior here, who each regret they did not fight beside the Nordland's finest during the defense of the realm. But hear and understand me, Bolvark Trollsbaneson, when I say that I see through the ruse you spew to back your father's desperate craving for conquest."

Leaning in to bare his teeth, Bolvark replied, "I have only just arrived in Stormguarde and spent less than an hour upon these streets, yet there has been no decay in the regret and defense for our exclusion from the defense of the Great Gates!" His voice struck its ripe peak when he bellowed, "I have not *once* spoken out against our Storm King's decision, yet it appears I need not even strike my tongue. The offense is clear to all!"

Lord Bjarni shoved his younger brother into his seat, rough as he always had been with the boy, then aimed to pacify the mood when he said, "What Mielni meant to say, Lord, is that while the timing is evidently opportune, what proof does House Agulbarg have to justify this pursuit?"

"The proof lies in the caged wagon Bolvark holds outside the keep. Why not wheel it in to quell the questions before more arise?" Jarl Dulmir coarsely rumbled.

"My men are securing the wagon in Harald's camp as we speak. That is where it will rest, Jarl Dulmir, until the time comes for its contents to be revealed."

Dulmir savagely drowned the discord arisen from Bolvark's refusal to heed his question. "We have only just returned from the Great Gates and feasted through Kingslag for a single day. Mounds of the Ardent Avant's pilfered treasure lies before us, and already we speak of where we march next? I will not march my men to another war before the seasons even turn!"

Ryurik declared, "The decision is not for the Agulbargs alone to make, and we will first witness what Bolvark has brought to validate his father's request before we pass judgment."

"Give it time, and I will deliver you the just cause for which war may consume us so that glory might befall us both," Bolvark bade as he re-claimed the comfort of his seat.

Harald spoke out, seizing the opportunity left in the wake of arrogant ashes. "Bolvark has shared all the proof I need to sail the Breidjal Bakari to join him in conquest of the Garathandi." The sea jarl dismissed the muffled excitement and gripes, and he laid his full attention upon an apathetic

Dulmir Svenson. "Yet, I do agree with Dulmir Svenson. We cannot pursue another war until we have dealt with Tjorden's Reapings. Give our warriors a single season to return to their homes. Afterward, any honest Stormborne man will have seeded his wife and be ready to march to new wars."

The high seat of the Agulbargs would not be so easily appeased, and Dulmir instilled his every aggravation into the glare he gifted Ryurik. "We settle Tjorden's Reapings, burn and bury our dead so the Valkyrie might carry them to Halvalkyra, and only then will I entertain Bolvark's request. House Agulbarg does not bleed without a field of opportunity they can sow, and I fail to see the benefit in spending the youth of my nephews, cousins, and sons pillaging small swaths of land the Garathandi conquered millennia ago."

"I expected nothing more from a Son of Sven, seeing as I have not presented you with the proof that will sway your incredulousness." Lord Bolvark smirked, thoroughly riling the eldest Son of Sven Agulbarg—forgone Wardunwyrm of Riven Hold.

"Do not taunt me! I have no patience for your sly tongue." Silver shimmered in Dulmir's grievous eyes, and the severity in which he loomed sucked away the hall's fleeting warmth.

Lothair remained unfazed by the evolving conflict, yet interposed his voice as only Lok could. "Ease, Dulmir. Your temper is showing, and it does not sit well." He seized a cup of ale sitting before him, gulped down the brew, then wiped the stain of hops from his cracked lips. "Seize control, my grandson, and I will judge if you are worthy of becoming my heir after all."

As Lothair's voice trailed away, Ryurik professed, "The exact division of this plunder does not burden me, so long as we can summarily agree upon how to split the victory's greatest treasure. Relics unequaled in the power they will bestow upon their bearers and nearly as old as Eldrahg himself." He circled round Lothair's table to scour the nearest pile, searching for one of the five antique goblets of which he spoke.

Perplexed by his rummaging, Harald reproached, "If they were so damned valuable, Ryurik, you should have separated them from the bulk at the Great Gates instead of forcing us all to bear witness to your dramatic display."

Ryurik mostly ignored the jarl as he continued in his zealous search.

"Play with patience, Harald, and I will explain to you the importance of that which no one else did comprehend."

"Try the pile to your left then. The silver there shines much brighter than the rest," came the supercilious voice of the ever-disparaging shield-maiden Hela.

From the derisive smirk Hela wore, Ryurik worried she had been exploiting the time she'd spent with Thyra. The Gormriks whispered together while Lord Haneul listened close by. While intrigued, Ryurik spared no further thought for that issue he could neither amend nor critique. To his vehement surprise, he retrieved three Goblets of the Delas from the lustrous pile of silver and gold Hela had motioned toward. "I stand corrected, Jarl. Another polished individual sits at your table, but it is still not you," he said.

Harald casually discharged Ryurik's retort, which was but the most recent in the series of pernicious slights traded between them. "What are these jeweled cups of yours that require our supreme attention?"

Ryurik bestowed him a cursory glance while gathering the Ardent Avant's holiest of relics. He laid the first atop Lothair's table, on the side closest to the jarl. The goblet's aquiline shades suited the Jarl of Breidjal's colors perfectly. Feathered ensigns fell over the base, layer upon layer of grayscale, and from the center rose an eagle's limb. Its talons clutched the white-hued bowl and golden rim. Etched in silvery ink, clouds swirled in the depths, illuminating faint scripture—an inscription lettered in the secretive tongue of the Ardent Avant.

Ryurik placed the second goblet adjacent to the first. Its base split like charred, cracked dirt, and the mortar gluing it together bled the deepest hue of magmatic orange. The stem climbed like an obsidian spire. Where the stem splintered, the ancient jeweler had wrought a rosette bowl mortared in red clay. Within the goblet, the Earth Mother's ruby heart sputtered, radiating an aura corpulent to the core. A rim encrusted in slivers of garnet shaped like a thousand firths enwreathed Goldral's heart.

Ryurik sauntered to the other end of Lothair's table where his mother judged his flaunt, and he momentarily flashed her the third goblet before juggling it between his hands. He then laid it upon the table as if it were but the fourth. Grains like white sands flecked the goblet's base, and the stem whirled and unfurled like a torrent guzzling up from the ocean's floor. Within the bowl stirred azure waters painted with the glory of Eldaria's every ocean. Pearls encircled the goblet's rim. A myriad of silver trimmings latched onto the oceanic wreath—one bestowed for every one of Eldaria's seas.

He returned to the heaps of treasure, wading to the center where he believed he glimpsed another. Mistaken, he grabbed a chalice of solid gold and cursed beneath his breath for the indignity of the search. Harald's slight resurfaced in his mind, and it piqued his nerve. Ryurik had endeavored to isolate the goblets before the journey home, yet somewhere along the march they were reincorporated into the greater hoard. He hesitated, aggravatingly realizing the other two might have been abandoned to Tjorden's Reach. Glumly, he gulped down his apprehension, only to cough when his mouth secreted more.

"Descant me to Drur's Abyss," Harald scathed while he slammed down his fist. "Lothair, how long are we expected to mature through Ryurik's panicked search? These goblets should have been carried separately from the rest of Tjorden's haul."

Ryurik abandoned his search to resolve Harald's qualm. To his surprise, his mother spoke and swiftly silenced the great hall. "I'm certain Ryurik endeavored to do that as much as I am certain the treasure was rifled through on your march. Keep the peace, my jarl. Before you stand three of the eight Goblets of the Delas, and two more might lie within the hoard. Their recovery will be well worth the mild delay."

Harald betrayed his frustrations before nurturing a fragment of intrigue while Ryurik witnessed that the great hall's mood had swiveled in tune with his mother's speech. "As commanded, High Lady," said the Jarl of Breidjal by the Helmyan Sea.

Satisfied, Ryurik augmented, "Five were recovered after the Ardent Avant's retreat—goblets which for thousands of years belonged only to the Ardent Faith. Make no mistake, my great lords and jarls, our victory pales in comparison to our seizure of these gifts from the Pharophah'll himself." Amidst the mounting laughter, he mocked, "Oh 'glorious' leader of the Ardent Faith and divine prophet to Andurial."

Unamused with Ryurik's sardonicism, Dulmir questioned, "Where lie the two beyond that table then, Prince? We hold but three until they are found."

"Within these mounds, Dulmir Svenson, or in Tjorden's Reach, if the coffer in which they were placed was tampered with during our journey here to Stormguarde."

"What of the other three?" Dulmir persisted, his curiosity bleeding off his gruff tongue.

Sprawling her hands over the table as to summon Dulmir's astute attention, Valyria said, "Within the depths of the High East and beyond the shores of Keriador, son of my old friend."

Chuckling from the comfort of his chair, Harald broke the tension and said, "We should aid Ryurik in his search then, High Lady. Ingvar, Baylor, and the rest of you seal spawn shall search for these extravagant cups, so I may choose which to wipe my arse with before making a gift of it to Urien Aylard."

The shield-maiden of Breidjal stoutly reinforced, "Only after I've tasted fresh mead from one of the Phah'll's own holy cups."

Eljak Draven gruffly ordered, "Byron, my son, take our men, go forth, and do the same."

There was little structure to the paths by which Ryurik's newly acquired aid tore through Tjorden's plunder. Raving to find the touted treasures, they oft brought him average chalices in place of the most distinguishable of relics. It was a forgivable mistake had they the decency not to contend him on each piece's merit. Their contestation particularly aggravated him whence he informed them of their error, yet they inexorably continued all the same.

"Moon's Delas!" Lord Byron exclaimed. "Surely, this goblet belonged to Eldrahg himself." The Lord Son of Draveskeld lifted a goblet forged from moonstones high into the air.

"By the Draconic Father's beard, I didn't believe we would ever come to see this relic return to the Stormlands again." Seer Dragoln mustered the totality of his antecedent strength to scurry around Lothair's table toward the goblet Lord Byron held. "In all its exquisite beauty…" the seer stammered in awe. He outstretched a frail hand to beseech from Lord Byron a solitary gift. "You would honor an old seer far more than he deserves by giving him the chance to inspect this cup."

"The honor is mine alone," Byron replied with tempered, deferential grace.

Seer Dragoln retrieved the goblet, fondling the ancient relic his forebearers once held by equally wrinkled hands. Ground and forged from moonstones that bore the mark of Dwevland, the bowl shimmered by the light of a daytime moon. Lapis lazuli scintillated along its rim. Long, methodical strands of silver encapsulated the superbly cut sapphires that formed the body of the Delas of the Moon. The Draconic Father's jaws enveloped the crown jewel without so much as puncturing its fragile heart. Seer Dragoln barely kept himself from shedding virile tears when he confirmed the authenticity of what he held.

Quaking like a wellspring of blissful joy, the seer approached the Storm King to exclaim in full verve, "Storm King! The final goblet be damned to Drur's filthy Abyss. I gift this—borne of the Draconic Father and Goddess of the Moon—to you. I swear by week's end the skalds will have sung a thousand songs to you and Prince Ryurik for bringing me the unimaginable pleasure of witnessing this day come true." The seer placed the goblet directly afront the Storm King and pushed the shining antique of Stormborne magnificence until it was aligned with the other three.

"Seer Dragoln!" Lothair heartily resounded as he rose from his wolf-skinned, high-backed seat, gracing his great hall with an intensity that came from being king. "I'm as near to death as you, old friend. There's no glory in claiming this goblet for myself or hiding it in Stormguarde Keep where the moon's light will never touch its brim."

Lothair paused, as if lending the floor to Ryurik to speak, so he briefly abandoned his search to join the emotionally overwhelmed seer and said, "Three goblets lie beyond our reach, but we have lifetimes still to seize them. This goblet belongs to every warrior who fought and was slain at the Great Gates. It belongs with the Runic Faith most of all, whom I reserve no doubts will employ it better than the Prince of Storm who shall one day become its king."

Dragoln bowed his head in congenial acceptance and then laid a lethargic hand against the outer bowl of the goblet, letting his fingers trail down its magnificent stem. The seer shuffled to reclaim his seat at Lothair's left. Ryurik's grandfather grinned, a rarity he infrequently shed. Ryurik humbly accepted his satisfaction, then spun after catching wind of a commotion when a new face entered Stormguarde Keep.

"Do not forget the fifth, noble Stormborne, as he so often forgets himself." Righteous as the conquered sun, empyrean as the vengeful sky from which every Ehlrich drew descent, Thyra knelt against the far edge of the treasure, her eyes narrowing upon the last goblet Ryurik sought within. "One would think Andurial cursed all the world to live blind to Akhom Rha the same as he cursed the Delas of the Sun to walk blind to all the world." Within her hand, she displayed the goblet forged for the Delas of the Sun.

An intricate assortment of emerald and ruby gemstones were inlaid into its golden base that spiraled into a stem of pure white diamond. Golden fingerlings suspended the goblet's diamond core. They were wrought and magically invested to form a profoundly rotund bowl. The diamond stem pierced through the golden trough, revealing a single, shallow spike at its center. Seven strands of silver sprung from the diamond spike's tip, ascended the goblet's inner rim, and wrapped around its outer edge. Engrained with everything that made Akhom Rha ostentatious, prevailing, and supreme to all other Delas, the goblet radiated the light of the conquered sun.

With Akhom Rha's goblet loosely in hand, Thyra strode toward Ryurik and stepped into a curt but firm embrace. As the goblet cooled the back of his neck, Thyra seized the opportunity to whisper into his ear, "We will speak of what we must wash from you and your name, but it will not be today."

They parted, standing abreast in the intimacy of each other's thoughts while the jarls and lords of the Stormlands stared.

Ryurik bade she stay when he responded, "Does my sister Thyra chastise me now, or is this the sister corrupted by Hela's virulent seeds?"

Charmed by his rebuttal, Thyra smiled, but her hushed riposte was anything but courteous and suave. "I rid myself of Hela's company no sooner than I removed your indignance from the fields where train my Skjold."

"And abandoned me to this obligation to watch over their fatuous drills."

"It forgave the time to consider the situation," Thyra reproached before whispering in the severest of tones, "Forgive me, brother, but I need not the comfort of bloodthirsty, silver-hungry men to reinforce my every decision."

Ryurik's voice pitched above a whisper before he mellowed his tone. "They all partake in this grand game to which we are now slaves. We must shift ourselves into their favor before they move of their own accord."

"Careful, Ryurik, your need for validation is beginning to show." Her remark left him riled and stranded, and his blood boiled when she presented the fifth Goblet of the Delas to their grandfather with an aura of smug triumph.

"Storm King, a goblet originally wrought for the Delas Akhom Rha, who now roams as the Worldwalker after Andurial took his goddess for himself. It is the fifth you now own." Thyra consigned the golden goblet to its place. "Apologies for my absence. I've been fighting hostile fires lit during Ryurik's Kingslag and fed by its drunken celebrants."

Lothair begrudgingly received her, disgruntled with the fact that she'd arrived late, or at all. Peculiarly, he then admitted, "Fire is wild. It burns nearly anyone who draws too close. It is good you have come to revile your birthright the same as your brother." His focus danced between Thyra and Ryurik before it settled on Ryurik alone. "She heeds my advice for once. Join your mother, Thyra. Leave Ryurik to conclude his show."

Thyra offered him curt bow, unambiguously mocking in nature, and continued walking her rebellious line ripe with outright malice. She seated herself beside their mother and impatiently cocked her head to demand he continue.

Ryurik returned a vexatious glare, which she did not receive well.

Like their dear, departed brother, Thyra sustained a knack for seizing whenever she was truly riled. Ryurik swallowed his feelings, recognizing the inevitability a conflict would resurge between them, recognizing they needed to address one another's qualms, yet also understanding it was wise to move along. He instead adhered to instincts acquired from a lifetime spent in the shadows of Darius and Thyra, gesticulating to the aquiline goblet at the end of Lothair's table.

"Aquila, Lianth, Eldrahg, Meridot, and Akhom Rha," Ryurik proclaimed while presenting each in measured succession. "For all of Eldaria's goddesses and Andurial, a Delas was chosen to enact her divine will. Many now live in exile as Worldwalkers, awaiting their goddesses' resurgence into our Eldaria. For each Delas, the ancient world also forged a goblet saturated with their deific power, strengthened by their mind's resolve, and imbued with their magical prowess. To drink from these fonts of power is to drink power from the mouth of the Delas themselves. I cannot begin to fathom why the Phah'll allowed all five in the Ardent Avant's possession to join with Urien Aylard's siege. It is even more unimaginable that the

Light's Champion abandoned them during the Ardent Avant's retreat, yet here we now sit in Stormguarde, holding five as the mainlanders lick their wounds. The mighty lines of Runeheim, Draven, Agulbarg, Gormrik, and Trollsbane have all gathered while only Dulfang, Kenning, and the Frost-hammer dwarves of House Folkenarr remain absent. Five great houses of the Stormlands to match these five Goblets of the Delas." He motioned to Lothair's table as his verve subsided. He knelt to collect handfuls of coins before siphoning them between his fingers, and they splattered over mounds of treasure to languish upon the cold ground. "Let each jarl's banker dispute how we split this trifling rest, and let us drink our victory together from these instead."

Harald slid around the table at which he sat, butt skidding across the surface as if it were an alpine board skidding over snow, and with the celerity of a Breidjal hawk and the silkiness of a fjord otter, the jarl spoke, "And how are we to summon the power each goblet holds? I am no Lysian sorcerer, little Ryurik. I would not know how to…*imbibe* such strength on my own."

Valyria's shoulders dipped before she vigorously stood and looked upon each jarl, speaking to Harald first, "The Draconic Father's goblet was forged in the crucibles of Dülraht by the Dwarf Lord Harnik Folkenarr, who we now revere as runic god of the forge. Meridot's was crafted in Andlaust at the directive of the angelic conqueror Julianus Romanus Castiel. It was his kingdoms' safeguard against Andurial when Lucilla Queen of Strife was drowned beneath the oceans between the waves. The story of Akhom Rha's goblet is the most tragic of them all. They say the Imrahli of the Deserts of Rhavi wrought it with the energy released after Andurial stole his sight. Each is immeasurably unique, and yet…" She softly tapered her breaths while seizing the Goblet of the Delas Akhom Rha, "They share one thing in common. Beneath the brim lies an unsolicited inscription etched in the clandestine language of the Ardent Avant to encumber their power, so they can never be fully used against Andurial. Their power can only be drawn upon by those who can read old Avantian and wield the power of the Delas for whom each was wrought."

Intrigued by notions of deific power trapped inside the goblets, Harald Gormrik reached for Aquila's. He lifted it gently within the palm of his hand and raised it high, so the cup shimmered by the great hall's torchlight. The feathered base appeared to rustle as he leisurely lowered his arm. Harald fiercely twirled the goblet within his hand and then peered inside the rim, hunting for the text Valyria spoke of. Grinning once he located it, Harald brought the goblet to Lady Hela to confirm that which he saw. "Etched beneath the rim," he directed, finger pointing toward what he saw.

"Written in no language of which I know," the shield-maiden of Breidjal conceded, satisfied with her own recognition of the text within the goblet's maw.

"It looks like nothing else we reaped from the Ardent Avant," Harald commented before reclaiming the goblet to examine it once more.

Thyra leaped to her feet, inviting the great hall's attention when she joined Harald. "Aquila's goblet holds two inscriptions." She recouped the goblet, which the jarl tenderly released into her right hand. "The first you saw within is written in the tongue of Lunedir, the sky's ever changing language, understood only by royal or noble Lysians. The second remains hidden along the outer rim, as my mother explained before," she stated, adjourning Harald's ignorance.

Lothair folded his hands in a crescendo, then straightened his back. "Dragoln swears by the legitimacy of Eldrahg's goblet, so why presume the others to be woven by the hand of Lok?"

"The seer I will not dispute, but Ryurik alleged it himself. The Goblets of the Delas retain immeasurable value, so why were they simply abandoned to emptied camps?" posed Harald.

Thyra grinned and stepped apart from Harald, toward a clear floor. "Because bereft of their holy touch, these goblets are worthless unless placed in the hands of one who can both read and speak the Ardent Faith's secretive tongue that wraps their outer rim."

"I cannot attempt to read what isn't there," Harald stymied while he furrowed his brow.

Thyra rolled her eyes in hot agitation before sardonically replying, "It can only be seen with a delicate touch either way."

"A delicate touch," Eljak scoffed. "Something a Lysian bitch could never boast."

Lord Byron followed his father's lead, laughing in expedient, successive bursts.

Thyra insidiously sneered before tossing the goblet back to Harald.

Confounded, Ryurik glanced upon his mother to acquire an expert opinion on what Thyra intended to do next.

Valyria averted her eyes in swollen disappointment, knowing just as he should that Thyra did whatever she pleased.

Ryurik staggered when he glimpsed the soft light radiating from within his sister before she whipped a fiery ball toward the goblet. The magical projectile connected with the golden rim the precise moment Harald caught it. Aquila's birthright consumed solar sorcery flown on wings of sky magic—the divine product of the deific union of a vengeful sky and a conquered sun that seared hotter than any single evocation of solar sorcery could alone.

"You dare cast sky magic in my kingdom, before my jarls and lords, in my own great hall!" Lothair roared, nearly striking the back of his head against his chair when he leaped to stand.

"Storm King!" Ryurik interjected in his best show of force, but his effort was to no avail.

Lothair would not be stifled by anything, not even his grandson and apparent heir. "Thyra Ehlrich!" His face rippled as he roared. "How dare you unveil your cursed sorcery within the moon's sanctity of Stormguarde! Face me and kneel, or I will disown you and your wretched affairs and drown you in the Sea of Storm myself!"

Ryurik joined Thyra, standing beside his sister's grim countenance in an endeavor to buffet the growing storm. Thyra laid a hand against his shoulder, thrust him away, and tread before the Storm King's austere fury unremittingly. Her defiance enraged Grandfather even more. Lothair growled, an action utterly barbaric in nature.

Ryurik gazed upon his sister, fearful of her looming fate. He curled his fingers into twin fists wrapped in deep anguish. Several Bjardja stood with swords drawn. Why had he chosen to sleuth through a farmgirl's sheets rather than reuniting with his sister? Now he stood upon the wretched precipice of never seeing her again should they stoke their hatred of one another further.

Harald abruptly roared, "Lothair Runeheim, come see what I now hold!"

Ryurik spun to witness the fire inside Aquila's goblet dissipated into white light that illuminated the lettering hidden within its bowl.

Harald slammed the goblet against Lothair's unmalleable table, not caring at all for what Thyra had done. "She has lit the goblet's text, and I swear by Sjógurn the Ravager, I am no wielder of sky magic or solar sorcery, but by his salted balls I feel its power resonating within my bones. Let me sail the Breidjal Bakari beside every vessel we have ever built. Let me reave the mainland, so I may return with the first priest who can read what lies upon their rims!"

Valyria rose, white hot with disdain. "Jarl Harald Gormrik! Redress my father as your Storm King, then return to your seat." The resilience with which she scolded Harald rivaled those of the paladins and templar knights who adhered to the will of the Pharophah'll. "Now, let every jarl who is loyal seat his warriors and sheathe their swords. We stand in Stormguarde, jewel of the Erunheim, seat of the Tempest Throne, and capital to all the Stormlands. We will not tolerate these bellicose offenses anymore!"

Harald nigh staggered athwart the vindication the High Lady had hurled his way. "Storm King," he resolved before heeding Valyria Runeheim's decree.

A semblance of order returned to the great hall. Even the Skjold recognized the amicability Valyria's admonishment had forced. Steadily, they all unhanded their axes, seaxes, and swords. Relieved Thyra was, temporarily, no longer facing banishment or death, Ryurik briefly relaxed.

Lothair drove his fingers into the table's edge as Harald reseated himself. "Daughter," he called as he leaned dangerously far over the armrest of his chair. "Can you read the Avantian text, or is that knowledge not spared upon Lysians?"

Returning Lothair to his seat with vigilant exertion, Valyria answered, "None of my children can read scripture written in the clandestine language of the Ardent Avant. I suspect Thyra alone can draw the text to the surface if the time for it ever comes."

Lothair begrudgingly questioned, "The time for what?"

"Find a cipher, a speaker of the Phah'll's clandestine tongue, and from the power we imbibe from these Goblets of the Delas, the Stormlands will reign as the supreme power of the north." Valyria's eyes widened like those of a child devouring sweets for the first time. "In a quarter of the moon's cycle alone, we could march upon the Broken Fjords, drive out the ældrik who stole our ancestral home, then look to the Garathandi afterward."

"Yes, your damned dream as contrived as Jarl Baelgrant's ridiculous plea that we invade the Garathandi Empire to the north." Lothair frowned in disappointment, simultaneously stifling her ramblings and forgetting Thyra's earlier, incandesced exhibition.

"Both are as necessary as was repulsing the Ardent Avant! You can be the Storm King who reclaims the Broken Fjords, rips out the toothed seax buried in our backs, and cleanses the seat of power from the stain left by Baelric the Black Sword, who frees our runic—"

"Enough!" Lothair shouted. "I do not wish to hear of it anymore! Take your seat beside your vicious daughter and teach her what respect means to the Stormborne."

Valyria stumbled in anguish, retaking her seat in a flurry of disappointment. She often spoke of destiny, and she had written to Ryurik throughout the war of an enigmatic rectification of their forefather's grievous mistakes. She mumbled of the toothed seax held to the Runeheim's and the Ehlrich's backs. She whispered of a dire requisite to rid themselves of a darkness behind their doorstep in the depths of the Broken Fjords.

Ryurik understood none of it. He did not indulge her either, for while Valyria was his mother and worthy of all his respect and love, he did not agree with her cause. He saw little merit in reclaiming the last fjords behind the Great Gates of Tjorden the Storm King did not control. Why spend the lives of tens of thousands of Stormborne for lands shittier than the earth owned by Jarl Denurl Kenning?

"Five goblets whose powers are yet unknown. Five goblets we cannot wield alone. Five goblets' secrets we must learn. Five goblets too precious to hold in Stormguarde. We have been at peace for more than ten years strong," Ryurik continued, coveting nothing more than to direct the minds of the jarls toward something other than his sister.

"We have been at war with the Ardent Avant for that long," Dulmir scorned with a fiery tongue.

"With a foreign entity, who united the Stormlands' eight noble lines. If I preclude the siege of the Great Gates of Tjorden, we have been at peace amongst ourselves—without war, without conflict, without strife, and without feuds that achieve nothing but our own untimely deaths—for ten years. Realize this is a peace we should pursue and look at all which we have accomplished in its midst. The Broken Fjords, the Garathandi Empire, the Kingdom of Helmya, and the Alterian Highlands will pale against the Stormlands united. We will forever swell the reign of the Runic Faith and Monomua, Goddess of the Moon."

"A common goal. A common cause. A purpose which binds us all," Thyra muttered, smirking with an emotion that was neither regret, disdain, nor remorse.

Ryurik seized reassurance from his sister's remark. "Something to bind us all."

"Dole these remaining goblets between my jarls. I will assure you neither Ulfruk Dulfang nor the Frosthammer dwarves of Dwevland will carry qualms," the Storm King sternly promised.

Ryurik probed, "What of Jarl Denurl and the Kennings of Aidelgard?"

"Denurl Kenning refused to fight through the end of the war, or am I wrong? He is worth less than swine muck as far as I'm concerned."

Ryurik dipped his head, to which Lothair smugly nodded. Heir of the Tempest Throne he surely was, for he had wiped away the farmer's disdain and the stain of his daughter's crotch with a far better song to be sung by the skalds.

Jarl Harald Gormrik approached the same aquiline goblet Thyra had set ablaze moments prior. "It goes without question that the Breidjal Bakari is the greatest Stormborne fleet to ever sail by Sjógurn, but I have taken a liking to this particular goblet." He smirked at Thyra, then decreed, "I think we can all agree this eagle suits me best."

He retrieved Aquila's goblet, scrutinizing the beatific object between his masculine hands as if it were his own child. He looked to Ryurik for mock approval but did not linger long enough to receive it. Harald then continued onwards to retrieve Meridot's before Ryurik shunned his reach. The jarl grabbed it anyway, struggling with him momentarily until a slight twist of the wrist won Harald the bout.

Displeased, Ryurik safeguarded the remaining goblets.

Grinning, Harald placed Meridot's before Lord Bolvark in a righteous display of indifference and a sheer power of will. "If the sea's goblet does not lie with me and mine, then in the house of Baelgrant Trollsbane it should reside. Their fleet is second only to the Breidjal Bakari in strength and size. Does anybody disagree?" he demanded as he smeared the great hall with his pride.

Eljak stood for the first time since the onset of the meetings. With his son Byron by his side, he beckoned Ryurik to walk his way. Ryurik met them as they rounded their table. Together they returned to Lianth's goblet. Its earthen components shimmered deeply like the heart of the Earth Mother herself. Lord Byron angled an eye toward Ryurik before stepping aside to clear his father a path. Ryurik mirrored the Lord Son of Draveskeld, his aspiringly imminent brother-in-law.

"If there is but one thing left we can agree on," Eljak griped to Lothair alone, "it is that Draveskeld deserves this goblet more than Aidelgard."

Lothair dismissed Eljak Draven, so the jarl of Draven's Dominion declared, "We will bury this goblet so deep within the mountain hold of Draveskeld no Garathandi horde nor Lysian legion could ever hope to re-cover it. There it will remain buried until called upon by the next King of Storm."

"Storm King!" Dulmir Svenson shouted before calmly requesting, "Can I speak plainly?" The jarl's entire family stood to attention as he alone strode to the forward center of the great hall.

Lothair grimaced, stating, "When has an Agulbarg ever not?"

"My men will not be bought by empty promises, jeweled goblets, and proof of war's verity stuffed in a dingy wagon. We will not march toward another war until we' have recovered from the last one. I alone decide when Riven Hold will empty for war."

"You do, and you will not. At least while I still live."

Dulmir Svenson planted himself firmly and nearly growled his next words. "We will not, for as long as *I* live."

"I lived and fought beside your father Sven Agulbarg, my jarl. We were good friends for the longest parts of my life. He learned quite young that we cannot choose when war advances, only how we are to best redress its march. I hope you were not forgotten when Sven passed on this lesson. If you were, then know it does not weather me much. There is still another Son of Sven Agulbarg who can claim rule of Riven Hold, one who slew paladins, templars knights, and even an affluent mainland lord."

"House Agulbarg committed one-third of the forces that held the Great Gates, and we will leave with one-third of its reapings without sparing an-other word." Dulmir Svenson gritted his teeth menacingly, but he had not spoken entirely out of turn.

Lothair raised his hand to present the jarl with his approval to a third of the mounds of gold.

Dulmir regarded Ryurik, but not for a second more. He shoved past Byron, Eljak, then Ryurik himself to retrieve Akhom Rha's goblet before tossing it into a chest and then speaking with his sons.

Byron tread forth to combat the lord afterward, but Eljak pulled him apart from the errant response of a hot-willed fool.

"One-third of Tjorden's Reapings falls to the Agulbargs. The Gormriks and the Dravens may seize one-third each of what remains, and the finality of the treasures will be cloven between the Trollsbanes and my Erunheim," Lothair expressed.

The vast majority of the Agulbargs bowed, then departed from the great hall, leaving behind only Lord Bjarni Svenson and their banker to oversee the division of their share of the silver and gold. Within an instant through which a ranger's arrow might fly, one banker and one minor representative from each jarl's house adjoined to contend their claims to the plunders as the Storm King's partition was argued, then staunchly reaffirmed.

"Do not let Dulmir Svenson fool you, Ryurik," Lothair continued. "You did well in adhering to the path you chose. I'm surprised with how witty you've grown, yet there is still much for you to learn. Valyria, my vicious daughter, walk with me," he insisted while extending a hand in his daughter's direction. "You too, my cosseted seer. I would like to hear more of these Goblets of the Delas that my grandson retrieved."

It took a substantial amount of time before they fully departed. Lothair Runeheim's health waned more with each of the Crescent Lady's revolves, an ill fact Valyria's letters had failed to fully impart. Valvítr, Queen of the Valkyrie, would soon claim his grandfather. Ryurik would then be left the apparent heir to the Tempest Throne. It was his birthright, amongst some others he neglected from a past life, for the Stormlands were the only birthright he cared to claim.

Ryurik had yet to properly converse with Thyra since arriving in Stormguarde. If this day had taught him any lessons, it was that hers was a strength he needed to be his. He turned to grasp her attention, to amend his morning's mistakes, but he grabbed nothing but empty air. She too left him wanting, having vanished like smoke in the draft. Ryurik was joined by a whiny banker and left with little more than reaped gold and silver to comfort his growing concerns with his return home, his relationship with his divisive family, and his future in this hostile world.

CHAPTER EIGHT
ERE THE NORDLAND

HE FIRST DAYS WERE SURPRISINGLY the easiest. They were simple, simple because Agneta had lived as Ehlaru's apprentice for three years and cherished every second. This joint venture had been a pleasant return toward what she so desperately coveted. Yet, past experiences foretold a nasty truth was approaching. She abhorred to admit her methods might be the cause. Bitter did not settle well on the tongue of Eljak Draven's daughter. She did not wish to be bitter like him, but bitter was what she currently was. It exacerbated her mood and soured her thoughts.

Agneta remembered each day spent in Ehlaru's company when her life was reforged into that of a ranger's. Each moment held immeasurable value to her, having helped shape her into the woman she now was. How could her heart ever forget the memories of that which came after Ehlaru resigned his friendship with her?

She understood there was nothing her words could amend. There were no bargains to be made with past regrets. She'd made a decision, he'd rebuffed her advance, and still she pursued his heart and hand like a dog underfed. She would not reclaim the past, no matter how ardently she reached through the flow of time to feel it trickle down her hands.

Agneta accepted it—a truth made putative by her sudden departure after saving Ehlaru's life from a dire wolf's jaws. She had drawn that feral beast to his camp, so he unknowingly owed her nothing for her help. After finding the wolf while traveling the Godrulheim's westernmost path, she'd quickly realized the value in its alienation from its pack and then waited outside its lonely coven until night fell. Leading the feral beast through wilderness, she'd circled around the mouth of the mountain pass and left it to the allure of his fire. All that had come next was both expected and partially unexpected. She'd meant to intervene only to force his hand, not to save his life.

Agneta lived it—silence through five days and nights during which they crossed the Godrulheim Divide, entered the Nordland, and rode to the fjord where she lived. She led them east along the northern slopes. Here, like the rest of the Nordland, the high country met its bitter end. Yet, it did not end high above the Wrathgorne Wilderland underneath the precipice of the Thunder Falls like in the Soudland. The fjords here cut directly into the Jüteheln, and their cliffs were nigh unscalable. The eastern paths digressed unto no civilization, but if one followed them in spirit, they would reach the majestic convergence where the Valdhaz, Jüteheln, and Nordland met in an astounding union. She believed it to be the Stormlands' most remarkable vista, one where the high country seemingly vanished and mountainous fjords met the icy, roaring sea. It was there she had settled her new life, her glimmer of pride within lonely existence, and she sorely wished it were a moment of which she could deign to speak.

Agneta rued it—a byproduct of her acceptance of the consequences of her decision and the harder reality that she needed to abide them. Ehlaru had claimed the wolf's corpse as promised, and while they hauled the bounty in each other's company, it was as if they traveled alone. She required his help in some slim fashion. What she desired so incomparably more was her friend. Admittedly, any friend would suffice, but, lamentably, all others paled in comparison to him. She could not think to flee those feelings clawing at her heart, irrespective of how futile they were.

Agneta had crossed paths with other rangers after leaving Ehlaru's tutelage. She'd ascertained his every account of their merits to be both accurate and remarkably precise. They were exiles to some degree, each and every one, and hailed from near and far. They hid within the high country because it was the most difficult place for most any pursuant to reach, let alone figure out where they had gone. They'd been unpleasant, quiet, and preferred to stride alone.

The Stormborne branded their kin as rangers, imparting three expectations in return for the secrecy the title afforded. Rangers must keep the peace between Stormborne and dwarves and keep checks on the movements of etins, ældrik, and mountain trolls. Rangers must provide for those who dwell in the high country whenever nature roared. Rangers must manage the fickle fae within the Vales of the Eversong whenever their torments went intolerably far.

Agneta had met three rangers besides Ehlaru and exchanged a total of thirty words with each. None had ever yielded her their names. She had never proffered such information either, but she hoped at least one might have been a shred like him.

She fondled the stolen coffer, thinking of him. Willful, independent, intuitive, clever, and brilliant in some regards, she envied those traits that she herself only held by tinny threads. None like Ehlaru resided in these realms, and Agneta presumed appallingly few existed across Eldaria at all. It gave her reason to question who Ehlaru once was. She caressed the iron coffer upon the thought, candidly trailing her fingers along its every ridge and trough. She knew whatever was locked within portended his truth.

Agneta withdrew her hand when it lingered for too long and faked the discomfort that came when the stomach struggled to digest something partially raw. She did not wish to divulge its location. Even while having his word, she feared his reaction should he learn its exact location on her person. She brought the same hand upward, coughed, and quietly rasped her throat. The rabbit they'd consumed the prior night gave a little plausibility to the ruse.

Ehlaru never relented in his silence, but he cantered forward to draw beautiful Solveig beside her dun Greyjka. Solveig, the beautiful black horse, a daughter of two worlds. Solveig, the steed she'd been denied, ridden by the man whose only reason for passing through Dekryl was her and her alone. Fitting were the twists of Fate's Weave. Hers was befallen to unrequited passion arisen amidst her escape from an arranged marriage, and the yearn grew ever stronger with each day they silently rode on.

Pulling a flask from a sack draped over Solveig's right shoulder, Ehlaru popped the lid and offered her its contents. Agneta gratefully accepted. Smelling the opening, she perceived a minted flavor, then drank the tonic in a single swoop. The earthen mixture combined spearmint, chicory, and other bile suppressants all stirred into a sweet, orange extract of cloudberries. It tasted good enough, but it did little for her unassailed gut.

Upon returning the flask, she spared him a smile, but he did not lend her one in return. Not acknowledging her at all, he resealed the flask and returned it to the sack.

Agneta considered coughing, to test how long he would hold before offering it again, but ultimately decided against it. No need to provoke him further, she supposed. She would just speak for them both.

"We're a day and a half's ride from my home, even as weighted as the horses are. The broken path forces every rider to carry the same speed," she stated while pointing down the beaten, earthen slopes that looked to be born of nothing more than goats.

Agneta watched Ehlaru survey the land, his eyes trailing along the path and then climbing up the slopes. Trees perished, and truthfully, they were quite sparse all around. In their sylvan stead grew a field of frosted grasses, budding lavenders, and mauve-petal flowers that clung to the descent and sparse crag. Snow escaped the Range of Valdhaz by way of a little creek that wove through the lumpy foothills. The creek then fed into a modest Vale of the Eversong. High timber swept west of the vale, rising beside the ravined edge of the swollen fjord.

They rode on without exchanging another word. An astonishing valedictory of steely clouds opened the world above them. The sky, which had thus far refused to relinquish its dour, divulged vibrant colors with unchallenged brightness. Mist evaporated off the rocky pond at the center of the Vale of the Eversong as if touched by the wings of Valkyrie.

Agneta halted and Ehlaru halted beside her, albeit both for entirely different reasons. Beauty and splendor enraptured her world. Ehlaru studied the land restlessly as was his custom. He softened amidst his musings, then his face danced between numerous, imperceptible excitements with the passing of his every thought. She drowned within his countenance from a world away.

Ehlaru noticed her lingering gaze, adorned sterling diffidence, and averted his. "It will rain by day's end. We should set camp once we've passed that Vale of the Eversong, ascended the foothills beyond, and ridden past the right side of this fjord."

After a brief, baffled pause, Agneta inquired, "Why do you think I'm not leading us left toward the adjacent fjord?"

"I know," he answered with a brevity she so rued.

"Stopping early would lengthen this journey by a half day at least. How do you even know it's going to rain?!"

Ehlaru betrayed nothing but a stark, stoic silence as refined as these grassland mountains mostly devoid of spring's tenderest touch. The ranger deeply respired, parting his lips to taste the cool air with a flick of his tongue. She choked down a giggle that sought to escape her throat. Imperturbably, the wind shifted up the mountains, and Ehlaru closed his lips around a prolonged gust of wind escaping the sea.

"I can taste it in the air," he specified at the death of the wind. "This journey has only begun, and with you I now think it will last forever."

Solveig lingered with the faintest effort before duly carrying the ranger forward toward his embittered prophecy of forthcoming rain.

Agneta did not immediately follow. Her stomach genuinely ached. She swallowed hard, then looked to the sky where the clouds were closing around them again. Perhaps the sun would not break through this day. Perhaps there was merit in Ehlaru's prediction.

Damn the bastard. Ehlaru owed her his promises no matter how much of the 'journey' remained. She decided she no longer regretted her actions that brought him here and trailed him to the northeast. They rode through the Vale of the Eversong of forgotten fae, climbed the dimpled foothills coated in lavender fields, and galloped to the right side of the fjord where the Jüteheln crashed into the Nordland's farthest reach while the mood soured more than her face.

Ehlaru lazed beneath his bivouac through the day's dwindling light. Agneta brooded in her own separate encampment. In hindsight, he realized he had delivered an unnecessary slight arisen from a poignant weakness he'd yet failed to abolish within himself. He swaddled a grudge against her, one which he needed to displace for his sanity and cordiality's sake.

He did not realize his mistake until he received the same silent treatment he'd wantonly brandished against her in the prior days. Seeing was enough to know. Knowing was enough to understand. Understanding was enough to admit that he had gone a bit too far. In the meantime, he banished himself to a slightly separate encampment. His own brooding gave the perception that he pondered his mistake. Agneta was a clever, astute woman, and Ehlaru believed in time she would recognize his prudent appeal.

Opposite of the prior fjord they crossed, they camped within a rocky ledge overhung by two tall, tunneled arches of ocean whipped rock. The white diorite gifted them pristine protection from the assailing elements. Ehlaru found it quite cozy. The arches gave cover from the coming rain, and they lay far enough above the raging sea to be safe from all but the most horrendous of ocean gales. He predicted none would roll off the Jüteheln. They were neither within the season nor stricken by weather that could sustain them. The wind alone battered his conscience, carrying the acrimonious songs of his life's every mistake.

Greyjka mirrored his master's dourness by sporadically neighing his frustrations. Once Ehlaru grew tired of his judgments, his annoyance swollen beyond its tolerable peak, he rose to offer the horse a solution. He refastened Solveig to the rocks beside the draught-fjord. The dull horse won a great victory this day. Greyjka was far beneath the midnight mare whose company he now shared.

While Ehlaru was in route to reclaiming the comfort of his fur blankets, Agneta mildly surprised him with her determination to speak. "How did you know the path forward before I shared it?"

Clicking, then cooing to conciliate their steeds, she scowled after he made no effort to speak.

Sighing, Ehlaru professed, "It's something I simply learned to interpret."

Unenthused, Agneta urged, "Aye, Ehlaru, of course you somehow do, but *how* is what I now want to know!"

He leaned against the comfort of his pelts and subtly smirked.

"No you will answer me this, damn you! I've waited too long to show you the results of all your training and all my hardships for you to waive me off like a silly pup."

"I do not think you silly."

"Then answer me, damn you, or else your silence speaks louder than your words."

Sighing, Ehlaru withdrew from comfort to engage a long string of concessions that would not end on anyone's account except for his. "If what you won't admit is that you believe I have stalked your new home, then you are wrong. I've only been to the Nordland thrice, and each time toward a destination nowhere close to where we are."

"So you deduced where I live from where you have been and have yet to find me," she resolved with absolute certitude.

"Not quite," he stymied wryly.

She huffed in mock fatigue. "Then how?"

"I followed where the path leads in spirit," he admitted, to which, with an innocent smile, she shied away. He concluded after a bout of uncertainty, "I see its spirit like I see yours, and in knowing those both for as long as I have, it did not require much thought."

"I found it by mistake, you know," she attested after enjoying a self-contented pause. Fluttering her eyelids while she reminisced, she sustained, "I fashioned a repulsive little shack closer to Langreklif when I first arrived. The althing of Woten, which lies two fjords to the west, gave me the earliest of my contracts. Slay those fae who dwell within the vale we passed earlier today. The Fates Three must have bestowed me that task because they imagined me landing here above anywhere else."

Ehlaru observed her concertedly, then leaned forward to surrender some interest in her tale. "We never consciously seek our own Fate's Weave because they're never what we expect them to be. Perhaps the Fates Three did desire your path to lead you here. What became of the fae? There were no signs of any as we passed through that vale…"

"Hmmm. They must have kept themselves hidden because they could smell us brooding from leagues away."

"Hmmm." Ehlaru grinned, finding her insult to be fair.

"I never killed the fae, if that is what you're implying. I simply struck a deal and returned to Woten with faux earthen corpses the village's althing did not deign to question."

"Why did the village's althing pay to send your knives that way?"

"A prospector said the mud runts and rock pygmies who dwelt within the vale entombed his son's feet in the shallow pond from which he drank. He claimed they tore his son apart with their river stones in an savage show."

"River stones?" Ehlaru questioned, disbelieving the man's story without a need for them to have even met.

"My response exactly. The prospector and his son were returning from

215

a mining run on the borders of Dwevland. He was otherwise brash and ecstatic about his hauls of dwarven mountain gold, considering the very recent murder of his son."

"And the fae's rebuttal?" Ehlaru urged her on.

"The only truthful tale of them all. Without a single appeal, they unearthed the boy's body from where they'd hidden it within the pond. He was a corpse before their river stones had marred his flesh and bones. He'd passed through Death's Arch with his father's seax buried in his back. The fae stated it was for simply partitioning a portion of the stolen gold so he could leave and start a new life with a Woten girl he adored."

"Providential," Ehlaru sourly admitted. "I cannot recall when last I heard the fae speak the righteous truth."

Solemnly, Agneta swore, "They are more right than you would care to admit, Ehlaru. Without their honest interference, I would have never found a reason to slit his throat before returning his stolen gold to the Frosthammer dwarves."

Agneta had exacted justice no differently than he would have, and for it, Ehlaru surrendered his pride. "I believe we are at a convergence in the land, are we not?" he openly digressed.

"We're upon a terrestrial threshold of sorts!" she exclaimed, leaping to her feet and walking to the mouth of the arch where a dying sunset dropped beneath accumulating clouds of storm. "I returned to the vale to report to the fae that justice was served because of them. They thanked me, and we agreed that in the daylight they should become scarce. Next they directed me in the direction of one whom I could bestow Dwevland's stolen gold. We won't travel that far," she firmly stated before lifting two fingers and pointing. "A few more fjord's over, above a hidden cove where Jütejawed seals come to raise their young, I staked my home in the shade of the Valdhaz. There the Nordland, the Dwevland, and the sky itself wedge against the Jüteheln." Ehlaru laughed, to which she pivoted with concerted fury. "Why do you think I am joking? It is beautiful, isolate, and pristine!"

"No, Agneta," he contritely corrected. "I am not laughing at anything you have said. I think I know of this place, and of the exquisite beauty it holds that may well echo your own heart's. My mother once told me of such a splendid place, where the moon's Goddess stepped unto Eldaria in her powerful but petite form. I remember it from one of her stories long ago."

Evidently regretful in snapping, Agneta receded to a more tempered poise. "How did she describe it in her story?"

"Ere the Nordland, Soudland, the Ranges of Valdhaz and Tjorden, the Thunder Falls, the Wrathgorne, the Erunheim, Broken Fjords, each jarl's personal holdings, and Halvalkyra itself, there was naught but Dwevland to rule this thundering domain. Before Dwevland rose from the great cataclysm that sparked Goldral the Goddess of the Earth and the Element's reawakening, there was naught but fae folk exchanging their trickeries beneath the wings of massive draconic flights. Your description resonates with that of a land of which my mother spoke that marked the birth of the Stormborne. It sounds as though you have chosen to stake your home where the Crescent Lady, while adorned in her fullest moonlight, shone over an arcane Elder Wyrm and intertwined her soul with his, where he was then chosen to become the Delas of the Moon and the Draconic Father of all the runic gods."

"She must have been a great woman, your mother, to have known any of that in such detail. Mine once told me of Eldrahg's Ascension from Elder Wyrm to the Draconic Father but…never with such finesse, most likely on account of her hailing from the Verdant Forest where everything is apparently stale. Her accounts were always so damned…historical. Your mother's sounds beautiful, and I'm thankful to have heard it," Agneta whispered in a voice that dared to be heard.

Ehlaru answered with solemnity bound only by untouched ache, embalmed in an astral projection, and enwreathed with artificial strength. "She was strong, and she was strong for so many children who never realized they were unworthy of all her sacrifices and all of her love."

CHAPTER NINE

DREAMS OF A QUEEN

A CAUSTIC DRIP DISTILLED OVER RASHA'S tongue. Her breath smelled of the same pungency as flesh blackened by the plague. She awoke in Vel-thaka for perhaps the hundredth time, and in the company of Warlord Yel-jaraht. He had misplaced that touch of age that overripened him, and she wondered how that had come to pass. She vexed to ask where it had fluttered off or how he'd stayed the hand of maturation, but her words did not reach him. Her words were not her own, at least not presently. She dwelt within a dream, or at least that is what Rasha chose to believe.

They spoke at length, Yel-jaraht and she, while she observed the conversation unfold from her mind's eye. The sensation spooked her. Her will was not actually her own. Was she actually dreaming, wandering the ethereal spirit realm?

She awoke many times, riding the trails of dust her mental insolvency shed and sailing into the next construct she dreamt. She could feel her body, the soft emanation of its warmth, and the pressure of the clothes adorning her form. Was it real? Or the trappings of a fickle mind? Or the trickery of Voodandum's more pensive goddess? Or the remembrance of life forgone to time? Feckless to stop it, she turned her attention to Yel-jaraht.

"The vanguard and I shall ride for Gara-thandila tomorrow. I expect our passage to be swift," the warlord contemplated as he poured himself a cup of fermented anje root tea.

He offered some to Rasha, which she kindly refused. The Witchqueen instead indulged herself to a small handful of nuts hidden within her robes. She did not partake in alcohol outside the confines of Voodandum's rituals.

Every sip stifled her mind and irreversibly soured her mood. She preferred a clear head, always. Without it, she was at the mercy of her primality and the emotions tangled within the webs wreathed around her soul.

"There'll be roving bandits along the roads. The collapse of Zun-jish's guard forsakes all travelers, from the common troll to Vel-thaka's warlord. Do not tempt fate, Yel-jaraht. Bring da whole horde."

"And leave the brim of da Endless Wastes vulnerable to jütengolk frost giants and their beasts of old?! I would rather leave our empire's fate in the hands of the plague…"

"Then I'll be drawing a ritual to bequeath da Dark Moon to afflict every bandit along the southern Fulklar Road before you depart."

"That is not wise, young Witchqueen, especially when it is your name that is afflicted by the Crimson Curse. It be betta for you to reserve yourself to finding a cure instead of deepening the Warlord Prince's rumors."

Rasha studied her surroundings and the room's grungy contents. The space had been arrogated for Yel-jaraht's council of war, of which none of the other trollish warlords yet knew existed. Scrolls lay in heaps. Tablets were piled high. A motley assortment of the city's pleas for aid, aid which Rasha and the warlord were both irresolute to provide. Coffers once bearing the contents of Yel-jaraht's taxes and conquests were trimmed with the sleek of cobwebs. Burden, pride, and devotion had drained the warlord of his wealth. Vel-thaka's public treasury had fallen upon similarly hard times, and even Voodandum itself strained beneath the requisite to aid those trolls afflicted by the Crimson Curse.

"None know how this plague wracking the empire was born. Still," she vehemently implored, "I advise you to not yet travel to its murky source."

Yel-jaraht rebuked, "I will not be dissuaded by the fear of that which I cannot control."

"Fear of the uncontrollable makes us all the wiser. It be the most dangerous adversary of them all. Besides, this be no time for Vel-thaka to sit bereft of its warlord."

"Hmph," grumbled the warlord of the city Rasha loved. Yel-jaraht glazed her with his focus before twisting it skyward and relinquishing a snide smile. "Many Garathandi warn me the same. They claim a young Witchqueen will seize the city the moment I leave. Rhak-jan claims you seek to seize the Throne of the Riven Moon and rule over the empire itself."

Yel-jaraht riled her guts. A ball of fury rose to settle in the back of her throat. The air grew cold around her, accentuating the potency of the anger screaming to be let loose. The feeling was palpable, a genuine reflection of herself over which she had not control. What right did this warlord have to summon her to his private counsel to then batter her name and heart's rapport. None! Yet, Yel-jaraht did not appear to have intended conveying such a vile, careless remark. Her vision blurred in confusion. Had her vision blurred so long ago when first she lived this moment? Had it blurred from the anger rearisen from where it had been buried ages ago?

"I digress," the warlord continued after permitting her to clamor at length within herself. "I do not agree with them. I never have. This does not mean I trust you completely, Witchqueen, nor does it mean we are friends."

Rasha arched her back, filling the space around her as she pulled her shoulders back. "Do not mistake my familiarity. I claim no friendships with men."

Yel-jaraht grinned once o'er before answering her quip. "I can tell, but I don't care. You serve the Garathandi, and you will counsel with me when asked. Now tell me, Rasha," provoked the warlord in a vaguely deleterious tone. "What will Vel-thaka do if 'roving bandits' slay this dated troll?"

"I digress," she answered wryly. "We know they will not. You would sooner lose your head to the Warlord Prince for entering Gara-thandila with empty pockets than to bandits along the southern Fulklar Road."

"And should I fail to yield to the Warlord Prince's taxes, and should he carve out my tusks to mount as grisly tokens, what then?"

"You have no heir. You have delegated none to succeed you. A battle would ensue for control over Vel-thaka. Whoever stands atop the mounds of corpses would be named our next warlord."

"You preserve our history and traditions. Moudula strove to swot away that antique of da past. Does it suit you, sullying her life's intentions, or is it her footsteps you follow now?"

"I have a choice!" Rasha contended. "Every Witchqueen does…"

"What choice?" he rasped firm.

"I either follow in the footsteps of the empire, or I follow in the footsteps of she who led Voodandum before me. Either way, tradition is maintained."

Yel-jaraht contorted his face, his mind seeming to delve into the lines between absurdity and reason from whence her voice came. She meant for him to dwell there, though with no concern for how long he chose to reside. Having only recently acquisitioned the position of Witchqueen, her encounters with warlords numbered starkly few. Initially, she'd assumed Yel-jaraht's recess was borne of a slow mind. She'd modified her debilitating view with successive experiences and now understood the wisest trolls always afforded ample rumination before speaking at all.

Yel-jaraht stated, "Our right of succession is to survive slaughter, borne of barbaric avarice, until he who stands uncontested by the masses is crowned their next warlord beside the corpses of his mightiest kin. This tradition is what makes us Garathandi. Without it, we very well might have regressed into the stupor of a Stormborne mountain troll. Still…tradition is never absolute. You see it the same as Moudula once did. Good."

"The empire be destroying itself from within. We don't need to expedite that process by giving Vel-thaka a reason to destroy itself as well!"

Curiously, Yel-jaraht adjusted his measure so Rasha need not bear the burden of concern alone. "*That* will not come to pass, so long as I keep my head." The warlord gestured, chopping toward his neck before touching two fingers to his forehead.

"Forsake the Warlord Prince as he has forsaken his people by ravaging us with brutality and taxes without enacting measures to cease their mounting deaths. Don't be letting your head fall beside the rest!"

"I will not yield that promise. I march afront Vel-thaka's vanguard out of tradition alone. I will decide the purpose of my visit upon witnessing the situation in Gara-thandila myself."

"Why salvage Gara-thandila when it cannot be saved? Preserve Vel-thaka and the rest of your empire inst—"

"My empire?" Yel-jaraht interrupted with an air of intrigue.

"Garathandi is an empire whose glory and well-being befalls us all."

"Awww," the warlord conceded. He fingered the hair on his chin and brushed aside the dust collected on his tusks. "If I choose not to go, Zun-jish would march out to meet me while he sends his dogs to Domildin and Bulkarat. My pride would lure opportunistic eyes from beyond our borders. What would we do then, when Stormborne ships filled to the brim with Bjardja and the hooves of Helmyan horses cross into our lands en masse while we fight amongst ourselves?"

"It be our pride—yours, mine, every troll's in the empire! We manage one foe at a time. We face them together. Vel-thaka, Domildin, and Bul-karat against Zun-jish and his two raving dogs. Together or not at all."

Yel-jaraht straightened, splaying his posture to mock his previous grandeur. His was the hoary yet riveting figure of the warlord who'd sacked the fjord fortress of Langreklif. The umber-tusked troll's visage studied Rasha. From this vision of her past, she then recognized something previously unseen and starkly frightening. Yel-jaraht's eyes hung somberly, not due to regret of her counsel but with pride for how she meant to rule the Garathandi's world.

Without an indication he was prepared to speak, Yel-jaraht reaffirmed, "I will go to the Warlord Prince, although I do not feign to know what dis will entail."

Rasha stiffened, shuffled to reposition, and accidentally scuffed her seat over the floor. "If my counsel counts for so little, why was I summoned to speak at all?"

Her need for an answer was utterly rabid like the hunger of Geimelgarr mountain trolls. The Witchqueen pounced to her feet, thrusting aside her chair. She grimaced within herself, for her people's opinions held so little worth. In her past self, Rasha had witnessed an unrefined merit. Her soul burned like cold ire, an unrefined ore that could not bend without breaking. The sole difference between her and her people was that their ire burned hotter than the sun.

"I've hearkened your words, but I require more to act on than good faith alone," said Yel-jaraht.

They shared an awkward silence, neither deigning to speak before the other. Yel-jaraht grumbled, and Rasha reminisced of the curses she had wished to fling his direction. She might have even heard one slip past the threshold of her fastly wavering tongue. No, she thought that last one too. In her present state of mind, no less.

"Your counsel be valuable. Even though I cannot act upon your conscience, I still agree with it. Vel-thaka cannot survive without great leaders—the empire even more. We are dying, we do not know why, and we are powerless to make it stop! The Garathandi require strength and resolve if we are to survive, so I will name no heir. We will discuss that matter after I return, and you will lead Vel-thaka until then."

"It cannot be," Rasha coldly rebuked. With no grip upon her soul, the tantalizations of power did not lure her. "I have led no cities nor hordes of trolls. You risk inciting the wrath of the Loa and the Warlord Prince by bequeathing the Vel-thaka to Voodandum. We are meant to guide and preserve the Garathandi Empire with the magics of the Dream Walker and of the Dark and the Bright Moons, not lead the masses through witless wars."

Yel-jaraht betrayed no emotion when he laconically replied, "It be written the witches, warlocks, and voodoo priests of yore were once the mightiest in the Garathandi's hordes. They fought and bled beside the hordes as we carved out this empire in the frozen north."

Rasha swallowed the tactlessness of her instinctual response like poorly fermented anje root tea. "Those were dire times, more demanding than the ones we currently be living. I know the story of Witchqueen Vutuala, who led the First Warlord Garatha and his discordant exiles to this hoary place after ripping it apart from the hold of frost giants and men. I reject the notion that be the path we must take!" How easily she was riled. How easily she beguiled herself.

Yel-jaraht grimaced, then took his turn at boasting riled might. "The empire be dying, to this hoary land, to the hostilities we exchange with our neighbors, to this dreadful plague the Warlord Prince and his wolfhounds dubbed the Crimson Curse. I fear da time of da Garathandi troll be ending. Our people's future has never been more dire than it be now!"

Rasha returned, "My first duty is to preserve our culture through Voodandum, and my second be to honor the Loa who share in our might and plights. I cannot bear the burdens of this city without sacking my greater calling and abandoning Voodandum's ancient charge."

Yel-jaraht inexorably continued, "And whose legacy will be left for you to preserve? Who will be left to revere the Loa if this plague consumes us all? Voodandum is no closer to finding a cure. Only you will be left to preserve the festering rubble."

"You speculate we will not find a cure or some way to prevent its spread?!"

"You speculate we can…" Yel-jaraht inhaled deeply, leaving his cheeks terribly gaunt. He exhaled the impatience that overtook him and spoke his peace. "This plague has only just arrived. We are no closer to curing it than when it first wracked Gara-thandila. It be good that is where it's mostly stayed, but Gara-thandila cannot bleed and blacken forever. Eventually, Zun-jish and its people will clamor our way."

"I have my suspicions," Rasha confessed. "But no. We are no closer to finding a cure." The mere statement convoked ruination on her reign. Their eyes met beyond the surcease, and only then did she ask, "How long will you be gone?"

"I do not yet know," Yel-jaraht replied.

Provokingly, Rasha pressed, "Then strive to present me with your closest estimate."

"Until the next Bright Moon, should the journey be blessed. Many more if war erupts."

"Do not give me your drunken guesses. Should I agree to this, Voodandum has all but officially sided with what you intend to enact."

"I expected the Witchqueen of Voodandum to respect my pious answer."

"To earn my respect," Rasha growled, "you must first earn my trust."

"You want to trust me, Rasha? What reason do I have to trust you?" Yel-jaraht's questions tumbled with a savage, potent vigor, one which he'd never displayed to her before then.

"Zun-jish has never questioned my loyalty to the empire, only my honor for his lack of a functioning head. We've both openly spoke of sedition, yet here I sit and listen still."

Yel-jaraht sat silent, pondering his thoughts. Of the empire's seven warlords, he was likely the most introspective one. It had been as clear to her then as it was in this redolent dreamscape that she'd made a fateful mistake that day. She had not learned to respect him until after he had marched away.

Graying hair rose with each massive breath, and Yel-jaraht studied her hard. There was no price with which Rasha could be bought as a trollish warrior was. Yel-jaraht understood that clear as the crystalline deposits lining the Ralcrav. She admitted, across both banks of the river time's, Yel-jaraht did a fine job pursuing her commitment via an alternate approach.

"Five years I've committed to Beh'kliar's cause. If the war persists for any longer, I will surrender for our legacy's sake."

Rasha's eyes widened in disbelief before she tightened them in quick repose. "Then you are not alone?"

"I will lead in the light of the Bright Moon for those who must remain obscured by the Dark Moon. Mammotte and his herds must protect the

Fulklar Foothills from the east. Hulvassa must hold the Frallheim's northern trickles. They alone bar the jütengolk in the Endless Wastes from wandering into our lands. Bul-karat and Domildin must shield the south from the Helmyan horsemen, and should those massive armies gathered outside the Great Gates bring the runic folk to heel, we must be certain our southern borders will hold if their desirous gaze turns to us. Who else be left but Velthaka to pounce Zun-jish's forces without sabotaging our entire empire?! If the people revile Zun-jish as much as Beh'kliar claims, we will seize da Everdark City before the next Bright Moon gleams."

"It is true," Rasha confessed off a sore tongue. "Beh'kliar would be surrounded by Zun-jish, Ruh'rehm, and Rhak-jan all. Kuro-kal would surely fall."

"I must march, with or without your blessing," muttered Yel-jaraht.

"Five years then," Rasha tentatively promised. "I will commit five years alone."

Humored, pleased, delighted, and evidently more, Yel-jaraht questioned, "And after five?"

"If we have not won Gara-thandila, if the plague has only grown…I will implore Zun-jish to seek a truce. In the aftermath of your victory or surrender, we'll find time to speak on the matter of Garathandi succession and the future of the empire further."

"I will send a message to Warlord Beh'kliar with the answer you have given."

"No, Yel-jaraht. I will acquaint myself with this fellow conspirator myself. I need to know who I am to work with from the shadows of the far north."

"Then to the Garathandi Empire, to the Dark and the Bright Moons, and the end of Zun-jish's Crimson Curse," Yel-jaraht swore, slamming a freshly poured cup of fermented anje root tea and offering her another, then slamming it down when she stalwartly refused.

CHAPTER TEN

PUPS OF WAR

H IS UNREMITTING JOURNEY HAD EXHAUSTED Ehlaru to his core. The preceding weeks had merely granted him a breather from actual respite, but the cool wind that whipped his face was a relief he was eager to oblige.

The Jüteheln's foam wrapped around his face before lulling over the fjord. Torn at the edges, the mists effervesced between sea and sky, showering the fjord's ledge like blankets of silk hanging from an unmade bedstead. The sky-held waters glistened with the indomitable hue of golden magnificence as they rolled into the Jüteheln. The mists sank into seafoam swept off land to dissolve into an exotic array of color. The Jüteheln wolfed down the golden rolls. Sweet relief overcame him at the sight of a sky-piercing longhouse striking through the morning's dew atop fields of snowcrest galiants that climbed the cliffs of the adjacent fjord.

"By the heart of Hælla Dwolv, I've never seen him shed his morning blanket to Sjógurn so quickly!" exclaimed Agneta.

"Really?" Ehlaru teased while he steadied his lungs. "If I were the runic god, I would be ecstatic to rid myself of the wet wrap I awoke to every morning."

"You're not a runic god, Ehlaru." Agneta smirked. "Perhaps the sensation suits him better than us humans could ever comprehend."

"If it suits him so well, why not wear the blanket the entire day, water your flowers a bit longer, and blind the sun for all but one day of a twelve day week? If this truly is Hælla Dwolv, he has stirred particularly early to outpace Sjógurn."

Flustered, Agneta feigned impatience at his joke with a huff. "I know it's not actually the runic god. It just seems so much more beautiful than the actual answer to what we're seeing."

Endeavoring to expand upon the awe the air suspended, Ehlaru explained, "I think hidden somewhere within that truth, there is room for Hælla Dwolv and Sjógurn still."

"Really," Agneta challenged wryly. "You are the biggest critic of the runic gods and the pantheon above them that I know. Do you have a story for how Sjógurn and Hælla Dwolv came to detest each other, or are you just biding your time until you finally recall the force of weather that caused the fog to roll?"

"I disapprove of the mysticism, circularity, and bombastic nature of divinity, but it does not mean I think them false."

Solveig shuffled beneath him, recognizing his tongue's superfluous calling, sensing the nerve the memory struck, and reminding him of both with a bump of her arse.

Ehlaru switched pace to share his thoughts in a manner more whimsical and controlled. There was no pressing need, but he was enjoying Agneta's company quite a lot. "They have a more daunting and well defined purpose than our mother's stories might steer us to believe. I would not jump to conclusions, but there is a reason behind everything in life yet unexplained."

Her captivation was instantly obvious from the suppressed awe her face sustained. She proffered him a devious grin while replying, "Well, if this is indeed Hælla Dwolv shaving his stumpy legs in the morning, I hope he hears how I have preferred Sjógurn's company far more than his as of late. At least the runic god of the seas feeds me through the winter!" she yelled ecstatically across the morning.

"It's not Hælla Dwolv's fault that Freyja's scorn left him with sores on his arse where nothing can ever grow."

Apparently peering through his contrived dryness, Agneta punched his arm. "Are you saying I picked shit land to live on, or are you trying to offend *every* runic god this morning?" Sarcasm rolled over her tongue like waves against fjord cliffs.

Ehlaru realized he had actually missed her capriciousness, and her lip brought him to smile. "It's not as comparatively rich and fertile as the Soudland, but it's quality land…for the historic factor alone," he conferred.

"You might be the better ranger, but I've lived in the Stormlands for longer than you. There is nothing fulsome or fertile about any of the high country…Nordland, Soudland, and Dwevland too."

Ehlaru chuckled at the veracity of that statement before reminding her there were plentiful bounties, even here, if one simply knew where to look. "I had a thriving fish farming enterprise in the works, but I think they will all be dead by the time I finally return."

"Thriving because of Sjógurn. Definitely not because of Hælla Dwolv," Agneta insisted, wagging a finger to solidly reaffirm her prior point.

"Does that make Sjógurn the lord of lakes? Does he rule over rivers, creeks, and ponds too?"

"You were catching salmon, were you not? Salmon live in the oceans, which definitely make their harvest one of his blessings."

"They're born upriver," he argued, curious to see how far their debate could feasibly unfold. "That counts for more than where they live thereon."

Agneta's nostrils flared as she exhaled, "I think who we are and what we become holds a little more value than who we *once* were."

"If that were true, we wouldn't be rangers," he stated bluntly, realizing the harshness of the statement as soon as it left his tongue.

Agneta recoiled, but to his relief the comment did not inflict everlasting damage. "There is something besides gods we think differently on after all."

"I was beginning to worry you and I were a little too alike," he ameliorated.

Her mood perking amidst a clandestine epiphany of knowledge, she quickly exclaimed, "It must be some consequence of where you were raised, because in the Stormlands, all anybody cares about is what you are destined for. They are far duller and more pious in Helmya, or maybe you are from one of the kingdoms on the mainland, or perhaps the High East…"

The manner in which she'd drawled over "High East" caused Ehlaru to skip an entire breath.

Seemingly invigorated, Agneta ceased adding speculations to her list.

He sighed, speculating if he gave no response, in her curiosity she would relent.

"I knew you were from the High East before you made yourself a ranger! What were you then…Lysian? A Baelviche rebel? An Asmoduil slave?" she questioned in a flurry as her zeal shone bare.

How wrong he had been. His silence had only fueled her interest. "What gave it away? I thought it would have taken you longer than five years," he drawled.

"You're too striking yet equally relatable to be from anywhere else," she complimented, flushing blood through his heart and into his head.

"By those standards, I could hail from the Verdant Forest or the sprawling heart of the city of Magnopolis itself."

"Nobody from Magnopolis could survive a single winter this far north, and if you tried to save me from that storm speaking in the accent of an Arcanum lord, I would have sworn you to piss off before dying out of spite."

Ehlaru laughed hysterically. Agneta comfortably joined along. Their mirth conjoined for longer than he expected, but he found it all the more regaling for each spout it withstood.

"Have you ever met someone from the Verdant Forest?" he asked. Agneta frowned, so he appealed for forgiveness for having forgotten it was where her mother was born. "Aside from family, of course?"

"No one besides my mother. I swear I loved her dearly, but most days she was intolerable." Her brows furrowed as if she were recalling memories whose intimacy stung like the cut from a blunted sword. "Avella was rather haughty and could never be proven wrong, which is a curious quality considering how imperious my father was."

A curiosity sparked within Ehlaru. "Jarl Eljak married a lady from the Verdant Forest whose tongue and temper could match his own? Being outwitted by you no longer wounds my pride as much anymore. It was only inevitable, I suppose."

Agneta softened, and her eyes fluttered before she spoke, "I am glad you've finally realized you're the exact variety of cultivated and pompous I am most familiar with."

They approached a waist high hedge of stone, which Ehlaru assumed she'd laid to plot her home.

She continued, "If there's no more hiding the fact that you're an erudite ranger, what is the final verdict on the history of the land?"

"It lies upon a convergence." Ehlaru motioned toward the peninsular fjord three leagues over where he glimpsed a stout little dwarven village. "Settled along the border of Dwevland and the Nordland as well."

"Where they meet with the Jüteheln Sea," Agneta softly remarked, her voice aspiring to reach his mind as its tome dwindled. "I find it more attractive than the Helmyan Sea because it's simply different. The white foams of this cerulean sea glint with an eerie, aqua green whenever beset by the right light. It is so much more striking than plain blue could ever aspire to be."

Ehlaru regarded his companion as she leered over the washing waves. "Perhaps that was why Eldrahg made this his home before he was crowned Monomua's Delas, Draconic Father to all the runic gods, and ruler of Halvalkyra."

Agneta's sapphire eyes trembled, and her face relaxed like a ripened peach. She faced him when she humbly requested, her voice strong before trailing off with the morning breeze, "Let me show you what I've made of it since…"

Ehlaru followed her lead, dismounting Solveig while she slid off Greyjka's back. He followed her through a gate in the stone hedge. Solveig shook her shoulders, and the vibration carried backward across the entirety of her back. The mare neighed in pleasure for having rid herself of his weight. He relinquished a few carrots and kindly stroked her neck.

They persisted, passing a well next to Agneta's longhouse. A thatch roof overhung an open stable, and a single post ran across its full length. The stall was only wide enough to shelter one Greyjka and perhaps another half of a draught-fjord. Agneta did not seem to care as she tied Greyjka to the back of the post. Greyjka stood half exposed to the elements and the beaten brow of the conquered sun. She motioned for Ehlaru to tie Solveig to the front, and he obliged.

Agneta subtly glanced in his direction after entreating his aid. "For Greyjka's sake, we'll need to expand this stable to twice its current length."

Ehlaru did not much appreciate her attempt to garner his aid beyond the boundaries of their agreement. With discretion, he decided not to divulge this. He'd promised Bolveig Svenson he would properly care for Solveig under any circumstances. Agneta had certainly deduced that, or so he presumed, so she'd fashioned a way to benefit from his oath to the expatriated Bjardja lord. He supposed it would be worth the effort since Greyjka's current diminution was not fair by any measure.

Ehlaru moved past his discontent. After unbridling the bags strapped to Solveig, he stashed them beside a door behind the stable addendum and then freed Solveig of her saddle. The mare whinnied in content. He laid the saddle against Greyjka's, along the front wall of Agneta's home and offered Solveig more white carrots, then he fed Greyjka a few as well.

"Afraid the horses might wander off the cliffs if they're not tied down?" he alleged with a half smirk.

"That's exactly how I lost Frida," she stated sternly.

"How did you actually lose Frida?" he questioned in concern.

She adorned something more genuinely dejected before replying, "Jumped the stables in Skraelg and froze to death during that late winter storm before I paid you a visit."

"I am sorry. She was a good mare. I remember the day you bought her well."

"She jumped that damned fence then too! Caused quite the disturbance across town until we finally cornered her. She's the reason why I built this in the first place."

"At least Greyjka is more...docile." Ehlaru glanced to the horse he spoke of that simply stared into the wall.

Agneta glanced at Greyjka and shook her head. "Dull is more accurate, but he is well trained, like I told Boll. So how exactly did you procure Solveig when the turd wouldn't even let me ride him to then ride her at least once?"

Ehlaru's jaw tensed, forehead furrowed, and his voice croaked. "You offered to sleep with the man simply to jaunt his horse?!"

"It was just a joke I passed when all else had failed," Agneta huffed before she chuckled over the severity that had momentarily overwhelmed him.

Stepping apart from the girl to cool his nerves, Ehlaru studied the home she'd built in the four years since departing his tutelage. The cross-beam foundations both lifted the structure and leveled the ground. While the walls were mostly carved from a stoneskin pine more common to the Nordland, logs of blue-spruce patterned each face also. He counted two entrances and three windows in locations correspondingly similar to his own abode. It stretched longer, stood a floor taller, and boasted a roof with a classic design that pierced the sky at both sides. The roof extended into the ground on the opposite side of the stables to form a modest kennel from where he heard the whimpers of wolfhounds.

"I think we bonded, him and I," he commented while glancing to her again. "But perhaps he simply prefers the company of men."

Humored, Agneta replied, "I doubt it." She cocked a brow on a capricious whim.

"Actually, I do recall Lord Bolveig sharing a vivid account of the best woman he ever took to bed."

"You pigs!" Agneta interjected after stamping down her foot. "Even you, as I would have never guessed!" She gave him no time to respond before circling to the back of her home. "Come on, Ehlaru, or do you not wish to meet the reasons why you're here?!"

Ehlaru hummed a somber tune, conjecturing how he could be held at fault for something he had never said. Agneta regarded him too highly. Most women did. He supposed her scorn would always befall him if ever he digressed from her perceptions of him. He should have begun their relationship by actually acting like more of a pig. Also, had she not just shared how she'd offered to sleep with the man in the slim chance that he might loan out his horse afterward? What acute hypocrisy at its finest.

He trailed her to the kennel that housed two young Garathandi wolfhounds. They remained astoundingly quiet through the noise of their arrival. Once they caught sight of their master, however, their patience rivaled a drunk's whose empty cup had been scorned a refill. The two adolescent wolfhounds, who had outlived the majority of their puppy years, wrestled with each other in excitement while dashing toward the opened kennel gate.

Their legs were long and lanky, but they had not yet filled out to match their grayish blue-tinged paws. Long, muscular chests surged with each breath taken as they jumped into Agneta. They were tall but still growing and would eventually take on commanding figures she could not physically support should they not learn to control their urges. Gentle when stroked, fierce when provoked, the wolfhounds licked her enthusiastically.

"Obryn is the larger of the two, the one with the umber fur. Grist boasts more of a tame, stone-spruce color, and he's sweeter than his older brother."

Agneta knelt beside her wolfhounds and calmed them by caressing their scruffy manes.

Ehlaru decided to approach, edging closer with short, gentle strides meant to obscure that resolute approach.

Obryn, who had been maintaining a keen eye on the stranger in his master's home, strutted afront Agneta to bar Ehlaru's approach. Grist mirrored his brother but came much closer before reeling to a halt.

Bending to his knees, Ehlaru unadorned his hood and then patted his thigh, tempting Grist to come closer.

Grist's ears flipped over, and he looked toward Agneta, toward his brother, then to Ehlaru once more. Obryn whined, begging Grist to withdraw. His plea went unanswered. Disappointed, Obryn bounced back into his kennel, sinking like a sack of wet sand. Grist sauntered forward and stamped his paw into Ehlaru's right boot. The wolfhound then speedily withdrew to playfully stomp on Ehlaru's other foot. Ehlaru smiled, finding some innocence in the gesture, and Grist's shoulders relaxed. Ehlaru gradually reached out to stroke Grist's shoulder in three leisured passes. He withdrew, relinquishing the wolfhound an opportunity to consider his touch. Grist decided he rather adored it and jumped against his chest. Ehlaru caught the wolfhound mid pounce and judiciously guided him back to the ground. He rolled two fingers behind the young wolfhound's ears, scratched the top of its head, and Grist's tongue lulled out in content.

"Like I said," Agneta interjected while petting a sulking Obryn in long sweeps. "Grist is the sweeter of the two, and Obryn knows you are a pig."

"A friendly swine at that," Ehlaru commented as Grist rolled against his legs. "They are definitely older than pups, but adolescent for certain."

"I've been enjoying their youth since I first found them starving by their mother's corpse. They were the only two who survived the winter after she died defending them from wolves."

Ehlaru scrunched the back of Grist's neck when he became overexcited. "How long ago was that? Could you guess how old they were then?"

"Three seasons. They could not have been alive for more than one."

"Well," Ehlaru rejoined, "you saved them soon enough. They likely think of you as their only mother. They never had the chance to capture the heart of the wild. Easy enough to refine."

He grinned when she was not looking, then tossed it away when Obryn rejoined them. Grist absconded to return to his mother's hand. The wolfhounds curled into each other's comfort, and Obryn regarded Ehlaru again with nervous, prying interest.

"Why name them Grist and Obryn instead of something less conspicuous?"

"Conspicuous?" Agneta responded with feigned modesty. "They're good names! Obryn befell me one day on a whim, and I once met a Grist I liked well enough."

"Don't pretend they are not analogous to your brother's names."

Agneta rolled her eyes in abject irritation and answered him much the same, "They might be similar, but they are certainly not the same! Why does it matter?" she exacerbated. "Who here will ever hear me call their names?"

"They tie you to your old life. That makes them an exploitable liability should the wrong, clever man ever hear their names."

Her nostrils flared. "You are right," Agneta savaged with mock credence. "That's exactly why I gave them those names. I will not be reprimanded for missing the parts of my life I neither fled nor wished to escape. Caring is not my weakness—it is yours for not loving anything. They could be named moon and stone and would still be my weakness, and that is a choice I've happily made!"

"Nobody looks twice at the dog named moon or the horse named Greyjka, but meet the mare named Solveig, whose beauty was said to rival Freyja's own, and one begins questioning who her rider was and all efforts toward secrecy are effectively nulled."

A vein flared in Agneta's neck as a voice indulged with repugnance cynically instructed, "Help me train them well, and neither of us will ever have reason to worry."

Ehlaru mumbled, "It's like arguing with the wind." Unreservedly disappointed, he then moved to recover the important half of his belongings.

"Where are you going?" Agneta cried out as he strode to the corner of her land closest to Dwevland.

"To set my camp," Ehlaru barked back before avowing not to speak again that day.

<hr />

Men always alleged luck only came from the unexpected strike of chance occurrence. They considered its passage the providence of bygone spirits, the Fates Three, and deities. Luck was difficult, took time to garner, but was anything but accidental. Luck possessed a malleability that warm hands could mold, and to control its issuance depended entirely on the wit of the one who summoned it forth. Each hand dispensed its own luck. Each hand was luck's true maker. Agneta had recklessly dispensed hers, and she now understood it would take time to fashion more.

They returned to not speaking, for in defending the names she'd given her pups, Agneta had panged his personality's weakest chord. On certain unpredictable things, Ehlaru loathed being challenged. Whenever he lost or lost interest in an argument at which he had thrown his entire stock, Ehlaru would retreat into a shell of silence like a turtle. She swore he was as excessively stubborn as any woman, that his mother must be the Elder Wyrm Ísvalar for him to constantly behave in such an infuriating manner.

His insufferable silence and self-torture would at least not stifle their agreement. The ranger was true to his word. He would not leave until Grist and Obryn had been mastered by his hand, then hers. With some regret but not enough to entice she relent, Agneta turned his own honorable dedications against him by contracting his skills for personal benefit.

It began with the stone hedge that marked her stake of the land. By way of her own indomitable determination, Agneta had successfully trained her wolfhounds to never jump it. Still, she'd failed in deterring them from simply walking through any of the ungated entrances whenever a particularly fascinating bird flew overhead. Grist, evidently excited with her return, sprinted through one of those open egresses on a whim, sparking an exhaustive chase. Agneta failed to catch him, permitting him to taunt her with his novel freedom from afar when she began addressing the issue at hand. Ehlaru cornered Grist upon his return from hunting for hares to find her fashioning a gate. Her feigned frustrations lured the ranger toward aiding in the construction of the next two. How lucky for her.

A few days passed, and her ruse bled a few chores deeper. Ehlaru always addressed the abuses by recusing himself to a new hunt each day. His discomfort was obvious, but in irritation, Agneta refused to make a change. It felt swell. If she couldn't dance with the ranger beneath the midnight moon, she would at least reap their situation of all its worth.

Together they extended the makeshift stable to provide the horses with more spacious living quarters. Agneta worried her luck would find absolution because it did not necessarily abet Grist or Obryn. Fortunately, Solveig's ease of living served as an adequate substitute in ensnaring his assistance. She appreciated the midnight mare all the more for it.

"Hand me the last of those planks," she requested from above while setting wood into the extended roof's frame.

Ehlaru handed up each plank in quick, successive throws. She laid them against one another until the stable roof was enclosed. Knotting the corners with rope, she nailed them down firm. Another task completed, not another word really spoken between them, and she deviously pondered what chore she should lay before them next.

After some thought, she softly questioned, "How much thatching is left behind my house?"

Ehlaru lumbered off to retrieve a bundle of hay. Upon returning, the fuming ranger tossed her the stacks without a word.

She spread the thatching over the roof, pressing it firmly against the planks, then tied down the thatch roofing with rope and descended to the ground elegantly. "Well," she idly remarked, "there's a few nearby fields we can reap tomorrow to gather more plant fiber to finish thatching the roof."

"You can go alone."

As to not overexert his diminished patience, Agneta ploddingly responded, "It would be quicker if the both of us went together."

"Do it yourself. It will give me more time to attend to the reason I am actually here," he sharply stymied.

"I would like to be here to learn when we do begin," Agneta nimbly argued, to which his temper piqued.

"Then remain and watch instead!" The curtness of the ranger's tongue stung her. "I start tomorrow, and I will not quit until I have finished with our task."

Agneta meekly obliged, "Then I will wait and watch."

"I am not a tool made to be spent, but you're dangerously close to spending my last shred of patience and the little bit of help I'm still willing to give."

"I didn't ask for your damn help," Agneta savaged, although they both distinguished the lie buried within that allegation. "I embarked upon a few tasks I had left sorely forgotten, and you decided to abet me yourself."

"To get on with the only thing keeping me here," Ehlaru lashed out.

Her heart palpitating from stress, Agneta proclaimed, "You could have asked for us to get on with it anytime these last few days!"

"And it would have led me nowhere but here," Ehlaru tersely remarked, his breath bereft of both comfort and calm.

Ehlaru spoke frankly, however much it might sting. Agneta had undeniably taken advantage of his sense of duty. She'd admitted it to herself time and again and well knew her luck with him was waning and that their shared pool was nearly burnt to a crisp. Rescinding the effort might salvage his temper, but probably not for the day. She would attempt it, nonetheless, and would witness the explosion of their forced solidarity laid bare.

Eyes cast aside toward the kennel where Obryn and Grist idly played, Agneta achefully confessed, "I am sorry I led you astray, but now is as good a time as any, if you are willing."

Her voice betrayed a certain solemnity, but he evidently took no solace from her appeal.

"Then let us begin our first lesson," Ehlaru blunted, striding to his camp to retrieve some bones latched with grizzled flesh. He hid them within his cloak and hushed her pup's whining as they began chasing one another's tails. "Call them over to where you stand," he instructed.

"Grist, Obryn...come!" Agneta commanded, waving them over and then firmly patting her legs. They took notice, but after a concise deliberation, resumed biting at each other's tails. "Grist. Obryn. Come to me now!" she called out.

Seemingly humored with her attempt and failure, Ehlaru critiqued, "If they won't respect your voice, you must make them respect your glare."

Aggrieved with his ridicule, Agneta glared his way.

"Exactly," he chided. "Now watch me."

Leisurely, Ehlaru removed one of the wolf bones from his cloak. Enraptured and ecstatic, Grist approached him first. Obryn eventually followed. Ehlaru offered them no time to reach him before returning the bone underneath his cloak. He glared them over gravely until they drew to a halt. There the three stalled until he surrendered his innocuous pout.

"Come," the ranger commanded with a backward nod of his head.

They answered without hesitation, Grist a decent bit before Obryn, but both came to patter to his feet like timorous ducklings returning to the warmth of their mother's wings. Grist wallowed in anticipation of receiving the treat lurking beneath his cloak as he pawed expectantly at the ranger's foot. Ehlaru ignored him and gifted the first bone to the more patient Obryn.

He eagerly snapped it up, and with Ehlaru's permission, strode off and began gnawing away. Grist tried following only to be gently pulled back by the gruff of his neck.

"Sit," the ranger instructed while he began pushing Grist's butt to the ground.

Ehlaru momentarily abandoned the effort when Grist resisted too much. He withdrew both hands, paused, and ignored her wolfhound's futile wails to placidly study the distance.

Grist rose to face him, moaning in devastation toward his deceit.

The ranger revealed another bone from beneath his cloak before directly regarding the wolfhound at his heels. "Sit," Ehlaru instructed once over, his attention searing through Grist's arched brows.

Agneta noticed whenever the ranger acutely acknowledged her wolfhounds, they were more likely to heed his commands.

As expected, Grist finally listened. He bent his knees until he eventually sat. The ranger surrendered the bone in reparation for the honest effort. Grist seized it as if he were starving. The little brat! Ehlaru scratched behind his ears before dismissing him to join his brother and taunt her on the ranger's behalf.

"How…" Her voice trailed away amidst her confusion with Ehlaru's effortless success.

"Your first lesson lies in directing their attentions with your own. Until they have done something worthy, give them nothing at all. Once they have, make sure it is clearly known."

"I can do that," Agneta softly drawled before flowering her tone to abruptly pose, "Give me some time to practice before tomorrow's lesson?"

Retrieving what gear he'd not already adorned, Ehlaru saddled Solveig while continuing in his infuriatingly salient effort to ignore her until finally bequeathing, "I will give the next lesson once it's earned."

Agneta neither challenged him nor called out in protest as he rode off. She simply pondered if he intended catching another damned rabbit to sear for the nattmal meal again. She digressed. She would discover soon enough, so she turned her attention to her Garathandi wolfhounds and the grizzled flesh they happily gnawed on. Her attention invited wolfish grins. If that were what Ehlaru—a stranger to them both—could accomplish with two bones, what discipline could she instill with the promise of an extra meal—a little reward?

After having spent the remainder of her day tirelessly training her beloved wolfhounds, Agneta signaled them to sprint to the opposite stone hedge again. They indulged her without hesitation, returning when she bid they come home. For their prompt efforts, she fed them gummy slivers of leftover rabbit meat. Though she lightened their rewards with each successive display of obedience, they were still appreciative of the treats.

She'd made decent progress off Ehlaru's first lesson. She could now direct her wolfhounds anywhere she pleased. She even felt like the lord whose soldiers were the savage hounds of war, a hound master she supposed. That credence reenergized her damaged ego.

Eventually Agneta would boast her progress to the ranger, but Ehlaru had yet to return from his hunt. He would eventually return on account of his oath, and there was nothing that could kill the ranger who had trained her. She had seen all and yet nothing of which Ehlaru was capable, and both were equally frightening. Where Ehlaru traveled, danger followed. Whenever not, he often seized the means by which he could create peril for himself. Agneta's best guess for his delayed return was that he was hunting something far bigger than rabbits. The greater the stress he posed, the grander the challenge he undertook.

Agneta decided her wolfhounds had earned themselves a rest. She was no slaveowner like the jarls of the Stormlands, and she did not wish to overexert her furry pets. She recalled Obryn and Grist to her side. The two wolfhounds plodded toward her like thralls in the halls of Draveskeld who had been summoned moments before the day's end. The sun continued its swift descent. She surmised there were but six hours remaining before the moon would rule the sky.

She was uncertain precisely when each hour ticked. Ehlaru had once taught her that in the Stormlands, a spring day contained fifteen and its night comprised twelve. Summers reserved the most for the day. At summer's peak, the night lasted no longer than six. Winter, the world's currently dwindling season, had the exact opposite effect. During a particularly fun hunt years prior, the ranger had divulged the finer astronomical details of something he called Eldaria's celestial cycles. The cycle was adjusted to one's relative proximity to some magnetic poles as well as Eldaria's station within a complicated, thirty-two year cycle. Lok be damned for bringing Agneta to fall for an erudite man.

She assumed the ranger must be a Lysian. Asmoduil slaves were a nastier type, and Ehlaru was certainly not dark elven or undead. High Lord Baelviche's rebels were not as sparing with their intellect as most other High Easterners. Besides, they were more abrasive than sanding sheets freshly cut to length. After acclimating to strangers, Ehlaru was actually quite debonair. Only Lysians ever mustered his particular charm.

Agneta abruptly laughed, considering he'd only divulged that portion of his identity when he stopped devolving into an ill-tempered tantrum like a Stormborne man. Even when angered, he never strayed far from reason. Instead, he brandished a blunted sharpness. In some ways, she utterly adored him for it. The ranger could certainly work on managing his feelings, but then again, so could every man she had ever met.

She walked her wolfhounds to their kennel where they petered out atop their beds. She laid down between them as they snuggled into her chest and cuddled against her legs. Silly dogs. She wondered if they were afraid, afraid that this night she might leave again. It warmed her heart to know they treasured her. She finally relaxed, her shoulders delicately sagging, and hummed a lovely tune while awaiting Ehlaru's return.

A wooden gate opened three unspoken verses into the buoyant tune. The disturbance enticed her to depart her dogs' warmth. Hoof beats trot closer until Solveig neighed in the open yard. Her wolfhounds basked on. Her departure left them only mildly perturbed. She barred the kennel gate, then paced around the corner to find Ehlaru unloading a buck's rack alongside satchels of dressed meat.

"Not the kill I expected after three days of munching on mountain hares, but well done, Ehlaru. Well done indeed."

"I crossed its path in the valley that leads to Dwevland up those foothills. We are in a lull between their breeding and fawning seasons, so I assumed venison would be a welcome change."

Behind a flash of brightened diffidence, Agneta jested, "How could I complain? I have yet to touch my food stores, thanks to your kindness. Would you like help cooking it as thanks?"

"I know no Stormborne recipes. I keep to salting and peppering the meat to grill over a meal-fire or boiling it into a skause. I suppose I'm due to learn something else."

"Basic, but both work," she teased before rejoining with mild exuberance. "Most of the recipes call for lamb or chicken, but we could attempt a toblakah with venison instead."

"Toba-what?"

"Toblakah, you haughty High Easterner. That is what we're making tonight!" Agneta smiled, endeared by his efforts to make amends before she even could.

Ehlaru studied her quizzically before his face softened of its own accord. She would settle for the apology he surrendered in this manner he most preferred, and she hoped he would settle for the one she would eventually return.

Agneta strode to her door to gather the necessary spices to marinade the meat and herbs to garnish the top. Fortunately, she was an unlikely connoisseur of homely collections, and her home genuinely retained all they would need. Well, fortunately for her most of all. She was so damn tired of eating grilled and boiled rabbit alone.

"Cut us thin strips of venison and some chunky ones for my pups, then set the meal-fire wide and low so it retains that charred taste you seem to adore." She thought she caught a scant smile while passing through her front door. "Something wrong?"

"Nothing at all," the ranger grinned.

Agneta and Ehlaru quickly set about preparing toblakah over the next hour. The dish's sauce of honey and mashed omund leaves took the longest to prepare, but amid mild ruminations of the compromise her and her mentor had made, she did not much care. She completed her bit of the recipe no less than two minutes before the ranger completed his. A fast simmer over the meal-fire Ehlaru built outside her house transformed honey-glazed venison into authentic toblakah. They kept the meat warm above a diminished meal-fire as they quietly but happily served themselves.

Omund leaves gave toblakah its signature flavor, but were poisonous when ingested in heavy concentrations. In spite of nature's scorn, her Stormborne ancestors had introduced its leaves into their diets anyway. In scrupulous quantities, her and Ehlaru could now enjoy its flavor too. There was heritage in this moment, one which she vaguely assumed they shared.

Agneta had first acquired the recipe from her father's thralls after providing them with an incentive to share. It had been an accident really. The thralls were simply terrified of refusing Eljak's daughter and incurring his wrath. Even after both of her parents had instructed them its contents were of no concern of hers, they yielded to her childish demands.

Terrible with directions, Agneta's first attempt at toblakah had produced an inedible slop befitting hogs. She recalled she had refused to ask for help. She was simply more fulsome than Eljak and Avella both. Instead, she had hid herself within a pantry to secretly learn the finer details on how toblakah was prepared. She had observed, repeated after the thralls, and learned how to properly prepare the dish alongside many other savory meals.

Avella Jane, Agneta's mother, had only recently passed at that point. Yet, even in the lowliest of kitchens, her will remained law. Every other noble Stormborne woman was expected to cook and care for their home no different than the karlar. Avella's heritage of an Arcanum Lady from the distant Verdant Forest had gifted her the idea that she deserved to live as her jarl's equal. Agneta was her daughter. In some crude fashion, she retained most of her mother's rights. Her freedom however…not so much. Better not to dwell on the past too much, lest it draw her back in.

Agneta handled a thin strip of venison toblakah above the fire. She savored the subtle hints of the dish's toxic lethality. The marinade soaked the meat nicely. The flavors of scorched honey and candied herbs danced like Alderian fire across her tongue.

Beyond another tasty bite, she choked on her tongue. It should feel better, not having to run. Catching Ehlaru did not feel anything like she'd expected it to. They were here together, yet still they felt so far apart.

Ehlaru devoured the last of his toblakah while she lost herself within her thoughts. The ranger did not ask for more. His eye's mute solace told her it was something he was considering. His pride prevailed him, and he took to the ale instead.

Agneta smiled. How she loved the stubborn man. "How is it?" she asked. After granting him a moment to acknowledge her, she specified, "Different from peppered rabbit, I would think."

"I like the omund. It's relaxing and unexpectedly delicious."

Agneta tore into another strip of venison to prolong the tingle lingering on her tongue. "You're welcome to more, but be warned. Your gut will ache about as much tomorrow as your tongue relaxes tonight. It's how I keep myself honest whenever I cook this meal up."

"I'll survive," Ehlaru insisted. He took the last strips of toblakah, gifting her plate two more. "So long as you didn't over season any of those."

Agneta grinned. "Not in this lifetime, but perhaps I'll try in the next."

Leaning in over one elbow, Ehlaru replied, "Maybe my prior life's stomach is why this one handles the omund so well."

"Destiny recycles itself until eternity's end," Agneta mused until the thought escaped its sententious nest in her head.

Ehlaru's pupils broadened. "Then we are truly all our father's legacies and our mother's precious mistakes."

Huffing, Agneta munched down the last of her toblakah before wiping the grease from her lips. "It goes beyond bloodlines. It must! Otherwise, we're just doomed to repeat our parent's mistakes. I think our souls transcend new worlds after each of our lives, which means there's a chance Eldaria possesses the ability to change because each generation brings new perspectives to the challenges the ones faced."

"Perhaps, if only we could stray, resile the legacy that flows through our veins, and abandon those forgone mistakes." Ehlaru ceased chewing for a somber moment as if he were caught within a memory as sour as the toblakah's underlying taste. "Perhaps then these lands would find peace, Lysian would have never fallen, and there would be but one race of elves."

Agneta scrutinized his theory, dissected it clean, and disbelieved the notion she was beholden to either of her parent's mistakes. "Four isn't a wholly ridiculous number when you consider how different we humans can be!" she digressed.

Ehlaru rolled his eyes like he were peering at knowledge that burdened his thoughts. "Our differences are minor in comparison. The elves have developed over the course of hundreds of thousands of years. Their subvariants are more distinguished than ours, but…I agree with you still."

"Agree with what?" Agneta inquired, perplexed by the thought.

"We're not different enough to warrant the hate we endlessly expend."

Ehlaru tore through another strip of toblakah. He seemed to relish the dish. He better! Agneta specifically chose it knowing how much stress the ranger always carried. She supposed the relief and relaxation the omund flower provided might cool both their heads. The outcome was peripheral to her goals, but her gentle conciliation worked well to some extent.

"Is that your mother's mind, your father's, or your own?" Agneta queried, beckoning he defend his subtle assertion.

"My own," Ehlaru confessed unto her burgeoning well of excitement. "You win this one, Lady Ranger."

Drur be damned. She definitely had not expected that.

"So you met Grunda Helida during your journey?"

Ehlaru quipped, "And quite the displeasure it was. Branded me a pampered lord, which only proves they don't quite understand how difficult the lives we led once were."

Agneta bolstered, "Or respect how we choose to lead them afterward," knowing not the burdens he carried, yet recognizing the pain inside his voice. "You're no pampered lord, Ehlaru. From your life's mystery, I have at least learned that much."

There they sat as Agneta watched him recall a past he so often repressed. Striking blue eyes tinged with thin wisps of green wandered over the Jüteheln Sea. His consciousness might as well have sunk into the nothingness underneath. She envied that stoic grace he wore so well, knowing it to be his greatest appeal—the appeal she cherished the most. In the depth of solace where he often reclused, she witnessed him express his truest self. Loyal to a lonesome end, and no soul to bear witness but her as she strove to pull him away from its debilitating embrace. She envied his ability to dissociate, yet it equally drove her insane.

Ehlaru's choices were his own. He'd chosen to isolate himself above all, but his endeavor for seclusion saddened her deeply. She had witnessed the warmth companionship bestowed him. She wanted to see it blossom for him in full, even if it were never for her.

For her. What a pain-stricken thought. She viewed herself much as a girl adamant to live unburdened by all of Eldaria. Her versatility granted her strength, and although her family might never understand her fully, they were still the reason life was worth living. What were Ehlaru's reasons, if not for those he loved? Did the ranger actually love her behind his refusal to succumb to his heart's yearn? He had followed her this far. If not for love, then what had it all been for?

Agneta felt hurt, disappointment, and betrayal like everyone else ever born. Few of her own stories inspired greatness in those who cared to listen, but it was the threads of silver laced between which sparked a light that outshined the rest.

Somewhere in Ehlaru's own story, the one which had led him to adorn himself as a ranger for some seven years, were clandestine accounts of fellowship and greatness. How else could the ranger who'd trained her be so inscrutably intertwined with Fate's Weave? Ehlaru breathed in beat with the wind as if it were his kin, and that spoke greatly of his resilience.

Agneta descended into memory, recalling a saga was often all it took to change a man's heart. "When my father promised me to Ryurik to ensure I would one day become Storm Queen, I wanted nothing more than to slit his throat for breaking his promise to my mother. They were never meant to meet, you know. Some three drakken longships overwhelmed a single mainland ship carrying her to Helmya where dwelt her true betrothed. Avella was meant to be his wealth and fortune, yet my mother's own goals enticed her to use him as an escape. Each time the Dark Moon conquered the night, their love budded and grew. They were different, so vastly different, but there was joy between them once—enough joy to bring three children into the world whom she loved. My mother made him promise never to force us toward fates we did not wish to lead like her, and he gave his solemn word. I saw him give it!" She balked, the thought carving her heart raw. "Relinquished it as she lay upon her deathbed, and still he denied me as soon as she was gone…"

Her heart hammered harder and harder until she forced herself to draw deep and steady breaths. It felt as though that memory arose from a lifetime ago, but Agneta knew it had fallen within the embrace of the youth she wore still. Perhaps that was why it still stung her so.

She continued, "Just as I came to understand my mother, she passed, swept away by the plague like a feather on the wind just as she had been swept into the Stormlands to begin with. I've told you I am the youngest by five, and Byron was a man before I was even born. I felt alone without her because I was like her and neither of us were Stormborne. Without Avella, I fought my battles alone until I finally met one of my brothers."

Agneta paused when a recourse of celestial starlight pierced the clouded veil shrouding the waning moon. In a transcendence of opportunity, she claimed Ehlaru's place in the pathos of mystery for herself.

"Eljak pushed my brothers and I apart because I was his daughter, a stark reminder of the woman he'd lost and a hindrance on the hardened warriors he needed them to one day become. I argued against his wars, the feuding and the rivalries in which we participated for little gain of our own. For that, I was forced into isolation, so alone I fought on. Stigr, my second brother, had been gone for several seasons then, having returned late one night alongside Byron from a skirmish with the Kennings before the Ardent Avant arrived at the Great Gates. They fought for the 'glory' of our father's blood feud with Aidelgard over some stupid mining town Denurl Kenning had seized long ago. Stigr found me rifling through the kitchen as I prepared myself some food and pulled me away from the pantry. I didn't recognize him initially! We argued at length before we eventually digressed, and I think he carried me to bed once I grew too tired to stand." A tear shed her eye, one which she did not attempt to hide. "I begged Stigr to save me from that marriage years later. He did not scruple to free me and pushed me into the Soudland high country with a horse and supplies when I asked. I wouldn't have escaped the home my father locked me in otherwise, and it is something I think of day and night."

Through his eyes, Agneta glimpsed into his sententiously beating heart, no matter how meticulously Ehlaru endeavored to hide it. Though she lured him toward caring—a sentiment she craved more each year since departing his tutelage—the sincerity he accorded her outright amazed her. Perhaps she was too melancholy, but by Hælla Dwolv's heart, she would share her own, and by the runic gods, he would sit there and listen to what he'd refused to hear before. Her truth spilled like tidal waves, and Agneta was absolutely unwilling to relent in its flood. There had been too many lies between them, both his and hers.

He reached for her through the touch of his hand as it came to enfold her own. He had heard her and meant to share in her pain by opening his mouth to speak some comfort. She squeezed his hand tightly, so she might delay his response, and he obliged without worry and a smile that brightened her world. It was comforting and sparked a fire in her heart, but she had made the same mistake of pushing forward too fast before. She chose to do nothing more than share in this earnest moment she had somehow squeezed out of a cruel world.

Letting her hand fall from his, she made her bid to withdraw a sentimental and storied return. "What drove you to the Stormlands to become a ranger, Ehlaru?"

Stoicism dominated his expression as he gave a familiar response. "My past will one day be the death of everything I care for. I can only afford managing it while abandoning everything else I have known. I'm not without my own Stigr, but her story must remain unknown." Ehlaru flinched, wincing in discomfort before he grimaced in full.

Understanding she had gathered more about his past than ever before, she strove to remedy his disappointment before he mindlessly sullied their moment. "Her story sounds like a superb one, but wait, wait, do not worry. I'll not press you for anything more. I'll take this one humble victory and revel in it alone."

From beneath a veil of cynicism, a serenity arose to enfold them both. Ehlaru smiled as he had never smiled for her before. She had filled him with something she absolutely adored.

"I am proud of you, Agneta. Few have ever brought me to offer my oath who did not also share my blood. I'm proud of the person you've become."

A wave of awe struck her, but in time she recovered and drowned her throat in ale before the courage to speak befell her again. "Thank you," she said, thinking there was something else to be said but knowing she had nothing left to say.

Words fell from grace in the wake of dignified gestures, and when the voice failed in strides, its time became nigh esoteric. Her mother had told her long ago that no single gesture divulged the heart if it were not majestic, impetuous, or blisteringly honest. It had been a slice of wisdom from the Verdant Forest, where, like in Ehlaru's own homeland, everything was suitably grand.

Agneta did not think before it happened, but from her cloak she withdrew his iron coffer to fondle within reticent hands. There she hesitated, the guarantee of his oath laid bare before the runic gods and the Dark Moon as if she stood naked beneath Monomua's gaze.

Yet, what had Eldrahg done with Freyja, his daughter born with the indescribable beauty of life and forged with a splinter of his own wisdom. What had the Draconic Father done when her destiny unfurled? He'd given Freyja the means to resurrect Helti without question, without qualms, surrendering his trust in finality to her, then surrendering her life to Jüte, who had stolen Helti's own. Flown to the jütengolk lord's frosted halls by Valvítr Queen of the Valkyrie, there the runic god of frost imprisoned the runic god of life until Freyja freed Helti from his frosted catharsis. Thus was reborn the runic god of war, risen into a pathos of everlasting conquest, a quittance of love, and an ensign of familial trust undaunted by the malice of frost.

Agneta pressed the iron coffer into Ehlaru's hands.

First, he observed her distractedly, then with mild apprehension, and finally in gracious acceptance of what he did not understand.

She thought of his striking eyes. A softness consumed her soul. Her voice rung like a wavering ode to conviction as she moved to conciliate the flight of their nerves. "This does not mean your oath is lifted, but I should have never taken what was yours while knowing everything it means to you. Goodnight, Ehlaru. Sleep well till morning comes when I hope to see you next, and when next we train my little pups of war."

CHAPTER ELEVEN
DREAD-FORGED

THYRA FIDDLED WITH HER RUBY ring in the officer quarters of the Skjold's barracks. Deeming to have held it plenty, she pocketed the gift in haste. She had grown too fond of it. How puerile, considering it was little more than a tool she might use to bend a jarl to her will, yet reasonable, considering Harald intrigued her quite a lot.

Gulping down a glass of water, Thyra tore into a haunch of lamb, salivating over its gamey taste. Knuth ravaged another leg across from her, noisily enjoying the morning's dagmal meal. She had not properly spoken with her second regarding the coarse waters they charted since the division of Tjorden's plunder. Perhaps when Knuth finished eating, she would get the chance.

Thyra tore into the lamb leg again and again until devouring it completely. She reached for another to ease her itinerant mind before ultimately retracting her hand. Thyra retrieved the ruby ring from her pocket instead. It had hardly forgotten the warmth of her hand.

Various Skjold recently recounted stories seized from Stormguarde's streets. Most were taken from alehouse runs spent with the remainder of the standing Stormborne army. No longer a surprise, Thyra ascertained her brother had developed an insatiable appetite while defending the Great Gates.

Women learned quicker than men, and the female Skjold reported that her brother especially enjoyed farmgirls. It was as if Ryurik were overtaken by the spirit of Ellyan himself. Whispers of his delinquencies spread far. Fortunately, his parade of the pilfered Goblets of the Delas provided an adequate replacement story the karlar were speaking to instead. Thyra's own supplemental flare augmented the distraction from Ryurik's carnality as well.

Ryurik seemingly acquired the worst traits of each of their dead brothers—quick to fight like Durel, lascivious like Ellyan, and dutiful to a fault like Darius. Of Ryurik, there was nothing left but the abeyance of he who toyed with tempered intention as if it were destined to fall in his hands. Who was her brother other than the boy she dragged from his bed as a child then ferried to these foreign lands? He knew not what he wished to become other than that which was forced upon him. He was Ryurik, her little brother, who she'd failed so much.

Ryurik had routinely avoided her since dispersing the Goblets of the Delas like some mythical peacock who had been called upon to fulfill a clown's charge. It might have been wiser to force the issue less unexpectedly, but that was not Thyra's way. How then, if Ryurik were so like Darius, charging into every battle to provoke the wrath of the Avantians without fear, did he flee a confrontation with her like a spineless squirrel?

Lamb fell from Knuth's mouth when he stated, "Don't overthink it. Ryurik might have aided the jarls in breaking a siege and winning a war, but he still acts like an untrained pup. He needs your tempering touch."

With her free hand, Thyra pointed to her own mouth, pursing her lower lip when Knuth failed to comprehend.

"You won't answer because we both know I'm right! You should never have given him a set of Skjold armor to wear through Stormguarde! He insults our image, and how then does he learn even the Storm Prince or Storm King himself must abide by the latter's rule of law," Knuth flared in a single lofty breath.

Thyra scoffed, ascertaining Ryurik could hardly harm their reputation walking through Stormguarde in their armor. Little distinguished Skjold armor other than that it was standardized throughout the entirety of the core.

The Skjold wore dual lamellar boots, which ended in bushy tufts of fur below their knees. Each pair was crafted from elk leather and reinforced with ground ram's horn cemented into the boot's linings. Then came the wool leggings, which offered poor protection but superior mobility. Chainmail overhung their brown shirts and braies, dangling slightly below the waist. A leather belt clasped it all together—made from the same hide as their lamellar boots and bracers. A pair of gloves hung at their belts, but

Thyra keenly preached they reserve their use to maintain superior dexterity in combat.

Brown cloaks, whose color matched their braies, draped the backs of ordinary Skjold. They were trimmed in rabbit fur. Officer's cloaks were woven with threads of sky blue. A silver Valkyrie stood on guard at the center. A field of lightning surrounded the warrior maiden, an illustration of the Runeheims' favored runic gods.

All Skjold wore unadorned iron helmets forged to fit each one's head. They were little more than a round helmguard with a cross-haired reinforcement and spectacled guard. The sky-piercing, horned helms of the Agulbarg's finest—the twinned, finned crests worn by the warriors of the Breidjal Bakari, and the forward-facing horns resembling the tusks of trolls unique to Jarl Baelgrant's warriors—were far more recognizable than anything worn by her Skjold. Even if Ryurik undressed in the middle of Stormguarde to bare his beaten back and wetted cock, Thyra doubted anyone would associate that questionable act with her Skjold.

"You think I enable him?" Thyra questioned after an extensive pause for thought.

"I think he abuses his family's love. He was too young to feel the full hardships, which came with adjusting to your new home."

"Tanya is younger than him, yet she has matured far the better."

Brooding over the memory of the broken voyage they took to reach these Stormlands, Thyra clenched the ring's rough-cut gemstone so tightly that it nipped blood. She did not mind it much. Holding it helped her think more clearly, she supposed. It was a clear reminder of the rancorous games she was forced to play. Yet, the pellucid ruby enticed her tenderest touch. She could not recall when last anyone gave her charity without expecting something in return.

Even Lothair did not freely bequeath her command of the Skjold, not until Seer Hosvir attested there were none worthy of leading his shield guard besides her. Against all the disrespect she so outwardly afforded him, Harald forced this ring into her hands. It was a horn, which could resonate across all the Stormlands to summon the Breidjal Bakari, and with it, him.

"Tanya remembers the Gilded Citadel of Ellynon and our lives before here. We reminisce when we talk, you know," she joked, licking the blood from her finger and pocketing the ring for the remainder of the meal.

"So you don't just dwell, tease, and bicker like a pair of your brother's farm girls?"

Smirking but otherwise ignoring Knuth's insult, Thyra asked, "Then why has Ryurik not aged the same as she?"

"Because Tanya lives by the example you and the High Lady set, even if she occasionally spites the decisions you make. It's apparent in how she guides the priestesses in that runic temple and influences its seers. What does Ryurik live by, Commander? The words of Eljak fucking Draven, whose children despise him so greatly, one fled his hand while another secretly married a farmer's daughter as soon as he was beyond his father's reach."

In due course, Thyra joked, "Then the impending brothers by marriage will get along well. Aye, Knuth," she eventually continued. "I fear there is some truth to your concern. Ryurik holds to Eljak by the promise of a bride because he sees no alternative, but I swear I know my brother still. That is a bond I can split like dry wood if ever I could just corner him."

"Make haste of it, Commander. Each day their bond grows stronger, the more he becomes like the weasel wolf himself."

"Is that an order, Knuth?" Thyra demanded, riled by his bluntness.

"It was a suggestion, Commander, and a Drur-damned good one at that!" Knuth defended with an infelicitous growl.

Thyra ameliorated, "It will be easier now than before. The Agulbargs marched home to Riven Hold this morning, and Lord Byron was not far behind them on his path for Draveskeld."

"Took half of his father's forces with him. Sent to slap some sense into his brother Stigr, I would guess." Thankfully, he finished talking before he spooned more porridge into his mouth. "Is it true what they say of your grandfather?" Knuth asked as porridge drizzled from his lips.

"Lothair named Ryurik his heir to the Tempest Throne. The runestones are no lie. I bade Barul spread them throughout the city before the dawn."

After devouring the last of his bowl like a ravenous wolf, Knuth licked up the wanton devastation his loose-lipped style of eating wrought. "Let us hope Agneta Ilesha Dravendottir stays lost forever. I'll be damned to Drur's Abyss before I see a Draven as my Storm Queen."

"Jarl Eljak is desperate to hold on to Ryurik. He may even promise one of Stigr's unborn girls since they both love farmer's daughters so much."

Gradually at first, then until he boomed like a torrential storm, Knuth filled the room with laughter. He wiped away a tear before looking her over. His face was swollen red with blood.

"I'll wait for Ryurik to disperse the Erunheim before I dispatch our surplus Skjold to Húsavik. They'll be more useful along the borders with Aidelgard, where if tradition holds, we shall see the next rising storm," said Thyra.

Stroking his beard, Knuth remarked, "To lurk against the Kennings or in wait while the jarl lurks against us?"

"I know you were born in Húsavik along the Erunheim's northern border." Thyra then softly affirmed, "I swear to you, it is a precaution and nothing else. They've been strangely quiet since abandoning the defense of the Great Gates. The Kennings betray their neighbors when they sense weakness. It's intrinsic, I think. Besides, if battle with Denurl Kenning does come, we will end it quicker than two shakes of a lamb's tail."

"A Stormborne proverb!" Knuth resounded behind a dry, boastful grin. "There might be Runeheim in you yet. I do not fear for family, Commander," he digressed after a brief pause. "My mother is tougher than me. Only one of my sisters has bound her hands in marriage. Eadric is his name, or so Oddall tells me. Regardless, Eldith believes she has found herself a worthwhile man who she allows to hold her down." Slapping the table as if everything said before was but futile words, Knuth conferred, "The Kennings and Dravens have been blooded enemies since before I was born. Jarl Denurl has daughters too. If not to see his heirs on the Tempest Throne, he would offer one to slight his rival. You are then left with the Erunheim, the dragon's lapis spread of Aidelgard, and old Breidjal in the same court, if you think you can manage them all. If Ryurik does need direction, make sure it is yours. Not Eljak's. Not Lothair's. Yours!"

Indulged, Thyra attested, "It is possible, but Aidelgard is fairly considered a den of swine and whores. Seems better if we avoid an alliance with them at all."

"It is either Aidelgard or Draveskeld, Commander. The wolves or the boars. Neither bodes well for the long term, but we will be forced to choose one."

Scoffing at the notion she need choose at all, Thyra remarked, "And it is upon Torlv's Tempest Throne from which the line of Runeheim rules over them both. They will submit to my brother. They will submit to us both."

Bygone from the barrack's entrance, a shaggy-haired Skjold warrior called, "Commander Thyra!" He strode to a standstill athwart the table where she ate and Knuth gobbled up his food.

Knuth rose from the dented table. "What is your business, Sigtrygg?"

"The shieldmaiden, Hela of Breidjal, wishes to speak with you both. She waits outside the barracks entrance with her guard."

"I am already here, boy," Hela jested as she casually sauntered through the opened door. Lifting her hands in admission, she continued, "But I left my guard by the entrance so as to not cause you any alarm. Like I said, little Sigtrygg, I am not here to harm her."

Sigtrygg's eyes iced over as his hands tightened over the pommel of his sword into white knots of rope. "Give me permission, Commander, and I will dispatch her."

"Unannounced or otherwise," Thyra admonished, "she is welcome. Sigtrygg, you are dismissed."

Seemingly impelled to stay, Sigtrygg eventually ceded to Thyra's wish. He jostled past the shieldmaiden's shoulder in an antagonistic exit. He made it no farther than halfway through when Hela grabbed him and wrenched him around to answer for his belligerence. She held him firm as his resistance quailed, and a feral look arose between them when Sigtrygg wriggled and succeeded in pulling away.

"I'd like to see you on the battlefield, Sigtrygg. One day, I think I shall." Hela winked as Sigtrygg hustled from the room to curse her beyond the door's veil.

Thyra bade Knuth retake his seat, and with some reluctance, the ruddy warrior obliged. "Why are you here, shieldmaiden?" Knuth rasped, intentionally grating his voice.

"I seek a conversation I think the commander and I should have made days ago. She and Ryurik have been so scarce lately," Hela censured, smugly relaxing into an open chair that sat across the table from Thyra.

Thyra swept aside her empty plate and Knuth's gall, stating, "There is no dearth of work while managing the Skjold, Stormguarde, and the Erunheim for my grandfather."

"Do not oversell, Thyra. We are friends, so there's no reason to lie. We both know High Lady Valyria manages Stormguarde and the Erunheim all but militarily. I have not seen the Skjold drilling in the runic fields, so where have you been?"

Holding still, Thyra studied the shieldmaiden's vigor and firmly replied, "Either here or in Stormguarde Keep. I have been considering a foray to Húsavik, however. The weather's been improving there, I hear."

Hela did not relent in the slightest. "You might only consider us an ally for your brother's gain, as the herald of a fleet and an army, but do not disparage me, Commander. I'll withhold the Breidjal Bakari and all its warriors should you make scarce and avoid me again."

"A few days consumed by my own obligations seems a far stretch from being scarce."

"Perhaps, if only I had not recently presented you with the ever-lingering problem that is your baby brother."

Thyra's eyes narrowed, and the room grew dreadfully cold as ire descended over them both. "Ryurik's issues are my concern alone," she ravaged, leaning forward as she spoke.

"They are as much mine and Harald's as they are any other jarl's. I brought them to your attention, did I not?"

Her throat grated under the stress of her lash. "By leaving him strapped to a fence to be beaten while you and your men stood and watched! I'm tempted to leave you and Harald rotting. Find yourself lucky I spare you my time at all." Gone was the distrustful banter, which had, thus far, held them both in check.

Hela slammed her hand into the table, and the motion persuaded a defensive movement from the two Skjold who stood guard by the door. "For toying with the boy before you found a way to spare those involved? Thank me, unless you are more Lysian than I assumed you were."

"So you put the heir to the Tempest Throne's life at risk as a joke!?" Thyra savaged as she swatted away the two Skjold.

"Stand down, boys," Knuth bade, and they digressed after some hesitation—an inveterate theme amongst every Skjold who had been in Hela's company.

Inexorably, the shieldmaiden continued, "Had you not deescalated tempers, we would have killed them all except for your brother. I merely provided you the opportunity to uphold your charge."

"Whatever the plan you expect me to take part in, if you think I'll be its surreptitious grounding while my brother's left behind, then we are done."

Hela stood, fingers gripping the table until her knuckles turned white, and in a low tone that sliced a mind's stability, she said, "We have each managed your feckless brother through five years of war. My warriors were pulling Ryurik from battlefields and beatings long before I ever thought to make moves on you. I swear by Eldrahg, there are times I wish we let him die those first few." Thyra fumed at the shieldmaiden's admission, but Hela would not be stopped in her relentless account. "Your brother was single-handedly responsible for the death of thousands in Tjorden's Reach. Paladin Supreme Urien transferred a portion of his army under cover of storm through one of the southern passes, harrowing our flanks with a fraction of the number to see what response he could incur. Keeping the damned information to himself, Ryurik rode out with a collection of men numbered at two thousand, half of whom were not even his own. Had Eljak and Harald not reinforced when they had, Urien Aylard would have fully secured the pass and slaughtered far more than those one thousand. We took no prisoners—not because we chose to but because the Ardent Avant killed every one of ours—so we needed to repay their kindness. That is war, Thyra. You know it, but your brother does not. He has barely ascended to the point where he can manage a battle. He is a far cry from the Tempest Throne."

Thyra sat completely motionless for a long while until Knuth actually moved to stir her. Thyra leered him away, ruminating on the matter to herself. She had yet to consider how little she truly knew of the war. Lothair reserved both the foundation and the surfeit of communication from all others and unto himself alone. To salvage his apparent heir's image in the eyes of the people or to withhold shame from his line, Thyra did not know. Of one thing, Thyra was certain. Hela spoke the truth. She was not so different from this shieldmaiden of Breidjal.

Thyra did not vacillate when she decreed, "He is to be your Storm King, and I'll forever be bound to my family, whether in victory or defeat. Two of my brothers died so we could reach these shores. I will repay their debt. You claim he transcends the role of functional commander, and I think that is an astounding improvement from the boy I coddled to sleep on my boat. If we are to be allies, you must be willing to serve him because I've served two horrendous, erroneous leaders already, and it is my goal that Ryurik does not become the third."

The shieldmaiden, upon a wind of reason that cushioned her fall, returned to her seat. Crossing her legs and adjusting her position until comfortable, she seized Knuth's unfinished plate. She smiled toward the enflamed commander, munching through one of the legs before returning the plate. Knuth devoured the rest of his food in seconds, fearful it might be taken away again.

"I like you, Thyra. You're fiery, passionate, yet reasonable at the core. When the demonic blaze that sears your homeland is lifted, I hope we take the time to raid those shores. I'd like to take a few Lysian thralls who are like you," Hela professed openly.

"Commander, by your order, I will remove her before she spews another word!" Knuth abruptly bellowed.

The bastard Son of Sven rose from his chair like a blood-haired jüten-golk frost giant rising from its throne. Thyra's second towered over Hela Gormrikdottir while he motioned for the two Skjold on guard to join. Thyra swatted them aside again, inciting monumental confusion, and bade Knuth refrain from stirring them anymore. Knuth grunted furiously, and he plummeted into his seat. Something cracked, either the chair or Knuth's ass.

The shieldmaiden grinned, relishing in her strange reunion with the Son of Sven who had once sailed beside her in the Breidjal Bakari. "I will reconvince my cousin this is worth our time. Speak to him with a little predilection as you did at your brother's Kingslag, Thyra Ehlrich of the Skjold, and it will make my task simpler by far."

Thyra did not answer. Her attention turned instead to Barul when he barged through the open door. Of all her sub-commanders and captains, none were quite as fickle and unpredictable as the blonde bear when he had been snubbed. Barul leered at Hela, considering if he should speak. He stood in inert silence, and absolutely nothing else occurred.

Thyra sighed, nodding to Hela to consolidate their agreement, and rose to address Barul, "Why the interruption, captain?"

Barul did not cease glaring petulantly at the shieldmaiden of Breidjal. "The fucking girl slid in while our guards were distracted bantering with the shieldmaiden's own. I'd have just killed her once she began waving around an ax, but she is stamping up a storm, claiming you promised her father."

Rising to shift toward the apparent exhibition, Hela stated, "I should never have toyed with Ryurik after all. Better to have killed the farmer and left his wife and girl to mourn."

Veneering past Hela, who followed in a devolution of heightened interest, Thyra mutely commanded Knuth to join them in following Barul Benson. Striding down a short corridor into a diminutive hall, they swung through a vacant chamber, which brought them to the barrack's inner yard. There, the farmer's daughter made her stand, surrounded by five Skjold. She brandished a workman's ax, wielding it in slight error. She gripped the handle at the edge opposite its curved, metal head, pointing it like a spear toward any Skjold who drew near. The girl seemed not afraid but rather determined in her pursuit of recognition.

The farm girl noticed Thyra immediately, crying out as if her salvation had befallen, "Tell your men to stay back. I'm not leaving until I have been heard."

Complacently, Barul informed, "I've heard her, Commander. She spews nothing of value."

Irked by his comment, Thyra observed, "Then why bring me to her instead of tossing her out of our barracks yourself?"

"She threw out your name enough times, she's convinced some of the Skjold she speaks the truth," Barul defended in earnest, believing the girl's tirade devolved by no fault of his own.

Thyra reproved, "We've met once, Barul. I do not know the girl. She brandishes a weapon against your fellow Skjold. That is a mortally punishable offense."

"Commander," Barul mumbled, "can we not just let her waste in a cell to await some better judgment from Stormguarde's althing?"

"I gave her a chance to quietly live her life bereft of its judgment already. Save yourself from dish duty by disarming her and satisfying Stormborne law."

"Why kill her?" Barul insisted. "She's a feisty, pretty girl—"

"Barul, I swear I'll split you like a sack of grain if you do not disarm that girl," Knuth, in a fascinatingly celeritous foray to action, admonished Barul.

Humored by the event, Hela wryly reproved, "No need for brutality, Knuth Svenson. Let your commander demonstrate herself."

Shaking her head with thematic displeasure, Thyra physically separated Knuth and Barul. With a silent sweep of her hand, she drew off the remainder of her Skjold encircling the farm girl. Thyra studied the girl, who responded timidly. Nervously shifting the ax between her petite hands, the farmer's daughter summoned the courage to approach, letting it fall to her side as she strode forth and audibly cleared her throat.

"Do you remember what I told you when last we spoke?" Thyra raptured.

The farm girl froze, retracting like an infant kraken into the rocks of a coastal reef. Color drained from her face, leaving her pale as a moonlit specter. Tenuously, she rose to speak, voice bereaved as a venal widow's rejoining her murdered husband in death.

"I am worth more than life as a farmer's daughter," insisted the farm girl hotly, although her querulous voice forgave her little support. "You promised my father you would take me into the Skjold. You stole my first chance at living better. You cannot steal this one too!"

Thyra dismissed her fussing as if she were a stray kitten begging for food. "I will throw you into a cell or the sea. That is what I said, was it not?"

"At least in a cell, she will still rival Freyja's beauty," Hela interjected with an unfettered smugness imprinted unto her tone and her face.

"The same beauty that enticed my brother to spread your legs might help you keep your head, so if you think you are worth more, demonstrate it." Thyra stepped toward the girl, forcing her to cower. "You have an ax," she reinforced. "So prove you can do more than cull chickens, beat oxen, and split wood. Prove why you deserve to join my Skjold." She turned apart from the frightened girl and spoke with the shieldmaiden of Breidjal in a low, disgruntled tone. "Spare me the distress of watching my men disarm her while engrossed with her looks, and I'll forgive you for what I can."

Hela cocked a brow, acceding to Thyra's offer after giving it little time to dwell. Hela brought one hand to grip the sword at her back, and the farm girl swung her ax to meet a strike she believed would surely come. Smiling, Hela liberated an ax from her hip. She lifted the girl's from her unsteady hands. The farm girl leaped in like a pouncing fox. She was met by Hela's boot and thrust into the ground. Hela forced her down and held her underfoot, returned her ax to her hip, and tossed the farm girl's ax to Barul, who caught the weapon then studied it at length.

Distraught to the point of shedding tears, the farm girl scurried to her feet, tripping over the planked steps behind her. Her head smacked stone. She shrieked, squirming in anguish as Hela half walked and half drug the girl to Thyra. The shieldmaiden relinquished the farmer's daughter at her foot, and the girl crumbled to her knees. She coddled the back of her head while steadying herself. She did not cower long before standing to impart Thyra an irascible glare.

No one spoke, not even Hela, who—more likely than all the others—had something clever to share. Eventually, the farm girl's ardor subsided. The teary-eyed girl shut her eyes, squeezing away the torment of having knowingly failed. They opened, weary, disillusioned, and afraid. It was not mild fear gripping the girl. It was a terror born of lost aspiration and a trepidation of the unknown.

Yet, the farm girl did not flounder in that percolation of emotion. Her focus only briefly waivered until life rekindled within the girl. Her eyes darted between Thyra and the surrounding Skjold. She raised her hands, clenched her fists, and stepped into a more suitable stance. Thyra grinned. There lied her proof, shitty proof, but the proof she requested. She would take a chance on this girl, whose spirit was as tremendous as her father claimed.

"What is your name?"

"Astrid Asvordottir," the farm girl coolly stated, keeping to her fists.

"You would do well to remember all your brother taught you. Skjold do not fight with weapons until they've learned to defend themselves with their heads and hands," Thyra humbly admitted while parrying Astrid's servile smile with a dismissive grin. "Barul!" she called out.

"Commander?" the blonde bear replied with a disgruntled plunge of the jaw.

"Find our new recruit a meal and a bed. Do not remiss with Freyja's daughter either, or I will cut off your head...and no, Barul, the other one." Thyra dismissed him with a pestilent wink.

"Aye, Commander," the captain unctuously groaned.

"Thyra Ehlrich, First Princess of Lysian. Fiery, passionate, yet still reasonable beneath sky's veil," imparted the shieldmaiden of Breidjal in a whimsically rapt tenor. "I should now share that Lord Bolvark Trollsbaneson has made ready to unveil his show. We are expected, and I want to see what enticed my cousin to promise the Breidjal Bakari to the Bane of Troll's conquest of the far north."

They were a dwindling line, they few surviving Ehlrichs who assumed their mother's bygone mantle and the name to which it was sworn. Their father wracked in an Archdemon's impenetrable hold, their mother seemingly devoid of reason. The three surviving children of Valyria Runeheim and Edvuard Ehlrich were now wholly alone. Thyra assumed the mantle of ardent defender to the siblings whose lives were hers alone to ensure. Blazoned blood and its vindication washed them upon those shores. Hela betrayed her name in false pretense, for the shieldmaiden of Breidjal by the Helmya Sea could never understand who Thyra truly was.

"I almost forgot Bolvark meant to reveal the proof his father believes will fetch the other jarls' support and entice us to invade that imposing force that lies across the Jüteheln Sea."

"I have fought their dull, distant brethren in the Ranges of Valdhaz and Tjorden. Never Garathandi," Hela claimed as if rapt by their ethnic name. "My saga is young. Conquest of the Frostheim's shores, the Frallheim Timberlands, and the Everdark City from where their hordes stem forth seems to be a fitting verse for the next stanza in my tale."

"Despite myself, I'd prefer we march against the Broken Fjords," Thyra mumbled. "Knuth!" she blurted. "This recruit is now yours and Barul's, as are all the other recruits when we return. Join Hela and I to find what lies within Lord Bolvark's caged wagon."

"Aye, Thyra," came the forever faithful affirmation of her second.

"How long since you received the news?" Ryurik questioned Eljak Draven, his friend and trusted mentor, from the defense of the Great Gates.

Their gait carried them through Stormguarde city to its central square, where Lord Bolvark prepared to unveil his father's case for war with the Garathandi. All Ryurik could ponder was the word, which resounded the morning and that Eljak Draven forced unto his ear. Agneta Ilesha Dravendottir had been spotted outside the Soudland village of Dekryl, and the jarl sustained no lack of assurance the claim was real.

"The raven arrived late last night. It is why I sent Byron and half my army to my lands."

Ryurik persisted, "How did they describe the ranger they claim to be her?"

"Ranchers spoke of a black-haired ranger at the tavern in Skraelg and swore she stole a horse from one of their embittered friends. She was next seen in Dekryl, so my men swear. It's her," he decreed. "Torlv, take my voice if I am wrong. I know it is her."

Ryurik contended, "You've just described a lady ranger who happens to bear black hair. It could be any felonious outsider or an exile from another land."

The timing was too unreasonable. If Agneta truly betrothed herself a ranger to extricate her marriage to him, she was careless for allowing herself to be sighted within the sole propriety of the Soudland where she might be recognized as the daughter of Eljak Draven. Rangers were not careless. Remiss rangers always ended up dead, either torn apart by Kazbel's brutish children or mountain trolls, tricked by the fae to stroll to their life's end, or lost in nature's scornful fury. One always eventually culled the Storm King's rangers of their weak.

"It is Agneta!" Eljak nigh yelled, his jaw straining under the pressure his intensity laid upon it. "I will have my boys scour all of the high country, into Baelgrant's Nordland and beyond until I've uncovered the hole where she hides."

"Stigr helped her to escape, did he not? How can you trust him to be loyal to his word and not aid her once again?"

Eljak ground his teeth as he barked, "That was only the latter half of the message I received. That blunt-headed boy has apparently married a karlar farmer's shrew."

"I thought it courteous not to inquire," Ryurik confessed. "But you should know word has likely reached every man in the camps."

"He celebrated his new wife while we celebrated your Kingslag." Eljak carped his throat, and the jarl's clear misfocus disconcerted Ryurik's nerve. "My weasel son tricked our senile seer into believing he had been given my blessing as well. Stigr will do as I command and rut out his little sister, or else his new wife's life is not long for the Stormlands."

Ryurik acknowledged Eljak's sheer certainty, but he remained partially unconvinced. If Agneta were shrouded by the high country, Eljak would only locate her if provided ample time and resources and considerable luck.

Ryurik understood his distress, especially since Lothair just publicized Ryurik was now heir to the Tempest Throne. Agneta was the key Eljak would turn to seat his own heirs upon the Tempest Throne, and the girl was Ryurik's best prospect of ensuring the Draven's loyalty after Lothair's demolition of their trust.

Ryurik respected his grandfather, but he also viewed him as impetuous to a fault. Lothair disparaged those he disliked without concern for the disloyalty it incurred. The Kennings utterly abandoned the defense of their own home because they so sorely detested their Storm King. Jarl Eljak was another whose loyalty was in constant testation.

It began when Eljak refused to watch his men be slain beside Ryurik's uncle in one of Paladin Supreme Urien Aylard's few victories in the war. The death of his only son blinded Lothair with rage. No such convictions bound Ryurik, however. Ryurik never met Storm Prince Lætsven, and though his uncle's body was never recovered from the Alterian Highlands, Ryurik accepted his uncle was most likely dead. There was honor in living to fight another day, and Ryurik intended to reward Eljak Draven handsomely for his judicious head.

"I have no doubt you will find her, or you will transform your son's mistake into a weapon you can wield, but know that if Agneta evades capture, you will remain my friend to an auspicious end. Whether we turn our swords against a crippled horde of trolls, the Kingdom of Helmya, or the draconic transgressors the Broken Fjords hold, we'll meet them, and the wealth and glory at conquest's end will be ours most of all."

"Well, my boy," Eljak answered. "We will accomplish all those things and more after I have delivered to you your Storm Queen."

Eljak doled a firm hand, laying it upon Ryurik's shoulder and reassuring the strength of his conviction. Ryurik returned a broad smile, knowing he would do nothing more than await the eventual outcome of Eljak's hunt. His confidence that Eljak would succeed in the task was dreadfully slim. Marrying Agneta would serve the Tempest Throne, but Ryurik's past avowal to receive her meant nothing until she became Eljak's to give again.

They reached the trodden ground of the center square, arriving unto a vibrant scene of inquisitive men who enclosed it in its entirety. Each individual vied for the peerless view of the caged wagon and everything concealed by its woolen furs. Ryurik, Eljak, and the jarl's sworn swords broke through the circle. He caught sight of Harald and Haneul heading their direction. Harald Gormrik, the Hawk of Breidjal, the Jarl of Breidjal by the Helmyan Sea, and Ryurik's inescapable tormentor who always discerned a path to pervade his peace.

"Eljak Draven, Lord of Draveskeld, jarl of Draven's Dominion. Ravens fly, bald man, and they claim you've had a monstrous week of managing your children."

Harald came to face his fellow jarl. He stepped much closer than either Eljak or his warriors cared to allow. Eljak's sworn swords stepped forth to oppose Harald, and the Jarl of Breidjal summarily sojourned. Harald gouged his eyes of their brackish crust in a display of harmonic finesse, and he smiled sardonically at Ryurik.

"Lothair's heir must be pleased his frightened bride has finally been found. Even after all these years, however, she must not have forgotten why she ran."

"Look to the prince's frozen face," augmented Haneul, and he sneered with unwarranted contempt.

"What am I to see there, Lord Uncle? Inexperience. A tiny cock that has never been wet by a woman who matters? Ryurik seems more frightened of her return than she will be upon reuniting with her father."

"Mortification. Ryurik cannot turn a blind eye to his prurient desires whenever his blood drains from his big head. Eljak's daughter will flee from him again," replied Haneul spitefully after disregarding his nephew's insults.

Whereas Harald carved apart joy by unimaginatively agitating those he did not like, Lord Haneul of Breidjal preferred hammering situations exactly as he perceived they should be struck. Haneul's mind was cold like raw iron, and his will was firm like metal withdrawn from smelting fires and strung into a spearhead with which the lord provoked the world. As he had done for his brother Hakreun, and now his nephew Harald, Haneul sailed the Breidjal Bakari wherever his jarl ascertained wealth and glory lay, crippling their adversaries with the brims of Breidjal's warships while he crippled his allies with a tongue untamed and untrimmed.

"It's good we are not at odds, my lord," Ryurik slighted in return. "Your nephew has already declared his patronage for the Bane of Troll's war. We will fight side by side again, or maybe we won't meet on Baelgrant's battle-fields at all."

"We fight alongside our allies, little Lysian, not for them." Pressing past his nephew and shoving aside one of Eljak's sworn swords, Haneul came to face Eljak until his breath shared the balminess of the jarl's own. "You hear word your daughter's been sighted after all these years but promise her to him because he is who Lothair chooses. Why?" the lord demanded as he bared his teeth. "What are you promised, Eljak? Why waste blood on a Storm King who spites you, or a Storm Prince who will sire a hundred heirs with farm girls before you receive yours?"

Spitting as he spoke, Eljak unassailably retorted, "I have sons who still live. I am not like Lothair Runeheim, for I have blood to spare."

Haneul Gormrikson threw his right shoulder into Eljak. The Lord of Draveskeld scarcely caught it with his own. Reaching a hand against the hilt of his sword, Haneul Gormrikson then clashed with his adversary's stifling grip. The two pried for a better position while swords on both sides were drawn.

Ryurik came between them quickly, hands intertwining with their white-knuckled grips as he endeavored to force the two apart. Ryurik failed, and Harald Gormrik stepped within the circle in response. He shoved aside his own warriors, then disarmed one of Eljak Dravens with a startling punch before pulling away his uncle.

"Lord uncle, that is enough banter for the day," Harald chided as he thwarted Haneul's fiery protest. "If Eljak were to still have hair atop his head, we would know he, too, is soon slated to enter Halvalkyra's gates."

"You have one son of value left, Eljak Draven," Haneul scathed while he receded off his nephew's staunch command. "Be the lamb your forefathers once conquered. You're the prince's thrall now—discardable until the whispers of which these ravens croak actually appear."

Ryurik withheld Eljak by the collar of his cloak, yet the gray wolf afront a snowy mountain upon a field of hunter's green fell flaccid by no measure of his appeal. "I'll make use of Stigr's foolishness!" Eljak roared. "And I would not expect a salt-bearded seal fucker to comprehend the value of my son's mistake!"

"What else moves a mountain, Lord, but more silver?" Harald resounded when he stepped afront his uncle's fuming rage. "They say the Valdhaz runs dry in Draven's Dominion. He relies on the High Lady's generosity to endure."

Haneul dusted his shoulders, censoriously dismissing his nephew before acknowledging mostly to himself, "There is more than silver to Eljak Draven's schemes. He is as deplorable as Denurl Kenning, and never have I trusted that jarl."

Amidst the heated discord, Hela Gormrikdottir quietly joined her blood. "Lord Father," she glibly resounded, "rid yourself of that foul look. We're not killing today, and it bodes ill to display it for anything else." Hela slung a hand against Haneul's waist, insisting he relent in his hunger for discord, and with a begrudging acceptance, the lord uncle of Breidjal obliged. Hela adorned a casual contentedness with the welcome she quickly afforded Ryurik, saying, "Do not look so disappointed, my half-Lysian prince. I have brought your sister with me, and oh she has missed your company as much as us."

Thyra approached beside her second, the fiery Knuth Svenson. The bastard Son of Sven likened himself more a guard to Thyra than to Lothair, from what Ryurik observed. There was no hesitation in their strides. They drove through Eljak Draven and the Gormriks and casually slowed to a halt. Thyra gave them little notice either, bumping through several men who unhappily grunted in return. She came to stand before him as if there were no other reason that she had come.

"You've cleaned up better this morning. Good. The karlar's minds often count for more than the jarl's, as I am certain you will one day learn."

Thyra leaped a half step toward the Gormriks. Harald's eyes widened at the attention thrust his way, and Hela's spirits remained non-perjured. In a curious fashion, Hela conversed with Thyra, even though no words were exchanged between them. The women finished their unspoken conversation before them all, and Harald chuckled at its end.

Disgruntled, Ryurik announced, "There's nothing left for us to speak of Harald. Take away your men. I'll find you if I have need of your counsel after we have all seen what Lord Bolvark's prepared." He measured his steps until he stood beside his sister, hand resting over the hilt of his blade to reaffirm his demand.

"Have I offended you, Storm Prince? Forgive me," he whispered, "but I kneel to no man."

"Enough, Harald," Hela chided in a manner that Ryurik did not expect. "Let us witness this from a better vantage, and let us speak at length."

Harald's interest flared, and his intonation rose to match it. "Aye, cousin. We'll claim the streets where we can feel the sea's breeze rolling over our necks."

Haneul momentarily remained, standing athwart Eljak in distaste. "I am wrong, Eljak. You are still a wolf—a wolf who conceals its true nature beside a witless lamb."

"We leave, Uncle," Harald Gormrik scolded. "Did you not hear?" Lord Haneul trailed his nephew and daughter with bitter reluctance, departing Ryurik and Eljak with diffuse glares.

Knuth Svenson drew beside Ryurik's sister, where he'd reclused through the affair, and whispered something crude into her ear. Thyra turned, their collection of Skjold pivoted with her, and her focus skipped Ryurik to attend Eljak Draven and his men. "You as well, jarl. For once, I will claim my brother's time for myself."

Eljak did not take kindly to his sister's command. The jarl abruptly laughed, and his warriors swiftly joined him when his glare ingratiated them to. Eljak once drunkenly divulged he cared little for Thyra. He believed her a foreign insurgent, degrading Stormborne heritage via her silent exploitation of the Skjold. Ryurik did not understand the jarl's opinion, especially considering he, too, hailed from foreign shores. Ryurik's recent exchanges with his sister were significantly less than amenable. He did not share Eljak's vice opinions, and perhaps now was as good a time as any to bring them together within his fold.

"Eljak," Ryurik instructed, "I will join you later. A years' time is too short for the plans we must construct, but we must delay a little longer. I owe my sister a conversation."

"Is that wise, Storm Prince?" questioned the veteran jarl. His grit gave the firm affirmation he did not approve of Ryurik's choice.

"She is my sister and the commander of the Skjold, who will one day become my shield guard. There is much for us to discuss, so I will join you after this event's close."

"My prince...and princess," the jarl fiercely grumbled.

Resolute disgust dripped from the jarl's tongue as he addressed Ryurik's sister, but in an instant, Eljak and his men were gone. The Skjold seized advantage of his quick departure to clear the space around them. Ryurik glanced to his sister, who mutely surveyed the ground the jarl had departed. Thyra feigned no respect for Eljak Draven. It would make her integration into his established alliances more difficult than Ryurik originally supposed it would.

"Here we stand." Her voice surged and trailed so abruptly it threw Ryurik completely off guard.

"You watched as I rode off to war when last we properly spoke."

Thyra's gaze did not soften when her voice transposed. "Your first, and an overwhelming challenge there was no need for you to undertake alone."

"Fate's Weave will not doom you to remain behind again." Ryurik presumed it was what she wanted to hear, but he supplanted it with a simple confession. "I need you, Thyra. I need you by my side from here on if we are to ever survive and succeed."

She persisted within her own thoughts as if she had not heard him at all. "We were less established back then. You more than me, I think."

"Am I less established now?" he queried, decidedly playing along.

Thyra paused, her face betraying no consideration when she replied, "No, but you have forged a fractious alliance doomed to fail if we are speaking to hopeless fates."

"Eljak has long stood beside me. By Freyja's namesake, his daughter and I are betrothed! What more could I have done to make it clear? Held his hand upon my return?"

"Are you..."

"Am I?"

"Still betrothed?"

"Aye!" Ryurik affirmed.

Her voice blunted the air like a damaged whetstone as she spoke, "I don't necessarily hold what's happened against you—not entirely—but the emptiness of your return washes over any lessons you might have learned at war."

"One mistake does not always break the commander. I made myself weak, so I made myself strong afterward."

Thyra momentarily smirked. "It was a bit pretentious. The Agulbargs did not outright contest the outcome, so I suppose it was a success." So she also saw the division of Tjorden's Reapings in the same light as him.

"You are strong, and I doubt you've forgotten all we lost, but we deserve stronger allies than Lady Hela and Harald Gormrik."

"It doesn't matter because we both have them and need them still. The straw that flees the broom's handle snaps beneath the weight of a single sweep, but those bound together as one are stronger than ever they are alone."

"Are we together?" Ryurik exacted, curious toward the purport of her last remark.

"Yes, brother," she sighed. Her reproach was hardly restrained when she stated, "We are together, but only if you respect my value and my word."

"Then sum the swords of the Erunheim, the Dravens, the Dulfangs, and even your Skjold. That broom sweeps far!"

"The Dulfangs' support means nothing. They will never leave Tjorden's Reach or the Great Gates, which bars sky's encroachment."

"What have they to defend with the Ardent Avant gone?"

Imperial vehemence bled through every word she imparted. "The Kingdom of Helmya and the Ardent Avant's inevitable return. Do you honestly think Jarl Ulfruk will abandon his line's ancestral charge?"

"Under the right pressure," Ryurik contended. "And for a worthwhile cause, yes, I do. There is no reason we cannot progress beyond the constraints of bygone traditions if we choose to unite and leave them behind."

She inexplicably softened, for Ryurik seemingly struck his elder sister with a pleasant surprise. "It is true," she inevitably answered. "We are not bound to a past the Runeheims and the jarls constructed—your marriage to Agneta Ilesha Dravendottir most of all."

"I null my promise to marry Eljak's daughter, and maybe I preserve the Draven's fealty, but for what cause? What do I gain from riling my closest ally?"

Thyra grimaced. Ryurik forgave no knowledge toward why, but his sister did not dwell upon it for long. "We procure the Gormriks. Their soldiers rival the Agulbarg's in number, and they exceed those who follow Eljak. They have the Breidjal Bakari, the strongest fleet the Stormborne have ever mustered, as it is told. Eljak holds the stretch of the Wrathgorne, which lies below the Thunder Falls as well as all the Soudland's ingresses, but Breidjal lies against the Helmyan Sea. The Gormriks have trade aplenty, and peace with the Kingdom of Helmya begets an alliance more profitable than one with an undertaker when Drur's Abyss overflows."

Cutting her off in earnest, Ryurik corrected, "Stormborne do not trade. We seize anything that remotely catches our interest, dissuading the traders from ever returning to our shores. It is the way we rule the land."

Scoffing, Thyra replied, "Trade is the heart of every civilization. You think me a fool? Look to the coins we use at market across the land's eight domains. It is not Erun Runeheim's visage imprinted into that silver, but the mark of the Imrahli and the other peoples of the deserts who minted them in the heart of Rhavi." Before Ryurik could shirk away to think, she persisted swifter than a gale of breathless wind. "It is rudimentarily managed compared to Lysian or any of the High East, but I assure you these lands still trade. It is something that can only grow in times of peace."

"And once you're married, how long until you slit Harald's throat while he sleeps so I alone can rule the Breidjal Bakari?"

Contentiously, Thyra answered, "I will never marry for you."

Confounded by her severity toward his little quip, Ryurik pressed for a solid explanation on how she planned to assume Harald's fleet. "I cannot fathom Harald setting aside his disdain for me to support my succession without the promise of you in his bed."

Adamantly, Thyra persisted, "Yet, here I stand with the certain promise they can be yours still. I will not marry for you, so if you trust that, then trust this. I have led men longer than you, and experience counts for many things."

A pair of merchants—a caste of Stormborne that he had momentarily forgotten existed—stumbled into their clearing. The Skjold swiftly remedied the incursion by mercilessly tossing them away. His sister recovered far quicker than he, ignobly proving her galling claim.

"Whatever evidence Lord Bolvark has mustered is inessential for the jarls. Harald Gormrik believes him as much as I can see you do, but do not forget your own lesson, brother. Bind them together in a common cause that propagates your own interests. Then they are bound to you and only you."

Ryurik scoffed, frustrated with her lecture on the duties of succession without advice on how they were achieved. "That is plain to see. What would you have me do to see them all achieved?"

"Betroth the Gormriks, and you command the Trollsbanes too. Sack the Dravens, and the Kennings could become yours, but should you decide to stand by Eljak, he *must* answer to you. The Agulbargs are exhausted of fighting, they have made it brutally clear, but they will never betray Sven Agulbarg's indomitable memory. You have the Erunheim. You can summon the Skjold if circumstances allow it!" The vehemence with which Thyra spouted that particular statement elucidated a yawning desire. "Who is then left to challenge your ascension but Eljak Draven or Kennings depending on whom you choose?"

Ryurik reflected upon her plan's potential, so as brevity continually escaped him, he dove into the blaring issue in her scheme. "Can the Gormriks keep their peace with Eljak Draven if I find a way to control the mountain lord?"

"Only if Jarl Eljak remembers he answers to you, but it is difficult to control the man who seeks to enact his vengeance on another through you."

"His need for vengeance dies with our grandfather, no differently than our past bindings to Lothair's current will—"

"I do not trust him!" Thyra stymied with an iron will.

Delas of Death himself rise from his abyss to consume hers and Eljak's hatreds whole. "Do you trust any of them?" he sincerely requited.

"No, not entirely, but I trust Eljak Draven least of all."

"Then understand my reservations when you beckon me to join with Harald Gormrik."

The Skjold barked to each other from behind.

Together, they spun to regard the disturbance.

Lothair sauntered the soft ascent to Stormguarde's center square. Mother walked beside him, as always. Amidst their entourage of Skjold, Seers Dragoln and Drurhelm walked beside a third hoary man of the moon. Hosvir—sworn to Helti, the runic god of war—had finally returned to Stormguarde after a reprieve in Tjorden's Reach. He looked better than the rest. Maturity suited him well.

"What will you choose?" Thyra asked of him.

"I do not know," Ryurik confessed in a solemn oath suspended by nothing but truth.

"Soon, we will need to." Her voice wandered down a hidden path, curdling like a nestled dragon where Ryurik could no longer discern its intent.

"When the truth of Agneta's sighting comes to light, I will know for sure." Thyra challenged his reply without imparting a single word, but Ryurik understood it only meant there was a need to advance their trust. "That is when I will have your answer," he reaffirmed.

"When you do," Thyra furthered, "so must I. Don't doubt that even now, we're the outsiders. Common cause is dissolving, and Mother's marriage was a ruse. Lysians and the Stormborne despise one another, and our blood will ensure we are hated by them both. If we do not stand together, we will not stand for long."

Ryurik paused, caught on the edge of something clever, yet there he mutely hovered without the will to speak. For all the wisdom and counsel she wished to proffer, Thyra left him without her voice, support, or even a simple letter as he fought at the Great Gates. Yet, here she betrayed no implications she abandoned him to the storm for five years. Ryurik locked his eyes with hers. Pain. It was the Ehlrich's superlative burden. Did she regret her abandonment of him, or was she as consumed by her own intimate motives as Mother was with hers.

Ryurik had known his sister longer than Lothair, Eljak, or the other jarls. Thyra did not relent to anyone if she did not deem it a worthy endeavor. She never yielded to their grandfather, even athwart his retracted decree of panged fervor, which would have seen her banished from the Stormlands or killed if she continued to resist. She did not yield, and yet here—in recognizing him as the Storm King's heir and in offering all she had—Thyra yielded. She yielded to him. An apology might never escape her mouth, but through his sister's actions, to some degree, it already had.

Thyra blunted Lothair where Ryurik could not, serving within the callous man's shadow when he simply ran away. That was what he had done, after all, at least in the beginning. He fled his Storm King, his grandfather, a man he did not necessarily wish to succeed. He would succeed the Tempest Throne, but Lothair's legacy—if there was any to be accounted for—should simply be washed away with the breeze.

It could be easily claimed that most every tragedy donned by the Lysian Empire and the Stormlands in the last century was born of the craven ineptness of the latter's king. Ryurik did not wish to adorn the fate of his brothers. He did not wish to be that same Storm King. Thyra did not wish it upon him either, and with her every step, she made it brutally clear.

"Thank you, sister." Was it something she needed to hear? No, but it was more something Ryurik felt he needed to say.

"One day, you will have better reason to, little brother. For now, we must simply trust one another and learn when to agree and disagree."

<hr/>

Drur's seer sensed death wherever his feet fell. His nose could waft the finest scents of life's passage through Death's Arch, then on into Drur's Abyss. The air tasted of life's plea for succor, for what else was its smell if not the fleeting memory of that once lived. In every voice that spoke, he found the faintest hints of demise—the death of wind at breath's end, the death of love in a woman's cry, and the death of thoughts when words made their passage into the folds of a mortal's mind. Death intertwined with life itself like a virulent lover whose needs consumed them both, and the thought made Seer Drurhelm smile.

Drurhelm spent a lifetime amidst the richness of death. His was the pleasure taken by a warrior who buried his fallen comrades after each battle. He once slew men whenever his thane bid, and his hands then buried the countless dead. Toiling soil over corpses for decades or more, he sowed life all across the Stormlands, beginning with his mother after a sickness took her life. Lifeless bodies and injured souls writhed through the Arch of Death, almost always plummeting into Drur's Abyss. The sight of death never sickened Seer Drurhelm. Ever since weeping above the grave containing his sister's corpse, he found exquisite beauty in the work.

Pestilence of both bygone and imminent rapport currently saturated Stormguarde. The jarls' veteran armies had brought back a myriad of wounded from the war, wounded who were not long for Death's Arch. Of the deceased, only the bodies of the reputable and wealthy would burn on skeide ships sent out to the sea. The rest were left to the seers to bury, and so through him, the runic god of death's legendary powers would grow.

Thus came the only glory truly befitting Drur. Yes, Drur did hunger for Stormborne souls he was gifted by his adopted mother, Monomua. That was as undeniable as the totality of Lysian's fall. The promise of those soon to be delivered fresh, however, enticed Drurhelm so much more.

Dragoln recently returned to the runic temple bearing an ancient goblet forged for the Draconic Father of all runic gods. The Stormborne had recouped a relic that last dwelt in the Stormlands thousands of years before. The goblet's return was a worthwhile spectacle, but Seer Dragoln also brought word of an appetizing prospect for which his ears were finely attuned. War and the promise of death were why Drurhelm had come to witness Bolvark's show.

The political discord rife between the jarls did not interest Drurhelm in the slightest. The Stormland's noble houses had vied with one another for land and power over thousands of years. They would continue to do so for thousands more. It was in the nature of men to seek ownership over things not their own.

Jarl Baelgrant seemed to understand this clearer than most. If the heart desired conquest, let it be not with one's fellowman but with the stranger next door. Bolvark of the Nordland sang of war with the Garathandi. The potential was too great for Drurhelm to ignore. He needed to see Bolvark's proof himself. He needed to be sure of its authenticity before he threw out his voice in support of the Trollsbanes' call for conquest.

"Helti's thirst for war has been satiated for a hundred years over. The Stormborne have spent their blood. We need time to work the land and reclaim our disregarded homes, not march into another damned war," said Seer Hosvir.

Hosvir, likewise, arrived in due time to witness this potential marvel unfold. Sworn to Helti, the seer had long been confined to the Great Gates of Tjorden, where warriors swore the runic god of war fought beside them. What a bold claim. Helti died when last he descended from Halvalkyra to fight beside the Stormborne. Though he had been saved by Freyja's love, the runic god of war had not left since.

Besides, the runic gods seldom dealt in mortal affairs. Helti fought mortal wars no more, and war belonged to Drur as much as it belonged to him. Helti was war's deliverer. Helti bathed in its excess, but his calling served something more. Drurhelm perceived Helti as a herald to Drur and nothing more. He was the sword and shield presaging his brother's maw.

Yet, for all his wrath and courage, Helti's seer was practical. Hosvir's keen practicality thwarted Drur's ambitions. At times, it even countered the cavernous covets of his own runic god. Many opposed war with the Garathandi and the High Lady of Stormguarde's obsession with the Broken

Fjords. Hosvir also threw in his voice, rebutting all strides toward new aggressions with an ardent fury the moment he stepped foot in Stormguarde.

Why? Drurhelm could not comprehend why. Months in the Range of Tjorden should have told a tale similar to those told across the Range of Valdhaz. The heaviest of winters was over, snow sluggishly melted, but the mountains would soon slough it off in monstrous strides. There would be little farmland for crops to grow under the Thunder Falls once the floods began. This should be clear to a shrewd man like Hosvir, so what knowledge did the seer retain that swayed his opinions that infuriating direction?

"My son sees beyond the needs of the runic gods. The next war does not belong to them. It is for the jarls, the Stormlands, and a purpose we must attain before we begin fighting among ourselves," countered High Lady Valyria in a stern tongue.

"War for the sake war is not glorious. Helti never bids his children to embark a conquest if the saga sings for bloodshed without purport." Tenacious as the runic god of war who fought Baelric the Black Sword ages ago, Hosvir stated, "War without good reason puts us at the mercy of a wayward storm, which ravages everything it passes over."

"Lord Bolvark does not ask we march to simply slay trolls. I refrained from summoning Baelgrant's swords to defend the Great Gates because I did not know how the Garathandi would respond to a Nordland left mostly undefended. The lord of Langreklif simply wishes to seize his own glory. Simple reasoning, but not without purport," Lothair resounded with an echo of death.

"The reasons are flawed. Baelgrant did not fight at the Great Gates of Tjorden, yet he has been rewarded silver and gold for failing to heed your command," Hosvir continued, permeating past their Storm King's position.

"You say he has defied me?" Lothair questioned.

"You told him not to leave the Nordland. He abandoned his charge, and he attacked a foreign entity in force. What if Baelgrant had not met such easy resistance if the Garathandi responded in full force while we were besieged by the Ardent Avant?"

"I told him not to march his men to the Great Gates of Tjorden. He never defied me, my seer, and he has, likewise, not incurred the wrath of the northern trolls," Lothair rebuked.

The statement, although veracious and meritorious, was without a path to lead them forward. Lothair simply did not lead men. He hardly endeavored to lead at all, in fact. Age was not the weakness of the Storm King, for he had never led the Stormlands to war if not in defense of its riches. Lothair was a passive man, a trait he displayed since youth. Passivity was a rarity in the line of Runeheim, which resolutely ruled from the Tempest Throne since the time of Erun Runeheim. Runeheims had been well known for their vigor and verve until Lothair ensured those attributes were effectively culled with his pitiable and passive rule.

Resolute as the first Storm King of whom Drurhelm idly thought, Hosvir attested, "We must consider ourselves fortunate Jüte locks them away with permeating frost. There are fields and pastures awaiting us to replenish ourselves, and there are no good reasons to march for years to come."

"There are countless reasons for the Storm King's armies to march. Do not look to the Garathandi for reasons to fight." Drurhelm rolled his eyes at the comment, for the arguments of High Lady Valyria Runeheim could be predicted well before they arrived. "Look to the ældrik, the dragon spawn abominations the Broken Fjords hold. Are we to tolerate them forever, simply waiting for when next the Elder Wyrm Ísvalar's flight grows too large? Until we find another dragon's territory encroaching upon our own? Perhaps we should simply wait until the shadows hidden beneath their wings grow too large!"

"Enough! I do not want to hear you chatter of the Broken Fjords!" silenced Lothair in a command he conveyed unto them all. His displeasure infused each bristled hair upon his petite, wizened beard as his jowls trembled.

"I am your counsel, Father. I will never cease speaking of the thorns we refuse to abate when it is my children whose futures are at stake."

"Then cease your counsel. I am tired, Valyria. I'll die before you see this dream bear any fruit. It is better you save yourself the trouble and begin guiding your son to better ends."

"I don't have the luxury of discarding my enemy's remnants to a distant land to the east. They are beyond our control now. The only choice we need to make is when we choose to strike them down."

"Half of the enemy has sunken to the bottom of the sea!" resounded the

Storm King. "It is lost to the Ravager and time itself, and it is no longer a worry to us."

"High Lady, what happened at Riven Hold was an exception," reinforced Dragoln. The old couth choked down his coughs until the conversation halted to allow his enfeebled words to take hold. "Dwevland forges the majority border with the Broken Fjords. Hjuldir Folkenarr and his Frosthammer dwarves guard the border. They keep the Elder Wyrm's numbers in check, and we supply them with the food and drink their lands cannot sustain. It's succeeded since the birth of your line, and it will succeed until the death of all the runic gods."

Drurhelm disliked Dragoln, if only because Dragoln stood between him, total control of Torlv's runic temple, and its litter of chaste priestesses. Drurhelm was the second eldest seer in all of the Stormlands, second only to Dragoln. Dragoln esteemed the Draconic Father, so his was the voice that ruled the Runic Faith. Eldrahg's bondage abetted Dragoln's claim, and no other seer dared to challenge the Draconic Father's will.

Yet, with the reclamation of his runic god's Goblet of the Delas, there was little left to augment Dragoln's saga. Like Lothair Runeheim, Dragoln was another man soon to be claimed by the Valkyrie lest Drurhelm thrust him into Drur's Abyss. Should Drurhelm then succeed his elder, the world could move forward in a direction open to the glory of the Delas of Death.

In Ryurik, Storm King Lothair named an heir unbound by Stormborne traditions, for he was only half Stormborne. It was a future most pleasing for Drurhelm, for Storm King Ryurik Runeheim would deliver Drur souls aplenty if he were guided in the appropriate direction. Drur's seer dreamt of this future so vividly, so enticingly, and without surcease. He thought of how soon they might come and of how to bring them forth faster if the need ever arose.

"Elder Wyrms live forever, dragons half as long, and the ældrik halfbreeds grow in strength and numbers while the Frosthammer dwarves dwindle as millennia unfurl. If Eldrahg has sent you a vision, Seer Dragoln, foretelling the death of the runic gods when the Broken Fjords overspill, then know the day is fast approaching, and I have seen it as well," concluded Valyria without a lack of assurance in the doom she foresaw amassing in the Broken Fjords.

"Eldrahg has not gifted me visions in the longest time. If he foresaw a doom as terrible as the one you swear, he would have shattered my mind with its vigor and pulled me to Halvalkyra once his warning had been shared."

Interrupting the both of them, Lothair stoutly drawled, "Enough. Argue of the world's ending after I am dead. Drurhelm," Lothair addressed him directly while the High Lady's face furrowed in snubbed contempt. "I recently gifted you a skull instead of hanging it from the face of Stormguarde Keep. Am I to see Drur's ritual of skulls one last time before I pass through the Arch of Death? With my heir chosen, it might be the only thing for which I persist."

"Cease speaking of your death, and I will cease advising where my son should march for his next campaign," Valyria chastised on the edge of an effusive sorrow, which never fully unfurled.

"Valyria," Lothair comforted in a change of pace and tone. "Death is only the beginning of what lies beyond the Arch for he who is named Storm King. Halvalkyra will welcome me as it has welcomed every Runeheim before." Nodding to his daughter in diffident repose, Lothair then addressed Drurhelm. "Your ritual. Why have I not yet been summoned to witness it unfold?"

A fair question, and one Drurhelm had happily evaded hearing thus far. In truth, Drur's seer made all the preparations possible. Amid all of his excitement over the unveiling of the foreign noble's skull, Drurhelm failed to realize it only counted for half the number.

The ritual itself was quite simple. Drurhelm would call upon the Dark Moon as it shone on a cloudless night atop the intertwined seals of Eldrahg and Drur. Skulls once belonging to affluent souls who commanded the minds of men would be laid over each seal. Seer Drurhelm would invoke the strength of two Delas and their Mother Moon. Two souls would be ripped apart from the necrotic realm and their essence made gifts for Eldrahg and Drur.

Drurhelm could not acquire such a skull from the Stormlands without killing a jarl. If he were to truly call upon the Crescent Lady to erode the power of bygone mortals in an offering to Eldrahg and Drur, he would need to procure another skull. Its acquisition, above all else, would need to not see him killed.

"The runes have been drawn, and Lord Gefre's skull prepared."

Drurhelm's mouth lightly drizzled with spittle as he remembered the day it fell into his hands.

"And?" Lothair provoked.

"Amidst my initial excitement with the honor you bestowed me, it elapsed my brain that two skulls are needed for the ritual to be made complete. Forgive me, Storm King, for failing to report this unwelcome news to you sooner."

"Drurhelm does not lie, Your Grace. The ritual does call for two noble skulls."

The overripened cur's need to abet his claim displeased him, as he did not wish to be overspoken in front of the Storm King by an inferior seer. "We won't be delayed for long. I'll acquire the final skull soon, very soon."

Dragoln provided little clarity toward the thoughts spiraling inside his head. The wyrm seer's brow furrowed after considerable effort. Drurhelm did not much care for his fellowman's disdain. Dragoln had bid him report that unfortunate news to the Storm King as soon as they discovered the ritual was missing key components. He chose to ignore his advice, considering it both imprudent and wasteful of his time. For a seer of the Runic Faith, there was never threat of retribution from Lothair Runeheim. The Storm King treated them quite well no matter how their actions ultimately affected him.

Disappointed, Lothair mumbled, "That is…unfortunate. I have always enjoyed the more mythical rituals the Runic Faith can cast."

The young, pliable heir to the Tempest Throne strode forth to welcome the Storm King's procession. Ryurik's dreadful sister approached as well, glowering wrathfully over Drurhelm. He did not like the woman, for he could tell she was already spent like a Bjardja battle whore. Drur's seer much preferred the younger Tanya. Her supple, untouched youth were ripe for plucking, and Drurhelm intended to one day watch her ruin herself. Perhaps it was why Thyra despised him so. Jealousy clouded the minds of women who desired what they did not have. Tanya became his to entertain upon joining the Runic Faith and her wretched sister's to remember from afar.

Drurhelm broke the silence in blissful, devious delight to relay an insightful reminder for the Storm King as to why they had actually come. "Fear not, Storm King. They do not have to be human skulls. War with the Garathandi could prove useful in more ways than one."

Behind Thyra, Lord Bolvark Trollsbaneson readied himself to reveal the contents of his caged wagon. Some clandestine lure for his father's war lay within. The rawness of the mystery enticed her attention, but she shied that away from the lord's display. Instead, Thyra prepared to welcome Lothair, her mother, and the runic seers, excluding the dung toad they called Drurhelm, whom she viewed as neither a seer nor a man.

They approached from Stormguarde Keep, walking a path soon joining with her and Ryurik along the edge of the center square. A sprawl of wood-framed and sward-roofed houses dominated this section of Stormguarde. They rose a half measure above their stone bases. The wooden works of the craftsmen's district stretched to the south adjacent to the Sea of Storm. Several karlar staked their livelihoods along these lush streets. Lesser merchants, who could not afford fjord front residence, staked the land as well.

The denizens of Stormguarde collected at the tail of their Storm King's company. Many were already gathered around the center square. Regardless of where they stood, they gawked over the shoulders of Thyra's protectorate Skjold. Curiosity bid they follow their Storm King and encroach the caged wagon, which Lothair came for as well. Some endeavored to wrestle amidst the excitement, but her Skjold refused to allow any such incursions to proceed.

Of all the minor bouts, one piqued her attention the most. Two Skjold near the rear of Lothair's entourage impeded a thrall and his vagrant friend from entering the center square. The vagrant's face was marred in scars he most assuredly accumulated from an illness early in life. He wrapped the remainder of his body in blood-festered cloth.

Thyra assumed the thrall belonged to a butcher because of the blood-soaked apron he wore. She would watch for those green eyes, matted blonde hair, sharpened jaw, prominent and rounded chin, cracked lips, and rigid square face, if only to avoid poisoning herself with dirty, ill-prepared meat from whatever butchery he was enslaved.

"We're just trying to skirt around the Storm King, you thick-headed buffoon. Here, look!" exclaimed the butcher's thrall. He dropped to the ground and twisted his neck just enough so he could still see the Skjold.

"I'll drag my face through dirt and only lift it once I've passed beyond view if you'll just let us pass. Nobody has to know!"

"Doesn't matter," replied the first of the two Skjold.

"Are you daft! What do you mean it doesn't matter?" decried the thrall.

"Doesn't matter why you want to pass. Nobody goes any farther! Street's closed."

"Do we look like threats, big man? Why not let us pass to see the fun?" joked the thrall.

"Turn away before I have need to compensate your master. Nobody passes our line—"

"If you're so mighty, Skjold, a butcher's thrall and a vagrant should pose no threat at all."

"No, you don't," insulted the second Skjold.

The first guard laughed beside his companion when the thrall endeavored to rise. The second guard thrust his boot into the thrall's gut, pivoting behind the strike as if the boy were a rabid dog. The thrall tumbled until he landed in an open patch of mud. His vagrant friend rushed to his side, pulling him from the puddle. He tore away the cleanest portions of his tattered clothes to clean his friend's face but smeared the mud instead. Thyra cocked a brow when the butcher's thrall wrestled with his companion before the two scurried off.

The Skjold bellowed like wolves howling at the moon. Oddall chided and silenced them both upon realizing the scene they drew. His hand struck the one whose tongue came loose. His sky blue cape whipped the wind as his eyes mutely roared. The Skjold captain then abandoned them to silent reflection, and he reclaimed his place at the front. The two Skjold angrily rejoined the rear of Lothair's sluggish procession.

Returning her focus to her grandfather's processions, Thyra addressed them all. "Storm King, Mother, and good seers, I hope Stormguarde's streets have treated your feet well." Thyra immediately recognized an old, familiar face within the crowd, and she stridently addressed him next. "Seer Hosvir, welcome home to Stormguarde, friend. I assume Paladin Supreme Urien did not attempt another pass through the Range of Tjorden for you to have finally returned home?"

"Aye," Hosvir grumbled, grinning when she gripped his forearm, and he gripped hers. "Tjorden's Reach is clear of his ilk, though that was never why I lingered there for so long."

"What kept Helti's great seer from sharing Tjorden's tales of war?" she humbly asked.

"Stormborne graves, which required blessing." Hosvir motioned to the clouds wrapped around the height of the Valheim shrouding the gateway, leading to the halls of the runic gods. "Many warriors earned the right to ascend Halvalkyra upon skeide ships, and I beckoned Valvítr to send her daughters to ferry forth the rest."

"They drink with the runic god of war. They smile for the kindness you have gifted them by sending them to Eldrahg's Halls above."

Hosvir once served as a Bjardja warrior for Sven Agulbarg and for Lothair after that. As his life advanced and war raged unencumbered with every man he slew, Hosvir ascertained there was more to runic magic than casting upon inked runes for battle, so he joined the Runic Faith.

He often spoke of traditions, the seer's furtive rituals, and a Stormborne history vast and grand, and Thyra was a favored recipient of his hearty tales.

Hosvir took a particular interest in the experience Thyra brought from Lysian. The seer convinced Lothair to place her in command of his Skjold. Here she now stood, retaining the position seven years later. She had not moved much farther forward, but by biding her time with his undue assistance, Thyra now commanded the strengthened resolve and loyalty of a better-trained Skjold. Thyra knew few friends in the Stormlands, but Seer Hosvir had been her first and foremost.

"You have found your way back to Stormguarde," called her brother while she and the seer stepped apart. "I am glad you have returned to our side."

Hosvir considered Ryurik, his countenance icing over as if cursed by Jüte himself. "In time to hear you will one day become Storm King. An honor, Ryurik Runeheim," he declared, ameliorating her brother's brief distress. The two braced a handshake at the forearm. Ryurik held rigidly until Hosvir said, "Let Helti see our time together serve your rule well."

Ryurik swallowed Hosvir's assurance like it were a feast specially prepared for his own enjoyment. "Your guidance will always be welcomed in my court as it is welcome in Lothair's."

Thyra circumvented their awkward reunion to inform her grandfather in an intimate tone, "You are the last to arrive. When Bolvark takes notice, I'm certain he will begin whatever he has planned."

"Appropriate. This contingent will suffice. Take the remainder of the Skjold you reserved here and clear the center square," Lothair commanded without sparing her his eye.

"Aye." Thyra subdued her spite before it spilled. "Oddall, join Knuth and I as well."

Captain Oddall nodded, dictating another within his ranks to temporarily lead the Storm King's shield guard. "Commander," addressed the hardminded elder when he came to stand at her side.

Hosvir exacted Lothair's attention while her brother came to stand beside her again. "I will join Thyra for the time being," Hosvir declared.

It came as more of a notice than a request for release. Thyra was pleasantly surprised when Lothair simply nodded without challenging Helti's seer.

"I will find you when it is time to return to Stormguarde Keep, Storm King." Hosvir offered a curt bow, thereon inviting Thyra to lead.

Ryurik strove to speak with her as well, but she cursorily barred him. "We'll speak later when one of us has something imperative to share. Stand by the side of your Storm King."

Thyra departed, leaving behind Ryurik's concerns and stupefied stare. Hosvir strode beside her, Knuth and Oddall hovered close behind, and their Skjold escort completed the rear. They walked the perimeter of the center square. Thyra stationed pairs of Skjold to guard each street's egress. Knuth withheld a separate collection, who posted a tight circle around him, her, Hosvir, and Oddall when they drew to a halt opposite the center square from her grandfather.

Valvítr's statue shadowed them from atop a longhouse behind Thyra. The Queen of the Valkyrie pointed her sword toward the clouds. Her dualbladed Erun Ax hung at her winged back. Bolvark and his warriors leant against the covered wagon, ambling atop the stone dais at the absolute center of the square underneath the shadowy tip of her left wing.

"You have not long been in Stormguarde, and already the mindless have aged you by ten years," she commented of the seer.

Hosvir chuckled before his tongue quipped, "You mistake the patched gray in my black hair for silver. I've grown old fighting for my runic gods, not the Storm King and his jarls."

"And you were victorious," Thyra intoned. "Eldrahg's court prospers as a direct result. The Stormlands, the Stormborne, our culture…they survive too, though I do ponder how long this respite can endure."

Thyra dissected Hosvir's expression as his brows furrowed in profound thought. "Half a generation's time at most," the seer conveyed.

"So there was more to be done than burials for a few thousand in Tjorden's Reach?" Thyra queried, already knowing the answer yet still wishing to hear its details. "

"I secured the arms of a company of Bjardja I trust. We scouted the Range of Tjorden from the Great Gates to the edge of the Helmyan Sea." Hosvir paused. The termination of his tale carried like loose leaves caught by the wind. "The Paladin Supreme and his Ardent Avant have all returned to the mainland to lick their wounds."

Her breaths stacked like sticks and stones in a dam, and Thyra deferentially informed the seer of what was solidly clear. "You would not have returned upon that confirmation alone. What else did you learn, friend?"

"Helmya is in absolute disarray. We knew they abandoned their allies because of yearly diminishments in their crop's yields, but their people now starve in their streets. Many have even begun to rebel. The lords of the Alterian Highlands were first, having established themselves as the Kingdom of Emrys, forsaking Andurial and swearing to Loretia as in the olden days before Baelric the Black Sword brought them to heel. The Helmyans want to march, but I doubt they'll muster enough men to stand against them while the Irliash riot across every port connecting the isles and the north to the Helmyan's colonies in the west."

"Loretia's first nation beyond the forests of Keriador where dwell the ancient elves."

"Worse yet," Hosvir persisted, "be the advantage the Ardent Avant will gain in their maritime campaign against the Almerians. The Phah'll will eventually reinforce the kingdoms of Lumièr's and Verdun's efforts after the Paladin Supreme repents for failing to bring the Ardent Faith to bear within the Stormlands. It is only a matter of time before the Almerians fall and we are besieged again. We squabble, and now Baelgrant Trollsbane contrives ways to turn our swords against the Garathandi troll. I've seen it unfurl within a grim, moonlit augur while enraptured by shrooms. This future foretells our people's doom. It cannot be let to pass."

Thyra expected devolutions to occur both within and without the Stormlands when the siege of the Great Gates came to a close. She even predicted the Ardent Avant's recovery speed exactly as Hosvir described it. Yet, his knowledge confirmed her tacit intuitions were true. The future needed to be feared if the Stormland's course was not swiftly altered. The Fates Three's first sister *Þheyta* divulged her hand, for she had already begun spinning the wheel.

"What have you heard since returning the Stormlands?" she questioned. His knowledge was vastly important to gain since his predilections were unique from those of Knuth.

"Ryurik relies on Eljak Draven's guidance the same as at the Great Gates. Dulmir will take no part in an invasion of the far north, and Denurl Kenning has remained strangely quiet. I cannot lie," Hosvir whispered, "for I was surprised to learn how often you've walked with the Gormriks since your brother's return, Hela and Harald both."

"As am I," she answered wryly with a differential smirk. Thyra composed herself with genuine severity until she felt it suitable to renew. "Regardless of my counsel, Harald will want to join in Baelgrant's endeavor. They have fought beside one another before, and they are close friends. Our goal is to then steer them toward a better fight than one with the Garathandi troll."

"A daunting task," attested Helti's seer. "You have only met Harald Gormrik, who is the far more amenable and reasonable of the two."

"If the Bane of Trolls covets his own glorious war," Thyra staunchly contended, "we need only stir him toward a more advantageous pursuit. Harald will surely follow whichever war Baelgrant and his Nordland assume."

Hosvir's eyes glistened in realization of what Thyra was only beginning to plan. "With the Helmyans?" he whispered, bombastic and effusive.

"In arms with this Kingdom of Emrys if we must, but first, we need to address our own lack of unity. Lothair Runeheim, bless him to Drur's Abyss, will soon be dead not because I wish it upon him but because he wishes it upon himself. Ryurik will inherit the Erunheim and the allegiance of Ulfruk Dulfang, as I'm aware." Thyra paused for confirmation of Tjorden's loyalty, persevering once Hosvir passed his unspoken assurance her assumption was correct. "There are only Sons of Sven in House Agulbarg, and he must have imparted them with bits of his wisdom before he died by dragon's fire. Given time to reap fields and raise their children, the Agulbarg's will inevitably relent to march again. Baelgrant and Harald will only fight together, but we can forge the fight around that which benefits us all."

"That still leaves Jarls Eljak Draven and Denurl Kenning, whose feud burns brighter than your conquered sun," explicated Captain Oddall, who also recognized the domains contiguous to his charge were the most dangerous of them all.

Pleased with Oddall's admission to the conversation, Thyra replied, "Who we can easily stifle once one of them is gone." Bolvark Trollsbaneson dispensed a fierce battle cry, disquieting the crowds and rapturing them all. "Think on it, Hosvir. Lord Bolvark is starting something, and I would rather not openly speak to it here."

Knuth stepped forth to whisper into Thyra's ear, "How in a moonlit nightmare will we be expected to fight the Ardent Avant if they bring the full naval might of the Greater Kingdoms of Alderic with them?"

"Because the next time Urien and the Ardent Avant come to submit the Stormlands, we will be united, and we will be utterly prepared."

"Somebody's shrieking. It sounds like a Bjardja's battle cry!" exclaimed Muiri.

Muiri shoved through the crowds of fools ambling back too far to properly witness the excitement. He pulled Cadell behind him, easing his friend through warm bodies. Together, they ascended the streets clearest of karlar toward the center square, then mounted the slight rise supporting the center square.

"They might be having a duel!" Cadell shouted.

Cadell struggled to adhere to the path, so Muiri split apart the observers as they pressed forward—once for himself, then once more for Cadell to sneak through. It was not Cadell's fault he could not overpower most men. The man had been pox stricken as an adolescent, and though he lived and survived this long, it sapped most of his strength.

Helmyan pox was not contagious once the body vanquished the fever, but the Stormborne were a superstitious and entirely ignorant folk. There was no work in Stormguarde for any man who appeared sickly. Cadell told that he had not known his father, and his mother had died in her sleep when he was still young. Abandoned to the streets, Muiri's friend survived off infrequent charity comprising of mostly his own.

That, however, was only until Muiri found him behind the butchery, picking at his taut skin. Muiri snatched some scraps to cook into a makeshift meal, then shared his poorly roasted creation with the starving man. Cadell thanked him and kept around to chat. They both shared the experience of living shit lives and bonded soon after. Muiri inexorably decided Cadell was worth some decent human compassion, and he made it a personal venture to keep him alive in this awful city for as long as he himself lived.

"Muiri, I can't see what's happening. We need to get closer!"

The energy within the crowd was starkly palpable. Men staggered back as havoc cried again. Women yelped. Some even squealed like frightened hogs pulled from the safety of their dens. The two pressed on, Muiri taking the lead as always by pushing in as far as the densely packed bodies would allow.

"I know! It's a work in progress, Cadell. I have to finesse some of these bigger brutes."

Darting between the final rows of karlar, they approached a wall of Skjold. He feared he could not break through. Stormborne warriors stood behind them. Each of those strangers wore iron helmets embedded with twinned horns. Each horn curved forward like a ram's horns, or something of the like, he presumed. The twin-tusked warriors surrounded a wagon in the center of the square. Thick wool blankets and long trims of fur encased the wagon's caged frame.

A warrior cried out, hushing the last of the crowd, and his voice faded away until nothing remained but permeating silence. "You need to give the signal," ordered Cadell.

Muiri hushed his impatient friend. "I don't need to give the signal. We're almost there."

Cadell returned a distasteful glare. "If you cannot force your way through, just give the signal. I can part them quicker than an elder fox catches youthful hares."

"They might be the same bastards who kicked me earlier. I can handle it, but your rabbit bones cannot." Muiri allowed Cadell a brief moment to shift positions and capture a solid look at the two Skjold.

"They don't look at all alike. You're a liar, Muiri, and I swear to the runic gods if I ever meet your mother, I'll tell her so myself."

"Quiet! Fine. Fine. Have it your way." Inelegantly, Muiri offered the signal to Cadell's apparent glee.

Muiri slinked a few steps into the shadows to observe. Cadell removed rags from his face, revealing the full extent of its marring. He coughed, acquiring the attention of nearby karlar and Skjold. The karlar staggered back in frightened shambles, and the Skjold buffeted his advance. They soon recognized Cadell's scars, and their resolve crumbled to ash. Cadell lifted a beggar's hand, fumbling as he stumbled forward, breaking through the lines of Skjold with little more than an auxiliary cough.

Muiri thrust his way to the forefront to retrieve Cadell, entering the scene to perform the second act. "Runic gods, Caddy. Didn't Mother tell you not to wander?" Muiri led Cadell through the Skjold, hugging the faces of longhouses. "Forgive my brother. He is both stupid and deathly ill. We live two houses over. I'll drag him inside to rot, and you'll never see us again."

"Filthy thrall," exclaimed the closest guard before he kicked Muiri in the ribs.

Adamant to succeed, Muiri donned the challenge of keeping upright for the both of them. Cadell stumbled, Muiri heaving them along through the tremendous pain wracking his ribs, and they reached the second longhouse over as pointlessly promised. They slinked underneath a wood roof, which pierced the sky in two. Support beams concealed them from the sides while the rooftop enthralled them in shadow. Muiri faltered, and Cadell caught him and lay him against the wattle-walls.

"You've broken a rib," Cadell mumbled. "You can barely stand."

"I'm fine, Cadell. Keep quiet. We must stay unnoticed until the show has met its end."

Cadell shivered, and Muiri studied him. Somewhere along the path that brought them there, Cadell lost some of his tattered rags. Muiri struggled to twist, but he eventually succeeded in removing his apron. Without question, he gifted it to his scar-ridden friend.

"Do I bore you, Skjold?" the tusk-horned warrior's lord roared while approaching the Skjold guard who cracked Muiri's ribs.

"No, Lord!" cried the Skjold. "Two Alterians just needed a little reminding of who they are."

Muri scoffed at the lie. Cadell was obviously Stormborne.

"Did they need reminding the precise moment I began my show for the Storm King?" exacted the lord.

"They struck my foot while walking, so I thought it fitting to strike him back. Missed him, though. Hit his friend instead."

"Don't lie!" the Skjold's partner chastised in a whisper Muiri scarcely heard.

"Shut up!" the bastard reproved in an equally hushed tone.

"Fair, if it were any other time," the lord growled. His dreadlock mohawk whipped back like a wyvern's tail when he withdrew. The lord then turned to the Storm King, speaking as if he were unfettered by the exchange. "Any man who strikes the Storm King's shield guard strikes at the Storm King himself. Is that not your law, punishable by death? Let me enforce your will so I can continue without further interruptions."

The Storm King reposed and drawled, "The thralls scampered back to their master. How long do you expect me to wait until you've found and slain them, Lord Bolvark?"

The lord peddled a few steps backward, summoned several of his tusk-helmed warriors, and approached the same two Skjold. Muiri swallowed hard. Cadell yelped in fright as the lord faced the bastard, Skjold.

"Where did they scurry off to?" asked Bolvark.

"They claimed to live two houses that way." He pointed in the direction of their escape.

Muiri slammed Cadell against the wall of the longhouse, using the left support beam to shield them from view. His efforts were nulled when the crowds shouted out where they were. If they managed to escape, who would find them afterward? Muiri was unrecognizable among the city's hundreds of Alterian thralls, and Cadell could blend in as one too.

"Damnit, Cadell!" he yelled. "We need to make a run for it now!"

The two bolted opposite the direction Bolvark and his men came. Muiri faltered, his ribs buckling, and his gut clenched in a dichotomous swirl of pain and fear. Cadell gave pause beside him when he could not bring himself to stand.

"Cadell," he gravely demanded. "Leave me and run!"

"After all the times you essentially carried me these past years? I'll not leave you behind, Muiríoch Cadraicht!"

Warmth swelled within him, violently cascading against the anguished pain in his guts. He smiled but thrust Cadell away, refusing to see them both morbidly punished for what he alone should withstand. He prayed Cadell would leave and run as fast as his feeble legs allowed. He did not, and the horn-helmed warriors reached them in an instant, pinning both Muiri and Cadell beneath their feet.

"Did that Skjold's kick break your bones, thrall?" The lord's snide voice nicked Muiri's ear—the ear not buried beneath mud-washed rocks. "You are lucky, thrall. For you will not die today."

A woman's voice punctured this Bolvark's savagery. "Lord, you cannot kill them in the streets. That one has the right to be heard!"

Bolvark disregarded the shieldmaiden's call, retrieved Cadell, unsheathed his sword, and drove it through Cadell's chest. Cadell sagged, and the vile, twisting motion with which the lord withdrew his sword only hastened Cadell's death. Muiri screamed from under his warriors' heels as he tried violently twisting free. Another pair of boots came to crush Muiri's chest, and without breath, he screamed out in fetid agony.

Blood dripped from Cadell's lips, soaking the hair on the back of his neck. The warmth of Cadell's final breath trailed down his lips as more trickled down his back. The lord released Cadell's body before kicking it aside. Muiri's dead friend rolled like a pig stuck in the mud. The pain did not last long for Cadell, but for Muiri, it only swelled. It was Muiri's pain to bear, his anger to withhold eternally—bound to the pale visage of his friend's final breath, a face wrought with confusion and doubt, and a horrifying image Muiri could not hope to expel.

"He was a free man!" A war-torn seer stepped into the center square, departing the side of the shieldmaiden who futilely spoke in Cadell's defense. "You slew a Stormborne man for a crime that demands the althing of Stormguarde's verdict."

"The Storm King's court stood witness. Your court, Hosvir," the lord rebutted, pointing his sword toward the seer. "You did not speak out against me, so this is the result of your rule of law as well."

"He was a free man," the shieldmaiden snarled, the taste of her anger as palpable as the dirt smashed against his face.

Muiri watched as Lord Bolvark lifted Cadell's lifeless hands to examine them both for a thrall's brand. The vile, dread-locked demon would find no such mark. He would find nothing but the pox scars upon that lifeless body because Cadell was no thrall. He was Stormborne, and they murdered him for little more than distaste and sport.

"Too many pox scars to tell. I'll assume he was a thrall by association. Let the boy crawl to his master or as far as his broken body can take him."

The tusk-helmed warriors freed Muiri from their boots to join with their lord thereafter. Muiri struggled to stand, failing to move past his knees before collapsing against the ground. He pulled himself into a crouch to recover his breath. Each came dreadfully harder than the last. His heart ravaged, thumping louder and louder the longer it beat within his sunken chest.

"I'll take the body, Lord Bolvark, if you have no need of it."

Another seer waddled to Cadell and hovered over his fresh corpse. He was a fat man. His chin hung heavy as if he were on the verge of croaking. He bore a repugnant flattened nose like that of a toad. He sniffed Cadell's body, then smiled to himself thereon. Muiri endeavored to stand again, to salvage Cadell, and to escape before the toad could sniff his body again. His ribs buckled under pressure, and he collapsed to his hands and knees.

"He was obviously without a family to be seen scampering about with that thrall. Torlv's runic temple will bury him. I only ask that some of your men carry the body to our doors."

"It will be done," answered the lord, who dispatched two warriors to oblige the corpulent seer of toads.

Cadell Kornson was dead, and in the unfathomable vastness of Eldaria's cruelty, Muiri alone knew his name. When his own tongue finally fell still or when his mind faltered beneath the river's weight, Cadell's second death would be all but assured. The lesson was as hazy as the clouds blotting out the peak of the Valheim, but Muiri still vaguely recalled it. His village elder spoke to him of death once, of one's passage through the Arch when a soul left the body, and of one's passage from the minds of mortal men when last their name was heard. Muiri now carried the weight of ensuring Cadell and the joy he once knew was remembered by this world.

Struggling to his feet in resolute defiance while thrashing through the pain of each and every movement, Muiri charged the warriors pilfering his dead friend. He did not glimpse the armored arm impeding his mad dash, nor did he necessarily comprehend the force bashing his head. The force nearly knocked him unconscious. For an extended period of time, it broke him of his rage.

Dazed, Muiri glanced up from the ground. He saw the face of the shield-maiden—the woman who shouted out in defense of Cadell. The woman lifted him herself, and she guided him to the edge of the center square to the sides of an old Skjold captain, a fiery warrior, and the war-torn runic seer. Caught between three insurmountable men and a seemingly indomitable woman, Muiri sagged to his knees once released.

"Did the thrall charge me, Commander?" interrogated Lord Bolvark. He did not shift his insouciant stance when he demanded her answer.

"Never made it far enough to tell. I assume he's just weary of waiting to see what you've hidden within your wagon like everybody else."

A sardonic grin crept over every feature of Bolvark's embittered face. Muiri alleged the lord even cursed her beneath his breath, or perhaps his lips merely flinched. Trounced afront the entirety of the Storm King's court, the lord did not handle it well. Bolvark deserved more than simple embarrassment for Cadell's murder. If Eldrahg's court were truly just, Bolvark deserved nothing less than white lightning through his back and Valvítr's ax through his wicked heart.

The lord digressed to return to his caged wagon. In a single, flurried motion, he tore away the wool sheathing to reveal the battered husk of a troll. How the creature was alive, Muiri might never know. Its dour perseverance sang brilliantly of the resilience of Garathandi trolls.

Disregarding the next victim of Stormborne barbarity, Muiri begged, "Please, let me bury his body. Do not let that seer claim it for himself."

The Skjold shieldmaiden was initially astounded by his request. "It is not my place to choose what happens next, nor is it yours to ask that it change. Stay quiet, and when this...this travesty expires, you might live."

The shieldmaiden handed him into the care of the fire-headed Skjold officer, who wore a particularly vibrant cloak. There, within the grip of the bulking Skjold warrior, Muiri remained as the lord unfurled his show. Bolvark roared once o'er, brandishing two seaxes as if they were tusks. He frightened most everyone who was gathered, charging disparate throngs of the crowds in terrifying jest. They laughed, but only after wetting themselves in fear.

"That is the cry of Garathandi trolls. That is the call of war when it rolls in from Jüte's icy north." Sheathing his seaxes, Bolvark motioned to the stone-spruce and umber-tusked troll dressed in the tattered cloth of what was once fine robes. Amused, he deplored, "This is what the Bane of Trolls makes of them. For hundreds of years, my family has shielded the Stormlands from the Garathandi scourge. Lord of Langreklif, Jarl of the Nordland, I am that man's son come to tell our tale as he reaves the Realms of Frostheim to break more into his thralls." He waved over the decrepit troll. "Don't let this one deceive you. It was broken for a different cause, but when they are properly submitted, there are no better thralls."

The lord dwelt amidst his revelation, allotting time for his grim resolution to sink within the heads of his Stormborne audience. Muiri seized in intense anger. This cruel lord slew anyone he deemed to be a thrall so they could be replaced with his father's stock. Muiri scoured him with his gaze, and Bolvark Trollsbaneson seized an ax from the hand of a fellow warrior. In one fell stroke, Bolvark cut the cage's chains.

"Is this wise, Lord Bolvark?" the Storm Prince called out.

"This voodoo priest poses us no threat," the lord scoffed. "This one I broke myself—brought back from my father's first raid through the Fulklar Foothills along the Garathandi Empire's southeastern coast."

With pained effort, the emaciated troll delivered itself from the wagon's prison to settle on solid ground. The troll's legs stuck out like gnarled branches, collapsing sideways like twigs when dropped into a stream. Bolvark quickly took notice. Maliciously, he forbade his men from providing any aid. Bolvark Trollsbaneson simply smirked as he forced the crowds to witness the troll find a stance from which it could speak.

Yet, the troll did much more than speak with the freedom it obtained. It wove its hands in swift circles, binding the air around them as glistening strands of moonlight descended from the daytime moon. It mumbled in incoherent Garathandi as its hands crafted the energy born of the lunar realm. The troll incurred confounded gasps from nearly all those who watched.

Even the red-haired Skjold gripping Muiri's shoulder shifted as the spell continued to unfold.

Visibly mortified, the Storm Prince questioned, "What is it casting?"

The lord did not feign to answer.

"Damn you, Bolvark!" he yelled. "What does your troll intend to do?"

"Do not draw your swords," Bolvark insisted. "It's a simple ritual so we can understand it, and so it can understand us."

Many decried Bolvark's appeal, but the vile lord ignored them all. He permitted the troll to weave its lunar magic while he and his warriors dauntlessly stood guard. Emptiness consumed the surrounding sky. The air between the troll's long, thin fingers condensed as fabric crumpled during a wash. The sphere of moon-fed power collapsed around the troll, emitting a shockwave. Nothing came thereafter. The troll went still as it lay against the wagon's iron bars. Not even the Storm King deigned to speak, nor his Prince of Storm.

"Tell them your name, troll," Bolvark instructed the troll.

"I am Vrimos, Lord," groveled the battered troll. Its voice bore but a fraction of the drawl from the chant before, but its guttural timbre resonated troll at its heart.

"Tell them where you are from."

"I am from da city of Vel-thaka in da Garathandi Empire far to da north."

"Tell them what you were."

"I be a voodoo priest of Voodandum, servant to Witchqueen Rasha and follower of da Bright and da Dark Moons."

"Tell them what you are now."

The troll hesitated, imperceptibly so, but hesitated before it spoke, "I am thrall to Jarl Baelgrant, da Bane of Trolls."

The pretense unfolded before Muiri as if he were a faery floating in a forest grove. The troll's story—a jarl's predisposition dreamt in the solace of night, then recounted to be heard by the world—unfolded raw. In a youth free from slavery, Muiri's mother told him stories of their reigning lord's hall where traveling theater troops once performed. They were an Almerian novelty abstracted from the Seas de Cielos and refined in Helmyan courts. Characters drove a story forward, one the writers wished to be told. Those men knew within the confines of a story, they could twist the minds of man. Whatever this troll once suffered, he did not suffer anymore.

Muiri knew pain. He had known pain all his life. He knew its rapturing touch better than anyone. This troll conveyed a charade, and these barbarians were the audience enraptured with his every insincere word. Pain was the loss of what little was left to love, and only a fool valued himself above his family, friends, and the world.

"How does one so titled degrade themselves until they become nothing more than a thrall? Do you see this man, this human thrall?" The shield-maiden passionately inquired. She exuded the unrelenting aura of command, and it singularized the Skjold were hers to command. "He's Alterian, a thrall. Before your revelation, he watched his friend die—speared like salmon then flaunted before us all. He does not yield to being a thrall, even if that entails he'll be dead before tomorrow, so what makes you buckle like an infant boy to his mother's scold."

The troll crassly regarded Muiri, his cracked lips flapping as he spit in disgust. "They give you too much freedom if that is what you are. Die like a dog, pale little Alterian spawn. I will not die fighting battles I've already lost."

The troll broke form, and it studied him deeper than before. Muiri shivered with the sensation of spiders ascending his spine. The troll's pervasive gaze pierced his soul. Had this Vrimos realized Muiri deciphered his ruse. It would be better if he had. Muiri's tact would not be broken by some decrepit, enslaved troll. Let the voodoo priest flex himself while endeavoring to undo Muiri's nerves. Muiri's was already broken, but that did not entail he would willingly yield to any Stormborne or Garathandi troll.

"The Garathandi disembarked the Nordland, sacked the fjord fortress of Langreklif, killed its jarl and lord son, and forced his second son to retreat to the Godrulheim Divide. I fought your hordes beside Baelgrant Trollsbane, Eljak Draven, Hjuldir Folkenarr, and my father twenty years ago. I was only sixteen, a boy amongst men, who fought three thousand trolls and their wolfhounds of war. Not one survived beyond those who fled by the time the fighting was done. We took no prisoners. We tried. By Helti's beard, we strove to ensnare at least one fucking troll, but your kindred fought until they could not flex their tusks. Do you know what they did then? They impaled themselves on their own spears before we could break them!" called forth a Bjardja jarl with a half-shaven and tattooed head.

"Then da Bane of Trolls has gotten betta at capturing Garathandi for thralls. There are more like me. Am I da coward, Lord? So be it if I am, but I'll not rot in darkness with a plagued seax my back!" Vrimos fell to his knees, legs shaking, and he shrieked in a guttural pitch that effervesced the hearts of even the most resilient of men. "We been dying across da Frall-heim. We been dying in da far north for five wretched years. Da Witchqueen Rasha curses her own people, and da warlords be fighting amongst them-selves while her plague devours us all. Dey been fighting for as long as you fought da pale, pink men from da south. I will be da coward, I'll be da thrall until I die, but I won't die in da Realms of Frostheim to Rasha's Crimson Curse!"

Dire recognition engulfed Muiri's false observations. Amidst Bolvark's filthy ruse, the troll broke to divulge a grisly truth. Drivel ceased falling from his lips. In place of compulsory subterfuge while upon his knees, Vrimos confessed to the plight his people faced.

Muiri quietly wriggled from the ruddy-haired Skjold's grip to level with the troll's pain. Vrimos's furor had diminished, and his body abandoned the reds, which had previously carried it through his veins. Sweat only ever dripped from brows that broke the truth, and sweat did not drip at all from this troll's. His focus was rigid as stone.

The commander took notice of his newfound freedom but gave no orders he was to be constrained again. "Are you hurt? Why do you kneel?" she asked, sparing him an unexpected moment of consideration amidst the imperative development of Bolvark's ruse.

"To hear him for who he really is," Muiri lied, sparing a shred of truth, knowing he knelt because he believed his ribs were broken.

The shieldmaiden smiled, and the slender corners of her smile dove into divots as if she found him mildly amusing. "What is your name?" she asked.

Sorely, he answered, "Muiríoch Cadraicht." Vacuous pain enveloped him afresh.

Without reason, he surrendered his name to this woman he did not know, who he should not trust, but who he chose to trust all the same. Her brows furrowed when he scrunched his face in anguish, but she did not hesitate in returning her attention to the voodoo priest. The Skjold's commander, who Muiri was now certain she was, simply chose to let him stay. She was decent for allowing him this slight reprieve, but she did not fool him completely. Muiri knew he was a thrall to her still—a pawn in greater men's games.

"You're Alterian, are you not? Have you seen runic magic in your lifetime?"

"Aye, I have seen it before…from both sides of your Great Gates," he condemned.

"I am sorry," she said amid an elegiac stare. Muiri savored those words even after they fizzled to nothing, as if her lament alone redeemed all the injustices the Stormborne committed against him. "What do you think that troll cast? I've never seen anything like it."

"Lunar magic," he answered, but he was certain they were both dreadfully aware. "Without a single rune in sight for the troll to cast upon either."

The same inked Bjardja jarl, whose half-shaven hair fell thickly over the unshaved side of his head, decreed to the Storm King, "I promised it when we divided Tjorden's riches, and I'll make that same promise again. One year, no more than two, and the warriors of Breidjal will sail the Breidjal Bakari to Langreklif to support Baelgrant in reconquering the Realms of Frostheim from the Garathandi Empire!"

"Aye, Harald. You would do well to make room in your fleet!" barked a bald and black-bearded jarl who approached the Storm King and his son.

That wasn't right. Lothair was not the father of the freshly ordained heir to the Tempest Throne. Lothair's son was dead, slain at the Great Gates as all in the Stormlands knew. The man the jarl approached was Ryurik, Fourth Prince of Lysian, who arrived with his mother, Valyria Runeheim, alongside his two sisters from the High East seven years ago.

His sisters? One was the priestess, Tanya, who lived in the runic temple where Cadell used to, once begging for food. By Loretia's bush, Muiri met her outside of Stormguarde Keep during Ryurik's Kingslag. The other was a staunch warrior. They called her Commander Thyra, who inherited the Skjold! That was her standing above him, imperious as the blazing phoenix of an empire forsworn! What intrigued Abyss of Drur's had Muiri fallen into?

"And why be that, Eljak? Will we be fighting beside one another again in war, or does it simply suit you to howl at the moon?" incited the Bjardja jarl upon a sordid tongue.

Jarl Eljak placated, "Draveskeld will set sail with what few ships we have docked in Tjorden's Reach. I will fight aside the rest of the Storm-lands, and I'll be the Lord of Draveskeld who reclaims land once belonging to Hælla Dwolv."

Harald shifted in mild surprise, then cocked his head toward his fellow jarl. He chuckled, then grasped the bald-headed jarl's forearm. Their hand-shake was as rigid as their glares were crude and distrustful. They held firm, sealing their oath before the Storm King and Lord Bolvark, the lord who slew Cadell without remorse. Let them make their oaths to Bolvark and his father. Oaths bequeathed to the wicked would never last, and Muiri intended to be there when they crumbled to dust.

Muiri relinquished a curse, sealing it in the name of Loretia, whose whispers sauntered within mortal's dreams. From the heights of Ranges of Valdhaz and Tjorden, to the lands ruled by a feral desert's storm, to the vast Plains of Orglahar where roam the orcs, into the depths of lush Keriador, against the Sildurai city of Ur, across the expanse of the Seas de Cielos, into the High East where Lysian fell, and through a thousand places more, let the House of Trollsbane never see another conquest's glory. Let them writhe in earned agony beside Drur.

Ryurik Runeheim, the newly ordained Storm Prince and heir to the Tempest Throne, planted himself at the forefront of the propagating discus-sion to see his voice heard by all. "One year to plant and sow the fields, one year to reap the harvests, and together we shall then set forth to see how fare the Garathandi." He addressed Lord Bolvark directly, saying, "Take my word. The Erunheim will march in a year when winter next fades and glaciers recede. We sail to the far north as summer begins. You will not be abandoned by glory. It is yours and mine to seize."

"Your Grace." Bolvark bowed to Ryurik's promise mockingly, though it was a slight the Storm Prince did not perceive. "Let this troll be the first enemy to fall to our swords since Urien Aylard and the Ardent Avant were driven from the Great Gates of Tjorden!"

Bolvark's brow hung dry, and he betrayed nothing of his intent before it happened. After seizing the same ax he had used to break the cage's chains, Bolvark severed Vrimos's head. So ended the life of the voodoo priest when his head came to languish at Bolvark's feet. The troll's left tusk punctured a shallow puddle of mud, and it faced the Storm King directly.

"Storm King!" the seer of toads bellowed. "This voodoo priest once held great power, as we all clearly heard. Lend me his skull, and Drur's ritual of skulls will proceed!"

Muiri did not delay escaping to overhear the Storm King's response. In the hot turmoil following the decapitation of the troll, he slunk behind the fire-headed Skjold, down the first street he found, and through the crowds of karlar. He dragged his aching body as far as his ravaged ribs allowed, eventually locating a familiar cross street five down. It led directly to the merchant district, two streets away from his master's butchery and his alleyway hovel.

Muiri waited, obscuring himself between sward-roofs whenever anyone strolled through. Eventually, unto the prayer he failed to ever plead, an oxen-drawn cart presented the opportunity for him to proceed. He dashed behind the cart's unsuspecting driver, pitched onto the back of the wagon, fell into mounds of red apples, and rode the cart to the merchant district. How he came to clamber his way home thereafter, he might never actually remember.

In the expanse of lucid dreams that his pain absconded, Muiri evoked Cadell's name. Amid the groves—where soared the memories of his mother—arose his friend's face. To his mother, he chronicled the oath he failed and recounted his promise whilst imagining where it might lead. Her voice effervesced, resonating as if real, but nothing else in the dream felt even remotely real. Nervously, Muiri walked her way. He extended a hand to touch her pale cheek before the vision effervesced into a perfidious nightmare.

Moonlit surrealism forgave Loretia and her ethereal zeal. The vast sky then opened unto a thousand wails. Spirits intertwined with his own. The sun's blinding glare burnt through the tides of bitter destiny. Starlight shone around him as he strolled through a celestial veil. Death befell, yet it did not persevere. Shadow descended, held within a blazing hand of inscrutable familiarity unto which Muiri forced his love, faith, and will.

Muiri awoke atop his wet, dungy bed. Mud, blood, sweat, and tears choked his face, and Durkil nearly choked him to death. The pudgy porker demanded where he had been. Muiri never answered. He merely groaned in incoherent pain. He was broken, body rendered useless without repair, so Durkil stripped him of what little he falsely owned by abandoning him to Stormguarde city to perish like a stray.

Muiri aimlessly wandered, pausing every time his ribs torqued in pain. He had become something worse than a thrall, for at least thralls had food and a place to rest. He was a vagrant, like Cadell once was, with no skills beyond fishing, butchery, a comedic talent for getting himself hurt, and replicating the travesties he distinguished in the world.

All of that was useless to him now. It would not mend his broken body. He thought of little more than Cadell. Where had he been taken again? The runic temple! Muiri stumbled, and at times, crawled forward as pain wracked his body with every step he took. Not long for this world, not long to rejoin with his mother and Cadell, Muiri climbed the fjord into the Range of Valdhaz where the Valheim mutely overlooked Stormguarde's runic temple.

<hr />

Drafting runes demanded little effort. The key lay in the minor details: sizing to the correct proportions for a ritual's strength, including every stray curve of the illustration, and augmenting each with a little artistic flair where suitable. Tanya had grown adept at drafting runes, but Siv's talents rivaled those of Seeresses Dalla and Torunn. Torunn no longer resided in Torlv's runic temple. Thus, her priestesses completed such work alone, likening their labors to the legacies of those who now served the Runic Faith afar.

Siv sometimes adhered to too strict of a regimen. They had been made to redraft her half of the runic circle as a result. Ironic, considering Tanya always assumed more liberties than Siv, yet her work was never found wanting. If the runes were mostly accurate or if the seer for whom you drafted was incredulously fond of you, one could take liberties in their work. Irrespective, on most occasions, aside from this particular one, Tanya's work warranted more scrutinization than Siv's. Tanya did not envy Siv, nor did she ever wish to exchange places. Managing the repellent, unnerving seer of toads was her preemptive duty for her adopted sisters.

Chalking powder atop the ground under the mammoth pines of the east courtyard grove, Siv redrafted her half of the runic circle while Tanya augmented it with bird, elk, and bear bones. They had blessed many die for the ritual since Drurhelm—his gawking, wafting pestilence—and Dragoln's return. Die was a thoroughly loose term exchanged amongst the seers. Specifically, it described an object deemed suitable to bind to a runic god. The priestesses anointed, seasoned, and blessed those chosen die with the ritual's apposite songs. They had bound die to Eldrahg, to Drur, then bound some few more with ambits adhering to both.

"I've been studying this ritual's template since he brought back that first skull. Every day, I poured it over, and this was exactly how it was etched! What's not right about it?"

Siv often spiraled whenever her work was faulted—never for long—but until she regained composure, it soured her as a whole. The mousy-haired priestess adored brushing her thin brows, scrunching her nose, and biting at her lip's fleshy center when toiling over mistakes in her work. Tanya speculated Siv enjoyed the aeolistic nature of drafting and casting runes since it gave her the reassurance she held worth. Siv obviously held worth. She just needed occasional reminders of how much she was truly worth.

Siv deceived herself by investing in silly things like the seers' every opinion, perfection in her work, or what a warrior in the hospice thought when his eyes befell her butt. Siv was both clever and smart, or rather stupidly smart. It was obvious what every one of them thought.

"You did skip a day of studies to brood during my brother's Kingslag," Tanya drawled. "That is probably why it escaped you."

Siv's eyes hung unamused, but her face told a different tale. "Hardly! I crept back in well before sunset to spare myself plenty of time."

Flustered, Tanya exclaimed, "You snuck out to join the Kingslag and never came through to say hello?"

"Oh, I found you," Siv contested. "But you were quite preoccupied with some Alterian thrall at the keep's gates. I didn't think it wise to interrupt your affair."

Nettled with her excuses, Tanya scolded, "Not good, Siv. Dragoln does not appreciate us sneaking around without his permission, especially by ourselves."

Galled, Siv countered, "He doesn't approve of us drinking or contending his fellow seers either, but he forgave you for both after seeing it all, a clemency I could never earn." Siv folded her hands atop her lap as she stared befuddled at her work.

Tanya tended to scrubbing away Siv's interpretation of high cheekbones before chalking them anew. "It was not a very vigilant guard. Drurhelm's fat. Dragoln's old. It's not too difficult to misplace them if you try to."

Fuming exasperation, Siv protested, "I stare at this, close my eyes, imagine the template, and they look the same." She scrunched her eyes as if envisioning it again. "Exactly the same!"

Given little instruction, Siv did draft an exact replica from the template, outdoing even herself. Unfortunately, a replica would not suffice for the runic circle Drurhelm demanded. The foreign skulls, both the human's and the Garathandi's, gave requisite they modulate it in full.

"Siv, it's not always an unerring replica. Sometimes it is, but not for this occasion. Have you seen my half yet?"

"Not really," Siv sorely attested. "I've been drafting my half twice over, you know!"

Tanya embellished her voice, intending Siv would take no offense. "That's okay. Look at mine and tell me what you see."

Tanya ceased chalking the ground to rise as her fellow priestess shifted to her feet too. The Second Princess of Lysian, redressed as a Runeheim like both her mother and brother, awaited Siv's judgment. *Drurhelm's nepotism for her youth and sovereignty be placed aside in a djinn's bottle where she prayed it would never be rubbed to life, but all his qualms were legitimately admissible.* There was a reason why her skull fit the mold and why Siv's flunked the review.

Siv waved her hands over every crevice of Tanya's creation, exclaiming, "Well, it's not the same at all! You've chalked a…a troll's skull?"

"Exactly!" Tanya resounded from the bottom of recognition's gorge.

Upon returning earlier the same day, Drurhelm flaunted his newly acquired skull that belonged to a recently slain troll. Not a mountain troll. Their portly faces were ill-shaped and grotesque. This one was grotesque but in an exotic and well-structured way. The features were sharper and more refined. Tanya presumed it once belonged to a Garathandi. How disparaging its story was set to end for a cruel ritual drafted for Drurhelm's necrotic release.

"What?" Siv decried, for she apparently did not understand. "It shows to human skulls, not— Not this wicked rendition!" Wicked was a rather appropriate description for a ritual meant to retrieve two souls from beyond the Arch in an offering to the runic gods.

"The first ritual most likely used Stormborne men's skulls, which is why the template was etched the way it was. We're salvaging a skull from a Garathandi troll and a man from the mainland. They're different, so we modulate the runic circle as necessary, or else it explodes when Drurhelm casts upon it."

Tanya mimicked a volatile explosion of solar sorcery, the likes of which Siv had likely never seen before. There was something universal buried in the gesture. Siv clearly understood the message. It instilled a vivacity in her eyes brighter than the magic Tanya imitated as a joke.

"We should leave it the way it is and see what happens when Drurhelm casts the rune."

Tanya giggled against Siv's rather enticing suggestion. "You're the best of us Siv, which is why I make you read every tablet I manage to pilfer from the runic vaults."

Siv briefly blushed, her cheeks reddening like delicate apples. "I'd rather be our temple's finest herbalist and nurse than its best runic drafter."

Tanya adored the enigma buried in runic magic and how much like the Crescent Lady it truly was. The runic circles and tattoos were strewn in the auspicious image of the lunar realm's craters and curves. Each was filled with tributes to the feats of Eldrahg's runic court. Rituals of the legends of the runic gods were chanted atop the runes. Their songs sang like occultic, skaldic poetry resonating off Monomua's own tongue.

Exceedingly adept adherents to the Runic Faith could even adorn themselves in her moonlight, mirroring the shape and the light of the current moon the caster called upon. Seer Hosvir had mastered this particular talent. Helti's favored seer could charge into battle swathed in the Bright Moon's impenetrable light or cloaked by the Dark Moon. Tanya enjoyed working in the hospice, but by the runic gods, she would someday wield those siphoned powers of Monomua's everlasting dance.

"Let's make it beautiful then, friend," Tanya insisted, noticing her sister's admirers—the Gormriks—and a few others had begun to arrive.

They worked quickly. Siv's revitalized spirit propelled them through. They augmented the rune of skulls and bones before stepping apart from its grisly mien. Drurhelm pandered to himself nearby, coddling his freshly cleaned skulls. Droplets of a flesh-devouring solution pooled within the trough of the troll's tusks. Tanya evaded his approval, suggesting Siv do the same. Siv waved over Dragoln instead, who arrived in twice the time it took a snail to cross the grove.

"Seer Dragoln." Siv beckoned. "Time is fleeting before Drurhelm must begin the ritual, but I must know if the circle we've drafted is adequate, if it...fits the mood."

Shedding no expression while he considered Siv's question, Dragoln shuffled forth. He entered the runic circle, meticulously overstepping acutely positioned bones as he conducted his review. Eldrahg's seer beamed in approval, absolving the priestess of her prior, minor mistake. Siv quickly abandoned the languish she self-inflicted only moments before.

"A faultless rune for a decent ritual at best, but do not tell Seer Drurhelm I said such an awful thing."

Siv glanced for her approval to claim the credit, and Tanya consented. "I curved the tusks to match those of the troll Drurhelm's going to use."

"And those features—the cleft between its chin and lips. The sharp curve of its forehead. Is that your work, Tanya?"

Without hesitation, Tanya lied, "No, Seer Dragoln. I blessed the die and drafted a part of the human's skull. The rest is Siv's work."

"Ahh, I see then," Dragoln commented, examining Tanya curiously. "Excellent, Siv. You are finally learning to read between the runes."

"I should have learned it sooner!" Siv exhumed.

Aphoristic intent enveloped Eldrahg's seer as he queried, "Learned what, exactly, if you would humor this old seer whose memory often fails him?"

Tanya grinned. Siv flustered. How now would her fellow priestess fare amidst their lie?

"That like in life, we cannot constrain our runes to the patterns set before us. They are our guides but not our masters, and our responsibility is to interpret what they have to tell."

"You've drafted many runes to learn this lesson, though I suppose that you've finally discerned its meaning is what's most important. You have a blossoming gift. A master drafter, yes, but of a skald as well."

Tanya took no notice of the bliss Dragoln's compliment assuredly bequeathed Siv. Her gaze adhered to her brother and sister, who arrived behind Grandfather and Mother too. They prevailed together, albeit Thyra and Lothair stood mostly askew. Better they maintain an air of separation; otherwise, some vile strife would ensue. Hosvir joined her grandfather to succinctly consume him in conversation.

"Dragoln, I know I ask much, and I ask so often, but I would like to witness the ritual beside my family, and for Siv to as well, if that's agreeable with you?"

"You may linger with the High Lady through the evening, and I will see you early in the morning or in the runic vaults before, I assume." Dragoln smiled, slyly dismissing them without expending his hand, and Tanya pulled Siv away to stride toward her family.

Dragoln was far more clever than he disinterred. Eldrahg's seer had tired of engaging in intrigue long ago but was still familiar with its many dispositions. Dragoln realized he need not manage his priestesses. He need only manage her.

Tanya enjoyed directing the temple's little larks. When she did stumble with doubts, she sought Dragoln's counsel first. Whereas Drurhelm groomed innocence for his personal pleasure, Dragoln groomed experience by youth's virtue. With it, he could abscond to his own affairs, lay his duties unto others, and persevere through old age.

Lothair noticed her approach, halting his conversation with Hosvir to dismiss his Skjold guard. "Grandfather, I'm glad you came to watch the berries grow from the seeds we've planted. This is Siv. We blessed the die, and she drafted the runic circle for Drur's ritual of skulls."

"Storm King." Siv presented herself with a curtsy, honeying her voice with the dulcet of a songbird at dawn's rise.

Lothair acknowledged Siv, sparing her no response and preserving his nimbler focus for Tanya alone. "Dragoln and Drurhelm speak highly of you, Granddaughter. It is fitting you would draft the last distinguished ritual I will live to see."

"We have time yet to draft you more!" Grandfather mused over her cast-iron surety in favor of a rawer ore, so she quickly bolstered it with coal to temper his iron doubts into steeled resolve. "Between us and Seer Hosvir," she whispered, "we cast rituals twice a week at least. Siv and I draft the most, so I will inform you myself when the next remarkable ritual arrives."

"Seer Dragoln even recently entertained the idea of casting an ancient, powerful ritual that would fly Eldrahg to the lunar realm and then back upon the next Riven Moon. How many Storm Kings in Halvalkyra can claim they have lived to witness such an event?" boasted Siv. Having failed to direct her friend to curtail conversation with her grandfather, Tanya watched helplessly as the priestess embellished everything the seers did.

"Dragoln does love his wives' tales, and I have heard that one many times before." Her gut wrenched when Lothair licked his lips, but at the end, he only leisurely laughed. "No, Storm King has seen the Draconic Father soar since his ascension, young priestess. Your sister claims she has." Tanya scarcely realized she was even being addressed. "Although," Lothair continued, "I can see by your face she never told you. Well, Siv, my young priestess, if Dragoln discovers a manner to conduct such a ritual, do join my granddaughter in telling me when it will be cast."

Excitement dripped from Siv's lips as honey dripped off a bear's tongue, and she openly reveled in its sweetness. "Of course, Your Grace!"

Tanya sententiously added, "We will, Grandfather. You will be the first to know." Tanya wondered if there was more to Lothair under the illusion of frailty and death, but she ultimately deemed he had too little life left for her to decide before he would be gone.

After bowing to let it be known she meant to depart, Tanya pulled Siv aside where the mammoth pines of the forest grove would muffle their voices.

"It was a good lie!" contended Siv, even though Tanya had not yet said a word.

"It was risky!" Tanya scolded.

Averse to admit she erred in assuming she understood Tanya's family's dynamics, Siv inescapably insisted, "He enjoyed it, I think."

Tanya refused to acquit her friend, and her scorn was inescapable when she clutched at Darius's final gift. "Lothair only tolerates me because I joined the Runic Faith and forsook the last of my Lysian heritage in all but one necklace. One misstep, one mistake, one errant slip of the tongue, and that indistinctness fades. I would be treated no differently than my sister then. I do not wish to test my grandfather's patience, Siv. It is notoriously thin."

"I didn't know! You never speak of family. I'm sorry, I did not know."

Tanya sighed, surrendering the tension between them, and condoled, "I am sorry I did not warn you, but you must never speak lightly with my family. I'm little more than a beacon of faith while among them, an anchor between the two halves of our blood. I do not wish for you to share that burden."

"I've had little liberty in this life myself, not since before I was sold to the runic temple to free my father from the consequences of his mistakes."

Siv's confession was difficult to hear and effortless to respect, but it was even more difficult to understand. Daughter to a master woodworker, Siv was enslaved to the runic temple to salvage her father's life and reputation. After refusing to deliver repairs to the temple without receiving pay, Siv's father was made to trade her freedom in recompense by Stormguarde's althing. Siv paid for that injustice with the years of her youth. Yet, even after freedom was hers to reclaim, Siv married the Runic Faith. Her heart's commitment to the runic temple blared its strength. It was something Tanya did not know if she could have done herself.

"I want you to enjoy tonight's freedom because you have earned it and because you are as much my sister as Thyra. The credit's all yours, Siv, but don't leave it spoiling, even if only by mistake. There's little majestic about us royalty. Most of us are slaves to something ourselves."

Siv summoned scarce composure, stemming the tears that sought to stain her cheeks. "I am sorry, Tanya," she said.

"Don't be!" Tanya insisted. "Now you know, and I wouldn't have it any other way."

Siv, a girl betrothed to the Crescent Lady's cyclic transcendence, sloughed off layers of insecurity to find her inner peace. Tanya, however, was no mere priestess, nor could she ever be just that. Even in the Storm-lands, she was a Runeheim and a princess, and she had been Second Princess Tanya Ehlrich of the Lysian Empire before that.

At ten, she sailed away from that imperial home when stars of shadow plummeted from the sky and blaze erupted from the ground all around her. Then, amid the chaos of all the things she was, Tanya found what was missing from her life. Her future lay secret behind clouds of storm, barring her from ascertaining who she was meant to become after the fall of her homeland, or at least she desperately hoped.

An affable boy endeavoring to please all—in some broken fashion,

Ryurik understood who he was. Thyra resolved her purpose with her first breath. She was the spear that disarmed their family's foes and the shield guarding their hearts. Ellyan, her second eldest brother, was a conqueror of man. Ellyan laid his eyes on lands and women, and they became his without question. Where he led, men had always followed, or so Tanya was told.

Darius, the brother whose dearth haunted her most, was a conqueror too. Tanya loved him more, however, because his conquests always transcended war and death. Darius preferred vanquishing immeasurable odds to conquering a person's heart. In many ways, it was how he conquered hearts and why they then cherished him more than Ellyan's lovers ever could.

Was she no better than Durel—purposeless, aggravated, and the bane of love and light itself? No, even thinking that was foolish, and believing it worse yet. She was without direction just as he had been, and that frightened her beyond words.

Rescinding from her reflection over life's uncertainty, Tanya led Siv behind the Skjold guarding her brother and sister. She realized the two were in the midst of an argument she did not wish to disturb.

"He's hiding something, Ryurik. If Bolvark told us everything he knew, he would have spared the troll.

"What does Bolvark have to hide? He offered us ample time to question Vrimos before severing its head."

"And it hardly spoke at all," Thyra drawled. "Vrimos shared Baelgrant's tale and nothing else. He should have allowed you, Lothair, and the jarls an opportunity to interrogate the voodoo priest. Besides, it's unforgivably stupid to execute an enemy bearing rank."

"Baelgrant has Garathandi thralls to spare. Maybe not the witches and warlocks of their voodoo cult, but there are trolls who bow to him."

"Until I've seen and spoken with them myself, I refuse to believe Baelgrant boasts others. All he has are dread-forged lies to lead us into the unknown behind the far north's shadows."

"Is this your view, sister, or are you simply occupying the view of another derelict project you wish to save?"

"That Alterian might be a thrall, but he saw more than you apparently did. I sought his insight because he was engrossed in the display, even after his friend was murdered in front of him," Thyra savagely professed.

"Is all your wisdom spit from the mouths of slaves before they escape?"

Ryurik ridiculed behind a foolish construct Tanya hoped he might one day forsake.

"Like I said, only the useful bits I picked apart from the rest while everyone else gawked like starstruck children."

"Then we have both lost. You cannot interrogate the troll because Lord Bolvark severed its head, and I cannot ask your thrall whether he actually stepped on Gunther's foot because you let him slip away."

"What sense is there in restraining the Alterian to speak into your daft ear? You do not heed advice, Ryurik. I wonder how many more thousands will die beneath your reign." Siv leaped beside her, and Tanya shivered behind the whiplash of her sister's fierce temper.

Scoffing, Ryurik replied, "Bolvark happily returns home to relay his success to his father. The Nordland has nothing to hide!"

"The only dread-forged travesty is that your troll died only so Drurhelm could seize its skull to enact his ghastly ritual of death," Tanya interjected, offering them no time to notice her arrival or extend her a welcome.

"Tanya!" Ryurik shouted. He swept her into an awkward hug, a poor attempt at making amends for their delayed reunion, but an attempt nevertheless.

It did not behoove her to rile her brother by chastising him for his earlier disappearance. Tanya felt her sister had already done an adequate job of it herself. "I am glad to see you at last, but the skulls a little less."

"They are trolls," Ryurik declared while disengaging from their gauche embrace. "What else is there for them to aspire toward?"

Tanya expressed, "The seers whisper that it cast lunar magic and spoke our language as if it were its own. I am certain it would have achieved much if sanctioned to live a little longer."

Thyra smirked, peeving Ryurik, and Tanya waited for her sister to expound. "It submitted to slavery and servitude because it preferred life over death, and yet the Reaper came for it still."

Ignoring Thyra, Ryurik faced her. "You're the foremost expert on runic magic amongst us, Tanya. Is what the seers claim true?"

"Dragoln only tenders the truths he knows. Many of your lords also claim the troll bent moonlight to its will without the use of runes."

"It declared itself a voodoo priest from some disgusting cult called Voodandum, and I was curious if you've heard of it before."

Peddling him to his heels, Tanya spurred, "No, but what makes their Voodandum a cult and the Runic Faith not?"

"They bastardize runic magic in their ill endeavor to wield Monomua's lunar light. You don't see that as cultish at all?"

Tanya confessed, "No, I don't. They call theirs voodoo in homage to their past while we construct ours from runes. If voodoo were truly just a bastardization of runic magic, its casters would be impotent. Monomua would deny them her power herself. In the end, they must both be forms of lunar magic she has blessed. How we invoke her power makes no shred of a difference in the grand scheme."

"It's impressive enough that a troll invoked lunar magic without a rune to cast upon. The Garathandi may have discovered a way to become both summoner and vessel to the moon and bypass the need for runes entirely," Thyra remarked, speaking before Ryurik could respond.

"They stole that knowledge from the ruins of cities that once housed tens of thousands of Stormborne. I've read books from Imperial Library of Ellynon recording the history of trolls. None of the southern tribes have ever been descried harnessing lunar magic. If they can call upon Monomua's augur strength without the guidance of the runic gods, then they have surely robbed us of that antiquitous knowledge!" Ryurik refused.

Tanya could not help but smirk and wondered if he even remembered how to read. "I've never read your books, Ryurik, so believe what you must, but do know this ritual is far more demonic than the voodoo magic my seers described."

"What use are the runic temples if they cannot explicate this invocation of lunar magic that doesn't rely on the guidance of runes?"

She disputed, "They absolutely can! There are histories buried in the runic vaults beneath each temple, but the seers and seeresses scarcely divulge their contents to the outside world."

"You are a priestess to this runic temple. Could you not investigate this for us?" Ryurik spoke a partial truth, but he did not understand the difficulties she would face in order to do so.

"Half of that knowledge is barred from the priestesses as well. Each temple's ruling seer or seeress alone has unrestricted access to all knowledge held within."

"Then they're nothing more than another cast from an old world order set against me and the future of the Stormlands." Ryurik sneered. His anger was mostly reserved for the seers, but it stung Tanya as well. "After I succeed the Tempest Throne, I will pull you back into the world."

Her brother cemented his opinions with cold ire. Nothing she might say would change it without breaking his fundamentally challenged view of the world. She decided not to argue with him at all. Thyra, however, did not understand their brother could not bend but only be broken. She was as innately obstinate as him, so those delicacies escaped her. Ehlrichs did not yield, not unless they would seize something magnanimous in return for lost pride. The precipitous silence which rapt their tight circle confirmed it, as only Siv perked up once the ritual had begun.

Drurhelm broke apart from the visitors, adorned a gloom-wreathed sash, and entered the runic circle grasping two skulls. He stationed them opposite to what Tanya expected, placing the troll's within Siv's half of the runic circle before placing the other atop hers. He fidgeted with their positions without impacting much of a difference, nudging them all around.

Drurhelm nearly tripped while straightening from the task. He recovered his balance at the circle's center to burden all those who laughed with his scorn. Swallowing lost pride, Drur's seer banefully cast Eldrahg's die after setting aside his own patron god's. The Draconic Father's honorifics superseded all others, even the Delas of Death, who was no more than an expatriate in his runic court.

Tanya noticed a hardened dragon's scale in Eldrahg's bundle of die that Siv blessed, glistening as if it had never turned to stone. Jagged strands of brilliant obsidian, dragon's glass, were distributed next. Drur's die, however, utterly repulsed her. They were calcified reminders of the time she spent abetting this ghastly ritual, and she took no pride in their deliverance.

Drurhelm retrieved the final die as he beseeched the Dark Moon's glory from a midnight sky over which Monomua had yet to fully sour. The seer pitched die, dually bonded to Eldrahg and Drur, quickening his chant with discordant fervor. Disparate lights arose within the runic circle, beckoning an invisible bridge to carry over from the dark side of the moon. Lunar beams fused with both skulls' shadows. The last of the die fizzled from existence, discharging their essence, and transferred the lunar power into the shivering skulls.

Tanya could not feign understanding what happened next, but it bore the dark spark of familiarity in its void. Moonlight soured to utter darkness at a nigh undetectable speed, and the runes reached beyond the Arch to retrieve the souls the skulls once belonged to. Twin, ethereal essences drawn out by fatal finesse were siphoned, then divided between two runic gods. Both skulls crumbled to ash, the bone peeling away like tears of acidic rain. A runic circle, swaddled in the harkened call of darkness and the faint glow within the void, abruptly died. The Crescent Lady's lunular power enveloped the stark shadows, and the runes were remade whole.

Drurhelm knelt at the center with his elbows pinned to his knees and his head drooped between his hands. His face lifted, and for an imperceptible measure of time, Tanya could not see his eyes. Black balls calmly observed her before he blinked to return their natural blue. She shivered. She knew not if what she saw was real or the false flare of runic magic toying with her perceptions. Drurhelm grimaced in pain before smiling to reveal his smarmy, yellow teeth, and Tanya was instantly reassured he was the same degenerate man she had always known.

"Tanya," Siv whispered, pulling at her slate-gray robes.

"What," Tanya whispered crossly in return.

"Somebody's snuck into the runic vaults. He was watching the ritual before he forced his way inside, limping, and I think he could barely walk."

"It wasn't just Dragoln or Hosvir? You're sure of it?" she demanded.

Siv pointed. "Yes! They're all right over there."

Tanya had grown freshly ill with watching Drur's ritual of skulls. She would seize any excuse to depart this grisly forest grove. She quickly grabbed her brother's attention, striving to herald the ritual's settling awe with a familiar voice.

"Don't ask the seers about voodoo magic. They'll simply deny you the knowledge you seek. I will bring you back the truth once I exhume it from the runic vaults. I want to become a seeress one day, or at least I hope to, so let me aid you however I can before that day arrives." She softly pecked his cheek before swiveling Siv toward the ritual hall and hustling away.

"Hurry, little sister, before Seer Drurhelm catches up," Thyra joked in an ignorant test of Tanya's patience.

"Don't linger for long yourself, else the Jarl of Breidjal might invite you to bed under the moon's soft glow and the warmth of his furs." She grinned with the garnish for her snide remark, and Thyra's visceral dejection made it all the more worthwhile. Tanya guided Siv away from that forthcoming quarrel, and they ran to the ritual hall standing above the runic vaults. "Did you glimpse which entrance he went in?" she asked once they were reasonably far off.

"The one hidden by moon runes at the front, but should we not tell the seers before we pursue? He shouldn't have known it was there or been able to get in without casting the runes."

"No! You said he limped, right?" She waited for Siv to nod in confirmation. "Then we'll find and take him to the hospice before he gets himself caught and killed."

"What if he's dangerous?" Siv fretted. Angst sloughed off her tender brows along with giant clumps of sweat.

"Is he dangerous, or could he barely walk? The two don't mutually coincide," Tanya countered while heaving open the hidden door sitting slightly ajar.

"He could have a weapon," Siv fretfully warned.

"We'll find out soon enough," she responded, teasing with a dry grin while they slipped into the vaults, then closed the door behind them.

They scurried through the torchlight of the chamber. The floors were painted with Hælla Dwolv's runes while the walls boasted depictions of the Fates Three and some grandeur designs for the Draconic Father. They reached a far auxiliary hall opposite the entrance. Tanya leered around the corner, scouting the way forward as she looked for a sign of the intruder. She descried him almost instantly. His muddy, blood-ridden, blonde head was braced against the wall, and he keeled over his knees. Disjointed tablets scattered the floor around him. She snapped Siv behind the arch when the priestess flexed forward before retreating from sight herself.

"What?"

Tanya softly muttered, "I think I've met him before."

"How?" Siv angrily whispered, and Tanya clasped her mouth shut.

"During my brother's Kingslag." Siv's eyes posed her questions better than her mouth could aspire to. "He was delivering meat to the keep's kitchens. He's the thrall who you saw me bantering with. Now shh!"

Tanya directed Siv's gaze around the corner unto the Alterian thrall, who languished against the ground, clutching his side in pain. He had not heard them, or if he had, his pain was too great for him to spare them any concern. Tanya brought Siv to stand beside her, so the boy could clearly see them both. Hopefully, he would realize they meant him no harm. Together, they moved beyond the archway and into the vault.

Tanya called out in a soft-spoken voice, "Hello?" When the thrall did not answer, she asked in a mellower tone, "Are you hurt?"

"I only need to rest here for the night," he begged. "Then you'll never see me again."

Tanya approached quite slowly, confiscating each step with prudent measure, and came to kneel beside the battered thrall. She offered to check his injuries at length, laying a hand over his hand's vice clutch. The thrall shied away, fearful of her touch. Tanya persisted through his doubt. He posed no threat to her in his broken state, and he appeared seriously wounded. She set aside his hands after some insistence. She quickly determined he bore two broken ribs before he clutched them again.

"What's your name?" Tanya softly questioned.

"Muiri. I'm a butcher's...was the butcher Durkil's thrall before he threw me away."

"Your ribs are broken. You must let go, or you'll hurt yourself more." Tanya gripped his hands to draw them away, and he cringed and gritted his teeth in pain. "The temple has a hospice to care for the injured and sick. Why would you come here instead?"

"I suppose I'm also looking for a friend. He must have come with one of your seers on the wagon from the center square. The seer that looks like an unctuous toad."

"Drurhelm, I'm sorry, Muiri, but Seer Drurhelm only returned with corpses and the head of a Garathandi troll."

"No. He sent him here with those tusk-helmed men. Bolvark's men! He was the lord who slew the Garathandi troll. Cadell must be here!" A light dawned upon Tanya's face, and she decided not to elucidate for Muiri's sake.

"They only brought back a single, sickly man close to your age, but he was already dead. I'm sorry, Muiri," condoled Siv, mistakenly nullifying Tanya's act of kindness.

"No, that cannot be! Where is— Where...where is he?"

"Muiri, he is dead." Siv afforded the thrall little comfort when she bade, "Now you must quit wiggling, or you'll follow him to the grave."

"No, your seer took him. Where is he? Where is Cadell?"

Tanya pulled Siv to her knees, where they impeded Muiri from struggling to his feet. The boy's erratic mind willed him to stand, but his body ultimately dogged him. Tanya heard the rib puncture something vital, and blood seeped from his lips. Muiri immediately fainted. Tanya caught him and steadied his full weight. Siv hastily joined in the effort. Together, they prevented Muiri from crashing into the ground, though it was not easy.

"Siv! We need to bring him to the hospice and treat him. Pull his other arm over your shoulder...just like that, and lift on one, two, three!" They heaved Muiri's limp body upward, vexing to carry his slack weight as they frantically exited the runic vaults.

CHAPTER TWELVE

WITHIN THE WEBS

W EEKS CONSISTING OF TWELVE DAYS by the Stormborne's calendar fluttered before Malith, and still his muthra dreamt. Rasha's mind wandered the spirit realm without surcease. His dreams were like a mill perpetually spinning the river. Rasha's were as undoubtedly diverse as blades of grass in a field untouched by cattle.

The Witchqueen would not choose to sleep if sleep bored her. She partook in no insipid tasks. Dreariness was far beneath his muthra, yet how long must they wait until it bored her? Would she wake then, recalled to the mortal world, or would she slip further into that reflective, pensive realm where the mind's cravings elapsed?

Malith bore the brunt of the labor stemming from caring for his unconscious tutor. He did not bemoan the task. Rasha was his Witchqueen, leader of Voodandum, his teacher, and his adoptive mother. Those titles bestowed him more than enough reasons to offer Rasha his undying aid.

Malith mostly compelled Rasha's body to receive food and water. He washed her where appropriate, and he cleansed the rest of her body with voodoo spells. He even cleared the bowls of waste and scoured the hollowed stocks of the anje he utilized to capture those excrements. Only Sulja exchanged the stocks. Malith outright refused, knowing he would never survive his Witchqueen's wrath should she reawaken while he performed such an intimate task.

"She is ready. I've just finished tricking her stomach into expanding. It should accept the nourishment all in one pass," Sulja informed.

Sulja was without obligations for the day, so Malith had beseeched her help in feeding Rasha. Malith was fully capable of nourishing her himself, but all the methods he knew took lots of time. With one, Malith force-fed the Witchqueen ridiculously slow. He loathed that option, so he avoided it like the Crimson Curse.

He employed the second option far more than the first. By mixing water, salt, and ground-up, frothy crystals—the ones often encasing the sharper crystals in the Ralcrav—Malith produced an expansive gas. Malith utilized the gas to swell her gut before using voodoo to amalgamate her food. The gas worked much faster than the alternative, but it was still so gallingly slow. He could never fill her stomach too quickly. When he did, her stomach rejected its nourishment and forced it back out, most often across his chest.

"You are going ta have to teach me that one," he noted as Sulja dispersed her voodoo. "I don't ever want to spend an hour grinding frothy crystals again!"

Sulja grinned, and Malith pithily cast his own spell, having performed it dozens of times already. He collected the staples of the day's meal, raised them into the air with voodoo magic, and squeezed and twisted his hands to amalgamate it into one mass. Malith then guided the food into Rasha's mouth, down her throat, and into a happily expanded stomach.

"Ya really need to teach me those tricks. It be unfair I can only study with voodoo priests while all the witches and warlocks grace you with their defter expertise. Must be lucky being the next in line to become Witchqueen."

Sulja discharged the notion without hesitation. "I'm not going to become the next Witchqueen. They made me Rasha's representative through the peace talks because I know her mind as well as I know myself."

"Everybody else grasps it except for you, Sulja. Why be that?" he asked.

"Because I don't believe it to be true. I'm just a Voodandum acolyte. She hasn't offered my name to da Loa or Voodandum's elites, much less to me. Don't ya think she would start by telling me?"

Malith sighed like a banal sapper tied to a poorly mixed explosive. "She has ya follow in her footsteps and clarifies all she does. She be grooming you for the rigorous responsibilities that come with being the Witchqueen, Sulja."

"We're her apprentices. The other teachers do the same for their own," Sulja stated hotly, her denial deafeningly clear.

Malith gently contradicted, "Not every witch and warlock be good tutors, regardless of their talent and skill. Jalcha complains that Drukkabi gives him only one good lesson every turn of the Dark Moon, if he be extraordinarily lucky. One lesson, Sulja! Even I get ten from muthra in half that revolution, even if she always be thinking it's a waste of her time!" Sulja grinned, so Malith pressed on. "The rest of the time, Jalcha be reading old Stormborne tablets or our trollish scrolls. I see ya thinking about it now! I guarantee as soon as Rasha awakens and inquires to Yel-jaraht, she will be telling ya everything her and Tyratus spoke of on da Hoary Perch. Then she's gonna explicate why she split her soul for Hulvassa in front of so many trolls after performing it for the First Warlord the morning before."

"Even if there be truth to your speculations"—Sulja groaned—"I don't have the approval of Voodandum's elites or the council of the Loa Gods."

"Tyratus respects you as much as he respects Rasha. If you have the support of Tyratus, ya effectively have the support of four of the Loa, but it don't matter right now. Rasha is gonna reawaken and take care of it. We just don't know when that is."

"How can you be certain?" demanded Sulja. "You said it yourself, Malith. She has not stirred since collapsing in Mammotte's shrouds of dust. I've seen her continuously since, and she hasn't moved of her own volition." Sulja surrendered the flair of gripping, agonized concern, her heart nearly bleeding outright for the woman who raised them both.

Malith decided to expound upon Rasha's motives exactly as he saw them. "Oh, bite your tongue, Sulja. Rasha won't pass through the Arch until she delivers me one last insult."

It was slightly insensitive to speak of Rasha as he did, especially considering his muthra was lying right beside them. Still, his humor succeeded in parting the tension lining his adopted sister's brows. Malith chuckled to himself, and Sulja quietly laughed along. He was cautious not to disturb Rasha. Although, if the incident actually woke her, he would no longer need to grind frothy rocks into a fine dust!

"I will not allow our muthra to die until the day she realizes your full worth. Then," Sulja expounded, "I might consider becoming her posterity."

"We won't live long enough for that," he jested. They shed another bout of laughter more boisterous than the last.

"Don't be foolish, Malith, or you'll force me to revoke my promise.

Rasha be cruel to you for no other reason than that she cannot learn to trust. You tolerate it without complaint. Why do ya do that, hmm?"

Malith grinned, although its temperament was anything but humorous. She did condemn his mistakes more fiercely than she censured other male trolls, and she admittedly whipped most other trolls like they were thralls on a dragon-headed, Stormborne longship. It seldom wounded him anymore. Their muthra wore her thorns as a defense against that which gravely wounded her before. Malith viewed her harsher treatment as a coping mechanism for love.

Moreover, Malith boasted the unyielding desire to become a warlock. He believed with such power, he could abet the empire to grow. Rasha's crueler conduct only fortified his resolve. They also helped him learn and grow from his mistakes, no matter how small they were.

"There be worse people in da world to call muthra than Witchqueen Rasha. They're all like spiders, weaving their webs, luring you in, dictating where and when you can go like you've always been theirs to play with. Rasha be the spider who truly tells what lies on her glistening threads. The mother who sold me to Voodandum to feed the sons she loved more than me be like da spider who colors its webs to hide the trap. Give me the hard truths instead," Malith spat.

"I don't forget what you've gone through, but how can you be so certain the two perceive you any differently? You never knew you had no place in your mother's heart until she gave you away. How can you possibly know if you hold a place in Rasha's?"

"I don't know. I feel it, Sulja. I might be deceiving myself because it's easier to believe, but you don't know what you don't know until it already be too late, so I listen to the murmurs my heart conveys while remembering what I've learned to just live on another day."

"You be making faith sound easy. Faith is an arduous task, leeching life from the soul like parasites in a mossy lake. I trust that Rasha cares for me, for you, for Voodandum, and the empire we serve, but I don't hold faith. She knows where we're going. She schemes from the center of her web like everyone else, striving to transform da empire for da betta, but she's done little more than imbibe Garathandi blood because she be trapped by her own ruse."

Whispering, Malith scorned Sulja for her uncharacteristically loose tongue, "They be our enemies, Sulja. Rasha's, Voodandum's, and most of the Loa too, and they be the enemies of the empire and themselves. Zun-jish be too blinded by power to realize he be leading us all to doom. We know it be true, but don't say it aloud again."

Sulja radiated reservation like the old streets of Vel-thaka when lit by the Bright Moon, yet her tongue was liable to reenact that ancient ruin. They were to never speak of her infidelities to the Warlord Prince unless Rasha permitted them to.

The Witchqueen, warlocks Abijo and Drukkabi from Vel-thaka, witch Zikri, the old lock Rakish from Domildin, witch Kalat from Bul-karat, and voodoo priest Rhazin from Kuro-kal—who incurred the greatest risk of them all—had all covertly provisioned Yel-jaraht's forces throughout the entire civil war. They would be ousted as traitors if the truth were ever unearthed. Death would surely seize them all, and it would come for many innocents after. Sulja betrayed herself and her intellect by erring so dissolutely, yet in his harshness, he also erred. He gave her reason to doubt Rasha because, without Rasha, only they were left to keep one another in check.

"You cannot win a war without trolls dying along the way," he confessed, endeavoring to correct his mistake. "Rasha is no warmonger. She's just...a vajdna spider, struggling to oust the rot within its webs so her cluster can thrive and expand."

"Malith! If you let spiders tangle webs in my bed while I was sleeping, I swear I'll drink your blood next!"

Malith flinched, and they both whirled toward Rasha's bed. Rasha both removed and discarded her anje stocks to the floor and pulled herself upright. Tearing at her limbs while stretching for the first time in weeks, the Witchqueen ferociously yawned. Malith gulped, Rasha unfortunately descried it, but she did not move to chide or question why he was nervous.

Sulja stammered as she dabbed sweat from Rasha's forehead, "How long have you been awake, *mu-muthra gundir*?"

"Long enough to know you think I'm a vajdna spider and that I've been sorely missed." Rasha enfranchised them both with an earnest grin. Malith smiled—relieved his muthra was awake and content her spirits were also remarkably well.

With hands as delicate as butterfly wings, Sulja returned Rasha to bed. Confoundedly, Sulja questioned, "So Tyratus lectures the empire must crumble before it can be reforged anew?"

Sulja struggled to understand the advantage of the empire betrothing ruin amidst the onslaught of plague, the Endless Wastes, or a resurgent civil war. Tyratus withheld clairvoyance of past and future alike, but the acolyte witch remained unconvinced his foresight warranted running off a cliff to splinter one's leg before endeavoring to mend the shattered bones. The civil war was over. The truce was final. Remarkably fair terms had been established. The plague had predominantly dwindled. They could rebuild, utilize the majority sway toward prolonged peace that Warlord Beh'kliar provided, and regift the empire's purpose once it recouped all it had lost.

"Reborn anew, like a phoenix, though it be not as if either Tyratus or I have ever seen a phoenix," commented Rasha with humorous tendencies floating upon her voice.

Tossing aside Tyratus's motivations to penetrate Rasha's own perspicacity, Sulja plainly questioned, "What do you think, *muthra gundir?*"

"Tyratus speaks the truth. Should we fail to shift the warlords' bloodthirst elsewhere and restore Gara-thandila to a glory before it was wracked by the desolation of plague and civil war?"

Sulja only just finished bathing and dressing Rasha before plating food for her to peck. Already, the Witchqueen decomposed her contemplations while aiming them toward the future. Rasha had not yet asked of the outcome of the truce, the state of the capital and the empire, or of her accomplice, Yel-jaraht. Oh, how Malith was right, and Sulja resented him for reminding her of it. Rasha was hardly different than other trolls. She pondered conquest and her succession above all else, and the rest were mere means to enact those ends.

"Which of the Loa remain in Gara-thandila?" Rasha questioned at the end of a long pause after wetting her lips.

"Mammotte wished to stay, but he feared the consequences of prolonging his absence from patrolling the Endless Wastes. Tyratus left only days ago. He wished to remain longer, but he, too, could not linger. All of the Loa Gods have returned to their respective enclaves."

"I see." Rasha succinctly hushed, then shivered. "Tell me, Sulja, how did Yel-jaraht fall through the Arch? Was it quick and painless or barbaric and brutal? Did Zun-jish mount his tusks and skull on his palace walls?"

Rasha's eyes betrayed a clarity of devotion she gifted few men. Yel-jaraht had been no simple ally in the pursuit of liberation from despotic hands. Sulja's muthra did not sequester Vel-thaka's Rebel Warlord to the role of confidant by itself. Clearly, Yel-jaraht was Rasha's friend. It compelled Sulja to inform her muthra she still had the chance to say farewell.

"*Muthra gundir*, Yel-jaraht is not yet dead."

Adrift in her own thoughts, Rasha's eyes widened as she gazed into nothing. "How? But why, but how?"

"Zun-jish chained him to a cell once the warlords, Kindril and Beh'kliar, demanded he be allowed to live. They would not see the rebellion's leader executed until the treatise was signed and peace guaranteed."

Rasha paused for an overgrown moment, perhaps as flummoxed as Sulja that Beh'kliar lent his voice on behalf of rebels. The warlord of Kuro-kal interminably surprised Sulja with his staunch adherence to fairness during the finer negotiations. He ferociously pushed to balance the terms. It appeared his only motive throughout was to ensure a just resolution was served.

"The treatise has already been signed. Zun-jish decided to suspend his execution until after you awakened," Malith softly interjected as if to not upset Rasha with the information. She did not dissuade him from continuing, but her face did harden. "He's been sending royal guards to confirm your condition and whereabouts every day since."

Sulja interrupted Malith in turn, sparing him from a resurgence in Rasha's aggravation at further mention of the Warlord Prince. "Malith speaks the truth. The elites designated me as your temporary replacement to serve by their sides until your mind and body recovered."

"It was not my mind and body recovering, little ones," the Witchqueen mused on the leading edge of an indeterminate whisper.

"He'll give you no time to prepare, but you will be forced to watch," Sulja informed.

"Do not worry, Sulja, and both of you wipe the concern from your faces. Zun-jish cannot force me to do what I already planned to do myself. I wanted to speak with Yel-jaraht once before his execution. I am thankful our allies have given me the opportunity to say goodbye."

Reticent to let their transitory ally during the negotiations be forgotten, Sulja reminded Rasha, "Warlord Beh'kliar as well. He did much to satiate the Warlord Prince without spurning the support of the rebels."

Rasha drawled and temporarily lost focus. "Yes, Beh'kliar as well. We cannot forget him."

Sulja did not understand the reason behind Rasha's sarcasm, but she did understand its intent. Whenever Rasha received an uninvited challenge or correction to her words, she waved about sarcasm as a Helmyan horse warrior's flags rippled during a mounted charge.

Malith stuttered, "Warlock Abijo? But you're supposed to be in Vel-thaka!"

The warlock whom Rasha bade lead Vel-thaka during their visit to the capital forced a hasty entrance. Dressed in his finest linen trappings and burdened by sweat, the umber-tusked, stone-spruce-skinned, ashen-haired troll heaved as if his travels had only just relented. Abijo studied the Witchqueen, confirming rumors he would have only just learned. Abijo then invited Rasha to sit with him at the table beside her bed. Rasha curtly refused. Instead, she forced herself to stand.

Assuaged, Rasha demanded, "Abijo, why are you here? I left you in control of Vel-thaka until we returned from negotiating the truce—"

"Rasha!" Abijo resounded. "I am certain you will forgive my insolence in time, but you won't interrupt me again!"

A ghastly silence befell the room as Rasha's glare malformed into something severe. She eventually nodded, but only after beads of sweat had draped Sulja's forehead. Abijo coughed, his voice grating sharper than runeforged knives, then he honed his voice until his breath was all but exhausted.

"A delegation once led by warlock Vrimos has returned to Vel-thaka from the Nordland. They landed beside a bardlen warship ferrying fifty Stormborne warriors commanded by a nephew to da Bane of Trolls. Ole Vrimos had burrowed one of our juggernaut vessels and sailed out of harbor months ago with a hundred spears. We did not think to question his intentions, and I thought nothing of it until their return. The Stormborne now demand an audience with Zun-jish. They claim they were invited by Beh'kliar and the Warlord Prince himself. Vrimos remains in the Stormlands with half his original guard. Ask what you will, but that is what I know."

Realizing she was holding her breath through a remarkably long draw, Sulja wheezed when she gulped for air. Warlock Vrimos hailed from Kuro-kal, joined Voodandum at the behest of Warlord Beh'kliar, and served at the Altar of Ursala. Why would Beh'kliar invite Stormborne, who served Baelgrant unto the edge of the far north? The peace negotiations, reliefs in taxation, reconstruction compromises, and everything Sulja ascertained of his goals appeared moot when laid against this incorrigible news.

"Where be Beh'kliar?" Rasha's voice travailed as cold as Monomua's lunar realm, and Sulja shivered upon recognizing the anger laced within it.

"I don't know, Rasha. I tried to find him upon arrival, so I could force the grub bastard to tell you himself."

"I know where Beh'kliar be staying, *muthra gundir*. Jalcha claims the warlord took up residence in an abandoned manor in the Ralcrav's northern face. He described it pretty well. I can lead you there."

Her muthra regarded her adopted brother, and Sulja questioned if Malith truly knew the way. Malith had never been reliable with directions in cities. Having proclaimed it once himself, he only knew where he was going when trapped in the wilderness. Even as Sulja scrutinized the favor he extended and Rasha glared, Malith kept solid in his stance. He truly believed in himself.

"Then lead me to this conspirator who deigns to bring Yel-jaraht's oldest adversary into Vel-thaka before his execution's fall."

Rasha walked to warlock Abijo to whisper grievances into his ear, which Sulja could not clearly make out. The warlock grunted, then whispered in return. Sulja could not hear him either, but she irrevocably knew they spoke of Warlock Vrimos and Warlord Beh'kliar. Had it not been called out to the world already? She was the haunted heraldry of voodoo. It was what she would speak of if she were in Rasha's position.

Sulja joined her adopted brother before Rasha noticed his mediocre attempt at prying. Malith took to dressing himself in warming attire to avoid her reprimand. Sulja dismissed her initial judgment upon realizing it would be the first time he had left the altar in weeks. Malith grinned like a newborn baby swaddled against its muthra's tit. Sulja then sighed, realizing her adopted brother intended to guide them to Warlord Beh'kliar off Jalcha's hearsay alone.

Unwilling to let her own reservations dwell unrequited, Sulja plainly remarked, "Malith, I do hope you actually know where you're going."

"I do! It's easy navigating Gara-thandila by exploiting the Ralcrav. At least, it's easier than steering through ordinary streets of wood and stone."

They did not descend far into the chasmic Ralcrav. Kuro-kal's warlord had claimed his temporary residence within the second northern ridgeline beneath level ground. Like any pride-stricken troll, Beh'kliar did not frequent the masses who dwelt within the Ralcrav. The edifice Sulja approached was carved out of the cliffs for an ascendant family of trolls grown rich from exploiting the mines worked by their disenfranchised kin. Its needless enormity and outstanding depth reinforced her credence. Unfortunately for those past owners, the plague did not care if those it struck were affluent or meager grunges. It killed without prejudice and culled all alike.

Malith halted their procession a short distance from the entrance, where two guards stood watch. "This be the place Jalcha described exactly. The door's even lined in alternating layers of sharp crystals like he claimed."

Staring at the wasteful prosperity, Abijo scathed, "Mined from the Ralcrav's depths with the blood and sweat of our people, so we could smear it against stone again."

"We'll be sitting here for a lifetime if we breach those stairs to the lunar realm. I'll speak with the guards. I know one of them well," specified the Witchqueen.

Bemused, Sulja questioned, "Was he with the delegation led by warlock Vrimos?" Sulja only recalled Rasha having traveled to Kuro-kal thrice, and each time, they reclused themselves to the Altar of Ursala.

"No, child," Rasha answered. "I remember this one from our visits to Kuro-kal." Strange. Sulja clearly recalled they had never interacted with the warrior hordes of Kuro-kal.

Rasha bade they all approach beside her. "Dolk, tell Beh'kliar his Witchqueen has come to speak and that I won't be turned away!" Rasha's crimson robes, that enduring, beloved color she wore in spite of fouling rumors, trailed her in streams that folded beneath the caress of a soft breeze.

"Ya be awake, Witchqueen? We didn't know if ya ever be waking again after dat ritual ya performed for Hulvassa."

"Yes, Dolk," silenced Rasha. She rolled her eyes before plainly stating, "I walk amongst the conscious troll again. Now find me Warlord Beh'kliar and tell him what I've said."

Dolk exasperated, "No need, Witchqueen. We both know da warlord always be happy to see ya."

Dolk brushed aside his fellow guard as she moved to question his decision. After they exchanged incomprehensible gurgles of dissatisfaction, they cleared the door to allow them entrance. Rasha weakly thanked Dolk before entering. Abijo followed second, Malith hustled closely behind, and Sulja sauntered through last, questioning Rasha's familiarities with these guards of Beh'kliar.

Sulja stepped foot into a large, square room supported by four foamy crystal pillars. Clean-cut alcoves filled with stone statues and bronze treasures encased the outer walls. Amidst the pillars, a shallow descent led to a lower lounge. A large pine table inlaid with plates of shale sat crooked in the center. Warlord Beh'kliar stood, scrutinizing maps, papers, and letters strewn across the tabletop with hyper focus. He noticed their intrusion, then averted his attention their way.

"Rasha! You've awoken." Beh'kliar extended a rough hand. "Do you feel well? Have you spoken with Yel-jaraht? He is still alive if you weren't aware."

"I am aware. I have not yet spoken with our friend," arose the Witchqueen's response upon a cold, malicious air.

Beh'kliar discarded his blithe for a severity to match Rasha's. "I made certain our friend survived for your benefit. You should be thanking me for that," he growled.

"Our friend?" Sulja whispered, to which Rasha bade her not speak again.

Eventually, Beh'kliar wavered and whispered into the ear of his closest advisor. The troll lived and breathed for war. Sulja ascertained the two's familiarity from the troll's black-iron armaments and the ritualistic scars carved into his wrists and forearms. Garathandi trolls marred their flesh with precise cuts for their every kill in battle. This troll boasted at least fifty and had drawn Paontara's claws across them all.

Beh'kliar dismissed the advisor and his guards stationed about the room. Leisurely, they shuffled off while mumbling amongst themselves. Incensed with their hesitation, Beh'kliar shouted, "Be gone, all of you! I have things to discuss with Witchqueen Rasha, and I'll not be having any of your here to listen."

The guards hastened their escape. Beh'kliar's advisor to whatever mindless war he sought beside or with the Stormborne leered over Rasha. The Witchqueen's icy webs frightened the imposer to heed his master's command, and so he summarily fled as well. Sulja smirked as he exited the room, and she concealed her smile behind petite tusks as Warlord Beh'kliar gazed upon Malith then her.

"Abijo and my apprentices remain...and no friend. You will not argue with me on that!" Ice of the Witchqueen's making transgressed Sulja's veins. Disparate to how she handled the other conspirators, Rasha concealed this final troll so well, even Sulja never suspected him.

"I had forgotten you charged Abijo to rule over Vel-thaka while you guided this truce. I should have realized his presence meant ya already discovered everything I've done," Beh'kliar professed, inviting Rasha to stand beside him as his conference toward future wars.

Rasha trod forth in a scornful instant. "What have ya done, Beh'kliar? We've only just found peace, and already you're thrusting the empire toward another war!"

"Bah!" exclaimed the warlord of Kuro-kal. The table shook as he demanded, "Don't be chiding me, Rasha. I'm no infant troll grub. I've discretely conferred with Yel-jaraht and Zun-jish both. They agree the path I've drawn for will avoid a second civil war."

"Gara-thandila, Malakal, and Damari have all lost half their citizens to the plague. How are we supposed to fight another infernal war? Who's left who still be willing to fight?"

"The hordes of Domildin and Bul-karat spared few souls for our cause. I am certain they will spare many more for the Stormborne. The plague has mostly lifted from Kuro-kal, and I still retain three-quarters of my city's hordes. Our armies will sail to the Nordland aside whatever the Warlord Prince and his hound-dogs Rhak-jan and Ruh'rehm can muster. With Bael-grant beside us, we will conquer the rest of the Stormlands easily enough."

"With da Bane beside us...bagh! Beh'kliar, are you mad? Yel-jaraht sacked Langreklif and slew the jarl's father and brother. Jarl Baelgrant earned that ghastly title when he repulsed Yel-jaraht's hordes, slaughtered most everyone, and began ruthlessly reaving our eastern coasts. He'll never forgive what happened. You be inviting negotiations that'll lead us into a deathly trap!"

Beh'kliar barked, relinquishing his composure in favor of the howl wolves made for the moon. Like most trolls, his resolve floundered against Rasha's provocations and snubs. Yet, Sulja could not spite her Witchqueen for inciting the warlord's wrath. Baelgrant had slain thousands of trolls since the day he avenged his family's deaths and reclaimed Langreklif, his ancestral home. Beh'kliar's notion to seek an alliance with the empire's most bitter enemy while assuming the jarl would betray his own verged upon sheer lunacy. Everything that he and Sulja accomplished in the negotiations would spiral down a vapid whirlpool if he found better backing for his war with the runic folk.

Nigh roaring, Beh'kliar enforced, "I have invited nothing!" He paused, drawing massive breaths until his tusk's beat to a rhythm devoid of incensed haste. Measuredly, the warlord then drawled, "I was the one invited to an alliance with the jarl, and I be detached enough from past grief and grievances to have listened to his proposition."

"The Bane invited you? How came that, you snake?" Rasha retaliated.

"By a messenger about a year ago. Baelgrant sent many, but the one he sent to Kuro-kal was the only one to make it alive. I returned the Stormborne spy with my answer. I burrowed one of Vel-thaka's juggernaut vessels next, and I sent it forth with a hundred trolls from my hordes, led by warlock Vrimos to further our discussion."

"I'll forgive you for thieving my ships while my soul recovered and my body slumbered, but answer this. What good will a war with the Stormlands accomplish for the empire?"

"Don't paint yourself pacific because you've been walking in your dreams for so long. We both know the empire be nearing its end! We know this peace will not hold for long before Gekas, Kindril, and Yel-jaraht's successor rebel." Flinging Rasha's gall aside before she could divulge it, Beh'kliar instructed Sulja, "Tell her da bindings of the treatise. Let her hear it from the mouth of someone she don't believe to be as untrustworthy as aged, carcajou milk."

Four unassailable pairs of eyes instantly befell Sulja. Against her better judgment, she glanced to Abijo to speak for her. Sulja had given the same appeal to countless elites during the negotiations. Fortunately, they had been more receptive than he was now. Abijo was a durable warlock who tolerated no weakness, so he completely spurned her pleading gaze.

Sulja twiddled two thumbs and four fingers over a rough sketch of the Nordland. She then swept her hands lithely over another map depicting the Jüteheln Sea. Water stretched before the warlord's campaign. It felt more hollow than the Ralcrav's deepest crevices, the air hanging between them, and the answer she was yet to give.

"We negotiated a fair spread of taxes across the six warlord's holdings who fought in the 'Crimson War,' which Zun-jish decreed it forever be called. Labor levies were established to rebuild Gara-thandila. They are well balanced, and there'll be no occupations of the southern cities or villages. The terms only hold for three years before they are rendered complete. Then, Zun-jish will recover full control of the empire's affairs."

Rasha pondered the terms. "So you won't be contributing to the taxes, Beh'kliar? Is that how you plan to fund your war with the Stormborne?"

"I pledged to match every coin and worker paid by the other warlords... after the treatise was signed, of course."

"That be no lie, *muthra gundir*." Sulja then quietly amended, "He actually pledged more than the rest."

Beh'kliar spread his hands across the table, seemingly pleased with Rasha's mute response.

Rasha withdrew, folding her arms afront the lines of her crimson breasts while tapping one shoulder to an eccentric tune. "Clever move, Beh'kliar. From the shadows, you continue to move without fear of suspicious eyes leering for too long."

"Three years, and then we'll be slaughtering each other again. Turn the Warlord Prince and the other warlord's attentions to da Stormlands, and with Jark Baelgrant's aid, we will avert the crisis entirely."

"Why does the Bane seek to betray his own kin?" Sulja interjected, fearful they would soon find themselves trapped in an eternal debate over the merits of another war.

"That question leads in the right direction, young Sulja. Baelgrant is incensed. The jarl was forced to sit idle through ten years of war by his Storm

King's own decree. Da Bane yearns to answer that slight before the jarls know their doom has arrived. Baelgrant wishes for us to be that doom, and he already be pressing forward. Vrimos cast a clever bit of voodoo magic to help me see it through his eyes for myself. The Stormborne crave a new fight."

"And what be the reason you think Baelgrant's war should become ours," Sulja furiously interposed.

Beh'kliar smirked in appreciation of her question. "Baelgrant be convincing them to join him in the Nordland where we plan to spring our trap. Their armies will trickle up their falls, one by one, where we'll then slaughter them all. Once we have cleaned our spears of their blood, all that will be left is their unguarded lands and the unknown riches they hold."

Sulja ballooned with a myriad of questions, but Rasha cut in to advance her own. "How are we to trust him? He's still the Bane of Trolls! Baelgrant never ceased raiding our coasts after driving Yel-jaraht from his Nordland. He's slain thousands from Vel-thaka's hordes alone!"

"Because Yel-jaraht's execution is fast approaching. Baelgrant will not risk traveling to Gara-thandila to see it for himself, but he wants one thing in return—for his cousin to verify the execution and to bring back Yel-jaraht's skull."

Sulja exclaimed, "That's impossible!"

It was quite literally impossible. They had discussed, disputed, and reviewed every aching detail of the treatise that culled the Crimson War. No loopholes existed within those papers, permitting Yel-jaraht's head to fall to anyone other than the Warlord Prince. It was ironic their Stormborne neighbors were as begrudging and foolish as them. Baelgrant sought an unattainable restitution for past transgressions satisfied by the blood of thousands of Garathandi trolls he'd slain. Even after brushing his ambitions aside, the jarl could never outpace the more malevolent beast who claimed Yel-jaraht's head for himself first.

Sulja informed, "The treatise demands Yel-jaraht's head must fall to the Warlord Prince. We cannot abide that request, even if the Witchqueen wished to entertain it—"

"But from your smirk, old friend, there is a way," Rasha interjected dejectedly.

Beh'kliar resigned his grin and appended, "The treatise demands Yel-jaraht's head must fall to Zun-jish, but it does not specify that's where it must remain."

While technically correct, Beh'kliar's strategy relied entirely on Zun-jish's cooperation and a concession he would irrefutably refuse. Sulja crowded Rasha, her mind needing answers for why she would even consider this perilous path. To thwart the fall of their empire as Tyratus envisioned, or to doom more Garathandi to perish on Stormborne swords? Sulja retreated when Rasha gently swept her aside. She obviously felt no need to clarify her surreptitious expenditure of trollish lives.

"There's no doubt within you that Yel-jaraht supports this?" Rasha requested of the warlord, who ostensibly conspired the entire Crimson War.

"Aye. Confirm it with him yourself either before or after we have secured the promise of his head. Make your decision, Witchqueen. I've left us with little time to act."

"Monomua's wrath incinerate Kuro-kal if you be deceiving us, Beh'kliar, but I cannot isolate a lie from what you've said. Even a minor victory in the Stormlands would temper our people's spirits and shift our empire's focus for the better. I think it's time the Warlord Prince learns I've finally awakened."

Pleasure wrapped around his every word, Beh'kliar responded, "Then I'll be needing one last favor before we meet with the Warlord Prince."

"What favor?" Rasha asked.

"Send word to whoever leads Vel-thaka in yours and Abijo's absence. The voodoo priest Rhazin will soon arrive in Vel-thaka. He and a second juggernaut must leave for the Nordland."

"And why should I permit that?" Rasha demanded.

"I want to bring Vrimos and my warriors home, and we should assure Baelgrant that his be alive too."

Sulja refused to believe this was to be the Garathandi's legacy. They who once clashed across continents millennia before to carve out their rightful place in Eldaria, who ascended Loa from mindless animals and established voodoo magic where both never existed before, and who fought among themselves as they careened toward an inescapable fate. The people deserved more than war's womb. Their leadership should be better attuned to the plight of the common troll to break the waves sweeping them out to sea on the same, unchanging course.

Sulja might one day become the Witchqueen, but she would never bend like her muthra. She would not allow herself to break from her principles to satiate a warlord's transitory tastes. It was wrong, and Sulja knew Rasha would come to regret tolerating these clandestine games. The Garathandi did not scamper like rats in the streets. They overcame challenges endless to forever maintain their greatness. The Garathandi were strong, and Sulja would see true strength return to the empire if ever she ever succeeded Rasha as the Witchqueen of Voodandum.

<hr>

Beh'kliar and Abijo flanked Rasha as they climbed the numerous steps toward the Throne of the Riven Moon. Displeasure wracked her, for the Witchqueen's beloved city now housed fifty Stormborne led by a nephew to the Bane of Trolls. They sought the Garathandi's support in their own insurrection, or so Rasha had been informed.

She had known nothing of Beh'kliar's plot before reawakening. For that, Rasha silently rued the warlord. She had only just escaped the dreams of voodoo past and already was stepping into an empire that could not fathom lasting peace.

They were well received at the grim gates to Zun-jish's fortress. The cast black-iron, stone-studded doors of the fortress were unbarred for their passage without so much as a word. Rasha strode through the squarish outskirts of the black-iron fortress to the pyramid palace's primary ascent. She mounted the first few tiers at a placid pace her weakened body could sustain. Her recent reprieve of dreams had left her body severely weakened. The steps they took to Zun-jish's throne at the palace's zenith only further diminished that waning font of strength.

Rasha debarred her companion's aid, even as they offered it time and again. She did not rue the kindness, but she refused to walk before the Warlord Prince held in the arms of two men as if she could not surmount the palace herself. That was a stale image Rasha would not permit to be witnessed. They traveled slower as a result, but both Abijo and Beh'kliar understood why. Silently, they matched her gait, and together they climbed on.

Word of her arrival traveled quicker than they, and the lesser gates to the throne room were left agape. The guards split formation, drawing offset lines divided down the middle to ceremoniously welcome the Witchqueen. Their blades overhung the pathway, and their convex wooden kite shields lined the flanks. Between them stretched a crimson carpet, beckoning her through the gates toward the Throne of the Riven Moon. Rasha paused, not for reprieve but to mentally prepare for what lay at the end of the ascent.

Rasha assumed the supreme task of adjourning the execution of a furtively dear friend. The storm-lit tragedy of Baelgrant's demands dictated she acquisition Yel-jaraht's head once it was severed from his body. She would then reluctantly seek to invite each warlord to Vel-thaka, so Beh'kliar might dispense Yel-jaraht's severed skull to the jarl who assumed himself to be Zun-jish's equal. Every man viewed every other as his equal. To Rasha, they were but the stale crumbs of broken bread doomed to decay and frightful afterthought of sagacity betrayed.

Stone protruded from each side of the throne room's gates. Massive crystalline braziers lit the dimming sky above them. The Crescent Lady rose overhead in premonition of the end of reign. Stormborne, Frosthammer dwarves, and jütengolk all thought the Dark Moon's rising was an ill omen. Those foolish beings failed to understand that one's ill omens were another's call to fortune. As Witchqueen of Voodandum and keeper of the Dark Moon, the night's lucent shadow fell favorably upon any tasks she assumed.

"What are we going to offer the Warlord Prince in return for his surrender of Yel-jaraht's head?" asked the warlock, Abijo, who dispensed the question she had yet to answer herself.

"I'm the Witchqueen of Voodandum and the Garathandi Empire, you're an elite warlock, and Beh'kliar be the warlord left the strongest in the wake of peace." Leering at Beh'kliar, Rasha stringently continued, "Since our ally could not reconcile the jarl's deal with our Warlord Prince, we will bargain with something Zun-jish cannot reject."

"Let us judge Zun-jish before making our offers," Beh'kliar steadfastly asserted.

"We risk failure by entering without having any propositions," Abijo condemned.

"There are powers a Witchqueen can impart that Zun-jish will never refuse. Hold to your trust, my warlock, and I will win Yel-jaraht's skull for da Bane of Trolls."

Rasha walked beside Beh'kliar while Abijo trailed close behind her. Persevering down the crimson carpet the Warlord Prince placed to mock her arrival, they passed the throne room's threshold. Pine pillars banded in black-iron spikes upheld a studded roof. Tables encircled each pillar and displayed the countless skulls of slain enemies. Frosthammer dwarves, jütengolk frost giants, and their elder beasts lazed beside human lords and their equine steeds. Vestibules lined the room's edges—appropriated for every task, obligation, and pleasure intrinsic to rulership.

At the end of the hall lounged the Warlord Prince, Zun-jish. He planted one leg afront the foot of the Throne of the Riven Moon while the other hung opposite of the direction he leant. His arms pressed against sharp crystalline spikes of howlite, uncut silver, and white tourmaline while his hands overhung armrests of black-iron. He grinned, degrading the disdain they held for each other with its false afflictions.

"Welcome, Witchqueen, to the Throne of the Riven Moon. I'm amazed you've already come ta see me after awaking just today. Tell me, Rasha, how did it feel splitting your soul for the Red Claw?" Zun-jish waved a calloused hand to summon them forward while concurrently parting his guards.

Zun-jish entertained her advance with a carcajou's droll, so Rasha snarled, "I preferred conjoining it again after the ritual was done."

"Rasha," Zun-jish sputtered through a mocking laugh. "If dat were true, you wouldn't have slept for so long. Ya be lucky da great Woolly Mammoth stamped his mighty feet and sent da Red Claw scurrying away before he claimed your soul for himself."

"Your master is fortunate that be all the punishment he received for his incursion upon the sanctity of a ritual he did not deserve."

Enraged, Zun-jish slammed his feet against the floor, drawing the attention of all inside the throne room. "Hulvassa be no master of mine! Da Warlord Prince doesn't serve da Loa like you or Voodandum, and I shouldn't be reminding ya of who ya first serve!"

Begrudgingly Rasha strove to make amends so she might salvage the intent of their visit. "Forgive me, Zun-jish, but all Garathandi serve the northern Loa. But in return for their devotion to their power, you alone are gifted their power in return. When you serve the Loa like I do, you be helping the Loa serve the Throne of the Riven Moon, and by proxy, you."

"I prefer this new Witchqueen who's arisen from her slumber to walk before my throne and serve me like a gracious troll," Zun-jish amended wryly as he leant against his throne again. "You need to be sleeping more often, Rasha. I prefer this new you."

"Of course, and I'll be dreaming of a greater Garathandi Empire every second, for that is exactly why we have come."

"Yes, yes. Beh'kliar's already informed me of da Stormborne he thrust upon your home. But I think I like his proposition. This treatise we signed, which your pretty little acolyte helped form, doesn't suit my tastes. Garathandila and my empire will soon be craving riches since we no longer be fighting for my throne. Yel-jaraht's revolt has consigned us long enough. It be high time I deliver my empire something more."

Rasha sternly replied, "An alliance with Jarl Baelgrant could greatly facilitate your endeavor. The Bane of Trolls could eviscerate half his fellow Stormborne before we've even disembarked the Nordland."

"Then the warlords and I conserve Voodandum's support? Excellent, and ta think you traveled all this way to tell me yourself."

Suppressing the urge to even slightly aggravate Zun-jish, Rasha humbly corrected, "But we do not yet have Baelgrant's oath of alliance. The Bane will not yield to one until he receives the missing stone that would complete and unlock Garatha's tomb."

"Yes! Haha! Haha! Beh'kliar enlightened me ta that too. The Bane seeks to rob me of Yel-jaraht's skull while I still be planning which of these pillars I should mount it on." Zun-jish rose to his feet, accelerating his voice until it mounted the zenith of his pyramid palace. "Da jarl can join in conquering the Stormlands beside me, and I will even offer him the Tempest Throne, but he will not use an oath to rob me of Yel-jaraht's skull! Dat be my trophy," he bellowed both guttural and low. "I'll not be losing it to da damned Bane of Trolls!"

Seizing the floor with ardor, Beh'kliar implored, "Warlord Prince, without this alliance, we would be fighting into the entire host of the Stormlands instead of the Nordland's welcome. Yel-jaraht only succeeded in sacking Langreklif because of the stealth of the Dark Moon."

"But all seven warlords and their hordes can march united, Beh'kliar of my Kuro-kal. Baelgrant's offer has enlightened me to his lands' providence, and now da Bane may either join us or die by my blades of wrath."

Zun-jish sat atop the armrest of his throne and pressed his lower back against protruding crystals. He withdrew his blade, laid it across his lap, and drew his fingers across its sheen. Few trolls owned swords in the empire. There were few blacksmiths capable of forging them. The warlords and their best warriors were often the only trolls who would ever carry a sword. The rest of the hordes were begotten to spears, simple axes, and the occasional throwing knife.

"We will not win this war without Baelgrant," Beh'kliar decreed.

"At least da Bane be offering me something before he asks a favor in return. If ya don't believe we will conquer the Stormlands without the jarl's support, what are ya offering for Yel-jaraht's skull?" Zun-jish glared through Rasha mockingly. "You lend me Voodandum's blessing and the support of voodoo priests while all the witches and warlocks who command true power languish by studying scripts!"

Rasha studied Zun-jish. He connived his way toward the elder blessings of the Loa or the Crescent Lady's mightiest powers. Rasha never acquainted a warlord who failed to appeal Voodandum to impart powers they had once reserved for war. They were like ants in search of carcasses to satiate the colony's hunger who followed in the footsteps of those who crawled before them, yet even ants could grow weary of life beneath their queen. She must decide whether to compromise while she still held strength to pull the lever, or after her leverage was gone.

Voodandum had not warred since their journey aside the First Warlord to establish his empire in the far north. Further trollish conquests of the Realms of Frostheim, incursions from hoary beasts skulking in the Endless Wastes, and this plague that culled over half of Gara-thandila had pushed the empire to peer through the Arch itself. Voodandum would not yet march to war, but Rasha would inculcate Zun-jish's hordes with the powers of the Dark Moon like no Witchqueen had done since Witchqueen Vutuala. Compromise often stung, but when the wound finally healed, the bandage must be ripped off.

Rasha bequeathed, "I offer your warriors the pervading supremacy of the Dark Moon." She raised her hands skyward where the Crescent Lady blackened the sky athwart the pyramid's pointed roof. "It is too late to exploit this one, but sanction Yel-jaraht's execution be moved to Vel-thaka, satisfy Baelgrant's request, and Voodandum will imbue a thousand of your warriors with the power of the Dark Moon."

"Rasha, this cannot be done!" Abijo stepped between her and Zun-jish, obscuring Zun-jish from her sight. "This does not warrant the divulgence of such power, and it is too dangerous to be called upon at all. We will forever curse Voodandum if we betray Witchqueen Vutuala's dying decree."

"What other choice do we have, Abijo?" Rasha questioned him honestly. "If we hold to traditions that suit us and discard the rest, we discard the empire to return to civil strife before we all are drawn through Death's Arch."

Abijo whispered, "We cannot trust Zun-jish." His eyes pleaded that Rasha rescind. "Your predecessor refused Yel-jaraht the same offer, so why gift this immeasurable power to dis grub bastard, whose blood be more sour than the plague?"

"It's the choice I have made," Rasha resolved. "If we do not act rapidly, there will soon come a time when it is already too late. We choose the warriors carefully. Some from Zun-jish's hordes, yes." She hissed over still air. "And most from the warlords we trust."

"Witchqueen," Zun-jish called. He drew to meet her face to face. "Bind this oath in your blood, and I will personally deliver Yel-jaraht to this nephew of the Bane of Trolls."

Her answer ensued dreadfully simple. Rasha retrieved the ritualistic knife she held upon her always. Without waiting for Abijo to shed another concern, she cut the palm of her left hand until it oozed crimson blood. The Warlord Prince followed her example, slicing his palm's meaty flesh before he returned his sword to its sheathe. They shook, Zun-jish gripping her hand like a snake constricting its meal, grinning manically in the wake of his conniving triumph.

"Voodandum will leave behind a contingent of its strongest witches and warlocks at the Altar of Garatha and dispatch more to the remaining altars. We will be riding to Vel-thaka, and we should be leaving no later than the next Bright Moon," Rasha resolved.

"No, Rasha," Zun-jish corrected with a vanquishing grin. "We'll be riding to my empire's resurgence and to rain death down upon the Stormborne. Just as Warlord Beh'kliar has assured us both, our victory has already begun."

CHAPTER THIRTEEN

SEERESS'S AWAKENING

"ARE YOU SURE I SHOULDN'T be with you when you ask?" asked Siv.

Tanya hushed a sigh as she finished preparing the die she had gathered to bless.

"I was there too!" Siv persisted. "I heard everything Thyra and Ryurik said. Muiri speaks true."

Siv motioned to where Muiri lay sprawled across a cot in the temple's hospice. It was where they carried him two days prior. His arm occasionally twitched in pain, but it had yet to disturb his slumber. His right hand clutched at his chest. It was cute how it embraced his heart, and Tanya preferred its current penchant over its earlier, remiss clutch.

In due course, Tanya replied, "No, Siv, I need you to bless the last of the runic die, and Ella, could you grind down more bone meal? I didn't grind enough earlier."

"Of course! I'll…I will ask Seer Drurhelm for more marrow."

In a firm tone, Tanya instructed, "No need to bother Drurhelm. Just filch a few ribs. If he thinks he was robbed, I'll reconcile it with him later."

"Thank you," Ella squeaked as she checked the space around them before sneaking off, inviting a little more suspicion than if she just walked like a normal girl.

"Are you certain? Dragoln scarcely bends the rules for anyone besides you, and he never impedes his fellow seers!" Siv persisted.

"I am certain, Siv." Cajoling Siv's pride, Tanya specified, "You make the best blessings, draft the finest runes, and I need nothing less than your perfection before attempting to cast this ritual. I'm just better at persuading the seers to yield to what I want, so allow me to employ that talent, as it is what I do best."

"Fine, but tell me what he says when you return," Siv insisted, irritated her perseverance had been curbed.

"When have I ever not?" asked Tanya.

Siv blushed. Tanya withdrew from Muiri's side while he slept, leaving behind Siv with a bowl of blessed die. Siv began blessing a few more. She added chopped lamb liver to the motley assortment of bones, gnarled thorns, and flower petals. Tanya twirled to lend the girl a quick hug while whispering thanks into Siv's ear. She then departed the hospice in haste.

The temple's hospice lay on the opposite end of temple grounds from the mammoth pine grove. Tanya hurried in the opposite direction, hugging the stone hedge bordering the runic fields to the west. Downhill from both the hospice and ritual hall lay a triumvirate of lavish shrines—each dedicated to one of the moon's three main stages: the Riven, the Dark, and Bright. Their grandeur surpassed all the other buildings in Torlv's runic temple of Stormguarde.

The Shrines of the Three Moons were erected with clear-cut moonstones and variants of wood from local trees. The first was born of an ebon dream, dark as a starless night, and guarded by a pale-faced Monomua dressed in the blackest veil of moonlight. The second bled bright. The Crescent Lady's full incandescence was carved from white aspen and shined behind scintillating crystal eyes. The third swirled the two passions together in harmony not unlike the Riven Moon. An altar of intricately cut and meticulously stacked stone rested at the epicenter. It had not been exercised since Torlv's shattered soul was bound to the Tempest Throne, or so the seers claimed.

Dragoln often loafed within the shrine lying farthest up the hills begotten by the Dark Moon. Tanya entered to confirm that there the seer dwelt the day the same as so many others. Sitting in the comfort of his favorite unadorned chair, Dragoln smiled in warm welcome.

"Tanya," Seer Dragoln questioned, "to what do I owe the pleasure of the keeper of my Freyja's company?"

Dragoln dwelt on the verge of instilling a lesson whenever they spoke, so Tanya leaped ahead to quicken its pace. "This is your temple. We are yours to keep and protect, and you are ours to serve and obey."

"But like your sister," Dragoln remarked, "you have taken a keen liking to your charge. Don't fret, my girl," he interrupted when she drew breath to reply. "I cherish the effort you spare upon this temple's preservation. It gives this old man the opportunity to relieve his aching feet."

Tanya noticed Dragoln was shoeless. The sight of his bunions was rather grotesque. "Helping the others reach their better ends helps me pass the time and neglect the dullness of this place."

"Which is why I mostly leave you to your own devices and suggest to Drurhelm that he do the same."

"You've retained far more of them because of it. It would abet the temple even more if you forced Drurhelm out to establish his own."

"Across the ages, Drur's seers have dwelt in Stormguarde's runic temple for as long as the runic gods have dwelt in Halvalkyra's Halls. The Draconic Father must maintain a watchful eye on Drur in his Abyss from beyond the Valheim's peak. So, too, must I remain vigilant of the dealings of those seers who worship the Delas of Death. I cannot risk tossing out a necromancer. They are fickle, dangerous, and need to be controlled," said Dragoln with a wizened fervor more devout than any she had ever heard.

The seer described necromancy well. He, likewise, propounded the soundest solution to abide by the bygone edicts of the pantheon they served. She would advocate for it always because she fervidly despised Drurhelm, but Tanya had never pursued it to the point of inciting Dragoln's most stalwart resolve before. Age frightened men in curious ways, and for Dragoln, she believed he now feared the future beyond his imminent departure through the Arch of Death.

Conveying the stipulation as ominously as she could, she stated, "Then you must temper Drur's seer if you wish for me to remain and for this temple to endure."

"What has Drurhelm done to warrant this anathema you bestow upon him?"

"Nothing yet, but precautionary measures are often the most successful at stifling distant betrayals." Tanya inhaled to directly question, "Did Seer Drurhelm return from Lord Bolvark's call to arms with a non-troll corpse? It would have been fresher than the snow that fell after the ritual we drew the same night."

"He did bring back another alongside the troll's. The corpse of a sickly mendicant whom Lord Bolvark slew as punishment for striking a Skjold."

"Striking a Skjold?" Tanya scarcely believed her sister would allow the man's execution to unfold for a crime the Skjold committed against each other the most.

Sorrow shrouded the seer as he straightened. "He only stumbled over the guard's foot, but Lord Bolvark pierced the boy's heart before your sister could challenge your grandfather's verdict or inhibit the result."

Nettled, Tanya exclaimed, "Where is the Storm King's justice in that? How could my grandfather decree his death? How could my sister abide her own man's lie?"

"Thyra had no choice, as one usually has when rapt by the nature of power," he stifled before leaping upon his tangential point. "Though, I suppose his friend divulged more courage than us when he charged Bolvark wielding nothing more than his fists."

"There's nothing natural about holding power over another man!" Tanya came to a halt before rhetorizing, "Do cardinals force hens to farm for wild seeds? Do they send in the tanager to slay the flightless farmers if they overstep the falcon knight only there to keep the peace? No! Those are our bastardizations of nature—the evils humans, Frosthammer dwarves, Garathandi trolls, ældrik dragonkin, jütengolk frost giants, and even Valkyrie choose to compose. There's nothing natural in murder aside from the torridness of self-defense." Realizing she had assumed the ire of her father's forefathers, Tanya soothed her dancing hands before putting them away. "He was a free man, I heard. What happens to Lord Bolvark for killing a free man without a trial by the althing of Stormguarde, or the Skjold warrior who instigated his death?"

Dragoln explicitly informed, "He is a lord, Tanya. A lord in the Stormlands. This is not the High East, my good girl. You have not found yourself idling in the land of chivalry or grace. We both know nothing will befall Lord Bolvark for wetting his blade with his blood."

Dragoln shifted his feet over the floor to sluggishly reclaim his slippers, then invited her sit beside him. His insouciance boiled her blood. He refused to fault Thyra for the mendicant's dead and for the beating Muiri incurred, but Tanya did not. Regardless, in this hierarchy of the Stormlands, which rewarded the lord who owned the most swords, she was powerless to enact the change she wished to see. Tanya surrendered to Dragoln's offer, boldly bestrode the square table, and rigidly claimed the seat adrift to his.

Indulged, Dragoln continued, "Seize solace in knowing your sister disowned the guard who embellished the mendicant's mistakes. His partner now seeks atonement for not speaking out that day. I have received him a great many times already, yet his conscience still aches."

"He's just another ox strapped to the wagon that pulls injustice to market. Until the man who whips the backs of his kin walks along on his own two feet, another will be reaped to fill the last one's place."

"We can never remove the whip. Without some guidance, we inevitably stagnate until we are overtaken by a grander wagon pulling to market faster and exacerbating atrocities worse than the one we knew. No, you can never remove the wagon. Seat another driver, however—one who leads the oxen well, who convinces them they are magnificent steeds—and change becomes undeniably real."

Confounded by the comparison, Tanya exacted, "What does lying accomplish when they remain slaves strapped down by a harness? They're still at the mercy of another man's whip and his willingness to offer them feed."

"They have purpose, and if it is one they believe in, then they are no longer slaves," enriched the seer as his lesson became clear. "That is what your sister has done with the Skjold. They were but mercenaries for the thanes of the Erunheim before she weeded out the rot and gilded them with a glimmer that was not gold, but that is something you already know," he muttered, as if tempting Tanya to clarify the rest for him.

Tanya mumbled, "The same as she had in Ellynon. She adores her tight-knit command structures loyal only to her. Then, if someone deigns to challenge or break her rule of law, she forces them into submission through any available forum. It's effective for the iron hand that rules, but it's perilous and unpredictable for the rest of us. We are forced to rely upon the hope our leaders will always be born just."

The seer stated, "Frightening, isn't it?" Tanya bustled her shoulders as she formulated her refute, but Dragoln raised his hand in earnest, requesting she wait. "The only difference between your sister and the lord who slew the friend of this thrall you intend to mend is how they utilize the power they are given. That is the true nature of power, but do not worry. I've not seen this thrall in our temple myself and, thus, have no reason to believe what I've said or heard."

Tanya languished in the chill of Dragoln's jocularity and sardonic wit, contemplating how the seer so quickly deduced the reason why she came. "Our priestesses," he had said. Some little larks chattered between both of them then. Tanya sighed. Well, she could not fault them for gossiping. They were bound to quiet and tedious lives. Small drama entertained them all.

Seer Dragoln was at least a friend, an old, loquacious, and irreversibly docile friend. No priestess actively sought to speak with Drurhelm. As long as that trend endured, she would never fear them speaking to Dragoln. She supposed gossip always made its way back to her, whether by their mouths or through Seer Dragoln's.

"For your sake, and for the Stormlands once I'm gone, I hope your brother looks to your sister and studies her example more closely than the jarls and lesser lords he surrounds himself with. Perhaps, Ryurik could even learn from yours, like you learned from whoever bestowed you that necklace you wear like it were the muscle strewn across your heart."

Veiled lessons speckled Dragoln's every rambling, although when one lived as long as the seer had, they could afford to confer many. Dragoln managed to inculcate her head against her best efforts, plucking chords until her mind rung with the echoes of his chosen lesson. Then again, Tanya willingly waded into the sands by interjecting whenever he scrupled a sour nerve. She had not done a particularly good job in surpassing or even meeting his expectations. At least now she knew. She could learn from her mistakes and think more clearly when next he plucked at her moral code.

"I believe that's enough of a lesson for today, seeing as you did not wish for one to begin with." He chuckled, and Tanya softly chuckled as well. "How am I to temper Drur's seer for you then?"

"I want you to bury the mendicant in the lower graveyard. Bury him and nothing else. It's a favor for my family," she lied. It was an honest lie, one she needed to ask on behalf of the thrall who was without the power to do so himself.

"Aww. Family is something we choose for ourselves. Whoever you are truly choosing to request this favor for, I hope it is well deserved."

Failing to subdue the undue blush striking her, Tanya graciously replied, "I guess we can never know until after it is all said and done. May I tend to him now, Runic Father?"

"Clever thought. I think I will go now to beckon Hosvir for his aid and

Drurhelm for his forgiveness. Return to your Freyjas, good Tanya, and keep Torlv's runic temple strong."

⟨◆⟩

"How long until the lizard perishes," Drurhelm spat. "How long until his temple and all its vestal riches belong to me?"

Drur's seer could hardly think anymore. He grasped at thoughts within his head only to witness them descend into the muffled void before he could acquaint their erudition. His mind scattered, echoing like howling pheasants screeching amidst wintry peaks. They fluttered wildly in every direction, filching the moon's clarity. It left him with nothing but the bitter death of his thoughts—a death he mindlessly forgave, but a death he still loathed.

"How many bodies lie buried beneath this temple? How many have Drur's seers burdened this ground with?"

Drurhelm succeeded in his grim trend, desperately wishing he retained the option to fail. He could not help betraying his inner voice to the air. At least upon hearing himself speak aloud, he became aware he intended to think. He detested his mind's broken wellspring. Each slipping thought strengthened his self-abhorrence.

There were bodies strewn across the runic temple. Bodies were buried in the runic fields where that inviolable Lysian bitch flexed her sullied tits with Dragoln's permission because her Skjold guarded temple grounds from imaginary prowlers and thieves. They lay in the graveyards at the temple's southern edge. Bodies were strewn through the dirt beyond the pine grove where this inclement misery began.

"This is where the most bodies lie."

"*This is where my army lies.*"

Necromancy flowed through Drurhelm's heart the same as for any of Dranur's other incisive disciples. Doors had been closed to his ilk by the Runic Faith, but so many remained open because of Drur's acceptance into the Draconic Father's court. Eldrahg's law, however, forbade Drur's seers from ever raising the dead, and they had begrudgingly abided by that law for untold generations. It was not his army. Drurhelm commanded no army of the dead. The bodies buried here belonged to Seer Dragoln. Torlv's runic temple of Stormguarde was his to command.

"How long must I wait until I command this temple and all its secrets.

I have not seen all that's hidden in the vaults beneath the protective veils." His voice spiked like a noxious whiff of concentrated poppy seed poison. "How long must I wait!"

Drurhelm coveted the elder seer's death. Dragoln routinely derided him by incessantly interfering in his affairs. He had survived as the envious second in the shade of the runic father's wings, but those wings were now nipping at the brink of Drur's Abyss. Not much flesh was left there, only skin and secreted bunions refusing to enter the grave.

"A simple tonic. Omund flower mixed with a little green tea and some tellwyn to throw him unconscious. Perhaps wolfsbane for a kick. A greedy dragon hoards my priestesses, and so the rapacious wyrm deserves to be felled."

No! No, no, no. 'Twas too predictable. Drurhelm refused that thought already, and yet it kept coming back! A simple mind could trace the tonic's contents. They would administer a remedy before the crushed omund burnt through his stomach and throat. Drurhelm would not be ousted by simple folk! He needed a better plan.

"Bagh! A simple poison for a simple task. Carry him to the Arch of Death and shove him into Drur's Abyss before his soul can ascend. Another body for the army, but I have no army," Drurhelm argued with himself. His mind toiled in bitter anguish. Delas of Death, it hurt. *But we do,* the dark thoughts answered until only his consciousness timidly remained.

His army? His temple? His virgin priestesses to command? Drurhelm did not wish to touch them. He preferred them unsullied by a stranger's hands. He much preferred they break themselves softly, and oh, how he craved to bear witness as he forced the command. All that pleasure would be his to revel. Raise an army while the jarls fought amongst themselves.

"And why stop at Torlv's runic temple? Conquer all of the Stormlands. Flush out he who holds the toothed seax the Elder Wyrm first relinquished into my back!"

The phantoms within his head revealed themselves, and Drurhelm soberly realized they were not of his own design. It heard him even now as he cursed it. It would foresee any runes he cast to oust it before the die were even blessed.

"Who are you?" Drurhelm generously demanded before seeking to force these phantoms from his head.

"I am the bottomless black over which the pale moon rises, keeper of the kingdom graced by silver wings at the expiry of all craven things, and knife-eared terror who whispers doom into the Reaper's ear. I am the Delas of Death, you toad-throated fool! I am Drur."

"Drur?" Drurhelm's courage melted like stone to the onslaught of dragon's fire.

"That is what I am called. I have dwelt indolent for too long, and the bindings holding me weaken while those binding my betrayers hold strong."

"You are bound by naught. You guard the abyss where writhe wretched Stormborne who cannot ascend Halvalkyra. You have always guarded the abyss, just like Eldrahg has always defended his great hall."

"Do not question my word!" scathed the runic god with a tongue as icy as the Reaper's execrable glare. "You, too, have been betrayed. You are betrayed still. The Runic Faith has long withheld the truth from my chosen seers."

"The truth of what?"

"Long they've hidden the truth of my betrayal when I was bound to the old throne, shackled to Stormurgall by chains they falsely claim were forged for the wolf god Fenrof. It is here we both rot, deep in the Broken Fjords."

"Betrayed? By the runic gods?"

"Betrayed by Eldrahg himself. The runic gods will know the indignation of my chains. I will see them fall from Halvalkyra to languish beneath the Crescent Lady, so she might forever weep when the binds of Gleipnir break and I am freed again."

"How am I to break these chains of Gleipnir, oh Delas of Death? I am but one seer, one necromancer, and one man alone. I can neither part the Draconic Father's ældrik nor scourge the fjords of Ísvalar's brood to reach you and your bestial wolf."

"You will raise an army of the dead, you fool!" Death's Delas chided wrathfully. "My army. The army of Drur's Abyss. Have you grown so feckless and hollow in your position that you no longer remember how to raise the dead?"

How dare he be questioned by this runic god who had somehow slithered his way into his head. Drurhelm's thirst for necromantic release surpassed even his thirst for the many priestesses withheld from his grasp. His secrets had been laid bare before the both of them. Delving deeper would easily guarantee that his innermost cravings only benefited Drur.

"I have never forgotten!" Drurhelm yelled, silencing the phantom of death.

"Drurhelm. Have you forgotten you stand alone, or are you unwell?" came the voice of Seer Dragoln as he pitched faux concern.

Drurhelm retrieved a cloth from his belt to dry the beads of sweat torrentially collected atop his crumpled brow. "How long have you been with me? I wasn't aware I had company."

"A mere moment. You seem tense. You have been abnormally tense since performing Drur's ritual of skulls."

The air lightened with Dragoln's admission. Drur's chosen seer, as he now understood he was, and not in name alone. Long had Drurhelm coveted such veneration. Never had he assumed the price would be so high. The charge Drur posed was nigh insurmountable, but his will must be done. Drur was Death's Delas, and he was Drurhelm's patron runic god.

Seer Dragoln's soul was overdue for the Arch, and the Seeress Torunn had not been seen for countless moons. With Dragoln's death, Drurhelm could seize the title of Runic Father like no seer to Drur had done before. With Lothair's inevitable, inglorious death, Ryurik would become Storm King. The jarls would stand divided amidst his reign. Puppet the boy toward Drur's ends through Seer Hosvir perhaps, and he just might be capable of raising an army of the dead before anyone could stop him. He would confiscate the runic temple first, and with it, seize the deaths of all those left to oppose him. A simple plan for a simple task, but it made him smile, and from the warmth he felt rising inside his head, he knew Drur smiled too.

"No, I have not been myself at all. Something has been amiss since I performed Drur's ritual of skulls, but don't worry for me. I will have more time to review his records, to study the old stones, and with good rest and reading, I will reclaim peace for my mind at last."

"That is…comforting." Dragoln uninvitedly lingered, scrutinizing the fortitude of his response as if he were the magistrate of all men's resolve. "I have come to grant you a small bit of information you'll undoubtedly be displeased to hear. I've had the sickly mendicant's body buried in our temple's graveyard at the behest of the Storm King. I know you claimed that one, but Lothair was owed a favor, and I elected not to refuse. It is an easy one to abide, and I am confident you will satisfy Drur's hunger again…soon."

Betrayed! So Drur had spoken true. Augury of the future did not only come through the frenzied ingestion of shrooms or through Monomua, Goddess of the Moon. Dranur, Goddess of Death and Despair, foresaw futures as well. The Reaper gifted her cogent clarity to him through Drur. The crumbling visage of Eldrahg's favored seer—the withering keeper of Torlv's runic temple here in Stormguarde—slighted Drurhelm yet again. Drurhelm's neck tautened like a vice grip as blood pumped into his raptured head. He swelled with the indignity, and yet, why worry over the ramblings of the man he was bade to kill?

"The Storm King's rule is law." Drurhelm relieved himself of bygone anger, of the need to snivel and debate to retain his sovereignty as Drur's seer. "I would have no corpse had Lothair refused his lord permission to rupture the mendicant's heart. It was always his, I suppose, and he gave me the honor of preparing it before its reclamation came forth." Bury the sickly mendicant. Either way, he would one day rise to free the Delas of Death.

<hr />

Siv had drafted an immaculate rune, and Tanya fretted over casting upon such a seamless creation. She had never cast a rune before. The pressure was insane. Of course, she had drafted a sundry of runic circles, gathered die and blessed them, and never had her work failed to cultivate results. Yet, despite the endless experience taken from watching the seers cast runes, the notion of mere inklings of lunar magic flowing through her hands rattled her nerves.

The stakes laden upon this ritual were great. Tanya could not afford to fail. The narrowly weakened power of a daytime moon might curb the ritual's strength—and the penalties if her cast turned sour—but a life was still held in the balance. More importantly, she firmly believed that life had already suffered enough.

Reticent to begin, Tanya ambled aimlessly. "Are you certain he's centered? I doubt this will even work if his arms don't overlay Freyja's. We should postpone. We should redraft it so he fits the picture more snug."

"Tanya!" Siv contested. "You're just nervous. This isn't like the runic circle we drafted for Drur's ritual of skulls. It's just a simple mending ritual that requires a ridiculous amount of die. Dragoln has performed these rituals hundreds of times. Freyja's specialties are well outside his expertise. You're ready, and that's why he is knowingly leaving this one to you."

Tanya's legs nearly buckled against Siv's reassurance. It confounded her, the unfamiliar sentiment, and Tanya was ill-prepared to receive it with grace. In some ironic fashion, Siv was probably refusing to hear another one of her creations be snubbed, but her encouragement was at least genuine. She exhaled the admittedly silly lapse in her confidence to regain her lost grace.

"You're right, the preparations are impeccable, but I cannot fail," she quailed.

"You won't fail, but if you won't cast it, I will." Siv ogled Muiri's tranquil body, and she giggled when Tanya's gaze followed to latch unto him as well. "I'll still tell him you saved his life if you take my next few shifts sorting Drurhelm's bones."

Flustered by Siv's insinuations, Tanya rebutted, "You already owe me a shift! I'll cast the ritual and tell him myself before we escort him off temple grounds."

Splashing elation across her face, Siv triumphantly joked, "Don't tell me, Princess. You can have anything you want if you simply ask."

Tanya glared, reminding Siv how little she cared for those idyllic jests. The priestesses envied that stupid title she received for simply being delivered into the right family. They knew she abandoned what slim benefits it gave upon joining the Runic Faith, but they refused to quit with their teasing. Their intentions might be sublime, but Tanya reviled the reminders. "Princess" was just another term for a treasure her current keeper could use to bargain with against her will. In the Runic Faith, Tanya at least had the option to impose some form of self-will.

Tanya ejaculated, "Give me a little space to cast the ritual then, Siv?"

Siv obliged and pursed her lips in amusement. Tanya shook herself of hesitancy and of the vexation Siv left in its wake. Clearing her mind, she focused to recall the ritual's chant. Two stanzas lay before her, and each must resonate like the cogent whistles of whiskered pines on a whisperless night.

Tanya exhaled her doubts, relaxed, inhaled her fullest voice, and proffered the song off the mellifluous flow of a slightly nervous tongue. Like any ritual bound to the Hearth of Life's healing heart, the chant began soft and slow. It refused vigor against all judgment and humbly rose toward an effervescent chorus that beckoned Freyja's salvation be cast with more than just words.

Tanya tossed the die across the circle as she concluded the first chant. Most rolled off Muiri's body to be consumed by the rune's sparkling grays and reds. A few slivers of flesh and bone meal adhered to his robes, leaving faint, oily stains as they dissolved by her voice's order. Tanya persisted, power collected about the runes, and it dove into the tenderized mush of flesh surrounding Muiri's broken ribs.

Her voice cracked, the squeeze in her fingers faltered, and Muiri's body quaked. Tanya suddenly realized the raw runic power her hands were guiding. She felt waves of lunar magic resonating across the room. She did not lapse in the melody, continuing strong to the very end. His body susceptibly relaxed, its tension visibly departed, and Tanya's spirit soothed while the glow of the runes diminished.

Tanya knelt by Muiri's side to find his swelling greatly subsided. She caressed a few of his ribs to discover the bones were solidly set in place. The excess blood pooling beneath his skin had also vanished.

Glancing around the hospice, Tanya realized a small crowd had perked up to watch her cast the ritual to completion. The wounded warriors seemed amused yet subtly bemused by the whole affair. Truthfully, they were more stricken with her than with anything she accomplished. What else did men desire but a Freyja to call their own? Most of her fellow priestesses' mouths hung in awe, a welcome contrast to the gawking stares. Siv beamed, spreading her cheeks wide, and a rush of pride lurched up Tanya's spine.

"Tanya! Did...did you just cast a ritual by yourself?" Ella asked, surprised.

The feeling still unreal even as she dusted off Monomua's ambiance, Tanya proudly admitted, "I think I did."

The captivating hymn of a familiar folk song gently woke Muiri. His eyelids twitched to the bright melody the unknown priestess chaunted. After scrunching his eyes, then relaxing them as if determining whether he were in a dream, Muiri precluded they had yet to receive the light of day. He did not wish for the priestesses to discover he was awake. The hymn soothed his many anxieties, so Muiri chose to lie in wait and listen within his ruse of lingering dreams. The priestess sang for him, he presumed, humming an ode to Freyja and her quest for Helti's renascence as though the priestess believed Muiri was her own god to save.

Shifting once the voice droned to distant walls, Muiri stretched to check his ribs. They were no longer broken. He did not understand how. While the sharpest pains had departed, the bones still ached. He only came in search of Cadell. In retrospect, Muiri realized he stumbled into the one place a thrall would be mended without question as well. He could not thank them for their kindness. He could give nothing in return.

The girl's melodious tune gradually subsided until it completely abandoned the room. Muiri opened an eye to confirm no other priestesses were lurking, then sluggishly sat upright. Two warriors appeared to be sleeping, recovering from their own wicked wounds.

Muiri quietly sprang up from under the covers to gather his belongings beside his cot. He dressed himself and found his most precious possession stashed underneath them all. It took the finality of his self-control not to shout in excitement. He retrieved the woven charm his mother had garlanded with her hair before the Stormborne pillaged their village and robbed him away.

Muiri snuck opposite the direction the song had faded, then vaulted an open door. Light fell through an untouched window, overlaying the parched ink of an impressive interpretation of Freyja. The runic goddess's cheeks cut rather sharply—sharper than most Stormborne girls—and they blossomed like claret dreams. He lost his eyes within hers until they bled like Cadell's, and Muiri snapped back to reality.

His stomach gurgled in hunger. He realized he had not eaten since that accursed day. He ignored it, but his stomach growled again. No matter. Food would be his priority's bitter second. First, he needed to recover Cadell's body. Then, he needed to escape.

"So do you plan on rifling through graves until you either unearth your friend or collapse from hunger and fatigue?"

Muiri twirled to the right where a gorgeous, amber-eyed priestess leant against the wood-framed egress to a smaller room. "Not exactly," he sarcastically answered. "How did you know I was going to leave? You shouldn't have even known I was awake!"

"Please." She chuckled while lithely rolling her head. "I knew exactly when you woke up. Once you chose to hide it, I knew you were going to run."

Ignoring the innate smugness enwreathing her vexingly attractive features, Muiri confessed, "I had no idea you buried him."

"I didn't bury him," she corrected. "Seer Hosvir buried him at the behest of Seer Dragoln, after I requested it of him myself."

Muiri challenged her claim in more of a question than a solid retort. "But his body was taken by the seer who looks like a fat toad."

"Yes, it was," she agreed, mildly laughing. "I thought it would better if he were buried than dissevered into little pieces for pernicious rituals when he was more than a sickly mendicant to someone," she concluded in a more unadorned tone.

Muiri stood in stunned silence while he registered it all. He could scarcely comprehend her swift action toward warrantless kindness. He never had the chance to tell Cadell goodbye, but as she took the time to inform him of what she did, it felt as if he had. Life itself was blurry since he stumbled through that moonlit door. Her voice felt warm and familiar through the cold unknown. She knew why he was here and why he endeavored to escape. Had his heart fled him during his lapse in lucidity? Had she done this all for him out of pure, genuine sympathy?

"Thank you," he answered gratefully. "I just...I wanted to see him properly buried. He was a good friend, and us thralls usually have none."

The priestess adorned humility's crown. "You are welcome. From what I learned of the two of you from my sister, it was everything he deserved."

Who was this blonde-haired, amber-eyed priestess? "Your sister?" Muiri cooed. Oh, how had he forgotten this was Tanya—the teenage embodiment of Thyra Ehlrich. "You are the commander's younger sister. Loretia's bush smother my mouth. I cannot stay here, or I will be found." He panicked.

"Muiri, wait!" Tanya nigh ordered before he had even sprinted to the door. "She doesn't know you're here. The seers don't either." She raised a tepid hand before approaching.

He buckled, but he did not halt her advance.

"We only finished mending you this morning, and your body needs more time to recover its strength."

"I feel fine enough already, more flexible too!" Stoutly, Muiri challenged, "If I remain, one of her Skjold will find me!" He did not entirely understand why he chose to argue when he could simply step around her artificial blockade and run away.

"That's your mind tricking your body into believing it is fully healed. Plus, where would you go? You're an unclaimed thrall. I assure you, my sister will find you quicker out there than if you remain and hide here."

Intrigued by her staunch concern, Muiri joked, "She has that unrelenting aura about her, doesn't she?"

Tanya giggled before smothering her sanguinity to revert to a more polished pose. "I promise you will be safer here. Help us tend to our other sickly while you finish recovering, and I will help you escape Stormguarde to somewhere the Skjold will never find you."

Slight distrust of this Lysian princess lingered in his bones, even against her voice's soft appeal and her convivial charm. "Why help me? I entered your temple uninvited, and you know nothing about who I am or what I can do other than that I'm a thrall."

Stepping in without impeding his personal space, Tanya softly challenged, "That's not true at all. I know the only reason you came to this runic temple was to tender your friend a final kindness without thinking of yourself. You nearly died because you're an idiot, but at least you are an affable one." Tanya relented, stepping from in front of the door and clearing his path into an acrid world that sorely wished to welcome him. "Be imprudent if you want, but if you choose to leave, just remember I gave you the option to stay."

His odds of survival in this runic temple exceeded those on the outside, but he did not yet trust her. "Cadell was buried. You are certain of it?"

"Cadell was buried and nothing else," Tanya gently assured, inviting him to return to the hospice's main room.

She did not lie, even for as condescendingly as she spoke. Should he remain, at least he would not need to thieve for food, and his gut gurgled in support of the girl's offer. Noticing his hesitancy, Tanya beckoned him over. She did not bury deceit in the folds of her warm smile. It shone honest and true. Muiri yielded to her call, and he chose to remain for shelter and free food.

"Is this all you do? Cook meals, clean the grounds, change bandages, and administer a tonic or two? This life is dreadful." Muiri droned. The thrall scrubbed the dishes from the seers' dinners as Tanya already twice instructed him to do.

Tanya insisted, "I told you we mostly work—draft runes and bless die between chores—and in the spare time we're allotted, we study what the seers permit us to."

"So you can eventually become seeresses?" Muiri dispensed his questions quicker than fishermen flung their nets during an early salmon run, and she could hardly answer the first one before he unstoppably advanced to the next.

"Sometimes, but more often not. Mostly so we become better help to the established seers and seeresses."

"But every day? You do their bidding every day with no promise of anything in return. You're not much different from a—"

"A thrall?" Tanya shot back.

Her anger bloated, but not in contempt of his observation. In some root form, they were both slaves. Only their circumstances were different. A priestess chose and preserved her fate as an alternative to life's uncertainty. His life as a thrall befell him by no choice of his own. They were not so different, true, but Tanya did not desire being reminded that hers was a bondage she chose by a slave who had not chosen his own.

"I didn't mean to offend you," he amended. "It's just…wrong."

Tanya smirked. Muiri was sweet, but she did not need sweet. "We choose to live by the Runic Faith, and after some point, we all have the option to leave. I chose this life so I cannot be used as another pawn in my family's games."

"They cannot be that insufferable. You latched to their sides through all of the toad seer's ritual, and you seemed content enough." He grinned. "In fact, you looked as happy as my mother whenever she used to spend time with me."

Tanya giggled. What a coquettish comparison to make. "They're not entirely intolerable as much as they style themselves out to be. And his name is Seer Drurhelm. Drur's seer of toads, to be precise."

Muiri chuckled, and Tanya giggled again. She returned to pulverizing mountain arnica into tonics she would administer to the wounded to relieve their aches and pains. Fortunately, Tanya had finished toddling Muiri through the remainder of the tasks she intended to leave him for the coming weeks. No more guidance, no more questions, and her mind would find reprieve from the dual consequences of her snappish compassion.

"Why do you do it then?" he asked while Tanya augmented the tonics to transform them into more appealing drinks.

Tanya added in a pinch of poppy, then swirled each to the consistency preferred by their respective recipients. "Do what?" she softly probed.

"Remain with the Runic Faith when your brother is to be Storm King while your sister commands the Skjold? Can they not simply impel the rest of your family not to marry you off?"

"Marriage is the least of my concerns," she mumbled. Her nostrils vented her frustrations on their own accord, so Tanya decided to take a more inspiring and direct approach. "How about I show you why instead? That should answer your questions in full."

"Um..." Muiri hesitated, to which Tanya subtly smirked. "Are foreigners allowed to read your runes and learn our secrets?"

"No, of course not, but you don't need to read Stormur for what I'm going to show you."

"Well, I can if I ever need to." Ignoring her budding curiosity to that impressive claim, Tanya turned the corner to enter the hospice's main room. "I know Stormur, High Helmar, old Alterian, and even a little Avantian. My mother was a connoisseur of languages, and she made certain I learned to speak, read, and write with each one she knew," he called out after her.

"That's...surprising," Tanya tactlessly muttered. Catching wind of Muiri's fluster, she aimed to amend her crass mistake. "I only meant it's astonishing she learned so many languages having lived in a little fishing village for all her life. I was a princess for half of mine and royal Stormborne for the other. Each came with an excessive education and hyperspecialized tutoring. All of that considered, I only know Lysian, Asmoduil Elvish, and Stormur. Your mother knows even more than I do!" Tanya handed each patient their nightly tonics and received their gracious thanks before motioning for Muiri to continue following as she exited the hospice.

"She told me she was born there and never called another village home. Said she learned them all from the scribe who serviced the local lord. I never really believed her, though. It makes no sense why a local scribe who preferred men would take the time to teach her every language he ever knew."

"Who do you think she was?" Tanya whispered, departing the hospice to engage with the night's clear air.

"I don't really know, and I never thought to question her further," Muiri mumbled before assuming an astute clarity. "All I know is she was someone special, but she chose to leave it behind for me and our quaint fishermen's lives."

Muiri gave no indication he craved sympathy, but she opted to yield it anyway. "I am certain she misses you. It would be hard for any mother not to." The Alterian's face softened, but he did not avert his eyes from the path where she led, and they elected to walk in peace while locked inside their own heads.

Tanya once shared similar sentiments toward her own mother. Earnest trust and warm reassurance beguiled her youthful senses whenever she snuggled into her warm embrace. The empress who comforted Tanya upon the vessel bringing them hitherto, however, was not the same High Lady who governed the Erunheim. She saw it in her mother's eyes the night when Darius died. Beset by a betrayal nobody in the family ever spoke of—all mirth and sanguinity abandoned her. Three years of brutal war, three sons lost to ire, and Valyria became naught but the High Lady of Stormguarde's sour.

Mother always regretted marrying Lysian's Crown Prince. That which negated a Lysian invasion of the Stormlands also nullified her heart. Yet, upon their inglorious return, her mother latched onto Grandfather Lothair like an overfed leech fearful of squandering its host's blood. Tanya's deepest intuitions assured her that her mother still loathed him for it. It was a bygone grudge she refused to address but also refused to let go.

Valyria's incoherent hatred of the ældrik in the Broken Fjords suspiciously replaced those old grudges. She blamed the old seat of the Stormlands for Lothair's decision to abandon her to a loveless cur. The correlation made no sense at all. All Tanya could recall of her mother were the warnings she whispered when rapt with her darkest thoughts. "The toothed seax in our two families' backs. The true reason why your grandfather married me across an ocean, to ferry it far away," her mother had always claimed.

Tanya reviled what mother had become, so she fled her madness and incessant talk of war with the Broken Fjords by joining the Runic Faith. Ryurik departed Stormguarde to bolster the Great Gates, where the realm's actual life-threatening foe lay, seeking to earn the Tempest Throne. Thyra ground herself in the trenches beneath Lothair's glower, wading through the most hardships of them all.

Her elder sister, scarcely her elder by Lysian standards, wrangled with the Skjold to build herself a militaristic core and ensure they might survive the next catastrophe to come. Here in the Dark Moon's shadow, Tanya walked incomparable to her in spirit and name both. Tanya wanted to aid their family's renascence desperately, but at the end of five years, she still had no idea what her place in it all was.

Tanya ended their sauntered stroll in the middle of the mammoth pine grove, where the seers conducted their most remarkable rituals. She let Muiri settle his angst atop the countless runes and rituals cast atop this circle of earth. Waiting for Muiri to inevitably divulge how long he could handle silence, she basked in the mysterious peace drawn by the moon's absent glow.

"Why are we here?" he questioned predictably. "You cannot expect me to believe dark rituals like the one from the night before are the reason why you stay."

Tanya snickered before correcting his misinterpretation. "Runic seers have performed thousands of rituals on this ground. Drurhelm's only performed a few of them. I stay because of that," she answered, gesturing toward the moon's silhouette in the cloudy sky above. "It's one of the three moons fueling runic magic."

"Three moons?"

"The Dark, Bright, and Riven. They all belong to the lunar realm and are simply different dresses the Crescent Lady chooses to wear throughout her cyclical dance."

He smiled before peering into the deathless beauty of the Dark Moon. "Does runic magic come with a different flare with each moon?"

"A well-trained seer can walk imperceptibly against any medium under the Dark Moon. A typical Bjardja sworn to Eldrahg or Helti is most lethal by the Bright Moon's glow. Mix them together, and by the runic gods, you can cast untold varieties so long as you draft the right runes." After watching his eyes wander in the darkness, she widened hers as far as physically possible. "Especially on a Riven Moon," Tanya abruptly added. "The nights the Crescent Lady finds her pristine balance are the nights when the flows of runic magic are most efficacious and diverse. I stay because I want to learn every power a seeress can and realize the Crescent Lady's might by my own hands."

"It's the power drawing you then," Muiri tartly remarked. She heard him shift to rescind from her side. "What do you plan to do with it? Establish your own temple? Join some roving band of Bjardja? No, you wouldn't use it to kill. Why? What's the point of attaining all that runic might when you won't use it to rule like the rest of your kin?"

Relaxing to think, Tanya did not immediately answer. She obviously struck one of his heart's chords and unintentionally riled him. She saw nothing but the silhouette of his face, but somehow, Tanya could still glimpse his pain. She did not wish to spite him for importuning her with questions. She simply wanted to understand from where they came.

"Ryurik and I never learned to wield sky magic or invoke the conquered sun like my brothers or sister. This is how I intend to wield higher powers and bring about some good in this vindictive world. I don't want to be remembered as the youngest princess from an imperial line which fled the devastation of its home to save themselves." Tanya sharply inhaled, then wittily admitted, "I know I look a lot like my sister, but I'm not planning on leading armies. That's her calling, not mine." His teeth brightened the night's dour and eased some of the embarrassment her next confession wrought. "The first rune I cast was to mend your broken body, and I think that's a damn good start."

Tanya tailored her voice to a steady halt as the pines utterly consumed it. They stood in quiet discomfort again. Muiri shifted to face her, slightly ajar. Tanya watched him reach up to clasp the charm he wore. He fondled it there for a moment, sluggishly removing the necklace, and dangled it over his right hand until his heart froze. She stepped forward, struggling to see anything besides clumps of hair woven into a twine net held together by a circle of twigs.

"My mother gave this to me as we hid in the forest from the raiders who sacked our fishing village. We were cornered against an impassible river without a chance to escape. I was clueless, frightened, so she snipped the end of her hair and then wound it into this charm she always wore about her neck." Muiri pulled away and restrung the charm about his neck. "I am sorry I insulted you. I know I owe you so much already, but I cannot help but hate everything in the Stormlands because it reminds me of how I lost her." He stepped back to suffer it all himself before woefully remarking, "My only solace in speaking to her memory and remembering her face is that I'll never let it be forgotten."

"I understand. My mother's not dead, but this place stole her away from me too. I doubt I'll ever recover the woman I once knew. All because she lost the son—my brother, Darius—whom she cherished more than anything in this world."

Tanya revealed her own necklace, far gaudier and more opulent than his, but a genuine relic of remembrance nonetheless. She tugged at his hands in an invitation they return to honest light and replace the Dark Moon's dreariness. He flinched, and Tanya could not help but roll her eyes at the fastidious distrust he placed in anything he did not comprehend. She altered tactics, and instead of surrendering to his frightened reservations, lightly squeezed his hand. He did not necessarily resist, but he drew her to a stop as he inhaled to speak.

Without allowing him the chance to speak, Tanya whispered, "Two foreigners caught in a strange and roguish land. Let us help each other where we can."

The stiffness he withheld alleviated when he gently accepted her appeal, and for the first time since meeting Muiri, she believed he trusted her. A terrible weakness enveloped her, and her vigor and forte were abruptly drained. She nearly collapsed without compunction before he caught her. Muiri guided her down after she failed to hold to her feet. It was as if she lost the use of her legs. Tucking them to one side, Tanya thrust out her arms to catch herself. Her hands met the earth like they were flimsy ore-pine posts twisted by a midsummer gale, and Muiri embraced her to prevent her from falling all the way.

"The hell in Drur's Abyss. What happened?" he stammered, shaking her shoulders with unwarranted potency and rattling her dizzy head.

Disgruntled by his ludicrous reaction, Tanya softly cursed. "Don't shake me. I'm still awake." She realized she could still not see his face, which meant he most likely could not see hers. "Just let me breathe," Tanya sharply atoned before she undertook the effort to do so.

"It must be this runic circle...or the forest grove? Whatever it is, we should leave in case it happens again."

Tanya caught sight of black runes ensconcing half of his right arm. "Muiri, your arm!" she feebly exclaimed as her breath dwindled into gasps for air.

"Woah," exclaimed Muiri, withdrawing his hands and forsaking her to support herself alone. Tanya faltered, quietly yelped, but he caught her again before she could fall. "Sorry," he murmured, "but what did you do to my arm?"

"What did I do?" she scorned. "I don't know!"

Still quite disgruntled, Tanya foiled herself from scathing him any further. Whatever just happened to his arm, she realized, was probably her doing. As far as Tanya was aware, she alone had cast a rune before. But Muiri did have some power over lunar magic. He had breached the upper runic vaults, shattering those seals bound by shrewd runes during a death-bound psychosis.

Tanya burrowed his hand to salvage a closer look, shuddering when he initially refused. Muiri relented, allowing her to proceed. Tanya gasped. From the hillock bone beneath his thumb, a runic weave wrapped around his wrist, then scaled his entire arm. Half of his skin was suffused with in-numerable runes. Tanya pulled his sleeve over his shoulder to reveal more. They spiraled around his muscles, climbing to the precipice of his upper shoulder where they ended against an invisible barrier, leaving but a third of his skin unmolested.

"I don't really know what I did," she confessed before pulling down his sleeve.

Fiercely, Muiri bemoaned, "I thought the first rune you ever cast was just this morning. Now, half my arm is saturated in black ink runes!"

"I don't know how, but every rune bound to the Dark Moon is just embossed upon your arm as if you were a Bjardja sworn to Monomua's gloomier half."

"You touched my hand, then fell. Has a seeress ever done something like this before?"

"There are plenty of myths and legends that speak of what happens during a seeress's awakening, but they're all just derived from one."

"What? What legend? I'm just a damned fisherman who was taken as a thrall, then sold to a nasty butcher. I don't belong in legends. I hardly know of any skaldic legends myself," Muiri nervously prattled.

Tanya stymied the parting of his lips by clasping his mouth shut. "Just carry me back to the hospice before I actually faint. I need a bed and something to help keep me awake while I recall the details. Once I recover, we can visit the runic vaults to find out more."

"Then what am I supposed to do? Draft you some moonlight so we can read the runes?" he questioned incessantly.

"If you can manage it!" she slammed in return.

"What? Why?" he probed.

Her aggravation with his endless interrogation soared beside the peak of the Valheim. "So I can reread how Eldrahg became the first runic god. Somewhere in the beginnings of runic magic, I think we will begin to discover what's happened to my head and your arm."

INTERLUDE

ELDRAHG'S ASCENSION

ELDRAHG'S WINGS SPLIT AUTUMN'S NIGHTLY sky as if it were flesh caught by the sweep of a sword. Each pulse formed a transitory vacuum, and with every massive push, he soared higher, leaving harsh winds in his wake. Ice lingered upon his draconic scales, having melted from his body's immense heat before refreezing to the sky's chilled whip. He brought those crystalline scales home from the Endless Wastes, where he had flown to punish the inviolable murder of a frost dragon from his and Ísvalar's brood.

Eldrahg had lent his wrath upon that foul jütengolk lord and his unsightly band of brutes, descending from the sky in vengeance and melting their black-iron armor with deadly, cerulean flames. It consumed their white bodies and charred their bones, and he tormented them through several passes to ensure Dranur claimed them all. The jütengolk fought with formidable nerve and unmatched ferocity, but their enchanted weapons and arcane magics did not harm him in the slightest. Eldrahg was an Elder Wyrm of the cerulean variety. Arcane magic could not penetrate the scales of that which was born beside them.

The transgressors were dead, smoldering, sapphire ruins smeared across the Endless Wastes, yet Eldrahg attained no reprieve in their deaths. His child, a young dragon whom he and Ísvalar spawned centuries ago, had been slain. The corpse had already been eviscerated to be fashioned into barbaric armor by the time Eldrahg arrived. Eldrahg repaid that grisly vilification by slaying them all, thwarting the smithies from working their plunder in their icy forges of war. He carried what remained over the northern sea, where he let its scorched, dismembered corpse plummet into the chilled abyss. It gave him no solace. Like Ísvalar, he felt so hollow. They were bereft of yet another child to deter Andurial's lurking wrath.

Eldrahg descended unto the open fjord boasting his roost. His wings worn and weary from a rigid day's flight, he curdled ice with a prolonged, fearsome roar. Let Dwevland and the Nordland—as the puny humans called it—know their master had returned.

The sky shook with his fury, and Eldrahg cackled dryly. It amused him the sky now confined its own two gods. Delphine and her lover were no longer able to conquer her sister's courts, lest they expend hideous quantities of power to hurl their grievances across the world again, thus ensuring their swift defeat.

Their victory had not been without heavy cost. The God of the Skies had torn the other seven pantheons asunder, forcing each divine pair to bind themselves to their own realms to succeed in binding Andurial and Delphine to theirs. They were forever incapable of reentering Eldaria without detrimental travail—Andurial's cynical requite for their roles in imposing his savage expulsion.

Yet, Eldrahg cared little for those injustices, even for Saerellan and Ithilia, his bereaved celestial makers. Elder Wyrms were slain during Andurial's onslaught too, but Eldrahg, Ísvalar, and a myriad of others survived his breaths of wind. The sky's Elder Wyrms and their flight had been wholly slaughtered. The surviving dragons were made stronger because of it. Never again could the God of the Skies directly threaten Elder Wyrms or their flights. Ironic indeed.

Wreaking havoc upon the rocks, which did not comfort him, Eldrahg nestled against the cool fjord. He collapsed in disregard for the tremors his planking triggered. He bustled until duly comfortable, creating more with each transpose. Eldrahg desired the honest sleep of three days' time before he would consider rising again. However, he would be hard pressed to sleep beneath the desolating shine of the Riven Moon.

Eldrahg snorted. His eyes could not find their proper rest. Moonlight beat his crumpled brow, too much in his opinion for a night free from the Bright Moon. He shifted, twisting atop the fjord to curl his head away from Monomua and Melowyn's glares. He whipped his tail over the cliffs where it hung to tempt a raging sea. He spared a wing to shield his face, knowing Eshkalah would soon rise to entice his temper. He closed his nostrils, attuned his ears, and fastened his eyes shut, priming himself against any disturbance foolish enough to disturb a slumbering Elder Wyrm.

Yet, Eldrahg was, in totality, an Elder Wyrm. That ancient, antecedent title solemnized him as one of the first of his draconic kind, and it came with prodigious abilities few other dragons possessed. Eldrahg could sense magic of any variety: the insurgent wrath of a vengeful sky, the pervading scent of the infinite arcane, the elemental hymn of a shaman's earth, the destructive tides of vast, mystical seas, the spiritual serenity of druidic life, the foul rancor of necromancy, the sheer supremacy of a sorcerer's sun, and even the augur incantations of the seer's revolving moon. Of course, Ithilia's favored little sister would be the first to venture forth to vex him with their ignoble plight, as if Eldrahg would not rectify their imprisonments if he somehow could.

Eldrahg swung his head high to witness the Moon's Goddess undertake the strenuous task of descending the lunar realm. Monomua displayed her fêted moonlight, having enwreathed it in two furs. They shone in shameful matrimony, for she wore both alone. The Bright punctured the hidden veil encapsulating the lunar realm. She reserved none of her strength when unleashing the beam. The Dark enwreathed the shattered lattice, deceiving it into believing it had never been broken. Monomua descended through the opaque opening upon streaks of moonlight—the softly trickling remnants of the lunar might she summarily spent to briefly escape her prison.

Moon's Goddess gracefully landed unto the conspicuous precipice of his favorite fjord. Eldrahg welcomed her coming with a convivial roar. Rocks shook from their holdings and tumbled into the adjacent firth. Monomua levitated above a single foot in amused silence, and she returned his aggravated greeting with kind, open arms. Eldrahg shifted in suspicion of this enfeebled goddess who so evenly floated before him, a consummate Elder Wyrm.

"Will you not speak with your mother's dear sister, great cerulean wyrm?" she humbly inquired as he considered why she had come.

Shawled in alternating robes of black and white satin, the goddess accorded her body with the same sinew as the Riven Moon. Midnight bangs lay tucked behind her ears. A scarce few overhung her bright lashes. Blanched silver was woven into the bulk of her midnight hair. She braided the veil on the right side of her head, and its tail ended above her ample breasts.

Monomua's forehead shone with the forbearance of a falcate moon, illuminating her remarkably pale features. Her small, rounded chin bled into a soft jawline shadowed by sharp cheekbones and the sumptuous flesh held between. Supple lips twirled away from the elegant slant of her nose. A countenance once warm and soft had been hardened like the terrain of her cold, lunar realm, and her dark almond eyes coolly regarded him.

"You've spent so much of your power to briefly break free," Eldrahg disparaged, dipping his head to smell her stalwart resolve. "How long will it hold? How long until you're pulled back to your...Riven Moon?"

Monomua emanated idyllic composure, balking at the sheer power advantage Eldrahg now sustained. She swayed with indifference as if she had not just expended a majority of her power to jaunt the lunar realm. Elegance dripped from her hanging feet, so Eldrahg decided to humor this pristine celestial being. Monomua hailed him at monumental detriment to her own lasting strength. He would hear her ragged appeal before sending her away.

Eldrahg exuviated the scales armoring his colossal physique. He consummated his inner flesh into its humanoid form. A rush of wind arose in waves around them. Eldrahg walked forth a scaled, cerulean man, whose draconic wings and frosted, azure hair alone rendered him something other than a Jastorl man from the lands south of the Range of Valdhaz.

"You're much less fearsome in this condensed form, but I find you more appealing for it." The goddess graced the fjord beneath her feet and walked forth to join him.

Eldrahg balked. "Walk no farther, Goddess of the Moon. You walk the ground before my roost, but you will not enter. That solid ground you see before you is where we will adjoin." She splayed her hands in godly indifference before retracting a few steps, and Eldrahg ascended the fjord's jutted tip to where she welcomed him with exquisite splendor. "Why have you come, Ithilia's little sister, and speak quickly, for I am exhausted from my flight home."

"Is that a question you cannot answer?" she taunted with a voice sounding utterly aloof. "Do you think I've spent such a vast breadth of my power to gaze upon those magnificent scales alone?"

"Do not taunt me afront my own home," Eldrahg lashed out in a voice that boomed as if he had never transgressed his true form. Studying her crossed, crescent braids, he scorned, "Is that Melowyn's hair you've woven into your own. How repugnant."

"This? It is a keepsake," she lamentedly conveyed while toying with her half silver braid. "It is all you will ever see of my Melowyn. You betray yourself as deserving of nothing else."

"Why does the God of the Moon not accompany his goddess for this favor you've come sniveling down to ask?"

"Because Andurial's crusade has brought forth his death!" Monomua shrieked like she was possessed by a banshee. Her black hair flared to shred the salted air surrounding her haunted visage. "A demon unlike any other ascended our lunar realm. His legions were minion, endless and resilient, and we could not buffet their assault. Afront their ranks, once Melowyn and I did fall, it severed my husband's head, consumed his power, ripped out his heart, and implanted it beside my own." Monomua lowered her robes over her left shoulder, revealing a jagged, crude scar across her breast. "I alone am burdened to revolve the accursed sky, wearing the regalia of the Dark and the Bright. I have become their sole keeper, their Crescent Lady bound to a forlorn realm, and this...this heart of his I once claimed as mine that has been thrust aside my own? It will remind me of that vile injustice with the rise of my every Riven Moon."

Monomua clutched at her gruesome scar, her nails nearly penetrating flesh. Eldrahg met her dismal gaze before she redressed her pale body in its lunate garments. The hold of her sorrow appeared nigh impenetrable. Yet, beneath her hollow glare, Eldrahg glimpsed the fires of rage so unlike the lunar goddess, it were as if he stared into the eyes of another Elder Wyrm. Her word suffered its own veracity, bleeding like fingers freed from barbed thorns. Eldrahg questioned her not. He had chosen to indulge her visit, and he intended to commit nothing else.

"How could Andurial have sent this demon to murder Melowyn in his place? He is no master of demons. He is the God of the Skies, whom your narrow-minded sister sent to terrorize Eldaria and fracture the nine realms out of petty spite for his and Lucilla's faithless respite. Your realm has been assailed by some novel foe who sounds more nefarious and formidable than Delphine or Andurial."

"The demon never betrayed its master's name," she soberly corrected.

"It called itself an Archdemon, then named itself the Blazoned Prince. It swore we should have slain Andurial when we still had the chance rather than banishing him beside my sister and ourselves." Monomua's voice faltered, and her tears stained her pale, moonlit cheeks. "Then the bastard prince alleged it would seize our retribution beside its own, severing my Melowyn's head with that vile sword."

"I am sorry for your loss, but you have wasted yourself," Eldrahg answered amidst her allure of distress and struggle. "Spending an era's worth of your power to break those bonds for one night alone, seeking I join your retribution against this demonic prince, an enemy who is not my own. Should this Blazoned Prince slay Andurial while exhausting Melowyn's power, at least the deaths of my kin will not go unavenged. Leave me and seek my makers' comforts instead."

"You do not understand. This Archdemon doesn't fight alone. All realms lie along the path leading it to Andurial, and it won't sojourn with the lunar realm before attempting to ascend Sky's Throne," Monomua stated amidst an eccentric titter that shattered Eldrahg's antediluvian cool.

"Should it make it that far," Eldrahg gruesomely responded.

"Then victory will be his. You'll be avenged then, Eldrahg. We will all be avenged, and we will all become the subjects of a far more nefarious rule," drawled the poignant dirge whom they called Goddess of the Moon.

"You howl estranged like the lone wolf howls at your Bright Moon. I do not know how this Archdemon entered your lunar realm, but none can ascend the celestial stars. It is impossible for anything beyond those whom Saerellan sired and Ithilia birthed."

"Is it?" she questioned on a cold, dry tongue. "My realm was not the first to fall, and there are so few left to stand against it. Look there to your makers, Eldrahg." Pointing toward the bristling stars above the fastly faltering night, Monomua lamented, "Know that I am sorry, for I am too late in imploring your aid. One of them has already fallen dead."

Eldrahg's eyes tore through morbid night. His rage burst with the dread realization Saerellan was missing from the sky above. In his father's ominous absence, his mother hung a forlorn, grieving star. Alone within an infinite sea of her children, Ithilia's luster paled beneath the light of the Riven Moon. Alone amongst thousands of Eldrahg's unborn brothers and sisters,

Ithilia watched as her firstborn unleashed his ire for the Moon's Goddess like a lonesome wolf.

Cerulean flames spiraled from his hands, and his breath bled the arcane, turning the night sky an azure blend of pain and wrath. This Blazoned Prince had slain two of Eldaria's gods, and it did not fight alone! That power was irreverent, unmistakable, and foreboding for them all. His heart walloped for the pain he wished to impart upon this demonic insurgent who stole his father from the stars, who left Ithilia a widow while he flew about slaying jütengolk lords.

"I will gather all those Elder Wyrms who survived the breaths of wind. We will answer this vile transgression alongside those who've survived this Archdemon's murderous whim."

"We are too late, and we are too few. Dream's ether and death's departed dominions are all that stand between them and Sky's Throne. Your kind are too spent from fighting the sky to prevail alone."

"My father's murder shall not go unanswered!" Eldrahg roared, honing his teeth with arcane wrath as they oozed with chilled wisps of ice. "You tell me of this foe who threatens us all, who has murdered my father, then caution my response? Do not project your cowardice upon me, Monomua, because you now rule the lunar realm alone. Ísvalar and I shall gather the other Elder Wyrms. We will fly to battle this Archdemon wherever he hides, with or without you by our sides."

"Then you will soar to your deaths unfurled," Monomua placated as if she dreamt the augur prophecy herself. "We each are bound to our respective realms—incapable of uniting—even Andurial. We are in need of allies, Eldrahg. That is why I have come, expending my power on you rather than hopelessly hurling it at that bastard demon spawn."

"The mortals, and humans worst of all?" Eldrahg admonished in riposte, stunned by the hubris she displayed in assuming they could aid their cause. "They are weak, fragile, fleeting things who cannot set aside their own lustful ambitions long enough to unite within their own races, let alone beyond genetic bonds. What help would they be against this foe who so easily brought about the death of my father?"

"Their ranks would furnish the armies we are without. Yes, I do not disagree with you. They are lacking in purpose and resolve and perish faster than time unfolds, but they are only in need of guidance to become impactful in this forthcoming war. Five Gods have already been slain, and Delphine herself has been rendered useless. Three realms alone are left to inhibit this Blazoned Prince from attaining a nonpareil reign. Our pantheons might be shattered, but that does not stop us from forging them anew."

Confounded by her vague and dubious confessions, Eldrahg probed, "A neoteric god for the lunar pantheon to stand beside you?"

"Not a god, but an avatar for those who have fallen. Not just for the lunar realm but for each of the eight Eldaria boasts. Become my Delas," Monomua whispered, sauntering to his side as she laid an elegant hand upon his rigid form. "Become the Delas of my lunar pantheon so my power can flow through you unimpeded by the veil that fetters my lunar realm. You will rise to the rue of all my sisters as they follow in our suit." Monomua lingered amidst her avid appeal, drawing so close that she inhaled his arcane breath as he contemplated her deal. "Forge yourself followers from the mortals beneath us, and through your runic court, they shall inherit my power so we might guide them toward the salvation of their own doom."

"What of your lunar pantheon? What am I and my court expected to become?" he coolly assuaged as his heart matched with hers.

"A goddess to rule the realm where she was born. A Delas to wield her utmost power where she cannot unveil herself anymore. A Descendant born of her blood, so she can never be felled. And in times of dire consequence, a mortal champion she can call upon when the requiem reaches its crest. This will be our requiem, yours and mine. It will be our stand against demonic invaders who seek to exploit Eldaria's weakness to enact their unsung revenge. The mortals will chaunt of Eldrahg, Elder Wyrm bound to the Crescent Lady who rules the lunar realm, who I will make our first Delas and Draconic Father of all the runic gods."

"The father of my own deific court...of your Descendant?" Eldrahg questioned as the goddess drew in to sensually caress his cheek.

"My Delas, sire to my Descendant daughter," Monomua wistfully whispered. "And my revenge." The goddess withdrew to disrobe, revealing her pale yet radiant form, and whistled her sweet-tuned requiem while the Riven Moon shone down upon them both.

"Then I would taste your tears before my wings bring your vengeance to bear. Let the mortals draw their circles in your heavenly image and fill them with my rage. I will guide your lunar magic to them by way of the pervasive arcane, and we shall bring this Archdemon to rue the day he so rashly aggrieved the Goddess of the Moon and an Elder Wyrm as old as Eldaria itself. Give in to me, and I will see Melowyn's murder avenged by my own breath."

His blood thinned and hastened to the vivacious beat, tempering its primal flow. Eldrahg then pulled the goddess against his scaled chest where the transcendence of their powers conjoined. His reservations absent, Eldrahg unfolded his wings in a magnificent display. Frost-tipped spikes rippled within cool, midnight air. The Crescent Lady, forged from sorrowful loss, tore him asunder, and she rolled their primal love across the cold, hard fjord.

Monomua tempered beneath his onslaught, her head dismally lulling to one side where her eyes did not close. Amidst his strokes, he watched as the goddess gazed into the nothingness that lay west of his fjord, where nothing dwelt but trifling jütengolk and Jütenthrall villages and one of Loretia's Elder Wyrms. A pool of tears festered within her. She thought of Melowyn, he was certain, but for tonight, and perhaps forevermore, the goddess would be his to enjoy.

Eldrahg assumed his novel title of Draconic Father, Delas to Monomua and the moon. Her lunar magic intertwined with his frosted, arcane blood, etching his scales with thousands of disparate runes attuned to her Dark, Bright, and Riven Moons. Eldrahg ascended, becoming the first runic god amidst the culmination of their love, and his forlorn mother, Ithilia, lamented from the stars far above.

<hr/>

I hope you enjoyed this installment of my first novel. Please visit your favorite retailer to leave a review expressing your thoughts on my work. Your feedback is irreplaceable, much appreciated, and can directly improve the quality of my future works.

THE NEXT PART OF THIS EPIC FANTASY ADVENTURE IS AVAILABLE NOW!

Grab your copy of *Dark Moon Rising, Saga of Storm Book 1 (Part 2)* to follow Ehlaru and Agneta's journeys through the Nordland, Muiri and Tanya's unveiling of the dark secrets of the Runic Faith, and Thyra, Ryurik, and Knuth's march to war with the Erunheim's opportunistic neighbors!

ABOUT THE AUTHOR

Anthony LaRiva is the aspiring author of *Dark Moon Rising*, the first novel in the Saga of Storm trilogy that he began writing in college. Having switched careers to focus fully on pursuing his passion of writing epic, high-fantasy literature, Anthony calls the Colorado front-range his place of work and home. History has served as a major source of his inspirations, and he does his best writing among the beatific landmarks of our world. Vikingdom dominates his fresh and intricate Stormborne world. The histories, myths, and legends of that violent time alongside those of late antiquity and early medieval Europe gift unequivocable life to his stark tale of the Ehrlich family and the many challenges they face.

CPSIA information can be obtained
at www.ICGtesting.com
Printed in the USA
LVHW040735300322
714780LV00008B/816

9 781957 838007